DARK ANGEL

A DARK ROMANCE: LONDON RUTHLESS SERIES
BOOK 1

SADIE KINCAID

RED HOUSE PRESS

First published in 2021 by Red House Press.

Cover Design: Red House Press

Red House Press

For my incredible boys.

PROLOGUE

SAMANTHA

The room spun around me as I clung to him, my arms wrapped around his neck and my body cradled in his strong arms. I could feel his heart thumping against my own chest, its rhythm matching mine. I pressed my face against his throat. He smelled so good. Of expensive aftershave and fresh sweat. My insides trembled at being held so close to him. Every nerve ending was alive with electricity. I pressed my lips lightly against his skin and could have sworn I heard him groan.

But I couldn't trust my own senses. Not tonight. And especially not around him. He kicked open the door to my bedroom before walking inside and placing me gently on the bed. He looked down at me. Those green eyes blazing full of fire.

Oh, God. This was it. The night I had been dreaming about for four long years. And finally, he was going to kiss me. Then he would slide those strong hands up my legs and slip his fingers beneath my little black dress until he found that spot where I ached to feel him the most.

'Are you okay, Samantha?' he asked, his voice full of concern. He stepped back, placing his hands in his trouser pockets.

'Yes,' I slurred. Then I felt the bile burning the back of my throat.

I sat bolt upright. 'I'm going to be sick,' I shouted, but he didn't flinch. He stayed right where he was.

Thankfully, it was a false alarm. I held my head in my hands and groaned loudly.

'Jesus. How much have you had to drink, kid?' he asked with a sigh.

Kid? I was eighteen! Only eight years younger than he was. Just as I was ready to give him some snarky comeback, my head started to spin again. I leaned back against the pillows and closed my eyes. I heard him walking out of the room and wondered if I had completely blown my chance. To my relief, he returned a few moments later with a wet face-cloth and a t-shirt of my father's.

'Here. Put this on,' he said as he handed me the t-shirt and turned his back while I changed.

I stood up on shaky legs and slipped out of my tiny black dress. I blinked back tears as I thought about how many times I had imagined it would be his hands sliding this fabric over my body tonight, instead of my own. I pulled the t-shirt over my head, the soft cotton cool against my hot skin, and then I sat back down on the bed.

'I'm done,' I said.

He turned around and I saw his eyes drawn to the exposed flesh of my thighs before he quickly looked away.

'Are you going to tell my dad?' I asked as I lay back against the pillows.

He ignored my question. 'If he'd been in the club tonight instead of me...' he started as he sat on the bed beside me. He smoothed my hair from my face before placing the cool cloth on my forehead. 'Are you stoned too?'

'It *is* my leaving party,' I said with a grin.

He cocked an eyebrow at me. 'Well, you certainly know how to leave a lasting impression.'

I shrugged. 'Not enough though, it seems.'

He stared at me. 'What do you mean?'

'Are you going to miss me, Gabe?' I asked. This was my last chance. Tonight hadn't quite worked out as I'd hoped. Along with my friends, I'd gone to the club where I knew Gabriel was working, with every intention of seducing him on my final night in Dagenham. I'd worn my sexiest little black dress and had flirted with him outrageously every single chance I got. But then the cocktails, the shots and the weed had kicked in. The next thing I knew, I could hardly stand. I couldn't find my friends and I was being 'helped' outside by some random guy I didn't even know. A guy who obviously didn't realise that my dad and his best mate owned the security firm that employed the bouncers in the club, and every other club within a two-mile radius. Everything got a bit hazy after that. But I did recall being carried out of the club by Gabriel and then driven home.

And now here we were. Him looking good enough to eat and acting like his usual calm and controlled self, and me a hot, drunken mess.

I was leaving for university tomorrow and if I didn't go for it now, I wondered if I'd regret it for the rest of my life. I had a feeling that leaving this place would change me in ways I couldn't even imagine. And part of me wanted to change. I wanted to stop longing for a man that I could never have. But I wasn't sure I could.

I was completely in love with Gabriel Sullivan and had been since I was fourteen years old.

'Of course I'll miss you,' he breathed. 'Even if you drive me crazier than anyone I have ever known.'

My heart started to hammer in my chest. There was something in his voice, in the way that his eyes held mine, that made me wonder if he suddenly saw me as more than his best friend's daughter.

'But you're going to set the world on fire, Samantha Donovan,' he said softly as he brushed my cheek with his fingertips.

'I would stay though,' I said. 'If you asked me to, I'd stay for you. I'm all yours if you want me.'

There, I'd said it. No going back now.

'Jesus, Sam,' he blew out a breath. 'What are you trying to do to me?'

I blinked at him. What did that even mean? I don't think he'd ever called me Sam before and I wondered why he did now. It was what my dad called me. On Gabriel's lips though, it felt intimate and ... I didn't know. It was something I couldn't quite figure out. Maybe if I wasn't stoned off my face, I'd have a better understanding of what was going on here.

'Ask me to stay with you,' I pleaded as my heartbeat thundered in my ears.

He took hold of my hand and pressed my fingers to his lips. 'My beautiful, sweet, Sam. I care about you far too much to ever ask you to do that.'

Then he stood up and kissed me lightly on the forehead before walking out of the room. I felt the sob catch in my throat as I watched him leave. Little did I know that by the time I saw him again, that sweet girl he'd once known would be long gone.

1. FOURTEEN YEARS LATER

SAMANTHA

I stepped off the bus into the grey London drizzle. Despite the gloomy weather and the fact that I'd forgotten my umbrella, I smiled as I hopped over a puddle. For the first time in twelve years, my every move wasn't scrutinised. I didn't have to worry about what to say, or consider the consequences of every single decision I made. I was finally free.

The door to Archangel Securities was as unwelcoming as it could possibly be without having a sign on it telling people to get lost. Pushing open the heavy black door, I stepped into the dimly lit interior. The reception area was empty as usual. Not that I needed anyone to announce my arrival. I was expected.

Walking into the back, I pushed open the door with a sign that simply read, 'The Boss.'

'Sam!' My father, Sebastian Donovan, bellowed as he rose from his seat and crossed the room in two strides before pulling me into a bear hug. 'I'm so glad you stopped by. How are the new digs, sweetheart?' He asked as he took a step back from me, a smile spreading across his face.

'They're great, Dad. The office and the apartment are both perfect. Thanks for helping me find them,' I replied, shaking the rain from my hair.

'Of course, love. Anything at all I can do to help. You know that. I'm just glad to have you back home where you belong. And those apartments have good security, you know?' he replied with a wink. Archangel Securities were responsible for maintaining the CCTV equipment in my new apartment building and they also employed the security guards that always manned the front desk.

I smiled at him. He was always worrying about me. Forever feeling guilty that he hadn't always been there for me. But from the moment he had come into my life, after my mum had died, he'd tried his hardest and I loved him for that. He'd done the best job he could with a stroppy teenager who was still grieving for the only parent she had ever known. I felt a pang of sadness blindside me. It felt like that girl no longer existed now.

Startled by a movement from the other side of the dim office, I flinched instinctively. It was an old habit. I hadn't noticed anyone else in there when I'd first entered the room. But of course, he'd be there. He and my father were business partners, and despite their eight year age gap, the best of friends. He knew all about what had happened to me that night. Not the sanitised version from the newspapers either, but the real, awful truth. My dad had told him because he told him everything. Not for any morbid reasons, but because he'd struggled so much with what happened to his daughter, and the fact that, despite who he was, he hadn't been able to prevent it.

'Hello, Samantha,' Gabriel Sullivan said as he stood up and walked towards me.

I felt my breath catch in my throat and my heart started to hammer in my chest. He was even more handsome than I remembered. Slightly taller than my dad, and wider too. Dark hair, broad shoulders and thick arms. With the most incredible green eyes, and a few days' worth of stubble, his presence dominated the room. And damn, that man was born to wear a suit.

I'd had a thing for him years earlier, when I'd been a love-struck, hormonal teenager. But, for obvious reasons, he had always been off limits — and to him, I was nothing more than his best mate's annoying teenage daughter. I hadn't seen Gabriel since I'd left for university fourteen years earlier. I'd heard from my dad that he'd got married and subsequently divorced. No doubt he had a string of women vying for his attention. And if he was anything like my father, I would bet my life on him taking advantage of them all.

I'd been fourteen when I first met Gabriel. My dad brought him to the house one night while I was asleep in bed — at least I was supposed to have been. I'd heard them come in and had crept downstairs, only to be met by the sight of a shirtless demigod standing in our kitchen with blood trickling down from his shoulder and onto his chest.

'Sam! Get to bed,' my dad had shouted as he came running into the kitchen.

'But I can help,' I'd insisted, desperate to feel useful for a change.

He had looked at me and made a split-second decision as his colleague stood bleeding all over our expensive floor tiles.

'Okay. Go and find me some needle and thread,' he'd ordered.

That had been my initiation into the dark and shady world that my father sometimes occupied. Gabriel had ended up with a neat scar from my dad's DIY stitching job, which he later had covered with a tattoo, and after whatever had gone on that night, the two of them had set up Archangel Securities together. Gabriel had been a regular feature in my life for the next four years.

As Gabriel reached me, he leaned in and gave me a gentle kiss on the cheek, lightly touching my arm as he did. I felt the electricity crackling between us. 'Nice to see you, Samantha,' he said.

My skin prickled in annoyance.

What happened to the bear hugs he used to give? Just like my dad?

Suddenly I felt exposed — and vulnerable. It was as though all he could see was what had happened to me. I was no longer the feisty, funny girl, who had once been able to make him laugh and scowl in equal measure, but poor little Samantha, whose husband almost killed her. It irritated me, making me feel uncomfortable as I stood there in front of him, as though my clothes had suddenly started to chafe my skin. Fortunately, I'd perfected the art of hiding my feelings a long time ago.

'Hey, Gabe,' I said, flashing him my biggest smile. He hated to be called Gabe. He always had. I used to call him it when I wanted to push his buttons. It seemed it still worked and I grinned as he bristled and excused himself.

2. GABRIEL

I had been about to leave when she'd walked into our office. Samantha Donovan – looking like a teenage boy's wet dream. Her long dark hair pulled to one side, exposing the creamy skin of her neck. In a skin-tight pencil skirt that clung to the curve of her hips. The top of her white shirt wet from the rain, making it almost transparent. She glided across the room in her expensive designer heels, like she'd been born in them. Even dishevelled by the rain, she looked like she'd just stepped out of a magazine. She shook the rain from her hair and I felt a familiar twitching in my dick.

I greeted her with all the restraint I could muster. Kissing her cheek, I could smell her sweet perfume — the heat and the rain making it more potent. I was afraid to hug her in case she felt just how happy I was to see her. And then she called me Gabe. I remembered how I used to pretend that it infuriated me. And it did, if anyone else called me it. But on her lips...

I left the room as quickly as I could and it had been a relief to walk outside into the fresh air before climbing into the waiting car. Now, sitting here, stuck in an endless snake of traffic, I could still smell her sweet scent. As though even a moment in her presence had left her lingering on me. Instead of preparing for the meeting I was on my way to, all I could think about was how she would taste; how her skin would feel underneath my fingertips; what she would look like bent over my desk. Leaning my head against the headrest, I closed my eyes and tried to clear the unwelcome thoughts from my mind.

Samantha Donovan was the last person I should be thinking about. Not only was she my best mate's daughter, but she deserved much better than me. She had been through enough already. Besides that, I had more important things to deal with than chasing women, even a woman like Samantha. The muscles in my chest and arms tensed as I thought about the man I was on my way to meet.

'You all right, Boss?' Scott, my driver for the afternoon asked, snapping me from my thoughts.

'Yeah,' I replied, thankful for the temporary distraction. Opening my eyes, I turned to him. 'Did you bring me what I asked for in case this meeting goes south?'

'Of course, Boss. In the glove box,' he replied with a nod.

I didn't need to open it to know that there would be a Beretta handgun inside. 'Good. Now get us to the docks so we can get this fucking charade over with.'

'Want me to come in with you?' Scott asked.

'No. I can handle Jimmy Fenton myself.'

Scott nodded and remained silent for the rest of the drive. He pulled up at the Fenton's builders yard near the docks. I slipped the gun out of the glove compartment and tucked it into the back waistband of my trousers. I had a set of brass knuckle dusters in my trouser pocket too — just in case.

'This shouldn't take more than half an hour, Scott,' I said as I stepped out of the car.

'And if it doesn't, Boss?' he asked with a cock of his eyebrow.

'Then you'd better call the cavalry.'

I buttoned my suit jacket as I walked across the court yard of Fenton's. I'd known Jimmy Fenton for over twenty years. I'd first met him when I was eighteen and I'd disliked him almost immediately. He was a snake. Jimmy Fenton had set up Fenton Security Services around the same time that Sebastian and I established Archangel and our two firms were always going to be rivals. But whilst Sebastian and I specialised in providing security for clubs and pubs, the Fentons focused on retail. So, for the most part, we had an uneasy truce.

As I walked through the yard and into Jimmy Fenton's office, I wondered how much longer that truce was going to last.

I sat back against the worn leather chair in Jimmy's office and watched him pour me a glass of Scotch that I hadn't asked for. I didn't drink much as a rule, especially with people I didn't like.

'It's good to see you, Gabriel,' Jimmy said as he placed the glass in front of me.

'You too,' I lied.

'How long's it been?' he stared at me as he sipped his own drink.

I shrugged. 'Fuck knows. Probably not long enough.'

Jimmy laughed before drinking back the rest of his whisky. 'I see you've come alone?'

'Why wouldn't I?' I asked. This was all a power display and it was becoming tedious already.

'Well, I thought you'd have your partner with you. Some men would think twice about coming to my place without some back up, that's all. Especially with all my lads hanging around outside.'

I thought about the gun I had tucked away. Jimmy would have one to hand too, I had no doubt about that. He wasn't stupid enough to invite me for a business meeting and then shoot me in the head, but who knew what he was up to? What I did know was that bringing Sebastian to a business meeting with the Fentons was a recipe for disaster. Sebastian hated them with a passion. He'd had a run in with Jimmy's brother, Martin years earlier that had left Sebastian with a six-inch scar across his neck and Martin deaf in one ear. It had been smoothed over by me and Jimmy, but understandably, Sebastian and Martin still held a grudge.

'Well, I assumed I wouldn't need any back up for a business meeting?' I snapped, my temper already frayed.

He laughed. 'Of course not.'

'So what was this proposition you had for me? You mentioned a new business venture?' I asked. It had come as a shock when Jimmy had phoned me a few days earlier asking me to meet to discuss a business proposal. I had little intention of going into business with the Fentons. I didn't work with people I didn't trust. But, my curiosity got the better of me, and I wanted to know what his plan was. Sebastian and I had been developing Archangel Securities, cultivating a new image and a kind of client that could bring in national contracts. I hoped that in a few years, the two of us would be able to take a back seat and reap the rewards of all our hard work now. So, if there was a new opportunity on the horizon, I at least wanted to know what it was.

'Well, it's more of a new business venture for me actually.' Jimmy replied.

I frowned at him, my fists clenched by my sides. 'Then why the fuck am I here?'

'I want to take over Archangel Securities.'

I must have misheard him because that was the funniest thing I'd heard all day. I started to laugh. Surely this was a wind up? 'Are you being serious?'

He glared at me. 'Yes,' he snapped. 'I'm fucking serious. I heard you were looking to go legit. This could be the perfect opportunity for you. Let me buy Archangel. We'll take over the clubs. You have a re-branding and stick with your new, less demanding, contracts.'

Fuck! He was serious. The arrogant little prick! I glared back at him as I felt my heart start pounding in my chest. I should have known Fenton was going to pull some shit — the man was a Grade A prick. 'Archangel Securities is not for sale.'

'Are you sure about that?' he challenged me.

'Yes, I'm sure.'

'Well, maybe it would be better to sell it now and walk away with a good profit before someone simply walks in and takes it from you, Gabriel?'

'Are you fucking threatening me?' I snarled at him, ready to launch myself across his desk and use his face as a stress ball.

Jimmy leaned across the table. 'Think about my offer, Sullivan. Don't forget how I helped you out back in the day,' he said with a grin, revealing his gold canine tooth. 'I think it's about time I called in that favour. Don't you?'

I felt the anger surging through my body and had to take a deep breath to stop myself from putting a bullet straight through Jimmy's head. I hated the fact that he had something on me. I had always known it was only a matter of time before he played that hand, but if I was honest, I was surprised the little snake had waited so long. It had been over twenty years. I wasn't even sure there would be much of a body left to find after all this time.

But Jimmy Fenton had just as much to lose as I did if that particular ghost ever resurfaced. Calvin Stewart certainly wasn't the only man I'd ever killed, but he was the first, and the only one who hadn't deserved it. I still saw his face in my dreams.

I stood up from my chair and couldn't help but smile when I saw Jimmy flinch. 'Fuck you!' I snarled before walking out of the office.

'Think about it, Sullivan,' he shouted after me.

3. SAMANTHA

I headed back to my office, unable to stop thinking about what had just happened. My first encounter with Gabriel Sullivan hadn't gone exactly as I'd hoped. The first time I saw him again, I was supposed to be groomed to perfection, not wearing my boring work clothes and dripping with rain! But then nothing about my interactions with him had ever worked out as planned in the past. Of course, teenage me was a trembling mess around him, I was a walking hormone bucket and he was hotter than molten lava, but come on! I was a grown woman now. Confident and successful. So, why did being around him still make me feel like I was a teenage girl?

And how dare he be so bloody polite and stand offish. As though I was just some random who'd dropped by, and not the same person who used to cook him bacon and eggs every Sunday morning. Someone who had almost been like a little sister. I shook my head in annoyance. Perhaps it was for the best. I didn't want him acting like my big brother anymore anyway. I already had one over-protective relative in my father and he was more than enough.

As I rounded the corner, I heard Nick Cook's distinctive laugh before I saw him, and then I almost bumped into him and a red-faced sign-writer.

'Samantha!' Nick said when he saw me. Grabbing me by the shoulders, he spun me around to face the row of offices.

He could barely speak for laughing. 'Look. Look what it says.'

I read the freshly painted sign aloud. 'Donovan Cock Solicitors! Oh, for God's sake, Nick. How old are you?' I snapped, still smarting from my encounter with Gabriel. I was aware that any other time I'd have been laughing along with him.

Nick Cook was my best friend and business partner. I'd met him at university, where we'd had a few unmemorable, drunken liaisons before we'd agreed we'd be much better off as friends. And we had been ever since. Despite my ex-husband Jackson's best efforts to cut me off from everyone I knew, Nick had managed to cling on like a limpet, and I loved him for it. I knew that it was in part due to Jackson's arrogance and his mistaken belief that Nick was absolutely no threat to him at all. And I supposed that Nick didn't look threatening. He was tall and lean and had a boyish look about him. He wore thick, dark rimmed glasses and could go days without shaving and still have barely a hint of stubble. But what Jackson didn't realise was that Nick was by far one of the smartest men I had ever met. People did tend to underestimate him when they first met him. He was quiet and unassuming — but that was his superpower, especially in the courtroom.

When I'd decided to move back to Dagenham, Nick had been looking to move on from the solicitor's firm he'd been working at too, and as we'd both recently made the change from criminal to family law, it had seemed like the perfect opportunity for us to open our own practice together. Although to look at him now, doubled over and barely able to control his bodily functions because of a juvenile spelling mistake, you'd never know he had one of the sharpest legal minds in England. Watching him laugh uncontrollably, I was reminded why I loved being around him so much.

I turned to the sign-writer, who was staring up at the sign and rubbing his chin, a mild look of confusion etched on his round face. 'Who in their right mind would open a solicitor's office called Donovan Cock?' I asked him.

He started to stutter, his face reddening further as he responded. 'I just copied what was on the paper, Miss.'

'Cook! Not Cock. Cook! How long before you can fix it?' I asked.

'Not long,' he said taking hold of his ladder and leaning it back against the front of the building. 'I'll get it sorted.'

Nick patted him on the back before following me up the few steps to our office. The tears were still rolling down his cheeks as he shouted. 'Thanks for that, mate. Made my week.'

Despite my bad mood, I smiled at him once we were inside. 'You're such a boy,' I gave him a playful nudge in the ribs.

Nick grinned at me. 'Oh, there you are, Samantha. I thought you'd been abducted by aliens or something. How could you not think that sign was hilarious?'

'Sorry, Nick,' I replied as I rubbed the back of my neck. 'I'm just feeling a bit wound up today, that's all.'

'Anything I can do?' he offered.

'No thanks. I'll be fine. Getting stuck into those case files will take my mind off it,' I lied before walking into my office and closing the door. There was only one person I could think of who could take my mind off it – Gabriel bloody Sullivan. I hadn't stopped thinking about him since I'd left Archangel Securities. Sinking into the chair in my office, I closed my eyes and allowed myself a few moments to imagine all the wonderful ways Gabriel could ease the tension in my neck and shoulders.

4. GABRIEL

I walked into my office at Archangel Securities to find Sebastian hunched over his laptop with a smile on his face.

'You're not watching porn, are you?' I asked.

Sebastian shook his head. 'Nah. I'm booking me and Kayleigh a holiday to Turkey,' he grinned.

'Kayleigh? I thought you two had called it a day?'

'What can I say? I'm an old romantic,' Sebastian laughed. 'Anyway, what did that prick Fenton want?'

I frowned. My visit to Jimmy Fenton had pissed me off and I had an idea it wasn't going to be the last we heard from him. I pulled up a chair across the desk from Sebastian.

'He wants to buy Archangel Securities.'

'What?' Sebastian snapped. 'What did you say to him?'

'I told him to fuck off, obviously.'

'And then what?'

'Well, in a nutshell, he basically threatened he'd take it from us if we didn't accept his offer.'

'What the fuck?' Sebastian snarled as he slammed his laptop shut. 'Who the fuck does that cheeky cunt think he is? Threatening us? Has he got a death wish or something?'

I shook my head. 'Who the fuck knows, mate?'

'So what are we going to do about it?'

'Nothing. For now.'

'What? Jimmy Fenton threatens to take our business from us and we do nothing? Are you fucking kidding me?' Sebastian shouted.

'Just for now, Seb. Let me think about what we do next. Fenton won't make a move yet. He's not stupid and he doesn't need a war. I need to figure out why he's suddenly trying to buy us out.'

'I'm not sure. Maybe now is the perfect time to make a move before they start getting any more ideas?'

'We don't do that anymore,' I reminded him. 'At least not quite so openly. We'd lose half of our new contracts if they knew that was how we did business.'

Sebastian shook his head. 'I know that you want us to be more legitimate now, Gabriel, and so do I, especially now that Samantha's back. But if we don't deal with people like Jimmy Fenton the minute they step out of line, people will start to take the fucking piss.'

'Let's just sit back and see what Fenton does next,' I suggested. 'I'm not saying we can't, or we won't do the lot of them in if we need to, but let's consider our options, eh?'

'Okay,' Sebastian replied with a sigh. 'But if I see any of Fenton's boys anywhere near one of our places I will personally shoot the fucking lot of them.'

I nodded. 'Fair enough.'

I sat back in my chair, stretching my legs and letting my head hang back between my shoulders and sighed. 'Any chance of a drink?' I asked.

Sebastian stood up and poured us both a generous measure of Scotch before handing one to me. 'Not like you to drink in the afternoon,' he said. 'Something else on your mind, mate?'

I took the drink and shook my head. 'Nah. Fenton just pissed me off, that's all,' I lied. How could I possibly tell my best mate that the other thing on my mind, was his daughter, and all the things I'd like to do to her.

5. SAMANTHA

It was almost dark by the time I reached Archangel Securities. I'd been planning on going there straight after work. I'd made some loose plans with my dad to go out for dinner, but Nick had persuaded me to have a quick drink with him. Two glasses of wine later, I remembered dinner with my dad and managed to make my escape. Peering out of the taxi window, I could see the office was still open and was relieved to see I hadn't missed him. Despite his penchant to be an over-protective tyrant at times, I adored my father and now that I had moved back to Dagenham, I intended to make up for all the time we'd missed out on.

After paying the driver, I stepped out of the cab and walked into Archangel Securities. Making my way through the dim reception area, I could see the faint light coming from his office.

Pushing open the door, I flashed my best smile. 'You still up for taking a hungry lady to dinner?' I asked.

'I'd love to, Samantha,' Gabriel replied as he looked up from his desk and smiled. The pale glow of the computer screen illuminated his handsome face and I blinked at the sight of him. 'But I already have plans.'

'Gabriel!' I blushed. I hadn't seen him since I'd walked into this same office two days earlier. 'I assumed my dad was here. Sorry. I didn't mean...'

'He's left already. He thought you'd changed your mind. And he has a hot date — apparently.'

I could feel the heat spreading up my neck and over my cheeks and desperately hoped that he didn't notice in the darkness of the room. 'What? Another one?' I asked breezily. 'My father has more girlfriends than Hugh Hefner. I'll be on my way then,' I smiled and started to turn for the door.

Gabriel rose from his chair. 'Hang on. Let me drive you home.'

'There's no need. I'll ring a cab,' I said. I didn't want to disturb whatever plans he had for the evening.

'Come on. I'm leaving anyway. Let me make up for not taking you to dinner.'

I looked at him. Twenty minutes in a confined space with this sex god, who turned me into a nervous wreck, and made me think very, very inappropriate things would be tough. But, I supposed that being driven home in the comfort of his nice warm car was infinitely better than having to make small talk with a cab driver. 'Okay. If you're sure?'

Gabriel turned off his laptop and walked towards me, crossing the office in two quick strides. He stopped in front of me, his body inches from mine, and then he leaned towards me. My breath caught in my throat. I could feel the heat from his body and smell his expensive aftershave, and it made me want to bury my face in his neck.

I imagined him pushing me up against the door and kissing me hungrily, with his hands in my hair and on my body. I wondered if they would feel as good as I'd always imagined they would. I looked up at him, but he only reached behind me to take his coat, brushing my arm as he did. I let out the breath I'd been holding in. God, he was such a bloody gentleman!

Gabriel looked at me and smiled. 'Ready?' he asked, his voice a low growl that I felt in my bones. I nodded in response, afraid to speak in case my voice betrayed my downright filthy thoughts.

A few seconds later, I was relieved to be outside with the cool air on the flushed skin of my cheeks. Gabriel locked the office and I followed him to his car. A beep and a flash brought it to life as he approached it — a sleek, black Jaguar with tinted windows. I smiled to myself. It was exactly the kind of car I'd imagined he'd drive. Sliding into the comfortable leather seat, I kicked off my shoes and rubbed the chafed skin on my heels before settling back into the seat.

As we drove through the streets of London, Gabriel was silent, keeping his eyes fixed firmly on the road ahead. I watched him for a while, wondering why he was so distant with me. Perhaps, he'd hardly thought about me at all in the last fourteen years? Maybe I was inconsequential to him now? I had once been something to him, if only his best mate's daughter, but that had been a very long time ago. After a few moments, I looked out of the window instead, watching the scenery go by, until I could stand the silence no longer. 'So, do you have a hot date too then, Gabe?' I asked.

He raised an eyebrow at me. 'Would you care if I did?'

Was he flirting with me? 'No, of course not,' I replied nonchalantly.

He didn't answer my question any further and we continued the rest of the drive in silence until he pulled up outside my apartment block.

'Thanks, Gabe. Enjoy your evening,' I said.

'You too, Samantha,' he replied with a smile.

Slipping on my heels, I opened the car door. Before I stepped out of the car, Gabriel touched my arm and I felt the heat from his warm hand, both on my arm and in the throbbing sensation that was starting to build between my thighs. 'For the record, I don't have a hot date. I'm going to a meeting. But, I'd much rather be taking you to dinner,' he said softly.

I smiled but didn't reply, not sure of how I could respond without giving myself away, and I didn't want him to have any more power over me than he already did. Silently, I climbed out of the car. I continued smiling as I walked to my apartment building, making sure I gave Gabriel a good view of my behind as I walked away. It pleased me far more than it should that he wasn't going out on a date.

As I closed my apartment door, I leaned my forehead against the cool wood and let out a long slow breath. God, what the hell was wrong with me? Hadn't I sworn off men? Well, at least anything remotely serious anyway. A twelve year marriage to a sadistic psychopath will do that to a girl. Besides, this was Gabe I was thinking about. He would only ever see me as Sebastian's daughter — or worse, as Jackson Carver's wife.

6. GABRIEL

I'd driven to Tommy Parkinson's nightclub as soon as I'd dropped Samantha off. This meeting had already been rearranged once and I was close to closing the deal. Otherwise I would have blown off my plans and insisted that Samantha allow me to take her out for dinner instead of her father.

I'd only been in the place for ten minutes and already I was fed up of negotiating with Tommy. This was our third meeting now where we had gone over the same old ground. I wasn't prepared to give him another inch. Sebastian and I were doing him a favour bailing him and his failing nightclub out. We were offering him a decent price and if he didn't accept today, then I was prepared to walk away from the deal.

'I don't have all fucking night,' I snapped at Tommy as I stood up to leave. 'You've got until tomorrow morning to decide if you want to accept our terms. If I don't hear from you by then, I'll assume the deal's off.'

'For fuck's sake, Gabriel. You're killing me here. You know my business is worth twice what you're offering me.' Tommy spat, his face red, spittle flying from the sides of his mouth as he spoke.

I glared at him. Tommy was a decent bloke and I'd known him for years. On any other night, I probably wouldn't be such a cunt to him. But I was still smarting from my meeting with Jimmy Fenton the day before. I should have known better than to even consider a business proposition from a Fenton. Jimmy, and the rest of his firm were a shower of cunts, but unfortunately they were well connected ones.

If that hadn't wound me up enough, I couldn't stop thinking about the fact that I could be having dinner with Samantha instead of sitting in Tommy's shit-box of an office negotiating with him.

I fastened the buttons of my jacket. 'By twelve tomorrow, Tommy. Or the deal's off.'

'You can be a right fucking cunt,' Tommy said. But all the anger in his voice had disappeared. His words may have been strong but he slumped back into his chair and rubbed his hands over his face. He knew he was beaten. 'Okay. It's a deal,' he said as he held out his hand.

I shook his outstretched hand and nodded. 'I'll have the papers drawn up tomorrow.'

As I drove home I couldn't stop thinking about Samantha, wondering if she'd eaten yet. I thought about phoning her and asking if she still wanted to go for dinner. Although she'd turned up at our office looking for her father, I was sure I could have persuaded her to settle for me as a stand-in. Maybe I could offer to bring her a take-away instead?

I fingered the call button on my steering wheel. God, she'd looked so fucking good earlier. She always looked good. I felt my cock stirring to attention as I thought about those tight little pencil skirts she wore.

Fuck! What was I thinking? There was no way I could phone her. It was complete madness. If only I could stop thinking about her for longer than five minutes. The way my hand brushed the skin of her thigh when I'd changed gear. How she always seemed to recoil from my touch. How her breathing changed whenever I got too close to her. Did she feel this tension between us too? Or was she afraid of me?

But how could she be? She'd known me almost all her life. Maybe I came on too strong? Maybe it was all too apparent that whenever I saw her all I could think about was fucking her?

7. SAMANTHA

The music thumped in my ears as I squeezed my way through the crowd at O'Malley's bar with four bottles of Budweiser in my hands. It was the closest pub to Donovan Cook and so Nick and I often went there for drinks after work. We'd invited our legal secretary, Sadie, and our receptionist, Beth, out with us too. It was Friday night, and the couple of drinks we'd had planned soon turned into several and the place was now jam packed. I finally made it back to our table, holding the four bottles up triumphantly.

'Where are the shots? You promised us tequila.' Nick said.

'Shit! I forgot,' I said, realising my mistake. 'Anyway how many hands do you think I have, Nicholas?'

He grinned at me. 'Two! Exactly the same number you had in uni when you could carry six bottles and six shots easily in one trip. Are you losing your edge, Samantha?'

I stuck my tongue out at him. It was true that in my first year of uni I had perfected the art of carrying our group's whole round in one trip. But that had been before I'd met Jackson – sometimes it felt like everything good in my life had been before I met him. I closed my eyes to clear the thoughts of him. 'Four shots of tequila coming up,' I replied.

I was worming my way back through the crowd towards the bar

when I saw him walking towards me. Gabriel bloody Sullivan. That was all I needed. As if I didn't think about that man enough, now there he was looking so good I would have done shots out of his navel. I pushed a stray strand of hair from my face and willed my treacherous body to behave itself.

'Hi, Samantha,' he said as he reached me.

'Hello, Gabe,' I flashed him a winning smile. 'What are you doing in here?'

The pub was noisy and he bent his head down to my ear. 'Working,' he said, his lips grazing my ear as he spoke, sending a shockwave through my entire body and making goose-bumps prickle along my forearms. I was suddenly very aware that our bodies were only centimetres apart and I felt the heat searing between my legs.

'In here?' I asked as I looked around. O'Malley's wasn't the type of place Archangel Securities usually did security for, although I'd noticed they did have bouncers on the door now.

He nodded and was about to speak when someone stumbled backwards into me, pushing me up against Gabriel's hard body. He put an arm out to catch me. 'Watch it,' he snapped to the large man behind me who had knocked me.

'Sorry, mate,' he shouted over the noise.

Gabriel kept his hand around my waist, keeping our bodies pressed together. I looked up at him and his eyes burned into mine. 'Are you okay?' he asked.

'Fine,' I breathed. Other than the fact that my internal organs felt like they had turned to hot lava.

He still held me there and I could feel my blood thundering around my body. My breathing became faster. He leaned his head towards me again. Was he going to say something? Kiss me? Dear God, Gabriel Sullivan was about to kiss me in the middle of the crowded pub and I might just come on the spot.

Suddenly, a well-manicured hand appeared on his shoulder. 'Gabriel,' the blonde woman behind him shouted. 'I've been looking everywhere for you.'

His head snapped up and annoyance flickered across his face as he half turned away from me. 'Gemma? You're late!'

He turned to me again, still with an arm around my waist, and smiled. 'Looks like I have to go.'

'I thought you were working?' I challenged him, annoyed at the unwelcome intrusion.

'I am. She's here for business, not pleasure,' he said with a wicked grin.

'Whatever you say,' I replied with a shrug, trying to appear as nonchalant as possible while my heart pounded in my chest.

Gabriel stared at me for a few seconds, his jaw working, and I wondered what he was thinking. Then he leaned in close to my ear again. 'Make sure you behave yourself, Sam. My bouncers will be watching you,' he said in that low growl of his that made my knees weak.

He called me Sam!

Then he walked away, following Gemma through the bar and out into the street.

I stared after him feeling almost breathless with wanton lust, and left with an intense throbbing between my thighs.

8. SAMANTHA

I had lounged around my apartment for most of the following day nursing the hangover from hell. I'd ended up staying out until midnight and drinking my own body weight in alcohol after Gabriel had left. I'd outstayed Nick and the rest of my colleagues and ended up grabbing a lift with one of the solicitors from another firm. He'd suggested coming upstairs for a coffee — which we all know is code for a quick fumble, but I refused. The only person I was interested in fumbling with was Gabriel. I could hardly stop thinking about him, and the blonde woman he'd met up with. He'd said it was work, but what kind of business would he have with her? She didn't look like one of Archangel Securities' usual customers.

Why couldn't I get him out of my head?

By mid-afternoon, my boredom had got the better of me and I headed to the gym before asking my dad if he fancied having dinner together later, which he had happily agreed to. How sad was I that my Saturday night date was my dad? I was sure Gabriel had more exciting plans than I did — no doubt with some young, hot Gemma lookalike.

. . .

I stood on my father's doorstep waiting for him to answer his front door. A few seconds later he opened it with a huge smile on his face. 'Sam,' he said as he pulled me inside and enveloped me in a bear hug. 'Come on through.'

I followed him into the kitchen, inhaling the aroma of the curry he was preparing. My dad was a great cook, and his curries were to die for. He usually made my favourite beef madras whenever I came over for dinner.

I walked into the kitchen and saw Gabriel standing there, leaning against the kitchen worktop with a mug of something hot in his hand. He blew lightly on the liquid before taking a sip, eyeing me over the rim of the cup. I didn't know whether to be delighted or annoyed that he was there. He seemed to be everywhere I was lately, which would be fine if all my encounters with him didn't leave me feeling like a trembling mess by the time I got home. My poor vibrator had never seen so much action.

'Hi Gabe,' I said as I took a seat at the table.

'Hello, Samantha,' he replied with a curt nod.

Moody sod!

'You don't mind if Gabriel joins us, do you Sam?' my father asked as he walked over to the stove and stirred the curry sauce.

'Not at all, Dad,' I replied, forcing a smile onto my face. Gabriel put his mug on the counter and walked across the room to sit opposite me. His shirt was open at the collar revealing a tiny fraction of one of the tattoos he had inked on his chest. I dragged my eyes away from his body and looked out of the huge patio doors instead. How the hell was I supposed to spend the whole evening sitting across from him and pretend like he had no effect on me? While my mind might behave itself, my body had other ideas and I could feel my insides churning. I put a hand on my neck to try and cool my flushed skin. As if the heat from the curry wasn't going to be enough to make me sweat, I also had to sit under the heat of Gabriel's intense gaze.

. . .

'I'll clear the dishes, Dad,' I told him as he stood up. 'Why don't you two take your beers into the sitting room and leave this to me? It's the least I can do after that beautiful meal.'

'Okay? If you're sure?'

'I'm only going to load the dishwasher,' I said with a smile. 'It's not a big deal. I'll join you in a few minutes.' Despite my earlier reservations, the three of us had enjoyed a lovely meal with pleasant conversation.

It seemed my father was the perfect buffer. It had almost been just like old times. I had spent most of my meals as a teenager stealing surreptitious glances at Gabriel too. Only now, I was sure I caught him stealing some right back.

'That sounds like a plan to me,' my father said with a smile. He kissed the top of my head. 'Come on, mate,' he said to Gabriel and then the two of them walked out of the room leaving me alone.

I was loading the dishwasher a few moments later when Gabriel strolled back into the kitchen. 'I came to see if you needed any help?' he said with a smile.

I stood up straight, blowing a stray strand of hair from my face. 'No thanks. I'm almost done now.'

He walked to the fridge and took out another bottle of Bud. 'Want one?' he asked.

'Yeah, go on,' I replied.

He twisted off the cap and handed it to me before taking another for himself. For a few moments, we stood in silence, sipping our beers and watching each other across the room.

'So, I heard you got lucky last night. Who was the fortunate recipient of your affections?' he eventually said.

'What?' I said, momentarily stunned by his question. What the hell was he on about?

'I came back to O'Malleys last night to see if you wanted a lift, but one of my bouncers told me you'd left with someone.'

I blinked at him. Was that why he was there last night? Checking up on me? 'Is it really any business of yours who I did or didn't leave with? I can't believe you were checking up on me.'

He frowned at me. 'I wasn't checking up on you at all. I was dropping Gemma off so I thought I'd offer you a lift home. My bouncer said you'd left with some bloke, that's all there is to it!'

'Oh, really?'

'Yes, really!' he growled.

'So you weren't spying on me for dear old dad, just like you used to?'

He stalked across the room towards me. 'I have never spied on you, Samantha. Not for anyone! But you should be careful going home with complete strangers that you hook up with in bars!'

I shook my head at the sheer cheek of him and his double standards. 'You're unbelievable. You and my father can go home with a different woman every night of the week, but I happen to get into a taxi with a man, who was a colleague by the way, and it's newsworthy!'

I slammed my bottle onto the counter and started to walk out of the room. He grabbed hold of my arm as I passed and I felt the heat from his skin burning mine. Despite my anger, his touch made my breath catch in my throat.

'I don't do that,' he said. 'And I wasn't checking up on you, Sam,' he said softly.

He called me Sam!

He had done last night too. Prior to that, he'd only ever called me Sam once before. It had been the night before I'd left for university. I had wrapped my arms around his neck and called him my Angel Gabriel. Then I had told him I would stay in Dagenham if he wanted me to. But of course, he hadn't wanted that at all. It had been our last encounter for fourteen years and I hadn't thought about it in a very long time.

'Please don't call me Sam,' I whispered. It hurt too much.

I saw something flash in Gabriel's eyes before he released my arm and I walked out of the kitchen.

9. GABRIEL

I left Sebastian's house earlier than I'd planned. I should never have stayed for dinner. But I'd stupidly thought that maybe I could be around Samantha and pretend I didn't want to bury myself inside her. It had worked for a while. We'd had a nice dinner, and I'd tried to remember that she was my best mate's daughter and completely off limits. I tried to be nice — but that just seemed to piss her off and push her away from me.

I'd gone back to O'Malley's last night to offer to drive her home. If I was honest, I was hoping that she might invite me up to her apartment for a drink. If I was completely honest, I was hoping that the night would end with some part of my body inside her. When one of my bouncers told me she'd left with some bloke, who wasn't her friend, Nick, I'd felt like I'd been punched in the gut.

Samantha had been through a lot in the last fourteen years. I knew that. It had changed her. Made her suspicious. Cautious – even of me. It infuriated me that I hadn't known about what she'd been going through while she was married to that cunt, Jackson. I would never forgive myself for not saving her. When she was a teenager and I'd spent almost every weekend helping her out of one sticky situation after another, she used to joke that I was her Angel Gabriel. I knew she was teasing me, but I had enjoyed being her rescuer. She was a good kid. Funny and smart and I'd always got on well with her.

Then she'd turned eighteen and it was like she'd transformed into a woman overnight. To my shame, I'd started to look at her as much more than Sebastian's daughter. To make matters worse, she would flirt with me constantly. It had taken every ounce of willpower I'd had not to flirt right back. Then the night before she left for uni, she asked me if I'd miss her. I was so close to telling her how much I would. I'd wanted to pull her into my arms and kiss every inch of her body, but she'd been completely wasted and I would never take advantage of anyone like that. Besides, she was about to set off on a whole new life. And I'd wanted that for her. If I had known what kind of life she was going to, I would have chained her to her bed and never let her go.

The next day, I'd gone over to Sebastian's house to say goodbye properly. I was going to ask her if I could visit her on campus and suggest we could grab a drink or a bite to eat some time. But when I got to Sebastian's house, she was gone. Too excited to wait a moment longer, he'd said. And I'd realised at that moment, that I was her past and had no place in her future.

I jogged down the steps and took my phone out of my pocket and saw a message from Jimmy Fenton.

You thought about my offer yet?

I scowled at the screen. As if I wasn't in a bad enough mood.

10. SAMANTHA

Before I knew it, Monday morning and the beginning of another working week had arrived. I was fortunate enough to love my job. Not only did I love being my own boss, but I also got to work with my best friend, Nick, every day. I was sorting through the post in my in-tray while he told me all about his latest spat with his ex-wife, Mandy, over their two children.

'I just wish she wasn't so bloody unreasonable all the time, Samantha,' he sighed.

I had always got on well with Mandy while she'd been married to Nick. She worked hard in her job as a paediatric nurse and she loved her kids, but she had cheated on Nick and broken his heart, and I would never forgive her for that. Despite that, I knew that Mandy wasn't generally an unreasonable woman.

'I'm sure it's hard for her, too. You're both used to living with the kids full time. This is a period of adjustment for all of you.'

Nick nodded. 'I know you're right, but it's fucking hard. I wasn't the one who went off and screwed someone else, but it's me and the kids who have to suffer.'

I was about to respond when I picked up the final letter from my tray. I recognised the distinctive writing immediately. The hairs on the back of my neck stood on end and my heart started to hammer against my ribcage.

Sensing the change in mood, Nick sat up straighter in his chair. 'What's wrong? Is it another one?'

I nodded. 'I think so.'

'Here, let me open it,' he offered as he reached out his hand.

I shook my head. 'No. I need to do it myself.'

Opening the letter, I pulled out the single sheet of paper and read the crudely written note. It was just as disgusting as the previous ones I'd received.

'What does it say?' Nick asked.

'The usual threats,' I sighed as I handed it to him.

Nick shook his head. 'I can't believe you're still getting these. Have the police done anything about it?'

I shrugged. 'What can they do? There are never any fingerprints. They always come with a different postmark. Besides, I'm sure it's nothing, just some nut-job I've upset trying to give me a scare.'

I heard the conviction in my words but the truth was the letters were starting to freak me out. I'd been receiving them for two months now. I'd certainly had my fair share of threats before. I'd been a criminal prosecutor for four years and now I worked in family law, so it was a hazard of the job. But these had become persistent, and whoever was sending them obviously knew what they were doing as they left no clue as to who they were.

'Maybe you should tell your dad about them?' Nick suggested.

'My dad? Why?'

Nick's face flushed slightly. 'Well, he does have certain *talents*, doesn't he? Maybe he could find out who's sending these things,' he held up the note in disgust. 'I'm worried about these now, Samantha. Even if you're not.'

'There's nothing my dad could do about them either, Nick. If the police can't help, then I'm sure my father isn't going to crack the case.'

'Well, I think you should tell him anyway.'

'And have him worrying and hovering over me. Not a chance. I'll log this one with the police too. Maybe they can get something from this one?'

Nick handed the note back to me. 'You and DS Phillips must be on a first name basis by now?'

I nodded. Detective Sergeant Carl Phillips had dealt with each of the letters and notes I'd been sent since I'd returned to Dagenham two months earlier. We had become quite friendly during that time. He'd given me his personal mobile in case I needed to update him when he was off duty. 'I'll give him a call and let him know,' I said.

'I bet that's not all he wants to know about,' Nick grinned at me.

I laughed. It was true that DS Phillips was a huge flirt. 'Probably not, but that's all I'm telling him anyway,' I said.

'You sure you're okay?' Nick asked, his voice full of concern.

I nodded. 'I'll be fine. Thanks, Nick. Do you fancy a fresh coffee?'

'No thanks,' he said, standing up from his chair. 'I'd better get back to it. I'm in court this afternoon.'

'Oh yes. The Banks case. Good luck,' I smiled.

'Thanks. I think I'm going to need it. Matthews is the judge.'

I rolled my eyes. 'Oh, Christ. Not him. He's a bloody dinosaur.'

'I know. I'd better get cracking then. See you later.'

'Okay. Let me know how you get on in court.'

I watched as Nick walked out of my office. I looked at the note again and my stomach sank. Sooner or later the writer of these notes was going to get bored with his vile scribblings and escalate to something more sinister. Taking my phone from my handbag, I dialled Detective Sergeant Phillips' number. He answered on the second ring.

11. SAMANTHA

It had been three days since I'd received the last threatening note and spoken with DS Phillips. He had been his usual helpful self, but there had been little he could do and no leads for him to follow. Until now, that was. I smiled as he and his colleague, Constable Meadows stood up to leave my office. The door opened before they reached it and I stifled a groan as I saw my father walking through it. It was just my luck that he had chosen this particular moment to visit me at work.

'We'll let you know if we pick him up,' DS Phillips said as he extended his hand to shake mine. 'Please be vigilant in the meantime.'

'Thanks, Carl,' I said as I shook his hand. 'I will.'

My father eyed the police officers suspiciously as they brushed past him.

'Pick who up? What's going on?' he asked.

'Nobody. It's just work, Dad,' I replied, hoping he wouldn't probe any further.

'It's not just work though, is it?' Nick said as he walked into the office.

I glared at him. I loved Nick dearly. He had been the best of friends to me, but at that moment I felt like wringing his neck.

Instead, I glowered at him as I sat at my desk. He had obviously been hanging around waiting for the police to leave.

'Glare at me all you like, Samantha. But he could have hurt you today,' Nick said. 'You need to start taking this seriously.'

'Who could have hurt you? Take what seriously?' my father snapped.

'Samantha has been getting threatening letters. And today someone grabbed her on her way in,' Nick said.

'What?' my dad shouted as he looked between Nick and me.

'He didn't grab me, he just tried to-' I started to say when Gabriel bounded into my office too.

'For God's sake!' I muttered under my breath.

'It's a nightmare to park around here,' Gabriel said before looking up at the three angry faces in the room and realising he'd walked into something. 'What's going on?' he asked.

My father responded before I had a chance to. 'Some fucking nut-job is threatening Samantha.'

'What?' Gabriel asked as he started to stare at me too.

'It's been going on for months,' Nick added unhelpfully.

'Nick!' I snapped, wishing he would shut up.

'For the love of God, what the fuck is going on?' my father shouted.

At this outburst, Gabriel walked over to my father and put a hand on his shoulder. 'Calm down, mate,' he said quietly. 'And let Samantha explain, eh?'

I looked at Gabriel and gave a slight nod of thanks. For a brief moment, our eyes locked and I felt a shiver run down the length of my spine until he looked away and back at my father's angry face.

My father sat down in a chair, his arms crossed over his chest and he nodded. 'Sorry, Sam,' he said sullenly. 'But what the fuck is going on?'

Gabriel sat on the chair beside him and Nick hung around by the office door. The three of them stared at me and the next thing I knew, they were watching me like an interview panel, while I explained that I'd started receiving the threatening letters about two months earlier, shortly after my return to Dagenham. Then earlier that morning, the estranged husband of one of my clients, Anthony Garvey, had been waiting for me outside the office and had jumped out on me, making a grab for me as I'd been opening up. Fortunately, a passing jogger had seen him and phoned the police and I had managed to get inside the building while Garvey had been distracted. The police turning up had obviously completely spooked him and he seemed to have disappeared. Given what he'd said when he'd approached me earlier that morning, the police believe he was the likely sender of the threatening letters too.

'So what are the police doing about it then?' my father asked when I'd finished.

'They're looking for him. He's well known to them and now that there's a warrant out for him, I doubt he'll get very far,' I responded.

He shook his head in disgust.

'What?' I snapped.

'I don't trust that lot. By the time they get their finger out, he could have-'

'He could have what, Dad?' I interrupted him as I stood up with my arms crossed across my chest.

'I think we can all agree that the police have never been particularly good at preventing pricks like Garvey hurting people before, can't we?' Gabriel interjected.

'Oh, you mean people like me?' I snapped.

Gabriel shook his head. 'I never said that.'

'But that's what you're thinking though, isn't it? That's what you're all thinking. Poor Samantha can't protect herself. She's so pathetic even the police couldn't protect her.'

Gabriel stood up. 'That's not what I meant,' he said, frowning at me.

My dad stood up then and started shouting about how useless the police were and how he was going to sort Garvey out himself. Nick began talking in the background too and I tried to block them out, to no avail. All I wanted was for them to go away and leave me the hell alone. It was bad enough that Garvey had ruined my morning and scared the hell out of me without the three musketeers carrying on as if I was some defenceless damsel in distress. If there was one thing I hated more than anything in the world, it was to feel pitied. I knew they meant well, but they were driving me crazy and I couldn't stand any more of it.

'Get out!' I finally shouted. 'Will the three of you shut up, and get out?'

They looked at me and then at each other.

'Out!' I repeated.

It was Gabriel who spoke. 'Come on,' he gestured to my father who stood up and followed him. Together the two of them bustled Nick out of the door and closed it behind them.

I sank down into my chair and rubbed my throbbing temples. Why couldn't my life just be simple for once? Unlike my father and Gabriel, I had every faith that the police would deal with Garvey. He had frightened the life out of me that morning, jumping out and trying to grab me, but I'd dealt with the situation. Despite what people thought, I was capable of looking after myself. What my father, Gabriel and Nick didn't seem to realise, was that compared to my ex-husband, Anthony Garvey was a pussycat.

12. GABRIEL

It had been an hour since we'd got back to our office at Archangel Securities, but Sebastian was still raging. I tried to calm him down as he shouted and threw things around the room. Sebastian's legendary temper, never easily controlled at the best of times, was always ignited to dangerous levels when there was any possible danger to Samantha – whom he still considered his little girl.

'We should find this cunt and sort him out,' Sebastian snapped.

'Calm the fuck down, Seb. Samantha said the police are dealing with it.'

'And we both know how fucking useless they are. Don't you think she's been through enough without worrying about some nutter threatening her?'

'I know, mate. But you know what she's like, she'll go ape-shit if she thinks you're trying to interfere. Let's just calm down and think about our next move, eh?'

Sebastian nodded but I doubted he was taking much in. Nevertheless, it was doing no-one any favours for him to be carrying on the way he was. Samantha was fiercely independent; she always had been. I knew that it had a lot to do with the way Sebastian had been when she was a kid. He was only sixteen when she'd been born and her mother's parents had taken their daughter and granddaughter and moved to Kent. They didn't approve of Sebastian and they claimed they had wanted better for their daughter and grandchild. Sebastian had always regretted not running after them — not fighting for them, but he had managed to convince himself that they were better off without him.

When Samantha's mother had died when she was just twelve, Sebastian had discovered that he was Samantha's only living relative, and he had stepped up and tried to be the best father that he could. But he felt so much guilt for not being in her life that he'd spoiled her. When she started to push boundaries, and became the teenager from hell, he became overly strict with her, because he didn't know how else to look after a rebellious teenage girl. He had ultimately pushed her away — and eventually into the arms of Jackson Carver. I knew that Sebastian felt more guilt over that than he would ever admit, and it was that which was also feeding his anxiety and fear over this new threat. I understood Sebastian's need to do something about it. The thought of someone threatening her now, and hanging around outside her office filled me with dread too. But, I also knew that thirty-two year old Samantha was even more headstrong and independent than her teenage self had ever been.

'What do we do in the meantime, Gabriel? What if that bastard is waiting for her somewhere? Following her? I don't fucking care if she goes ape-shit, as long as she's safe,' Sebastian bellowed across the office, ensuring that anyone in the vicinity heard him.

A couple of our employees had been waiting for us in the meeting room next door and I watched as they crept past our office and out of the main door. They would rather miss a meeting and get a bollocking when Sebastian was in a better mood than be a target for his epic rage at that moment.

I looked at my best mate and could see the worry and the fear in his eyes and hoped that he didn't see the same in mine. I let him continue raging, knowing that he'd burn himself out soon enough.

A few moments later, Sebastian's rage had subsided slightly and he sat down on the expensive leather chair at his desk and poured himself a glass of Scotch. 'Want one?' he asked.

I shook my head. 'One of us has to be fit to drive.'

'Sorry,' Sebastian muttered before downing his drink. 'But I might as well make the most of not being able to.' Then he poured himself another.

I shook my head. Sebastian had been caught drink driving four months earlier and had been banned for twelve months. It usually didn't cause too many problems as we had a team of employees who could drive us when the occasion called for it and I didn't usually drink much anyway. I didn't like the feeling of not being in control when I'd had too much alcohol. But sometimes, it was a pain in the arse always having to be the sensible one. Sebastian was eight years older than me, but most of the time it felt like I was the mature one in our partnership.

'So? Garvey?' Sebastian asked as he leaned back in his chair. 'What are we gonna do then?'

I had been thinking about the situation since we'd left Samantha's office. 'We're going to let the police deal with him,' I said and could see Sebastian tense. It obviously wasn't the answer he'd been hoping for. 'Because that's what Samantha wants. But we can make sure she's protected in the meantime.'

'Okay. How?'

I couldn't help but frown. Sometimes I got fed up of always being the rational one who had to come up with the solutions while my partner sat back — or worse still, went off half-cocked, often creating more problems than he solved.

'By doing what we do. We run a security company, Seb. There's already security in place at the flats. We'll put an extra body on the front desk. And for the foreseeable future, someone should probably drive her to and from work. It's likely this prick knows her routine.'

Sebastian nodded. 'Okay. But you'll have to drive her. You know that? I don't trust anyone else.'

For reasons unknown to both me and Sebastian, Samantha refused to drive. She could drive. She'd passed her test at the age of seventeen in her attempts to get as far away from the place where she'd grown up as fast as possible. A little over twelve months later, she'd packed up her little Metro and driven off to university where she had met Jackson Carver, and had never looked back — until a few months ago at least.

'Okay,' I agreed. As if I didn't have enough on my plate already. But Samantha would run rings around anyone else we put on the job. She had a fierce hatred of feeling like she was being protected — or mollycoddled, as she called it. Besides, I wasn't sure if I trusted anyone else enough to do it either. Samantha had once been like a little sister to me. And now she was ... well, I didn't want to think about that.

'Tell her I'm making you do it.' Sebastian added. 'She'll go easier on you then.'

I nodded. I would tell her that it was her father's idea. It would make things easier for me, but not for the reasons Sebastian thought. The truth was I wanted to protect Samantha as much as he did, and I couldn't admit that to him or her or they might realise I was starting to have feelings for her that I had no right having.

13. SAMANTHA

Rubbing my temples, I tried to ease the headache that was threatening. It had been a long day. Nick had tried to insist that I go home after the incident with Garvey earlier that morning, but I preferred to be in work and keeping busy. And that's exactly what I'd done, barely lifting my head to speak to anyone. I used my work as an escape. It had been one of my primary means of coping when I'd been married to Jackson. It was the one area of my life where he encouraged me to excel. I supposed it looked good for him that his wife was also a successful solicitor. He tried to pressure me into taking the bar and becoming a barrister a few times, but I was much happier being a solicitor.

The shrill ring of the phone on my desk broke my train of thought. Glancing at the caller display I saw the call was from reception.

'Yes, Beth?' I answered.

'There's a Gabriel Sullivan here to see you, Samantha.'

I shook my head in annoyance. What the hell was he doing here? I hadn't heard from him or my father since I'd chased them out of my office earlier. 'Send him through,' I replied with a sigh.

Walking into my office in a dark navy suit, and a white shirt, open at the collar, Gabriel oozed confidence. My breath caught in my throat at the sight of him. Did he have to look so damn fine all the time!

'Hey,' he smiled at me, his green eyes twinkling.

'Hi, Gabe. What can I do for you?'

I watched him take a deep breath, as if bracing himself for an onslaught, and my heart sank. I already knew I wasn't going to like what he had to say.

'Your dad asked me to drive you home.'

'What? Why?' I snapped.

'He wants to make sure you get home safely, that's all.'

I felt the colour flushing my cheeks. This was exactly what I'd been worried about. I had fought hard for my independence and I hated to be treated like someone who was incapable of looking after herself. Especially by Gabriel. I wanted him to look at me and see the strong woman I'd become, and not a little girl who still needed him to look out for her. 'Well, you've had a wasted journey. I'll be taking the tube home, like I do every night. I don't need a bodyguard.'

'You have to understand why he's doing this, Samantha?' Gabriel said with a sigh. 'He's worried about you. Some psycho is threatening to kill you. He just wants to protect you.'

'Tell my father I can protect myself. I'm not some fragile little girl, despite what he thinks. And as for a psychopath who wants to kill me, I lived with one for twelve years. And yet, here I am.'

Gabriel stood firm, and placed his hands in his trouser pockets, causing the material to stretch taut over his muscular thighs. I had to make a conscious effort not to stare at his whole trouser region.

'Well, I'm not leaving. I'm here to take you home. There will be a car at your apartment building every morning, and I'll be here every night until that nutter is where he belongs,' he said.

I glared at him. 'What the hell does that mean? I told you and my father that I don't want you doing anything about Garvey.'

Gabriel nodded. 'And we won't. But we can make sure you're safe until the police do their job.'

'And I get no say in this?' I snapped.

Gabriel shrugged. 'It's not just Garvey. He's worried that it might be Jackson trying to get to you.'

I shook my head. 'You don't understand. Jackson is not some wannabe gangster trying to take over your turf, or some dealer who's terrified of you. You have no idea what type of man he is, or what he's capable of. Trust me, if Jackson wants to get to me, no-one can stop him. Not my father — and certainly not you.'

Gabriel continued to stand there, showing no reaction to my outburst which conversely only served to annoy me more. Did they seriously think I was a child? Or a feeble woman unable to look after myself?

'Why are you here then, Gabriel? Why isn't my father here himself if he's so worried about me? Surely you have better ways to spend an evening? Isn't there some nineteen year old blonde somewhere, just dying for your company right now?'

'You already know your dad lost his licence. Besides, he's dealing with some other business.'

'Oh yes. He's the brains and you're the brawn — that's right, isn't it?'

Gabriel shrugged, his face still showing no hint of emotion.

'So you just do whatever he tells you?' I went on, desperate to provoke some sort of reaction from him. 'He says jump and you ask how high?'

I knew that wasn't true, aware that Gabriel and my father had an equal partnership and that they were more like brothers than friends, but I was so on edge and his presence was only making me feel more irritated.

Ignoring my barbs, Gabriel sat down on a chair in my office. 'I'll just wait here until you're ready to leave,' he said, his voice low and gravelly.

'Fine,' I snapped. 'But I work late most nights, so you're going to be here a while.'

He simply nodded in response.

I swore under my breath. I'd been planning on going home early, but would have to stay late now, if only to inconvenience Gabriel, hoping that he'd soon get fed up of babysitting me. Besides, the idea of keeping him from any potential nineteen year old blonde, or any woman for that matter, was surprisingly pleasing to me.

Realising I was going to be around for another couple of hours, I dialled reception. 'Beth, could you bring me a coffee please? You can head off home then.' I looked at Gabriel. 'Would you like one?'

He nodded. 'Black, no sugar.'

'Can you bring my bodyguard one too, please? Black. No sugar. Thanks.'

A few minutes later, Beth came in carrying two mugs of coffee. Looking at the dark brown liquid, I sighed. Beth was new to the job and always got my coffee wrong. I was tired of pointing this out to her and thanked her anyway. She handed Gabriel his coffee while smiling sweetly at him and I watched with interest as they exchanged a look that suggested they might do more than smile at each other if I wasn't in the room.

Engrossed in highlighting pages of witness testimony, I had almost forgotten about Gabriel, who had been reading his way through the magazines in my office, until he piped up.

'Why did you ask for coffee if you weren't going to drink it?' He nodded towards the untouched cup on my desk.

'It's not made how I like it. I can't touch it.' I said before realising that statement made me sound incredibly precious. 'I can only drink very weak coffee, with lots of milk and four sugars,' I replied, feeling the need to explain myself. 'I don't really like to taste the coffee. Beth never gets it right. I don't know why I bother. I'm sure she got yours right though?'

'Well, it's pretty hard to fuck up black coffee, isn't it?' he replied with a grin.

'Suppose so.' I smiled back before returning to my highlighting.

'So, why do you drink it then?'

'What?' my head snapped up. Couldn't he see I was busy?

'You said you don't like to taste the coffee. So why drink it?'

I studied him for a moment. How could I answer that question without revealing more about my life with Jackson? I couldn't. 'It's a long story,' I answered with a smile. 'Now, can you let me get back to work?'

'You look like you could do with a break. How about I make you a fresh coffee and then you can take five minutes off to tell me about it. Deal?'

I put down my highlighter pen and rubbed my temples. I could do with a break. I was tired, and I should go home — if only I wasn't being so stubborn. A hot coffee the way I liked it would be nice. 'Deal,' I relented.

A few moments later Gabriel walked back into my office and handed me a fresh drink. I could already tell from the pale colour that it was better than Beth's earlier effort. Taking a sip, I realised it was perfect. 'Thank you,' I said.

'So?' he smiled.

I sighed. I was going to sound like a fruit-loop. But a deal was a deal. 'I only drink coffee because Jackson would drink nothing but tea. Every morning he insisted on a fresh pot of tea. I'd never been a big fan of coffee or tea but he claimed that even the smell of coffee made him feel nauseous. So, we only ever had tea in the house, and in the office — even for guests or clients. He insisted that I drink tea too. How could I not like the taste of tea, right? So, as soon as I left him, I started drinking coffee. Like some small rebellion. But I don't actually like it that much. I'm learning to tolerate the taste of it — by adding lots of milk and sugar.'

I looked at him, waiting for some reaction. He stared at me for a few moments before nodding his head and sitting back in the chair. He continued to flick through one of the magazines and I wondered why he'd even bothered to ask.

It was dark outside when I finally finished working on my case. I looked up to see Gabriel. Of course, he was still there, staring out of the window with a frown on his face.

I watched him for a few moments and wondered what he was thinking about. 'I'm ready to go,' I finally said.

He nodded at me and stood up, handing me my coat and handbag as I walked around to his side of the desk.

Gabriel and I stepped out into the cold and took the short walk to his car. He opened the door to his car and I climbed inside. I was so tired. Leaning my head back against the plush leather seats, I closed my eyes.

'Wake up sleepy head,' Gabriel's voice jolted me awake and I realised I'd slept the whole way home.

I rubbed my eyes before picking up my handbag from the footwell.

'There will be a black Range Rover here at 8am, Samantha. The driver's name is Scott Thomas. If you don't get in the car, he'll never hear the end of it. In fact, your bad-tempered father is likely to fire him, so can you please just let him drive you to work?' Gabriel asked as he stared at me — his eyes full of concern.

I stared back at him. God, I hated the way he looked at me now — the pity was unbearable. I understood my father's desire to protect me from all that was wrong with the world. It was his job. And given what he'd learned of my life with Jackson Carver, I accepted that he would always be over-protective, despite me being a grown woman. But it made my heart physically hurt to know that was how Gabriel saw me too. I was so much more than what he saw before him, and he would never know. I choked back the emotion. Swallowing it down, the way I'd learned to.

'Okay,' I said. I didn't appreciate the emotional blackmail either. As much as I hated their fussing and over-protectiveness, I didn't want some poor unsuspecting employee of theirs getting into trouble. I wouldn't put it past my father to sack the poor man. I climbed out of the car without another word. Not even a mumbled thank-you for the lift home. As I walked to my apartment building I felt a pang of guilt and had to force myself not to look back and smile at Gabriel. Perhaps I'd send him a text to say thanks when I got inside?

No! I wouldn't. Hopefully he'd tell my father I'd acted like a complete bitch and he would refuse to babysit me ever again.

14. GABRIEL

I rubbed my temples as I sat in the dark booth of the half empty nightclub. I'd arranged for one of our most trusted employees to pick Samantha up from her apartment every morning and drive her to work. I had thought about doing it myself, as Sebastian had requested, but any time in her company always seemed to leave me with a throbbing head — and a throbbing cock. And both were things I could do without at the start of every day. Besides, I sensed Samantha's resentment at my intrusion into her life, and it pissed me off. There had been a time when she had enjoyed my company. There had been a time when she had flirted with me every chance she got.

One of the barmaids, Ellie, brought a large whisky over to my table and I downed it in one. I was so tightly wound, I thought I might explode if I didn't get some fucking relief soon. Ever since Samantha Donovan walked back into my life, she occupied my thoughts constantly. But God she was so fucking prickly. She'd changed so much from the girl I'd known. Well, of course she had. After what she'd been through, who wouldn't?

I still saw still glimpses of the old Samantha. The Samantha who could make me laugh harder than anyone else I knew. The Samantha who would cross the street to help a kid who'd fallen off their bike, or to stroke a stray dog. When she'd been telling me about the coffee, I'd sensed I was finally getting through her armour. But then she clammed up again, and barely spoke another word to me, except to make sarcastic comments. After that, all I could think about was putting that smart mouth of hers to much better use before fucking her brains out.

Ellie brought me a second whisky, interrupting my thoughts. 'Are you okay, Gabriel?' she asked with a smile.

'Yeah, thanks Ellie. Just having a rough night.'

She ran a fingertip over my bicep. 'I'm sure I could help you take the edge off?' she purred.

I considered her. She was pretty. Big blue eyes and high cheekbones. She was a hit with the customers and I could see why. Maybe I should take her up on her offer? It might make me feel better to bury my face in Ellie's neck and pretend that she was Samantha?

'I'm sure you could. But I need to get home,' I replied with a smile. It wasn't like I was against a quick, meaningless fuck. It was one of my favourite ways to relieve tension. But Ellie wasn't my type, and besides, I wasn't in the habit of fucking my employees.

'Okay. But you know where I am if you change your mind,' she said before walking back to the bar.

15. SAMANTHA

I was standing near the window of my large office when I saw Gabriel walking up the steps. Damn that man made a suit look like a work of art. I was sure he must have them all professionally tailored. They fit the contours of his body perfectly. It was the fourth day of him being my bodyguard and although I would never admit it, even to myself, I was starting to look forward to seeing him at the end of each day.

'We're all going clubbing tomorrow, Gabriel. Do you fancy coming?' my receptionist, Beth asked as she walked into my office behind him. 'It's for my birthday.'

He raised an eyebrow. 'I don't really do clubbing. Thanks for the invite though,' he replied, much to my relief. I could do without watching him and Beth flirting together all night. I thought I might have built up some resistance to him by now, but each encounter with him left me a hot, dripping mess.

Beth shrugged her shoulders. 'See you tomorrow, Samantha,' she chirped as she left.

I sat down at my desk with a stack of case files in front of me. If Gabriel was going to keep insisting on driving me home, then he would have to wait.

'Coffee?' he asked.

'Yes, please. Plenty of milk-'

'And thirty–four sugars. Yes, I remember,' he said with a smile before disappearing out of my office again.

A few moments later, he came back in carrying two mugs and handed me one.

'Are you off clubbing too then?' he asked.

'Yes, of course. I haven't been clubbing for years. And it can't be a team night out without one half of Donovan Cook now, can it?' I grinned at him.

It was Friday night in Dagenham's newest nightclub and Sadie and I were dancing on a table when a burly bouncer approached us.

'Can you both get down please?' he asked politely.

'Spoilsport!' We both laughed at him before climbing down and continuing to dance on the floor. Nick was sitting on a nearby stool grinning inanely and holding a bottle of Budweiser like it was his baby. I scanned the room to look for Beth and spotted her with her friend, Leon, who had come along with us, and saw them grinding against each other on the dance-floor.

'I'll go get us another drink,' Sadie mouthed over the deafening music.

A few minutes later, she returned from the bar with a bottle of champagne and two glasses.

'Compliments of the manager, apparently,' she shouted.

'Nice,' I shouted back picking up the bottle. 'What the hell? This is Cristal. Do you have any idea how much this costs in a place like this?'

She shrugged her shoulders. 'Who cares? Just open it!'

I peeled off the foil and popped the cork. Armed with a fresh glass of champagne each, we made sure our bouncer friend wasn't in the near vicinity, before climbing back onto the table to resume our earlier fun.

A few moments later, I was about to declare, for possibly the fiftieth time that night, that *this,* was in fact, my favourite song when a strong pair of hands grabbed hold of my waist, pulling me down from the table and into his arms.

'Haven't you already been told once to get down from there, young lady,' Gabriel growled in my ear. 'I thought my days of throwing you out of nightclubs were long over?' He looked into my eyes and I felt the heat from his gaze deep in my core. I had a sudden urge to wrap my arms around his neck and kiss him.

Thankfully, he set me down on my feet before I did, before helping Sadie down too. I stared at him. I should have been annoyed that he had ruined our fun, but all I could think about was how good it had felt to have him holding me.

'What are you doing here? This isn't one of your clubs. How did you even know I was here?' I asked.

'I didn't know you were here until I got here. I came to see the manager, he's a friend of mine.'

That explained the free champagne then. 'How long have you been here?'

'About an hour,' he shouted.

'Have you been spying on me?' I asked, not sure if I was annoyed or flattered. The champagne was making me feel like a giggly teenager. Or was that him?

'No! But when Tony told me that he was about to throw two women out because they wouldn't stop dancing on the tables, I had an idea you might be involved. I remember how much trouble you used to get me into because you refuse to dance on the floor like a normal person,' he said with a smile.

I suddenly felt very light-headed. Champagne always went straight to my head. 'I think I need to go home now.' I slurred.

Beth and her friend stayed on at the club, but Sadie, Nick and I tumbled into Gabriel's car. I sat in the front seat and kicked off my heels, putting my bare feet on the dashboard. My dress, which was already very short, had ridden up to the very top of my thigh, but

I didn't bother to pull it down. As we drove to drop off Sadie and Nick at their respective houses, I noticed Gabriel stealing surreptitious glances at my exposed thighs, and even in my inebriated state, I couldn't help but smile.

After we had dropped off Nick and Sadie, Gabriel finally spoke.

'What are you wearing, Samantha?'

'A dress, Gabriel.'

'If you could call it a dress,' he said as he raised an eyebrow at me. 'You sure it's not a top?'

'Yes, I'm sure. I was clubbing, wasn't I? And I'm not showing any boobs so it's fine.'

'Eh?'

'Boobs or legs — but never both — them's the rules.'

He laughed. 'You could get a man into a lot of trouble with those legs.'

I wouldn't mind getting you into a lot of trouble!

We drove along in silence for a while before I spoke again. 'I suppose you can't wait to tell my dad you had to drive me home after I got drunk at a club again, can you?' I asked him. I had intended it to come out like a joke, but instead couldn't help adding a hint of sarcasm.

He turned in his seat and frowned at me. 'What?'

'Just like when I was a kid, always running to tell my dad when I'd been naughty?'

'For the record, I never once told your father about any one of the many occasions I had to take you home or throw you out of a club.'

I blinked at him. Surely he was lying. Back when I was a rebellious teenager, he'd been as bad as my father for treating me like I was made of glass — hadn't he? 'What? Of course you did.'

He shook his head. 'Nope. Never.'

'But I thought ...'

'You were usually in enough trouble without me adding to the drama. Besides, if he'd known about half the things you used to get up to, your dad would have had you carted off to a nunnery.'

I stared at him with my mouth hanging open. This was a

complete shock to me. Gabriel broke the tension by starting to laugh. 'Remember that time I caught you trying to climb out of your bedroom window and you got stuck?'

In spite of myself, I laughed too. I blushed as I remembered it. I was sixteen and had been grounded for smoking weed. I was sneaking out to meet my boyfriend when I saw Gabriel's car pulling into our drive. I had tried to climb back into the window but instead had managed to wedge myself in somehow. Gabriel had shouted from the drive to stay where I was, and then he came inside and made an excuse to use the bathroom before sneaking upstairs and secretly hauling me back inside.

'If I recall, you never told him about that, actually.'

'I never told him about any of it,' he frowned at me. 'I thought you knew that?'

I shook my head. 'No. He was always annoyed with me for something, I just thought he knew about me sneaking into clubs and drinking too. I assumed your loyalty always lay with him?'

I watched as Gabriel clenched his jaw shut. 'It did.'

I nodded. Thought so!

'But it wasn't about loyalty,' he went on. 'It was about understanding that you were both struggling to adjust, and that you were both just doing your best.'

I stared at him and he kept his eyes fixed on the road ahead. 'And what about now, Gabe? Where does your loyalty lie? Would you still keep secrets from my father for me?' I teased him.

I heard a low growl in his throat.

'Well?' I asked again, placing my hand on his arm.

He turned to face me. 'That would depend entirely on what the secret was,' he said seriously before turning back to the road. Suddenly, the air was thick with tension again.

I looked out of the window. I was far too drunk to be having such deep conversations with a man who was too intense for words.

16. SAMANTHA

Despite my protestations, and several irate phone calls to my father, Gabriel continued to turn up at my office at five o'clock every evening. And every night, I made him wait for at least two hours. I never thanked him for the lift home. Instead, I made sarcastic comments and asked inappropriate questions about his personal life.

He was always polite to me. Answering my questions, or graciously refusing if they were too personal, rarely letting any emotion show at all. But, the less of a reaction I got from him, the more I wanted to provoke one. At first it was because I was annoyed at him — and my father. But, once I had resigned myself to the fact that he was going to be my lift home for the foreseeable future, it started to bother me that I never got anything back from him.

What was that about? He never showed any reaction, even when I was being incredibly rude to him. He never once swore at me, or told me to mind my own business. I could only conclude that it was because he felt sorry for me. Poor little Samantha whose husband beat her. Samantha who couldn't even protect herself. That realisation made me resent him and his presence in my life even more.

I was looking out of the window when I saw him walking up the steps to my office in his customary suit. He looked as handsome as ever and I felt my heart start pounding in my chest as I imagined how he would look naked — and preferably on top of me. My cheeks flushed at the thought until I heard Beth giggling outside my door. I heard the mumble of chatter and wondered what she and Gabriel were talking about, especially when I heard him laughing too. But when he walked into my office a moment later, only serious, solemn Gabriel was present. No trace of laughter remained. As usual, he took a seat in the chair opposite my desk and we began our regular evening routine.

'So how was your day?' I asked, my voice dripping with sarcasm, as I sat down behind my desk.

Gabriel glared at me. 'How about we strike a deal?'

'I'm listening,' I said. The last deal I'd struck with him had resulted in him making me coffee every evening so that had worked out well.

'You can go on asking me as many questions as you like. You can ask me anything at all, and I'll answer. But, I get to ask you one question — and you have to tell the truth.'

I studied his face as he stared at me. God, he was so damn hard to read.

'Deal?' he asked.

'Deal,' I replied. I could answer one question. How hard could that be? And now I got to ask him anything at all. So, I asked him about the one thing that I'd been desperate to know about. The thing that my father had warned me never to mention.

'So, I hear you were married too while I was away? Who was she? What happened?' I said as I leaned my elbows on the desk. I expected him to scowl at me but he maintained his cool facade.

'Her name was Jennifer. We were married for three years. We got divorced four years ago.'

'That's it? Come on, Gabe. Tell me what happened between the two of you? Did you love her? Why did you get divorced? We had a deal and your limited answers are really not cutting the mustard,' I said with a grin. I so enjoyed trying to push his buttons.

Gabriel stared at me and I thought I saw the flicker of a scowl, before his face returned to its usual impassive state when he was around me. 'Of course I loved her - I married her. But we grew apart. Me and your dad were building the business and I spent too much time doing that and not enough with her. She had an affair, and that was it.'

I almost fell off my chair. I'd had no idea. 'What? She had an affair?'

He did frown at me then. 'Yes. That's what I said.'

'I'm sorry, Gabriel. I didn't know,' I said, wishing now that I hadn't asked him about his ex-wife at all. Although I quite enjoyed annoying him, I hadn't want to cause him any genuine pain.

'Don't be,' he replied with a shrug. 'It was a long time ago. We've both moved on.'

I smiled at him and wondered how anyone could ever cheat on Gabriel? He was one of the good ones, wasn't he? Not to mention he was hotter than molten lava. But what would I know? Thinking of all the women who used to envy my relationship with Jackson, I shuddered — how little they knew!

Gabriel pulled up outside my apartment building and turned off the engine of his car. I turned to him. He still hadn't asked me a question and I was curious to know what it would be. Earlier on, it had seemed like he'd had a specific one in mind. Still feeling guilty for making him talk about his ex-wife, I was reminded that although it was annoying, Gabriel was only being my personal chauffeur because my father was so worried about me. It wasn't Gabriel's fault he was stuck in the middle of the two of us. Perhaps I should be a bit nicer to him?

'You still haven't asked me a question?' I said.

He turned in his seat. 'The night's not over yet,' he replied.

I smiled at him. 'Oh, really?'

'I think it's about time you made me a coffee for a change,' he said with a smile.

Not quite a question.

I considered him. What was his game plan? Maybe he wanted to know about Beth? I'd seen the flicker of fire in his eyes when he walked into my office every evening, after he'd been chatting to my young, blonde receptionist. Whatever it was he was intending to ask me, I was now desperate to know.

'Okay,' I said with a smile, trying to convey a confidence I hardly ever felt around him. 'Come up.'

17. SAMANTHA

Gabriel and I were standing in my kitchen, waiting for the kettle to boil when he finally spoke.

'So, I've answered all of your questions tonight, Samantha. Now it's my turn. And remember, you promised to answer it truthfully?'

I leaned against the kitchen counter, eyeing him warily, wondering what on earth he was about to ask. It had been hours since I'd agreed to his seemingly innocuous request. But there, in my kitchen, I was beginning to wonder if I'd made a huge mistake. Gabriel walked towards me until we were only inches apart. He was almost a foot taller than me and without my heels, I had to crane my neck to look up at him. I could feel the heat from his body; smell his distinctive aftershave. His breathing was slow and controlled. As always, he was the picture of calm and confidence.

I, on the other hand, could hear my own breathing becoming faster and heavier, my blood pounding in my ears, the flush creeping up my neck. I prayed that he didn't notice, but feared my voice alone would betray me.

'So what's your question, Gabriel?' I asked, my voice barely a whisper.

He looked into my eyes. I wanted to look away from him but I couldn't. He held me there, his green eyes almost black.

'Why are you such a bitch to me, Samantha?' he asked.

I opened my mouth in shock, trying desperately to think of a quick retort. But before I could respond, and reprimand him for his insult, he went on.

'At first I thought you'd just turned into a bitch, but I don't think that's true, is it? Because you're nice to everyone. Even your receptionist who can't even get your coffee right.'

He stared at me, waiting for an answer. Then he dipped his head lower.

'Then I thought maybe it's a mask. You pretend that's who you really are so no-one will take advantage of you, and I get that. But, you're not like that with anyone else, are you? So, why do you reserve this particular charming facet of your personality solely for me?'

I looked away from him, afraid that he would see the truth before I could think of a convincing lie. I could try to walk away from him but he was so close I wouldn't have been able to move without brushing past him, and I wasn't sure I could trust myself to touch him.

'You promised me the truth,' he reminded me.

I was trapped. Had I known he'd ask something so insightful, I would never have agreed to his stupid request. I couldn't even think of a good lie. He had shaken me — seen right through the confident facade I presented and saw the real Samantha – and therein lay the problem.

'Because I can't stand the way you look at me, Gabriel!' I shouted and he took a step back from me.

A look of confusion flashed across his face before disappearing behind his usual mask of certainty. 'But I've always been nothing but respectful to you. Haven't I?'

'Exactly. And that's my problem. I see the way you look at other women. I see the way you look at Beth.'

'Beth? Are you fucking kidding me?' He frowned at me.

'You never look at me that way, and it's because you will only ever see me as a victim. As someone to pity.'

He glared at me then. His eyes burning into mine. 'Of all the things I might feel for you, Sam, pity is not one of them. You are the strongest woman I know.'

He called me Sam!

I shook my head. I didn't believe him. How could I? 'Are you telling me that when you found out about what Jackson did, you didn't feel sorry for me?'

Gabriel ran his hands through his hair as he stared at me. 'I wouldn't call it feeling sorry for you, but yes, I felt sorry about what had happened to you. I'm only fucking human, Sam.'

'I don't want you to feel sorry for me. I want you to look at me and see me. Not some poor little victim who needs protecting.'

'I do see you. I don't feel sorry for you, but that doesn't mean I don't hate what that bastard did to you. And you think I want Beth? For an intelligent woman, you really are clueless sometimes,' he snapped.

'Clueless? You-'

Before I could finish my sentence, he was on me. His hands in my hair, his body pressing mine against the worktop. 'Yes,' he growled in my ear. 'Clueless, if you think that I want anyone other than you.'

He pushed his groin into mine and I could feel his erection pressing against me, just above where I ached to feel him the most. The throbbing between my thighs intensified and I could feel the warmth and the wetness pooling there already. Everything about him was driving me crazy. The smell of him. The weight of his body almost crushing mine. The scratch of his stubble against my throat as he growled in my ear. Even the way he spoke to me made my legs tremble. His lips grazed my neck as he moved his head to look at me, and my face flushed pink as I thought about what else I would like him to do with that mouth.

He smiled at me and then he whispered, 'I'm not sure you could handle me though, Sam.'

Mistaking his statement as a challenge, I grinned at him. 'I'm not sure you could handle me, Gabriel?' I breathed.

He moved so fast that I could barely process what was happening. Before I could even blink I was bent over and pinned to my kitchen table, with one of Gabriel's large hands on the back of my neck. I gasped in a lungful of air and willed my heart to stop racing. It should have been a huge turn off for me. My brain was telling me to run, but my body was physically aching for him, desperate for him to sate the constant feeling of need he instilled in me. The way he did everything with such confidence and certainty — on paper, it should put me off, but it only made me want him even more.

Bending over me, Gabriel pressed his groin into my behind and his mouth against my ear. 'Do you want to know what I've been thinking about when you've been making me wait in your office?'

'What?' I whispered, hoping that it involved him doing unspeakable things to me.

'I was thinking about how much I'd like to bend you over that desk of yours, and fuck your brains out,' he said and I felt my insides turn to hot liquid.

Gabriel stood up and removed his hand from my neck. 'Don't move, Sam,' he ordered.

I remained still, my hands splayed against the cool wood of my kitchen table as my legs trembled in anticipation of what this man was about to do to me. I felt his hands on my knees first, lifting the hem of my pencil skirt as he started to slowly slide it up my thighs towards my hips. His fingertips brushed against my skin, leaving trails of hot lava in their wake. He continued pushing the fabric up my thighs and over my backside, until my skirt was bunched around my waist. I could hear his steady breathing but otherwise he was silent, his movements confident and controlled.

I closed my eyes, wondering how he was able to maintain such control when I was on the edge of collapse. I let out a small whimper as his hands brushed over my behind and he slid a thumb under the edge of my black lace underwear. And then he was there. Right where I wanted him to be. Right where I had wanted him since I'd first saw him again. His fingers slid through my cleft easily, until he found my clit and he started to use two of his fingers to draw slow, teasing circles. I groaned in pleasure and frustration until he leaned over me, his mouth pressed to my ear again.

'Fuck!' he breathed. 'You're dripping wet. Do you get you off on arguing with me?'

The only response I could muster was a whimper.

'I'm going to make you come, Sam. And then I'm going to fuck you so hard you won't be able to remember your own name. Right here on this table. Is that what you want?'

His words alone almost tipped me over the edge. 'Yes,' I panted.

Obviously satisfied with my response, Gabriel started to work me into a frenzy with his fingers, massaging my clit over and over. Then using his other hand, he pushed a finger inside me, dipping in and out — the rhythm matching that of his other hand.

Slowly he inserted a second finger and I moaned loudly. Unable to stand the growing pressure in my core any longer, I started to buck my hips against him, but he stopped me, using one of his hands to pin me down again. 'God, don't stop,' I groaned.

He leaned over me again. 'I told you not to move,' he whispered in my ear. 'Are you going to be still? Or do I need to hold you down?'

'I'll be still,' I gasped, barely able to speak coherently.

Gabriel's hands set to work again and I could feel the orgasm building, but each time I almost reached a climax, he'd stop and changed his pace or his position — leaving me constantly teetering on the edge.

'Please, Gabriel?' I pleaded.

I heard his soft, throaty chuckle, then he was on me again, his lips grazing my throat as he whispered in my ear. 'I like hearing you beg. Do you want me to let you come now?'

I nodded. My face brushing against the grain of the table as Gabriel pushed two of his fingers inside, rubbing at that perfect spot while pressing down on my clit with just the right amount of pressure. I closed my eyes as every part of my core tightened, before my orgasm ripped through my body like black powder, the heat searing through my legs and stomach. To my shame, I screamed his name.

After he'd rubbed the last of my orgasm from my trembling body, Gabriel pulled me up from the table and turned me to face him. 'I've been thinking about doing that ever since you walked into my office,' he said with a wicked smile.

He ran his knuckles across my cheek and I could feel the dampness of my arousal on his fingers. I shuddered as he dragged his wet thumb across my lower lip. 'And I suppose I can fuck you on this table another time.'

I blinked. What? He was leaving? I opened my mouth to protest but no words came out. I was bereft. Despite the incredible orgasm he'd just given me, I wanted more. I wanted him. All of him. I wanted to feel him inside me.

Then to my surprise, he kissed me. Deep and lush. His tongue pushing into my mouth, confirming my suspicion that he was as skilled with it as he was with his hands. Already I could feel the familiar warmth spreading through my core again. I needed him. Reaching between the two of us, I grabbed hold of his cock and squeezed. He was rock hard — his trousers straining under the pressure and I wondered again at how he managed to stay so controlled when he was clearly as turned on as I was.

'Don't,' he whispered as he moved my hand.

I stared at him, feeling like a child who'd been chastised. Before I could protest he put his hand under my chin and tilted my face closer to his. 'Oh, you're going to get that. Don't worry. But not here. If this is our first time, I want to do it right. Where's the bedroom?'

Dear God! I grinned at him before taking his hand and leading him down the hallway and into my bedroom.

18. SAMANTHA

Gabriel closed the door behind us and stalked towards me, his green eyes burning into my skin. I physically trembled as he approached. Why did my body have such a strong physical reaction to him? As if he wasn't bloody cocky and hot enough, he could blatantly see the affect he was having on me. It was doing my image no good at all.

Gabriel stroked my cheek. 'Are you nervous, Sam?' he asked with a wicked glint in his eye. 'After what I just did to you?'

'No,' I said, my chin titled in defiance.

Gabriel raised an eyebrow and smiled. 'Good. I'll make sure you scream my name at least once more tonight.'

I swallowed hard. The truth was I was incredibly nervous which was unusual for me. I was never nervous about sex. But then, I'd never had sex with anyone who made me feel like Gabriel did. And given what had just happened on my kitchen table, I had a feeling that sex with him was going to be an enlightening experience.

Gabriel started to undress me, running his hands over every part of skin that he exposed to the cool air. 'God, you are so fucking beautiful,' he hissed when I was finally naked before him.

I blushed and took a step back from him, allowing his eyes to roam over my body. He reached out and pulled me into his arms, his hands resting on my backside as he pushed his body into mine. He looked at me then, his eyes searching mine. I sensed some hesitation.

'What is it?' I asked.

'Are you sure this is what you want?' he breathed.

I blinked at him. 'Well, I'm naked and you're standing in my bedroom with your hands on my arse. I'm practically panting here. So, what do you think, Einstein?' I said with a grin.

'You know that I like to be in control, Sam?'

'Yes. You're a control freak,' I replied with a nod. 'So?'

He moved his hands from my backside and took hold of my wrists. 'I'm a control freak when it comes to sex too. I don't just like to be in control. I need to be. I want you to do what I tell you, when I tell you to do it. I want to hold you down. I want to tie you up. I want you to be sitting at your desk tomorrow and not forget for one second that I've fucked you. I'm not sure you can do that?'

'Why? Because-'

'Because,' he interrupted me before I could finish my thought, never mind my sentence. 'In case you hadn't noticed, you don't respond well to being told what to do.'

'I did fine just now in my kitchen, didn't I?' I reminded him.

'You certainly did,' he said with a laugh as he tucked a loose strand of hair behind my ear. 'I won't ever hurt you, Sam. I promise. But can you trust me? Do you want to do this?'

I stared at him. I did trust him, or at least I wanted to. He was Gabe. I understood exactly how he felt about control. I liked to be in control too — out in the real world. I'd had so little control of anything when I'd been married to Jackson, that it almost felt like I had to over-compensate now and I felt an overriding need to have a say in every decision in my life, no matter how small. From the colour of the walls in the office reception, to the brand of coffee we bought for clients. It was exhausting. So, giving up control, right then, of my own free will and to Gabriel, felt like I could finally relax.

'I trust you, Gabe,' I whispered.

I saw the fire in his eyes before he pushed me onto the bed.

'Don't I get to see you too?' I asked and he glared at me. 'Please?' I smiled sweetly. He stared at me for a minute, obviously considering my request before obliging by taking all off his clothes. I watched as he undressed, my eyes fixed on his incredible body, all taut, toned muscle. I had waited so long for this; I could hardly believe it was happening.

'Like what you see?' he asked in that trademark menacing growl that I felt to my very core.

'Hell, yes!' I replied with a smile.

He crawled onto the bed, holding himself over me before smothering me with a kiss. Taking my hands, Gabriel placed them above my head. 'I won't tie you up. Not yet. But I want you to keep your hands here. Hold onto the pillow if you have to, but don't move.'

'What will happen if I do?' I asked.

'Then I'll stop doing whatever it is I'm doing, and make you suck my cock instead,' he replied before kissing my neck.

I wasn't entirely sure whether he was being serious or not but decided that I didn't want to find out. Not that the thought of sucking him off wasn't pleasing. It was something I was looking forward to, but if what he'd done earlier in the kitchen was anything to go by, I was certain I wouldn't want him to stop whatever it was he had planned.

Gabriel continued kissing my neck before slowly trailing his lips down my collarbone, rolling my nipples between his finger and thumb before giving them a gentle tug. Then his mouth was on them, licking and sucking and driving me crazy with wanton desire. I had never wanted to feel someone inside me so much in my life. I dug my fingernails into the pillow. I wanted to touch him, to run my fingers through his dark hair and guide him down to the place that was aching to feel his touch. But I did as I'd been instructed and held onto the pillow. Suddenly, his hands started to move lower, until he found that sweet spot — that place where it seemed every nerve of my body ended.

Dear God, he was so good with his hands. I could feel my orgasm building already. I moved my hips, grinding myself into his fingers, and this time he didn't stop me. Just as I was thinking that I couldn't take any more and was about to explode, he stopped and I gasped out loud. I almost pulled him back to me but then his fingers were replaced by his mouth and I entered a whole new realm of pleasure.

Gabriel licked the length of my slit with his hot, thick tongue. 'Jesus, Sam, you taste so fucking good,' he growled against me and the vibration of his speech as well as his words were my undoing. He placed his mouth directly over my clit and I climaxed, shouting his name as I did.

'Well, that was easy,' he chuckled as he looked up at me. 'Maybe you should make me work for the next one. Or should I make you work for it?' He teased as he bent his head low again.

Before I could protest that I couldn't take anymore, that I was too sensitive, his fingers were inside me. The methodical in and out driving me crazy. And his mouth. He could do things with his tongue that made me hear choirs of heavenly angels.

He nibbled and licked and sucked.

Over and over.

Stopping and starting.

My blood thundered around my body. My heart was pounding in my ears. My breathing short and ragged. I was lost to him. I raked my fingers through his hair, pulling him to me and away from me at the same time. Then he stopped — and I realised what I'd done. My hands were no longer on the pillow.

He looked up at me. 'I warned you, Samantha,' he said as he moved up the bed towards my face. I blinked at him, feeling a momentary flash of terror. I had heard those words so many times before. Gabriel saw it instantly and suddenly his eyes were full of concern.

'What's wrong?' he asked.

'Nothing,' I whispered.

'Sam! Please don't lie to me. This won't work if you're not honest with me. What is it?'

I shook my head. 'That phrase. I haven't heard it for a while, that's all. I'm okay.'

'Shit! I'm sorry. I knew I shouldn't have... We shouldn't have...' he started.

'Please stop feeling sorry for me, Gabriel. It's just a phrase I'd rather you didn't use, that's all. Aside from that, you don't have to treat me any differently than any other woman you have sex with.'

'You don't have to prove anything to me, Sam. We can stop-'

'What if I don't want to stop? You said you wouldn't hurt me. This is hurting me. You, treating me like glass. I won't break.'

He smoothed my hair from my face. 'I'm sorry. I know you won't,' he replied softly as he kissed me again, before edging his way back down the bed to resume where he left off.

'I moved my hands, remember?' I said. 'I don't want any special treatment.'

He grinned at me wickedly. 'And you won't be getting any. But, you can have *one* free pass. Next time, I might just tie you up. But I don't want to come in your mouth — not tonight.'

His fingers and his mouth returned to their previous endeavours and before long I was climaxing and screaming his name again.

Once he had rubbed the last of my orgasm from my trembling body, Gabriel held himself over me — his rock-hard erection pushing against me, opening me.

'Are you ready?' he asked.

I nodded and he pushed himself into me in one swift move. It took me a moment to adjust to accommodating him, but once I had he began to pound me, nailing me to the bed with each thrust. Then he was talking to me again, and I swore he could make me come from his words alone.

'Do you feel how hard I am for you? I've never wanted to be inside someone so much. You are driving me fucking crazy.' He tipped us both over the edge with his growling in my ear and I felt him explode inside me, hot and sticky.

'Christ, Sam,' he said through gritted teeth before collapsing on top of me. I held his head to my chest, running my fingers through his thick, dark hair.

'Are you on the pill?' he asked, his mouth brushing against my breasts.

'Well, it's a bit late now, isn't it? But yes, I am. Although I don't usually-'

'Neither do I,' he interrupted me. 'I'm sorry I didn't have a condom with me. I never thought we'd ...'

'What? You didn't see this coming?' I asked with a laugh.

He lifted his head to look into my eyes. 'No, I didn't. I didn't think you'd be interested in someone like me.'

I blinked in shock. 'Are you kidding me? Look at you! Women fall over themselves to even speak to you.'

'Not women like you. As soon as you walked into our office the other week, I wanted you. You looked and smelled so good, like you belonged on the arm of some billionaire. I felt like a kid with no money looking through the sweet shop window.'

'And then I was such a bitch to you, wasn't I? God, you must have really enjoyed spending time with me.'

'I did actually. I've told you what I used to think about while I waited in your office,' he said with a wicked glint in his eye. 'You being a bitch just made me want to fuck you even more.' He nipped me playfully. 'And now that I know you want me too, I intend to fuck you as frequently as possible.'

'Is that so?'

'Hmm,' he mumbled as he started to nuzzle my neck.

'Tell me more about your need to be in control. You wanting to tie me up and do as I'm told. What exactly would I be getting into with you, Gabe?'

Sitting up, he took hold of my hand. 'That's it. I like to be in control when we have sex. And yes, sometimes I'd like to tie you up.'

'Spanking?'

'If you're into it.'

'Do I need a safe word?'

'No, if you want me to stop doing something tell me to stop — simple as that. I can exercise some self-control, you know.'

I smiled. 'I had noticed that. So, what happens if I don't do as I'm told then?'

He flashed me a wicked grin that turned my core into molten lava. 'I've already told you that. I'll stop doing what I'm doing to you. I won't make you come.'

'That seems unusually harsh and cruel,' I replied with a flutter of my eyelashes. 'Especially as you're so good at it.'

'It's not just punishment for you, Sam. I love to make you come,' he replied, his voice low and husky. He moved towards me, pulling me beneath him until he was lying on top of me again.

'I still think it's unduly harsh,' I said with a flash of my eyebrows. 'And I'm not sure I can put up with such tyranny from you.'

He grinned at me 'I will always take care of you,' he whispered and then he kissed me.

'So, we're going to do this then? Be friends with benefits?' I asked.

His head snapped up and he looked at me. 'Friends with what?'

'Benefits! Fuck-buddies.'

'I know what it means, Sam. But I don't want that with you.'

'I thought you only did casual?'

Suddenly, serious Gabriel was back in the room. 'No! You assumed I only do casual and I didn't correct you. I wouldn't risk my relationship with your dad for a fuck-buddy. Is that all this is for you?'

I stared at him as I wondered how to possibly answer that question. I had wanted this man from the moment I laid eyes on him. I had fantasised about this forever and the reality had been a million times better than anything I had ever imagined. But I wasn't ready for anything more yet. I was only just divorced. I was still getting over the court case. I didn't even know who I was anymore. I had to figure that out before I jumped into another relationship, and especially one with Gabriel, a man who already had so much power over me.

'I just didn't realise ... I'm not sure I'm ready for a relationship yet, Gabe. I've only just ...'

Suddenly his face softened. 'Of course, Sam. I should have

realised that. I'm sorry,' he reached out his hand and stroked my hair. 'But I'm not interested in a fuck-buddy.'

'Then it looks like we're at an impasse?' I said with a smile. He might say that wasn't what he wanted but surely, he wouldn't object to a repeat performance of tonight — if he had enjoyed it half as much as I had, how could he refuse? I just needed a little more time.

He pulled back the covers and climbed out of bed.

'Where are you going?' I asked.

'I'm sorry, Samantha. This shouldn't have happened — for so many reasons. Please can we forget it did and go back to the way things were before?'

'What, with all the frowning and sarcasm and the sexual tension?' I asked with a flash of one eyebrow. 'Yeah, because that was a barrel of laughs.'

He started to laugh as he pulled on his trousers and for some reason the sound made me feel incredibly sad. 'Well, I promise to behave myself from now on. No more frowning or sexual tension. Deal?' he said.

I looked at him and had an urge to jump out of the bed and pull him back down on top of me. The truth was I would rather have all of that with him than nothing at all. How could he just pretend like this night hadn't happened? Just because I wasn't ready for a full-blown relationship — that was it!

'Good,' I snapped. 'It was starting to get a little tedious.'

I saw the hurt on his face and turned away from him. He continued getting dressed in silence.

'I'm sorry,' he said.

'Nothing to apologise for. We're both adults,' I replied with a shrug.

'Good,' he whispered. 'I'll see you then.'

'Yeah. See you,' I replied nonchalantly, despite feeling like my heart was going to crumble. What the hell was I doing? Run after him, Samantha! Tell him you'll be whatever he wants you to be!

No! I couldn't. I had spent far too much of my life doing that already. Instead I watched as he walked out of my bedroom. The next thing I heard was the soft clicking of my front door closing.

I lay back against the pillows and willed myself not to cry. I never cried. Crying had been a turn on for Jackson, it had always spurred him on to hurt me more. Besides, this was my choice. Not Gabriel's. Mine. I need to remember that.

19. SAMANTHA

As five o'clock approached the following day, I became increasingly fidgety. I checked my hair and make-up in the small mirror in my handbag. I had done nothing but think about Gabriel all day. I had done nothing but relive the incredibly hot sex we'd had every chance I got. The feeling of his expert hands and mouth. The relief my body felt at being full of him. There was a throbbing between my thighs that had been building for hours. I had been so distracted in the morning staff meeting, that Nick had thrown a banana at my head and I hadn't seen it coming at all. It had bounced off my forehead in what I can imagine was a very comedic fashion. He'd apologised profusely afterwards after almost passing out laughing first.

I wondered how on earth I was going to have Gabriel so close to me and not launch myself at him. I felt a bead of sweat trickle down my back and turned up the air con higher as I stood at my office window.

I saw the car pull up outside and a tall man climb out of it. But it wasn't Gabriel. It was Scott. My heart sank. Why had he sent Scott to pick me up instead of doing it himself? The coward! How dare he just palm me off on one of his employees.

A few moments later, Scott walked through my open office door.

'Gabriel asked me to pick you up tonight, Samantha. I hope that's okay?' he said with a warm smile.

I wanted to tell him that it wasn't okay at all, and that I would get the tube home in a declaration of protest. But Scott was so nice. I didn't want to get him into any trouble.

'Of course it is. Thanks, Scott,' I smiled.

For the next three nights, Scott continued to turn up at my office instead of Gabriel. I hadn't heard from him at all. I'd picked up my phone a few times and scrolled through my contacts, my finger hovering over his name, but I hadn't called him either. How could he just pretend that the other night hadn't even happened? I knew that I couldn't. I thought about him and his incredible body constantly. I had promised myself that I wouldn't jump into a new relationship with anyone. I had been with Jackson since I was nineteen and I had changed so much of myself to fit in with him and his wants and needs that I wasn't sure who I was without him. I had lost myself trying to fit Jackson's precise specifications.

I'd been happy being single. I'd been having fun figuring myself out with no-one to answer to. Then I'd let myself fall for Gabriel bloody Sullivan. It was bad enough when I simply lusted after him and enjoyed the fantasy of what it might be to penetrate his rock hard exterior, and run my hand over those rock-hard abs. But, now I knew what it was like, and the thought of not having him, or his abs, in my life was making me thoroughly miserable.

'Are you ready, Samantha?' Scott asked, snapping me from my train of thought.

'Yes, coming,' I said with a smile as I picked up my handbag and coat.

'You're going to your dad's, aren't you?' he asked me.

'Yep. Are you sure you're okay to drop me off there?' I asked. I had dinner with my father every Tuesday night and although I enjoyed spending time with him, I would have been equally happy tonight to go straight home, pour myself a large glass of red, order a pizza and watch some trashy television.

'Of course,' Scott said. 'Anywhere you want to go is fine with me.'

I smiled at him and resisted the urge to ask him to take me to Gabriel's house instead.

I knocked on the front door of my dad's house. He had given me a key, but it didn't feel right to use it. It wasn't my home any longer. He opened the door a few moments later.

'Sam,' he pulled me into a hug and slung his tea towel over his shoulder. 'I wish you'd use your key,' he said as he started to walk down the hallway. 'My sauce is going to burn.'

I followed him into the kitchen. Half expecting and fully hoping, to see Gabriel, but he was nowhere to be seen.

'Gabriel not joining us tonight?' I asked.

'No. He has a date. Didn't he tell you when he picked you up?'

I felt like someone had driven a hot poker through my heart. 'No,' I replied. So, Gabriel obviously hadn't told my father that he was neglecting his bodyguard duties.

'I've made his favourite as well, steak and peppercorn sauce. I hope you don't mind? I thought you might be fed up of curry?'

'Sounds like a nice change, Dad,' I smiled.

I watched my father as he busied himself at the stove. He loved to cook. He said it helped him deal with stress. When I was a teenager, he'd cooked a lot!

'So, who is this date with then?' I asked, trying to sound as casual as possible.

He shrugged. 'No idea. I hope it goes well though. He's been a moody sod this past week.'

'Oh?' I asked, feeling suddenly brighter that he may have been feeling as miserable as I was.

'Yeah. Haven't seen him like this since after Jennifer,' he said as he rubbed seasoning into the two juicy rump steaks on his chopping board.

'He must have dates all the time though?' I said.

'Gabriel?' my dad started to laugh. 'Nah! He's a soppy bastard. Not like me. He's an old romantic. It's all or nothing with him. Jennifer really did a number on him and I think he's worried he'll get his heart broken again.' My dad turned and looked at me then, his face full of emotion. 'I've told him it's about time to move on. Maybe his date tonight might work out? Maybe she's the one?' He rolled his eyes and went back to his steaks.

'Here's hoping,' I lied. There was nothing I wanted less in this world than for Gabriel to meet *the one*. I wanted to be his *one*. I just wasn't ready to be. If he could just wait for me? But a few days after the most incredible night of my life and he'd already moved on to his next target.

I stepped out of my dad's house and into the waiting cab. Taking out my phone I dialled Nick's number. He answered on the second ring.

'How do you fancy getting absolutely plastered?' I asked him.

'Shit-faced?' he replied.

'Exactly.'

'Count me in. Where and when?'

'O'Malley's in twenty minutes,' I told him.

'I'll be there in fifteen,' he replied with a laugh.

It was a Tuesday night and O'Malley's was relatively quiet, but even so it looked like all the tables were occupied. I looked around to see if Nick was at one of them but I couldn't see him. I continued scanning the bar, and then I saw him, Gabriel and the blonde from a few weeks earlier – Gemma. Yes, that was her name. I stood staring for a moment as they sat at a small table for two. She was laughing and he was smiling and suddenly I felt like I could hardly breathe. I had to get out of there before he saw me. I spun around and bumped right into Nick.

'Samantha,' he said with a smile. 'Let's get the drinks in?'

I shook my head. 'No. let's go somewhere else,' I said as I took hold of his arm.

'But we love O'Malley's. At least let's have one,' he insisted as he started to move towards the bar.

'Nick, please!' I hissed.

He turned to look at me then. 'What's wrong?' he asked, his voice full of concern.

'Let's just go,' I said as I looked around. Too late. Gabriel looked up and his eyes locked with mine.

'Please, Nick. Can we go? I'll explain over a drink.' I linked my arm through his and we walked towards the door.

We were walking along the road to the next pub when I heard him calling my name.

Nick spun around first while I was determined to keep walking.

'It's Gabriel,' Nick said. 'He's shouting you.' He pulled on my arm to stop me in my tracks.

I turned around too to see Gabriel running towards us. 'Samantha,' he said again as he reached us.

'Don't you need to get back to your date?' I snapped at him.

He frowned. 'It wasn't ... Can we talk?'

'Talk? You've ignored me all week and now you want to talk. Well, tough! Me and Nick are having a great night and I'd rather you didn't ruin it, thanks.'

Nick looked at me and then at Gabriel, his face a picture of confusion.

'Come on,' I said to him as I took hold of his arm again.

'Nick, would you mind giving us a few minutes please?' Gabriel asked.

'Of course-' Nick started.

'There's no need,' I interrupted him. 'Enjoy your evening, Gabriel,' I said with a smile before turning around and walking towards the nearest pub.

'Sorry,' I heard Nick say to him before he fell into step beside me. 'What the hell was that about?' he asked.

I shook my head. 'It's a long story!'

20. SAMANTHA

The following day, I was packing up my laptop ready to go home when I heard someone walk into my office behind me. I turned around expecting to see Scott but my heart leapt into my throat when I saw Gabriel walk into the room instead. He was wearing one of his finely tailored suits that fitted his muscular body perfectly. A few days worth of dark stubble covered his jaw and his green eyes burned into mine.

'Ready to go, Samantha? Or are you going to make me wait around for you tonight?' he said with a scowl.

'Where's Scott?' I snapped. 'I was hoping he'd be driving me home.'

He shrugged. 'Well, we don't always get what we want, do we?'

'I suppose not,' I agreed.

We drove to my apartment building in silence. I stared out of the window and tried not to think about the man sitting next to me. It was proving incredibly difficult. He even smelled good enough to eat.

When we finally pulled up outside my apartment building he turned to me. 'Why are you so pissed off with me?' he asked.

'Are you serious?'

'Yes!' he replied with a frown.

'Where shall I start? Palming me off on poor Scott because you didn't want to have to drive me home anymore. Going out on a date with that blonde woman you told me was *just business*.'

'God, you are fucking infuriating!' he said.

I opened the car door and climbed out, slamming it behind me. To my annoyance he got out too and started to follow me across the car park. 'Samantha! Sam!' he called.

I turned around. 'Don't call me Sam.' It hurt too much. He didn't get to call me Sam if he was screwing someone else.

He held his hands up in surrender or apology. 'I honestly thought you would prefer it if Scott drove you home. After what happened ...'

'Don't lie to me,' I snapped.

'It's true. But, you're right, that's not the only reason,' he said as he walked towards me. In a few strides, he was standing in front of me. My treacherous body leaned towards him of its own volition.

'I wasn't sure I could trust myself around you. I know the other night was just a bit of fun for you, but it meant much more than that to me.'

'So much that you needed Gemma to console you?' I sniped.

'I wasn't on a date. Did your dad tell you that? I just told him that to shut him up. It was a business meeting, I swear. She's a club promoter and we've just bought a nightclub. Besides, why do you even care what it was?'

I looked up at him and my head spun with so many emotions, I didn't know which one to feel first. I tried to focus on what it was that I really wanted — and the only answer I could find in that moment was him.

'The other night wasn't just a bit of fun for me, Gabe. It was incredible. It was terrifying. It was so much more than I was ready for.'

He stared at me. 'I know,' he said with a sigh.

'Will you come up for a coffee?' I asked him.

'I don't think that's a good idea, do you?'

I wrapped my arms around his neck and pulled his face to mine. 'No, I think it's a terrific idea.'

'Samantha,' he groaned. 'Don't do this to me.'

'I want you, Gabe,' I whispered in his ear. 'Please?'

'I don't want a friend with benefits. I'm sorry, but I need more than that.'

'Then I can give you more,' I replied. Now that I knew what it was like to be with him, I couldn't bear to be without him.

He shook his head. 'No. You've already told me you're not ready. I can't ... We can't do this. It's not right.'

'Then just give me one more night. I feel like I might implode if you don't touch me. Please, Gabe,' I breathed in his ear, pressing my body against his. I could feel his erection against my abdomen and it made me more determined. 'Just fuck me one more time,' I purred against his neck.

'For fuck's sake!' he growled. Then he took half a step back and I thought he was going to walk away, but he grabbed hold of my hand and marched me across the carpark towards my apartment building.

We walked silently up the stairs to my flat and I was starting to wonder if Gabriel was angry. Had I pushed him too far? The sexual tension still crackled between us and my body was acutely aware of the closeness of him. I closed the door to my apartment and turned around to find him standing right in front of me. I looked up at him. His eyes burned into mine. Then without warning, he pinned me against the door. Pushing his body against mine, he kissed me roughly and I responded greedily, savouring the taste of him. He pulled away and spun me around so my face was pressed against the cool wood and his erection was pressed against my back.

His hot mouth was on my ear. 'So you just want one more fuck, do you Samantha? A friend with benefits?'

I closed my eyes to try and gain some sense of control as my heart hammered in my chest and my blood thundered around my body.

'Do you let all of your friends do this then? Let them touch you like I do?' he said as he slid my skirt up my thighs until it was bunched around my waist.

'No,' I breathed as he slipped his hands inside my lace underwear. Then I heard the delicate fabric tearing in his strong hands and gasped as he pulled the material roughly over my skin. Pulling my hands behind my back, he tied my wrists with the shredded material.

'Is this all you want from me, Samantha? A good fucking?'

His stubble scratched my neck as he growled in my ear, grazing my skin with his teeth. He pressed me into the door with the full weight of his body until it felt like I could hardly move.

'Yes,' I groaned.

Then I heard the unmistakeable sound of his zipper opening.

'Are you wet?' he asked.

'Yes.'

'Good,' he growled and I felt his knees bending slightly before he pushed into me until I was full of him, pinioned to the door. He was quick and rough. 'This is what you want, isn't it?' he groaned.

'Yes, Gabe,' I whimpered before wondering at the ease in which I gave him complete control of my body.

'Tell me what you want me to do to you.'

'You already know,' I panted.

'Tell me,' he growled.

'I want you to fuck me.'

'And what else?'

'Make me come,' I breathed.

He started to pound into me relentlessly, over and over until we were both breathless.

'Do you have any idea how much I want to fuck you, Sam? Any idea how much I want to be inside you?'

He reached his hand around to my clit and started to rub with the same intensity that he used to thrust into me and it wasn't long before I was climaxing around him.

'I love to feel you come on my cock. Your tight little pussy squeezing every last drop from me,' he grunted as he came inside me.

When he was done, he untied my hands, his deft fingers making easy work of undoing the knot in the fabric. I turned around and he stared at me.

'One last fuck?' he said. 'Is that what that was?'

'God, I hope not,' I panted and he smiled.

'You enjoyed that? Being tied up and fucked against your front door?' he cocked an eyebrow at me.

'What do you think?' I put my arms around his neck and pulled him towards me. 'Will you stay tonight?'

He ran his hands down my body and squeezed my backside. 'Do fuck-buddies sleep over?' he asked with a grin.

I laughed, grateful for the chance to diffuse the tension. 'I have no idea. I've never had one before.'

'Me neither,' he said before kissing me.

The sun was streaming through the gap in the blinds as I opened my eyes the next morning. I could feel Gabriel's erection pressing into my back as he started to nuzzle my neck.

'I was wondering when you would wake up,' he said as he started to rub his warm hand over my hip and onto my stomach before making his way between my thighs. I stretched and smiled. I loved the feel of his rough fingertips on my soft skin. He lifted my leg up and hooked it over his before running his hand back up the inside of my thigh. I gasped as he slid a finger inside me.

'Hmm, always wet for me, Sam,' he whispered in my ear before pushing his rock-hard cock deep inside me. His skilled fingers quickly found my already swollen clit and he started to rub as he ground into me, growling in my ear the whole time. Telling me how much he loved to fuck me; how much he wanted to be inside me. I climaxed just before he did, whispering his name as I found my release.

Afterwards, I lay in Gabriel's arms wondering how on earth I had ever lived without him, and how I could ever live without him again.

'I think that's my absolute favourite way to wake up in the morning,' Gabriel said as he kissed the top of my head.

'Hmm. Me too. You fuck like it's your vocation. You know that, don't you?'

He lifted my chin, tilting my head to look at him, his smile taking over his whole face and his green eyes twinkling. 'I think fucking you *is* my vocation,' he growled.

I pulled him to me for a long, deep kiss.

God help me!

21. GABRIEL

It was early afternoon as Sebastian and I walked across the deserted builders' yard towards Jimmy Fenton's portacabin.

'This feels dodgy,' Seb whispered as we passed an empty skip.

'That's because it is fucking dodgy,' I replied. 'Fenton is a fucking snake. There's no way this isn't a set up. That's why we're here an hour early. And why we've brought back up,' I said, thinking about the Berettas we each had inside our coats.

'We're early?' Seb asked. 'Why don't you ever fill me in on your fucking plans until the last minute?'

'Because,' I grinned, 'you never ask.'

Seb shrugged. 'Fair enough.' No doubt happy just to be in the thick of it for a change. It wasn't often I favoured the violent, no holds barred, approach, these days. I tried to use my head instead of my fists as much as possible. But Jimmy Fenton had requested another meeting and he wasn't backing down with his offer to buy our company. And I was becoming increasingly impatient.

'Let's go in there and try and play nice first,' I said. 'And then if he refuses-'

'You mean *when* he refuses,' Sebastian interrupted.

I nodded, knowing that he was right. 'Well, then we'll do things your way.'

We approached the portacabin. I opened the door and stepped inside, with Sebastian close behind me.

'Hello, Jimmy.' I grinned as I saw Jimmy Fenton sitting at his desk being sucked off by a blonde who most definitely wasn't his red-headed wife, Colleen.

'Caught with your pants around your ankles, Jimmy,' Sebastian laughed.

'What the fuck are you two doing here?' Jimmy barked as he pushed the blonde away from him.

'Fucking hell, how old is she? Fourteen?' Sebastian said as the young girl scrabbled to her feet. 'You dirty bastard,' he snarled.

'She's fucking seventeen,' Jimmy snarled back. 'Not that it's any of your fucking business.'

'She ain't your wife, though, is she?' Sebastian sneered. 'And she's younger than your own fucking daughter.'

Jimmy was about to respond when the door of the portacabin burst open and his younger brother, Martin ran in.

'What the fuck's going on in here? You two are fucking early,' Martin shouted as he joined his brother, who was still fastening the belt on his trousers.

Seb glared at Martin. He would never forgive him for the scar he'd left him with seven years earlier. It ran from behind his left ear down to the bottom of his neck. Me and Jimmy had convinced the pair of them to let the whole thing go. We'd reached a truce after that showdown, and our rival security firms had gone our respective ways. That was until the Fentons had started making threats about taking Archangel Securities.

'Are we early?' I asked, looking at my watch. 'Sorry about that, gents. But now we're here we might as well get down to business.'

'Get out of here,' Jimmy told the young blonde as he pushed her roughly away from him. 'Wait in my car. I won't be long,' he added as he glared at me and Sebastian.

I took a twenty pound note from my pocket and handed it to her as she passed me. 'Get yourself a taxi, kid. We might be a while.' The last thing we needed was a young girl hanging around when there was about to be a kick off.

She took the money from me and scurried out of the office.

Jimmy continued to glare at me while Martin and Seb eyed each other suspiciously.

'So, why did you want to meet with us?' I asked eventually.

'You know why, Sullivan,' Jimmy snapped. 'We want Archangel Securities. We're prepared to make you a good offer.'

I could sense Sebastian getting increasingly agitated beside me. If Jimmy wasn't careful, he or Martin could get their heads blown off any minute. It was always a risk bringing Sebastian to meetings like this. He was a loose cannon. But Archangel Securities had to present a united front, and Sebastian's impulsiveness could be useful at times. It made sure people were always wary of him. In fact, most people were terrified of him. Ever since Martin had got the better of him all those years ago, by bringing a knife to a fist fight, the Fentons had been waiting for him to take his revenge.

'And I've told you, it's not for sale. So, fuck off,' I snapped.

Jimmy glared at me. 'This is your last chance, Sullivan.'

My right hand had remained in my coat pocket for the duration of our brief meeting. The shooters were our last resort. We'd only brought them because we knew Fenton had one in his office. If they came out, people would end up dead, and we could do without a war, or the police sniffing around us. So, I slipped on the brass knuckle duster I'd brought with me. 'No. This is your last chance, Fenton,' I said as I gave Sebastian the nod.

Before Martin could blink, Sebastian had him in a headlock and started punching him in the face and head. Jimmy went for his desk drawer where he kept his shooter, but before he could reach it I jumped over the desk and brought him crashing to the ground. I started pummelling Jimmy's head and he cried out in agony as my bronze-clad fist connected with his jaw. Jimmy was a strong bastard though and he came back at me with everything he had. Fortunately, I had the advantage being on top of him and gave him a hard knee to his groin which had him groaning in agony. I punched him again to the face and watched as his eye almost exploded out of its socket.

Sebastian was obviously enjoying himself as he continued punching and kicking Martin, who was also on the floor by this point. When Sebastian picked up the computer screen from Jimmy's desk and smashed it over Martin's head, I decided we'd done enough damage for one day.

'Don't you ever fucking take us for a pair of mugs again,' I spat as I tapped Sebastian on the shoulder to indicate we were done. 'If you ever come after our business again, we will fucking end the lot of you.'

With a parting kick to Jimmy's legs, I walked out of the porta-cabin, with Sebastian close behind. Looking over at Jimmy's car, I was relieved to see his young conquest hadn't hung around.

I put the car into gear and drove away from the Fenton's builders yard. As we pulled out of the gates, I saw the white transit van driving in.

'Reckon that must have been their back-up?' Sebastian asked.

I nodded. 'Of course. There's no way they'd have taken us on one-on-one. Pair of shit-houses'

'We should have fucking finished the two of them off, mate,' Sebastian said as he shook his head.

'Don't be fucking daft,' I snapped. 'You want to risk doing life for that pair of wankers? Because I don't. Everyone knows they're after our business, so we would be the prime suspects if those two ended up at the bottom of the Thames.'

'But they're cheeky fucking cunts,' Sebastian snarled. 'I told you people would start taking the piss if we tried to go legit. That's not how our business works.'

I sighed. I had a feeling Sebastian was right. How many more takeover bids would we have to fight off? Back in the day, when Sebastian and I had gone around maiming, and on occasion killing, our competitors, no-one had dared to take us on. But now that I was trying to make us a pair of respectable businessmen, the Fentons had had the cheek to try and take us over. 'The Fentons will back off. That's all we need for now, isn't it?'

'For now,' Sebastian replied as he checked his watch. 'It's nearly five. You'd better go and pick Samantha up, hadn't you?'

'Oh yeah,' I replied, trying to sound as casual as possible. Just the thought of seeing her and what I was going to do to her later made my cock stiffen.

'Is she still giving you a hard time?' Sebastian asked.

'You could say that,' I replied.

'Want me to come with you and smooth things over?' he offered.

'No. I'll be fine,' I replied. That was the last thing I wanted.

'Okay. Don't let her give you too much grief though, mate.'

'I won't,' I swallowed.

Fuck! I was going straight to hell.

22. SAMANTHA

Fresh from my shower, I strolled into my kitchen in my bathrobe. Sitting down, I watched Gabriel sip his coffee across the table from me, a frown flickering across his handsome face. Since he'd first stayed the night a week before, we'd hardly left my apartment except to go to work. And we had spent most of our time together in bed.

'What's up?' I asked him as I took a drink of my own coffee.

'Your dad,' he sighed. 'You know we've got to tell him about us?'

I groaned. 'Do we though?'

Gabriel looked at me. 'Yes, Samantha! He's your dad. He's my best mate, and my business partner. It's bad enough that I've even gone there with you, but if he finds out we've been seeing each other behind his back, he'll go nuclear. You know what he's like.'

I shrugged. 'He'll go nuclear anyway, no matter when we tell him. So why risk it until we know what this is?'

'What this is?' Gabriel frowned at me. 'I assumed we'd got past the fuck-buddy phase?'

'We have,' I agreed. It had very quickly become apparent that we could barely keep our hands off each other and a friends with benefits arrangement was never going to work for us. 'But, it's only been a week,' I said, trying to appear nonchalant.

The truth was my insides were churning. The thought of telling my over-protective father that I was seeing his best mate was the least of my worries. The last week with Gabriel had been a heady mix of lust and excitement. I could barely stop thinking about him for more than five seconds. I was feeling things for him I had never felt about anyone, and it was bloody terrifying.

Gabriel glared at me. 'A week where I have spent most of my time inside you, and you still don't think this is something worth telling him about?'

'I know what you're saying. And it's been an incredible week, but let's not get ahead of ourselves by declaring our undying devotion to my father. Because that is what he'll expect from us.'

'I wouldn't risk my relationship with Sebastian if I didn't want this to be something more than a casual thing though. I thought you understood that?'

I looked at him. He was struggling to keep his emotions in check, I could tell by the way his jaw was clenched shut. I wanted so much more than casual from him too. But it was so soon. It all felt too much. I had sworn no man would ever have any power over me ever again. And here was Gabriel Sullivan, one of the most feared men in London, asking me to be his significant other. I was torn between self-preservation, and wanting to spend every waking moment with him. But as well as that, I knew how much it was killing him to keep this from my father. They didn't keep secrets from each other. They were as close as brothers, and I knew that Gabriel felt like he was lying to him every time he saw him.

'Okay, we can tell him,' I relented. 'But I have some ground rules.' He looked up at me and I carried on talking. 'I will allow you to take control when it comes to sex but that's as far as it goes. I am in control of my own life in every other way.'

'Okay,' he nodded.

'You don't get to tell me what to wear or drink or eat. You don't get to tell me what to do. I will talk to who I want to, when I want to. I have male friends and I will go for coffee, or lunch, or dinner with them if I choose to. I will hug them, kiss them on the cheek and any other manner of things that friends do. I'm not a cheat, and I don't play games. I expect the same from you.'

He smiled. 'Anything else?'

'Yes. Honesty. I'm not a child, I don't need protecting from anything and certainly not from the truth. I expect you to be honest with me, even if it's something you think I'd rather not hear.'

'Does that apply to you too, Sam? Will you be honest with me?'

'Yes,' I nodded as I took a sip of my coffee. 'But I'm giving you notice that there might be things about me which you'd rather not know.'

He shrugged so I went on. 'The final, but most important rule, is that I am not your property. If you can accept that, then we can try and make a go of this.'

Gabriel pushed back his chair and stood so quickly that I was startled. He pulled me to my feet. 'It's very unfair of you to negotiate with me while you're almost naked, Sam,' he growled as he started to untie my belt. Kissing my neck, he pushed the robe over my shoulders. The delicate silk slid easily over my skin as it fell to the floor.

'It's unfair of you to try and distract me. Especially when you haven't answered my question yet,' I replied. Despite my words, my body was already responding to his touch and I leaned into him. He'd made me come more times than I could count the previous night, and again that morning, but I ached for him, desperate for his touch, longing to feel him inside me.

He whispered in my ear. 'I accept your terms, Sam. But, I have a few of my own.'

'Oh? What are they?' I purred as he continued kissing my neck.

'You have to let me fuck you senseless at least twice a day,' he growled and my pussy clenched in response. 'And don't ever lie to me.'

'I think I can live with that,' I breathed.

'Now, do you remember when I told you I was going to fuck you on this table,' he smiled at me as he slid his hand between my thighs. 'And I love that you're already wet for me, baby.' Then he unzipped his trousers and lifted me onto the table.

23. GABRIEL

My head was pounding as I drove to the office. I had no idea how I was going to tell Sebastian that I was sleeping with his daughter. How would I even start that conversation? I'd have preferred to have told him myself, but Samantha insisted that we do it together. One thing I did know was that he was going to go mental.

I hoped that he wouldn't be in the office when I got there. I could do with some time alone to wrap my head around the whole thing. I hated lying to Sebastian, and it felt like that's what I had been doing every single time I saw him and didn't tell him about me and Samantha. But everything had happened so fast. One minute it had felt like Samantha and I weren't even friends any more. Then after that night two weeks ago, everything had changed. She'd invited me up to her apartment for a coffee, and I had sworn that that was all it would be, but the next thing I knew I had her pinned to the kitchen table with my hands all over her.

When she'd told me that she wasn't interested in a relationship, I'd felt like she'd ripped out my heart, but I'd at least been able to reconcile the fact that it was probably for the best. How on earth would I navigate a relationship with my best mate's daughter? Then last week had changed all of that again.

Despite my headache, the memory of our epic fucking sessions made me smile. I had thought about what it would be like to fuck Samantha for so long, I'd wondered if the reality would ever live up to the fantasy. But it had been better than I could have imagined. Resting my head against the seat, I pictured her shouting my name as I made her come. I could still taste her. I could still smell her on me. I was definitely going straight to hell.

A car horn blared in my ears as the driver behind me signalled that the lights had changed to green. I drove off and my thoughts returned to Sebastian and the reality that he was going to completely lose his shit when he found out I was fucking his daughter.

24. SAMANTHA

The sun glared through the passenger window of the taxi, making me squint. There was a knot of anxiety making itself at home in my stomach and a bead of perspiration ran down my back. I wasn't particularly looking forward to meeting with my father and telling him about my burgeoning relationship with Gabriel. He was so bloody over-protective of me. I could understand why. In his mind, he had failed me twice. Once when I was born and he never came looking for me or my mother, and again when he failed to protect me from my psychopathic ex-husband. What he didn't understand was that I didn't hold him at all accountable for either of those things. He had been sixteen when I was born. He had no family. No money. No job. And besides all that, my grandparents hated him. They had sworn to cut my mother, and me, out of their lives if she stayed with him, so she did what she thought was the right thing and agreed to move to Kent with them and never see him again.

I also didn't blame him for failing to notice that my marriage to Jackson Carver had been a living nightmare. To the outside world we had been the perfect couple. I'd learned to hide my bruises and my scars well. I had become a damn good actress too. I was a chameleon. It had been the only way to survive. Nobody had known what Jackson was really like or how he made my life hell. I'd hidden it too well. I saw my father three times a year for our birthdays and on Boxing Day, and the rest of the time I kept him at arm's length.

Neither of my parents were perfect. Whose were? But they both made decisions that only ended up hurting themselves, and I believe they'd made them for entirely selfless reasons.

What my dad didn't seem to realise was that I was no longer that scared twelve year old girl who had been dumped on his doorstep. I was a grown woman who was more than capable of looking after myself. After all, if I could survive a marriage to Jackson Carver, I could survive anything.

Gabriel and my father were in their office when I arrived. I could hear them chatting, and it sounded much like their usually friendly banter, so that meant my father remained blissfully unaware of our relationship. I pushed open the door and saw my father's face break into a big grin when he saw me. Crossing the room, he pulled me into a hug.

'Sam. What a lovely surprise. What are you doing here? You're still coming for dinner tonight, aren't you?'

'Yes, Dad. I'll be there. I wouldn't miss it,' I replied.

I glanced at Gabriel, not wanting to make too much eye contact in case I gave the game away before we'd had a chance to explain.

He stood up and walked over to me and we both looked at my father. We hadn't discussed how this was going to go. I knew it was more difficult for Gabriel than it was for me. If any boundaries were being crossed, then he was the one crossing them in my father's eyes. So, I thought it might be better to come from me first.

'I've got something to tell you, Dad,' I said.

Gabriel was at my side in an instant. 'We've got something to tell you,' he added, taking hold of my hand.

The colour started to drain from my father's face and he glared at Gabriel. 'No!' he shouted. 'Tell me you're not ...'

'Sebastian,' Gabriel started. 'Just let us explain.'

'Explain what?' he snarled as he squared up to his best mate. 'I trusted you to look after her!'

'Dad,' I said as I put a hand on his arm, but he shrugged me off and put a hand around Gabriel's throat, pushing him back towards the wall. Gabriel offered no resistance while I stood there with my mouth hanging open.

'You fucking snake!' he spat. 'She's my fucking daughter. You've known her since she was a kid! You fucking pervert!'

'I know, Seb,' he said quietly. It was as though he agreed with my father's outrage. As though he somehow deserved what was happening. Well, he might, but I certainly didn't.

'Dad!' I shouted and he turned to look at me.

'I don't blame you for this, Sam,' he started. 'I know it's all his doing.'

'What?' I said, feeling the anger well inside my chest. 'I am a grown woman and I make my own decisions. I am thirty-two years old for Christ's sake. How dare you suggest that this is somehow all Gabriel's doing? I have chosen to have a relationship with him. The only two people who get to comment on that are me, and him. You most certainly don't get any say whatsoever!'

He blinked at me. I knew I'd hurt him, although I hadn't meant to. I knew that his guilt would be telling him that I was saying those things because he wasn't a very good father, even though that wasn't true.

'Let him go!' I snapped. 'Or I will walk out of here and you will never see me again.'

He dropped his hand and took a step back.

Gabriel rubbed at the skin on his throat. 'Sam,' he said. 'Why don't you leave this to us to sort out?' he suggested.

I glared at him. 'So, now you're treating me like a child too?'

'No! But your dad and me ... this is between us. Please?' he said.

I shook my head in frustration. My outburst had at least made me feel a little calmer. 'Okay! But I am warning you both now, neither of you get to make decisions for me. There will be no deciding what is best for me during your little chat!'

Gabriel nodded. 'Of course not.'

My father glared at me and I could tell he was anxious for me to leave the room so he could continue berating Gabriel.

'I'll go. But this is happening, Dad. Whether you approve of it or not. We didn't plan this. But I'm your daughter, and he's your best mate, so sooner or later you're going to have to deal with it.'

'We'll sort it,' Gabriel said.

'Fine. I need to get back to work,' I said as I started to walk out of the office. 'I'll see you later, Gabe?'

'Of course,' he smiled at me. 'Scott is in the reception. He'll drive you back.'

I heard the heavy footfall of steps towards my office and looked up to see that Gabriel had arrived early. His large frame filled the doorway and the sight of him set my pulse racing.

I smiled at him until I noticed the cut on his lip. 'What happened to your face?'

Touching his lip, he winked at me. 'Oh, nothing. You should see the other guy.'

'You didn't. Did you? You and my dad? How old are the pair of you? I thought you were just going to talk after I left?'

He walked in and perched himself on the edge of my desk. 'We did,' he said as his tongue flicked over the dried blood on his lip. 'And then he punched me.'

'He punched you! Is he okay?' I asked, wondering just how much of a fight they'd got into.

'He's fine. It's how we've always settled our differences,' he replied with a shrug.

'Did you hit him back?' I asked.

'Of course not,' he replied.

'Why not?' Although I was relieved my dad wasn't hurt, I also wondered why Gabriel hadn't defended himself.

'Why didn't I punch your dad in the face? Really?' he frowned.

'Yes. I don't condone violence, but I know you well enough to know that if someone hit you, under ordinary circumstances, you would hit them back.'

'Well, this isn't exactly ordinary, is it?'

'You agree with him, don't you? You think that you've done something wrong?' It was my turn to frown now.

He closed his eyes and sighed. 'Kind of,' he eventually said with a shrug. 'He's my best mate, Sam. You're his daughter. No matter how grown up you are, you will always be his little girl. He asked me to drive you home to keep you safe, and in his eyes, I took advantage of that. Maybe I did?'

I looked at him. I suppose I could see where my dad was coming from, as much as it annoyed me to admit it. But there was no way in hell I would give any credence to the assumption that I had been in any way taken advantage of. What was I, some poor defenceless princess with no mind of her own?

I stood up. 'You did not take advantage of me,' I said as I stepped forward until I was standing between his strong thighs. Being so close to him made all my nerve endings sizzle in anticipation. 'If anything, I think it was me who took advantage of you.'

He wrapped his arms around my waist and pulled me towards him, a wicked grin spreading across his face. 'Is that so?'

'I believe so, yes. You were just some weak, unsuspecting man, who was unable to resist my charms.'

He started to laugh. 'Did you just call me weak, Samantha Donovan?'

'Hmm,' I nodded. 'And unsuspecting.'

He pulled me tighter and bent his head to my neck, grazing his teeth across my sensitive skin. 'I'll put you across my knee if you're not careful,' he growled.

I shivered with excitement at the thought. What the hell was wrong with me? This man turned me into some crazed sex maniac.

'So, is my dad okay with us then?' I asked as Gabriel nibbled on my neck. My office door was open and I feared if he continued kissing me much longer, I was only mere moments away from unzipping his fly and riding him on my desk.

It had the desired effect and Gabriel stopped kissing my neck. 'Not exactly,' he said with a sigh.

'What? You let him punch you in the face and he's still not okay with us?' I asked.

'I didn't exactly let him punch me, Sam-'

'You didn't stop him though!' I said, knowing that Gabriel was faster and stronger than my father was.

'No. But it's complicated. He'll come around.'

'You should have let me handle him,' I said.

'Well, it's not you he's pissed off with. It's me. And I can handle it.'

'By letting him punch you in the face again?' I grinned.

'I would let him punch me in the face every single day if it means I get to be with you,' he said and before I could respond he silenced me with one of his incredible kisses.

25. SAMANTHA

An hour later, Gabriel pulled up outside my father's house and turned to me. 'I'll pick you up about nine,' he said.

'Are you sure you don't want to come in?' I asked him.

He shook his head. 'I think me and your dad have said all we need to say to each other for now. I'll speak to him in a few days when he cools off. Besides, I think he'd quite like you all to himself for a bit,' he smiled.

'Okay,' I replied with a sigh.

'If you want me to come for you any earlier, or later, just ring me,' he said as he took hold of my hand and kissed my fingertips.

'I will. I wish you'd just come in with me though. This is ridiculous!'

'Sam!' He said sternly. 'Just let us deal with this our own way. Please?'

'Okay! I'll see you later then.'

'Don't stay out too late,' he said with a wicked grin that turned my insides to jelly.

'I won't,' I replied.

I stood on my father's doorstep waiting for him to answer. Gabriel drove away as soon as the door was opened.

'Hi, Dad,' I said with a smile. I couldn't stay mad at him; despite the fact he'd punched Gabriel in the face a few hours earlier.

'Hiya, love,' he said, pulling me for a hug. He hugged me every time he saw me, but this one felt a little different. He held me tighter and for longer. 'I really wish you'd use your bloody key though,' he said as he pulled away.

I followed my father into his kitchen and could smell my favourite beef madras cooking.

'So, how are you?' I asked him as I leaned against the kitchen counter while he tended to his curry.

He shrugged. 'Do you mean how am I in general, or how am I feeling about my best mate shacking up with my daughter?'

I rolled my eyes. 'He is not shacking up with me! We're just dating, Dad,' I lied.

Actually, we hadn't been on a single date, we were just having lots of sex. Very hot, frequent sex.

'But he's my best mate, Sam. He's known you since you were a kid.'

'I know that. But I'm not a kid now, am I? I'm a grown woman, Dad! And he's only eight years older than me.'

'I thought you weren't interested in seeing anyone?' He crossed his arms over his chest and eyed me suspiciously. 'You said you'd had enough of men for life, as I recall!'

I laughed. 'You can talk! How many times have to told me you'd never get engaged again?'

'We're not talking about me!' he snapped.

'Well, that was certainly the plan,' I said with a shrug. 'But then I saw Gabriel, and well...'

'He's not pressuring you into anything, is he?'

'No, of course not! Why do you insist on treating me like a child?'

'Because you are my child, Sam!' he bellowed. 'Like it or not, you always will be. I know I've let you down in the past, but that will never happen again! And if that means I have to stick my nose in where it doesn't belong from time to time, then that's what I'll do. I should have done it when you were married to that cunt! But I didn't, and I'll regret it for the rest of my life!' he finished and I saw the tears in his eyes.

'Oh, Dad!' I said as I crossed the kitchen to him and wrapped my arms around his neck. 'You need to stop blaming yourself for what happened to me. Jackson was a master manipulator. He fooled everyone. Nobody had a clue what was going on.'

'It doesn't matter how many times you tell me that, a father is supposed to protect his daughter.'

I kissed him on the cheek. 'And you do. But you don't need to protect me from Gabriel, do you?'

He looked up at me. 'I suppose not,' he said.

'So, can you promise not to punch him in the face the next time you see him then?' I asked.

'That was nothing, Sam. It's how we deal with things. He's never let me win before though. I haven't got the better of that bastard since I met him.'

I shook my head and took a seat at the kitchen table and my father followed suit. 'Dinner will be ready soon,' he said and then he looked down at his hands. 'I always thought you never invited me round to your house in Knightsbridge because you were ashamed of me.'

'Dad! I have never been ashamed of you,' I said. Knowing that he had spent all those years thinking that made my heart feel like it was going to break.

'I know that now,' he replied.

'You must have been so disappointed in me, abandoning you. After everything you did for me?'

'No,' he shook his head. 'Not at all. I was proud of you for making something of yourself. You were always meant for better things, Sam. But now you're back. And you're with Gabriel – and I know it must be serious, because you've told me, and because that soppy bastard doesn't do anything else. You've only been back home five minutes and already you're being sucked back into our world. I want better for you.'

'This is my world too, Dad.'

He nodded. 'I know that.'

I sensed there was something else on his mind that he wasn't saying out loud.

'What's really bothering you, Dad?' I asked him as I placed my hand on his arm.

He stared at me. 'He's my family too, Sam. If something went wrong between the two of you...'

'I know that. But we're all adults. I would never ask you to choose sides. I'd never put you in the middle of us like that.'

He sat back against the chair and ran a hand over his beard. 'Well, if you really think you know what you're getting yourself into, then I suppose there's not a lot I can do about it,' he said with a shrug.

Rising from my chair, I hugged him. 'It means a lot that you're okay with this.'

'I never said I was okay with it,' he raised his eyebrows at me. 'But, I'll try and get used to it.'

26. GABRIEL

I put my mobile back into my trouser pocket. I'd just finished a few phone calls to my head bouncers, confirming there had still been no trouble from the Fenton brothers. It had been two weeks since Sebastian and I had visited them at their builders' yard, and so far, it seemed our warning had worked. I'd heard on the grapevine that Jimmy Fenton had needed twelve stitches in his right eye and had had a steel plate put in his jaw. Martin had suffered a few fractured ribs and a concussion. I just hoped it was enough to warn them off for good. Jimmy had mentioned no more about his threat to expose my secret and I hoped that would be the end of it. After all, he was implicated in Calvin Stewart's murder as much as I was.

Walking into my sitting room with two glasses of wine, I saw Samantha sitting cross legged on my sofa looking at a framed photograph of me and her father when we'd first opened Archangel Securities eighteen years earlier.

'Is everything okay?' she asked. 'I heard you shouting at someone.'

'We're just having a bit of trouble with a rival firm, that's all. Nothing for you to worry about,' I said as I handed her a glass.

'If it involves you and my father in trouble, then I beg to differ,' she said.

'It's nothing, Sam.'

'So, you get to know the intimate details of my life and be my own personal bodyguard, but I'm not allowed to know about yours, is that it?' she asked.

'No. But …' I started. She didn't need to be burdened with my problems. She had enough of her own to deal with.

'I'm not a child, Gabe. I know what you and my dad are into. Just tell me what's going on. I'll only worry if you don't.'

'Okay,' I said as I sat on the sofa beside her. 'There's another security firm who we had trouble with years ago. You know that scar on your dad's neck?'

'Yes. He tried to convince me it was from a cooking related accident.'

'Well, one of the brothers, Martin Fenton did that to him. He and your dad were having a straightener, there were supposed to be no weapons, but Fenton brought a knife. Fortunately, your dad got the better of him anyway. And after that, we … well we sent them a message in return, and we've had an uneasy truce for years. But for some reason, they've started making noises about taking over our business. We've increased security and I don't think they're a real threat, but I'd just rather they were dealt with.'

'So, who was on the phone?'

'Just one of our new bouncers. He let a couple of the Fenton's firm into one of our clubs last night and they tried to smash the place up. Fortunately, some of our other bouncers spotted them and threw them out before they could. But new guy will be lucky if he's still in employment by the end of the week.'

'That seems harsh. He is new,' she said. That was the Samantha I loved — always seeing the best in people.

'We're only as strong as our weakest link, Sam. We can't afford to have people on our team who don't know their shit, or who make mistakes. It puts too many people at risk.'

'I suppose so. I hadn't thought of it like that.'

I kissed the top of her head. 'What are you doing with that anyway?' I indicated the photograph in her hands.

'I took this picture. Remember? You both look so young,' she smiled.

I nodded my agreement. 'I do remember. Although, it seems like a lifetime ago now.'

Samantha took a sip of her wine. 'God, remember when we were young?' She said with a sigh. 'Do you remember the night before I left for uni and you caught me smoking weed in that club you worked in?' She started to laugh.

'I do, yes,' I replied. 'But I'm surprised you do, you were so wasted.'

'I offered myself to you on a plate.' She smiled at me. 'And you turned me down point blank. I was so pissed off at you.'

I shook my head. I thought about that night often and what would have happened if I'd said yes. 'God, I remember. You were wearing that tiny black dress, if you could call it a dress. It barely covered your arse.'

'But you weren't tempted?' she teased me.

'Of course I was. I'm not a fucking saint, Sam. But you were eighteen. You were stoned off your face, and you were my best mate's daughter.'

'I woke up the next morning in an old t-shirt of my father's and remembered I'd propositioned you and you'd turned me down. I was mortified.'

'Well, you had no reason to be mortified. I was very flattered. And *very* tempted.'

'You really were my Angel Gabriel, weren't you? Some men would have taken advantage of a girl in that state.'

'Yes, I know, which is exactly why I took you home. It's a good job your dad wasn't working that night, because he would've gone mental.'

Samantha rolled her eyes. 'He was always going mental at me. He barely let me move.'

'Well, he had his reasons,' I said.

'I fancied you so much. I never forgave you for turning me down.' She pretended to pout.

'You'd never have forgiven me if I hadn't. And more importantly, I don't think I'd have forgiven myself. You have no idea how hard it was for me to resist your continued efforts to seduce me.'

She stared at me open mouthed. 'Really? I never knew that. So, you liked me too then?'

'You are a beautiful woman, Sam. You're an incredible woman. But at eighteen...' I didn't finish my sentence. Fancying my best mate's eighteen year old daughter who was eight years younger than me wasn't exactly my proudest moment, but she had been something else.

I smiled at her. 'I lost count of how many dickheads your dad and I had to warn to stay away from you. And before you start on about being an independent woman, these were men you really didn't want to be involved with.'

Samantha blushed. 'God, I used to give you both such a hard time.'

'Well, we probably deserved it,' I shrugged.

'I wish I'd known, Gabe. Why didn't you say anything to me?'

'Because you were dangerous,' I admitted.

'Dangerous?' she laughed and the sound took me back fourteen years.

'Yes. You were only eighteen years old. You were gorgeous, and far too smart for your own good. I thought you'd be more trouble than I could handle. Besides, you went to uni the next day. And the next I heard you'd married some hotshot lawyer and were living in a fancy house in Knightsbridge. I didn't think there was a man alive who could tame the indomitable Samantha Donovan.'

'Well, you were right. He wasn't a man. He was a monster,' she replied and I saw the change in her instantly. Any mention of her ex-husband or her life in Knightsbridge could change the atmosphere in the room as quickly as flicking a switch.

She stood up and placed her wine glass on my coffee table, then she turned back and straddled me. She obviously didn't want to talk any longer.

Dipping her head, she started to kiss a trail down my neck

towards my chest. Then her soft fingertips were brushing my skin as she pulled my t-shirt over my head. I wrapped my arms around her and pulled her closer to me and she groaned, letting her head fall back and exposing the delicate skin of her neck. She smelled so good. I wanted to sink my teeth into her tender flesh, but I kissed her instead and she purred with pleasure as she moved her hips up and down, rubbing herself over my stiff cock until I couldn't stand it any longer. I needed to taste her. I needed to have some part of my body inside her. I pushed her onto her back on the sofa and tugged at the belt on her wrap dress until it fell open, exposing her beautiful body.

'Gabe,' she groaned and I felt my dick twitch.

'I know, baby,' I whispered as I slid my hand up her inner thigh and under the edge of her underwear. I closed my eyes and stifled a groan as I found her already dripping wet for me. It took all my restraint not to bury myself inside her. I would soon enough, but first I needed to make her scream my name.

27. GABRIEL

I stood on the doorstep of Sebastian's house with my hands in my pockets, waiting for him to answer. I hadn't seen him for three days — not since Samantha and I had told him about our relationship. We'd managed to avoid each other in work, but now I had something to discuss with him. And no matter what he thought about me and his daughter, there was no more time for his sulking. I was prepared to take another punch to the face, or even a few of them, just to have my best mate back again.

Sebastian answered the door a few seconds later and rolled his eyes when he saw me. 'What do you want?' he snapped.

'Can I come in?'

He glared at me for a moment but then he opened the door wider and allowed me inside. I followed him into his kitchen.

'So, what do you want?' Sebastian snapped.

'I've had the contracts through on the nightclub. They need your signature.'

'You could have left them at the office for me.'

'I did. With a giant fucking post-it note on saying sign here!'

Sebastian shook his head. 'I didn't see them.'

'How long are you going to punish me for, mate? Do you want to punch me again?' I held my arms out wide. 'Come on, then. If it will make you feel better?'

Sebastian glared at me. 'Did anything ever happen when she was a kid?'

I scowled at him. 'Of course it fucking didn't. What the fuck, Seb?'

'I just needed to know,' he said as he sat down at the kitchen table and ran a hand over his beard.

I sat down opposite him. 'Look, mate. I know this must be weird for you. But, I need you to know that I really care about her. I wouldn't risk my friendship with you if I didn't think this thing between me and Sam was a long-term thing.'

'If you ever hurt her...' Sebastian pointed a finger at me.

'I won't.' I shook my head.

'Then where's this fucking paperwork, then?' he asked as he held out his hand.

I pulled the envelope out of my inside pocket and handed it to him.

Half an hour later, I left Sebastian's house with the signed paperwork in my pocket and my relationship with my best mate back on track. I checked my watch and wondered if I had time to pay a quick visit to Samantha's place before I started my weekly checks on our clubs. I was usually happy to work at night and it had always been my job to check on our venues and bouncers weekly. It never used to bother me as I hardly slept anyway. At least I never used to. I had plenty to keep me awake at night. But something about being curled up to Samantha's warm body made me sleep like a baby.

If I went to her place now, the likelihood is I wouldn't make it back out again before morning. I couldn't afford to let things slide any further. Although we'd warned the Fentons off, they were still a threat. I pulled my car away from the kerb and sighed. The sooner I got this over with, the sooner I could get home to her.

28. SAMANTHA

I ran the brush through my hair as I waited for Gabriel to pick me up. He hadn't been able to drive me home from work, so had sent Scott instead, along with a request to be ready for a date at 7:30pm. It had been almost four weeks since we'd got together, but we'd never been on a proper date before, preferring to spend most of our time in bed.

I was looking forward to whatever he had planned. I hadn't been on a good date for as long as I could remember. I'd texted him to ask him where we were going but he'd refused to tell me. When I'd asked what I should wear, all he'd replied was 'Nothing fancy.' I'd dressed in a sweater dress and calf length boots and hoped that it would suffice.

A few moments later, I heard the knock at my door and opened it to Gabriel's smiling face.

'Are you ready?' he asked.

'Yes,' I replied as I grabbed my handbag and coat.

As we climbed into Gabriel's car, I noticed a couple of blankets and a cooler box in the back seat.

'So, are you going to tell me where we're going now then?' I asked.

He turned to me and smiled. 'To theatre in the park.'

Of all the things he might suggest, that had been the furthest from my mind, but it sounded incredible. 'Really? I've never been to one of those. What play?'

'Midsummer Night's Dream.'

'Well, Gabe, you old romantic, you!' I said with a laugh.

'Hey! Less of the old,' he replied as he lifted my hand to his lips and kissed the tips of my fingers.

When we got to the park, Gabriel steered us to a spot near the back of the audience, and off to the side where there were few people. I had suggested that we find a spot with a better view but he'd simply glared at me and I'd realised that there was always a method to his madness.

After we had finished eating the delicious food he'd brought from a local deli, I sat between Gabriel's outstretched legs and leaned back against his chest, nestling my head under his chin while I watched the play. He handed me some wine in a plastic glass and I sighed in contentment. It was certainly a great way to spend an evening.

'I think this might just be the perfect date, Mr Sullivan,' I said with a smile.

He kissed the top of my head. 'It certainly is.'

As the night grew colder, Gabriel reached for a spare blanket and pulled it over the two of us, draping it over my legs.

'Pull your knees up, Sam,' he ordered in my ear.

I looked around at the smattering of people who were nearby. None of them were close enough to hear, or see much in the dusk — no wonder he had chosen that particular spot. I did as instructed and he slipped his hand beneath the blanket before slowly sliding it between my legs. I could already feel that warm, pulling feeling in the base of my abdomen.

'What if someone sees us, Gabe?' I whispered.

'I'll make sure no-one does. I promise. Just relax,' he replied softly.

I let my legs fall apart slightly, giving him easier access to exactly where I wanted him. I gasped as he pushed my underwear aside and started to rub slow teasing circles around my clit. He kissed my neck periodically but most of the time he watched the play, no doubt keeping an eye out for anyone straying too close who may guess what he was doing. He continued lazily moving his fingers and I eventually stopped watching the play and leaned my head back against him until I could feel his erection pushing into my back. I closed my eyes so I could concentrate only on the feel of his fingers and what they were doing to me. My orgasm built so slowly, that when I finally came it felt like it washed over my whole body in a long rolling wave. I bit on the inside of my cheek to prevent myself from crying out.

Gabriel kept his hand between my legs and whispered in my ear. 'Did you enjoy that?'

'Hmmm, yes,' I said with a sigh. 'It was just like being sixteen again, getting drunk in a park while some boy tries to finger me.' I giggled, the wine and the fresh air making me feel giddy.

'Samantha!' He nipped at my earlobe. 'For the record, I didn't try and *finger you* as you so eloquently put it. I bet you want me to though, don't you? I bet you'd like me to slip my fingers inside and fuck you with them?'

I nodded and at that precise moment, I wouldn't have cared who saw us either. He could have flipped me over and fucked me right there on the grass and I wouldn't have resisted. He quickly slipped one large finger inside me and I moaned.

'Later, baby,' he laughed as he pulled his hand out from under the blanket.

I sat on Gabriel's old comfortable leather sofa, my cheeks flushed from the wine and the enjoyable evening. The play was wonderful. The food was delicious. Gabriel was fantastic. That had probably been the best date I'd ever had in my life. Gabriel walked into the living room with two bottles of Budweiser and handed one to me. Sitting down on the sofa he pulled my legs up so they were draped over his lap.

'So tell me about these boys who tried to finger you in parks when you were sixteen then?' he said with a smile.

'Not boys actually. Just one boy. Charlie Morrison, and he was my boyfriend.'

'Oh, yes I remember him. Pony tail. Always stunk of weed. I didn't know he was your boyfriend though.'

'Well, of course I would never have told you or my dad, would I?' I said with a flash of my eyebrow. 'He would have probably put poor Charlie's head on a spike outside our house to warn other boys away.'

'I don't think he was quite that bad, Sam,' he said as he took a swig of his beer. 'Was Charlie your first then?'

'No,' I replied. 'We never had sex at all, actually.'

'So who was your first then?'

'Nick.'

'Nick? Nick, your best mate?' He started to laugh. 'No way. Really?'

I frowned at him. 'Yes. Why is that so funny to you?'

He shook his head. 'He just doesn't seem your type, that's all. I can't imagine the two of you...'

'Well, good. I don't really want you imagining me and Nick, if you don't mind.'

Gabriel laughed. 'Did you two go out together for long?'

'God, no! We were awful together, at least in that way. After a few dates, we decided we were much better off as friends.'

'It's nice that you're such good mates now,' he said as he put an arm around me and pulled me towards him. I looked at him and could tell that he meant that. I had never dared tell Jackson that Nick and I had even so much as kissed.

Suddenly, Gabriel pulled back and looked at me. 'So, how old were you when you lost your virginity then?' he asked.

'Eighteen,' I replied.

'What? I don't believe it!' He started to laugh again.

'Why on earth not?' I snapped as I gave him a nudge with my elbow.

'It's just that you were such a wild child... I just assumed...'

'You assumed I'd slept around?'

'I *assumed* you'd had some experience, that's all. The way you used to constantly flirt with me.'

'Well, I never met anyone I wanted to go that far with. Then when I went to uni, I kind of felt I had to, and Nick seemed nice. I went out with another lad from my course for a few months. And then I met Jackson. And now there's you.'

Gabriel stared at me open mouthed. 'So you've only had sex with four people?'

Suddenly, this conversation had headed into a place I hadn't intended it to go. I felt my skin becoming clammy and I started to wring my hands unconsciously. I tried to remember to breathe the way I'd been taught to. Intensive EMDR therapy had helped me to process the many painful memories. They didn't hold the same terror and shame that they once had, but they still knocked the wind from me when they crept up unexpectedly.

'I never said that,' I said and pulled away from him.

'I'm sorry, Sam. I was just curious. It's not a big deal. I don't care if you've slept with four men or forty,' he said as he sat forward and put a hand on my arm.

'You think I'm worried that you're going to judge me for how many men I've slept with?' I snapped at him. I was being unfair to him. But this was hurting. I could feel my pulse starting to race and pushing him away was the only defence I had.

He blinked at me in confusion. 'No. I don't know where this is coming from, Sam? I asked you a question, if you don't want to answer it, that's fine.'

'But it's the reason why you think I don't want to answer it that's bothering me. Because you think I feel ashamed that I've either slept with too many or not enough?'

'No, I don't,' he said with a scowl.

'Really?' I crossed my arms over my chest. 'Because it certainly seems like that. Of course, if I'm uncomfortable talking about how many people I've had sex with, it must be because I'm ashamed of my number. There is no other possible reason.'

I saw the confusion in his face but I was spiralling and I didn't know how to stop.

'I never said that. But what is the reason then? If it's supposed to be so fucking obvious to me, tell me what it is? What the hell is wrong with you?' he asked.

That question felt like a slap to my face. I blinked back the tears. How dare he ask what was wrong with me? As if I was broken. It was bad enough when he treated me like I was made of glass, but to be treated like I was broken somehow, that was ten times worse. Because it touched on one of my deepest fears.

'What's wrong with me?' I shouted.

'I didn't mean ...' he started but I kept on shouting.

'There is nothing wrong with me! If you're really so desperate to know, then yes, I have only slept with four men of my own free will. But as for how many I've had sex with, well that would be eight.'

His face changed in an instant as what I had said registered with him. 'Sam,' he said.

'There. Feel better now you know, do you?' I snapped at him, even though I knew I was being irrational and unfair to him. How was he supposed to know what had happened to me while I'd been married to Jackson?

'I'm sorry, Sam. If I'd known ... I wouldn't have even asked.' He put his hand on my shoulder and I shrugged him off.

'Sam-' he said again.

'Don't, Gabe. I don't want your pity.'

'Why do you always mistake my concern for pity?'

'I think I need to go home,' I said, standing up. The memory was becoming too painful and I needed to process it alone, without Gabriel looking at me wondering if I was going to crack. Questioning if I really was broken.

He stared at me for a moment and I thought he was going to ask me to stay. But he didn't.

'I'll ring you a cab,' he said as he took his phone out of his pocket and dialled the number.

I sat in silence as I waited for my taxi to arrive and Gabriel did the same, watching me the whole time. When he received the alert to say it was outside, I stood up. He walked over to me and tried to pull me into a hug but I shrugged him off.

'Don't,' I said.

He dropped his arms by his sides. 'I'll call you tomorrow.'

'Okay,' I replied as I walked out of his house and climbed into the waiting taxi.

29. SAMANTHA

I twirled a paperclip around between my fingers as sat at my desk and thought about the previous night. Having to reveal some of my messed up past to Gabriel had been an unexpected turn of events. He hadn't asked for detail and I hadn't offered any, but I wondered if it was something I'd have to tell him about eventually. It was a part of my past that had taken me a long time to come to terms with. I had been young and naïve and the shame had weighed heavy on me for a long time. It was only through the wisdom of experience that I'd realised that shame was never mine to carry. It belonged squarely on the shoulders of others.

I knew I'd been unfair to Gabriel. I didn't doubt that he hadn't intended to cause me any pain. He couldn't possibly have known that one of Jackson's many methods of controlling me was to allow his friends to have sex with me when I had stepped out of line. He saved it for the most heinous of my crimes — trying to leave him, but it was a crime I committed often — until that last time, at least. After the trial, I had found an amazing therapist who had introduced me to EMDR therapy — a method of processing memories that enabled me to live with them without allowing them to overwhelm me, or have any power over me. It was effective, but it wasn't fool-proof.

But all the therapy in the world couldn't convince me that I wasn't broken. On good days, I believed that maybe I wasn't. I'd been married to a psychopath who had tried to destroy me and I was still standing. But on my darkest days, I would question whether I attracted all this pain into my life because I was fundamentally damaged in some way. Perhaps there was some malfunction in my brain that made me essentially unlovable and incapable of love in return? Wasn't that why I rebelled so much as a teenager and never had a long-term boyfriend like my friends did?

My therapist had helped me to realise that all my memories of my life before Jackson were viewed through the lens of my life with him — twisted by his lies and manipulation, until I no longer knew the truth. I don't recall ever feeling broken when I was younger. I had never wanted to be a burden to my father after my mum died. I wanted to be independent and fierce and I'm sure if I went back in time and spoke to that girl, she would tell me that she was. But of course she was broken. Because I am. That was why Jackson chose me.

I heard a noise and looked up to see Gabriel standing in my office doorway. I hadn't realised it was that time.

'Ah, my bodyguard,' I said, regretting my tone as soon as the words left my mouth.

If he was offended, he didn't show it. 'Are you ready, Sam?' he asked.

I looked at my open laptop and the papers strewn across my desk. I had hardly done any work all day. I had thought about my past, and about Gabriel and how he could possibly ever see a future with someone like me — who had more baggage than Heathrow's lost and found.

'Yes,' I said. 'I just need to tidy this up.'

He crossed the room. 'Let me help,' he said.

His hand brushed mine as he picked up some of the papers and I looked up at him. 'I'm sorry I ran away last night.'

He put the papers into the folder as I held it open. 'You have nothing to be sorry for,' he said softly.

I put the folder away in my drawer and locked it. 'Ready,' I said as

I walked around the desk and stood in front of him. Putting my hands on his waist, I pulled him towards me until our bodies were pressed together.

'Does what I told you make you see me any differently?' I asked.

He frowned at me. 'Of course it doesn't.' He reached up and stroked my cheek. 'I can't even imagine the things you've been through,' he said. 'I wish I'd known.'

'It's in the past. It's part of who I am, but it doesn't define me. I don't want it to define us. Please don't feel sorry for me.'

'I don't, Sam. But you can't tell me things like that and expect me not to react. I'm only human. I know you've worked hard to deal with your past, but what that bastard did to you will never be easy for me to hear. But that's not because I feel sorry for you, it's because I hate him and because the thought of anyone hurting you makes me feel sick.'

I stared at him unsure how to respond.

'All I'm asking is that you give me the benefit of the doubt. Despite how I might react, and what you think I'm thinking, please know that I am never feeling sorry for you.'

'Okay,' I agreed. 'If you can promise me that when I tell you something awful from my past, that you won't treat me like I'm fragile.'

'You are the least fragile person I know.' He bent his head and kissed my neck. 'Besides, we all have our demons, baby,' he said in that low growl of his that made my legs tremble.

'Even you?' I asked.

'Especially me,' he replied. Then before I could ask what those demons were, he ran his hands over my hips and onto my backside, pressing my body even closer to his as he kissed me long and hard. I could feel his erection growing as his tongue explored my mouth.

'Jesus, Gabe. Take me home,' I panted as we came up for air.

'Your wish is my command,' he said with a grin as he took my hand and led me out of the office.

30. SAMANTHA

Gabriel and I had eaten dinner and were sitting on the sofa together. He'd fucked me in the hallway as soon as we'd got to my apartment and our argument from the previous night had been forgotten. Now he was watching a documentary about polar bears and the melting ice caps as I sat with my legs draped over his. I absent-mindedly curled his hair around my fingertip.

'Are you bored?' he asked me with a grin.

'No, why?'

'Because you're staring at me. Is the plight of the poor polar bears not interesting enough for you?'

I smiled at him. 'Not half as interesting as you. Anyway, I don't like documentaries. I only like trashy reality television and soppy romance films. You know this.'

'Oh yes, of course. Nothing too highbrow for you. I remember now.'

He knew that it was another remnant from my dysfunctional marriage — another tiny form of rebellion. Jackson never let me watch what I wanted to on television. All he ever watched was the news, documentaries, or war films. So now I refused to watch anything vaguely educational, except for the news occasionally when some of my cases were involved.

'I do sometimes make exceptions for fluffy polar bears and other cute animals though,' I said.

Sensing that Jackson was on my mind, as he often was, Gabriel put his arm around me. 'Did you ever try and leave him?'

I looked at him. God, how naïve he was. As though leaving had been an option.

'Yes. In the beginning, I tried to leave all the time. But he would always find me, always bring me back. In the end, he got fed up with it, and so he made sure I never tried again.'

'Why, what did he do?' he asked as he turned the television off and faced me, his voice full of concern.

I stared at him. I had never told anyone except my therapist about it. I hadn't told the police during my interviews. I hadn't revealed it during the trial when I was cross examined over and over again – I couldn't bear the thought of all those people knowing. Could I talk about it now? The therapy I'd undergone had helped me to deal with the memories in a way that made them less painful to relive. But given my reaction last night to him asking me a perfectly innocent question, perhaps this was something he should know about. It probably explained so much about why I was the way I was.

I took a deep breath as I prepared to tell him about one of the worst experiences of my life.

'It was a few days after my twenty-fifth birthday. I'd left Jackson the week before, but he'd found me, like he always did, and brought me home like a runaway teenager. He'd been furious as usual. He'd threatened me. Then he'd threatened to hurt my dad. Sometimes, if it had taken him a while to find me, and he was really pissed off, he would invite one of his friends around to help keep me in line,' I swallowed as I looked up at Gabriel and saw him grimace.

He didn't say anything and I looked down at my trembling hands. I couldn't look at his face when I told him the next part. 'Anyway, a few days later, he bought me a beautiful dress and told me to put it on, because he was taking me somewhere special — somewhere that I'd never forget. I assumed the being nice and making up stage was about to begin. He was often on his best behaviour for a few weeks once he knew I was back to stay.

We drove to a big house in the country and he told me we were staying for the weekend. I had protested that I hadn't packed any clothes and he'd laughed and told me not to worry, because I wouldn't be needing any. I assumed the house was a little hotel, and that we'd be holed up in a room for the weekend — we'd done that before when he'd been trying to apologise for something. But it hadn't been that at all.'

I could feel my heart hammering in my chest now and I reached over to the coffee table and picked up the glass of water I'd left there earlier. I took a sip and tried to steady my erratic breathing.

Gabriel put a warm hand over mine. 'I'm here, Sam. Just take your time,' he said softly.

I looked up at him and nodded. 'It was the house of one of his friends. Four of his friends were already there, staying at the house too for the weekend. I'd met two of them before under similar circumstances, but it had only ever been one at a time before then.'

Gabriel sucked in a breath and I swallowed down the knot of fear and anxiety that was forming in my chest. I had to get the next part out, because then he would know, and I'd never have to talk about it again.

'They passed me around between themselves for the weekend. Sometimes Jackson joined in too. But mostly he just watched, or held me down when I got too feisty.' I let out a long shaky breath. I didn't tell Gabriel how they had laughed at me when I fought back and had tried to convince me that I was really enjoying myself.

'Jesus, Sam!' he growled. I saw his fists clenched at his sides, his whole body rigid like a piece of iron. 'I wish ... I would have ...' he shook his head as though he couldn't bring himself to finish the sentence. 'What the fuck!' he finally hissed.

'He told me it was my punishment for leaving. He wanted to remind me that I was his property and he could do whatever he liked with me. He told me if I ever tried to run again, I would suffer more of the same — or worse. I never tried to leave after that and he never did it again. But sometimes those same men would come to our house for a party, bringing their wives along too. They would leer at me, like I was some sort of party favour. They would try and talk to me and share crude inside jokes when their wives weren't around, as though they thought I had somehow enjoyed them raping me. Perhaps Jackson had told them that I did?'

I finished talking and stared at Gabriel, trying to figure out what was going through his mind. I hated to be pitied and he knew it. But, despite that, I knew that as hard it was for me to relive that experience, it would also have been hard for him to hear.

He pulled me into his arms, so I was sitting on his lap. He brushed the hair from my face. 'Give me their names, Sam, and I will make sure they suffer. I will make them feel more pain than they ever could have imagined,' he growled.

I shook my head. 'I appreciate the offer, but no. They're not worth it, Gabe. Besides, we're talking about some powerful people here.'

'I don't care how powerful they think they are,' he scowled at me. 'I will bury the fucking lot of them — including Carver.'

I placed my hand on his chest and felt his heart hammering underneath my fingertips. The anger radiated from him in waves. Somehow, my desire to calm him down, made my own anxiety easier to handle.

'Please, don't let them take up any space in your head, Gabe. I dealt with this a long time ago. It's not something I want to think about. It's certainly not something I want you to waste any energy on. I told you because it's part of what makes me the way I am. But it's in my past and I'd prefer to leave it there.'

'I don't know what else to say, Sam,' he said, his voice thick with emotion. 'I can't even imagine what you went through, and how you dealt with that.'

'I dealt with it by burying it — at least at first. Then I found a great therapist during the trial. She was amazing. She really helped me.'

He swallowed hard. 'No matter what you say, I need you to know that I will kill that fucker with my bare hands if he ever touches you again, Sam. I promise you that.'

I nodded. I didn't feel like it came from a place of pity, so I could understand that he would want to hurt the man who'd hurt me. I just hoped he never had to live up to the promise.

'I think you're wrong when you tell me you weren't made of glass,' he said as he stroked my cheek with his thumb.

I blinked at him. 'And why's that, Gabe?'

'Because you've walked through fire and have come through the other side, stronger and more beautiful than before.'

'You're such a poet,' I smiled at him and he pulled me towards him, wrapping his arms tighter around me. I never felt ashamed about my past any more. None of it was my fault. I knew that. But in my years as a solicitor I had come across so many people who judged victims of sexual abuse. People who assumed that she must have been asking for it. Or that she enjoyed it really. It used to make me so angry. As a defence solicitor, I often had to defend alleged perpetrators and I did it to the best of my ability. Everyone, guilty or innocent, was entitled to legal representation, and I believed in the justice system. But when I'd been asked to defend one of three young men who'd been accused of gang raping one of their college classmates, I'd quit and had taken a job working for the Crown Prosecution Service instead.

Jackson had been furious with me, but I couldn't do it anymore. The defence's primary tactic in the case had been to discredit the witness and paint the perpetrators as respectable, middle class young men. I'd known they were guilty because they'd told me, yet it was my job to be part of the legal team that would pull this young woman's sexual history apart on the stand and make her question whether she had in fact been asking for it — and make a jury do the same?

'Are you okay?' Gabriel asked softly.

I nodded. I was. But I also needed to know whether what I had told him, had changed the way that he saw me. I didn't want him to look at me and only see my past. I didn't want his pity.

I sat up and straddled him, guiding his hands down my body. 'Sam,' he groaned. 'What are you doing?'

'Please, Gabe. I need this,' I breathed against his neck.

He responded without hesitation then, understanding exactly what I needed from him.

31. SAMANTHA

I was filing away some papers when I heard the buzz of the external intercom. It was just after six and everyone else had gone home for the evening, even Nick had left early to pick up his kids from his ex-wife's house. They were spending the Easter bank holiday weekend with him and he'd been excited about it all day. I had some exciting plans myself. To celebrate our one month anniversary, Gabriel had invited me away for the weekend to his friend's cottage in the countryside. I had thought about little else all week. I'd arranged for him to pick me up at six o'clock instead of his usual five so I could get some office admin done and enjoy our weekend away without worrying if I'd missed something.

The outer doors of Donovan Cook could be opened by a button in my office. There was a similar one in Nick's too. It was only the reception desk though which allowed whoever was inside to speak to the visitor. I knew it would be Gabriel, and I'd almost finished the last of my filing, so I pressed the button to let him in rather than walking to reception and interrupting my work.

I heard the footsteps walking towards my office, and the squeaking of a soft shoe on the tiles. That was odd. Gabriel's shoes never squeaked. I felt my heart start to race.

Don't be stupid, Samantha! He's probably been to the gym and is wearing his trainers!

Despite telling myself that, I felt the uneasiness growing until it felt as though every nerve in my body was on edge. I swallowed and tried to steady my ragged breathing.

Where was my phone? Could I get to it quickly enough? Was there a weapon to hand?

I glanced at the letter opener just a few feet away from me on my desk. As I reached for it I looked up to see the door to my office opening.

Oh, God, please let it be Gabriel!

32. GABRIEL

'Fucking traffic,' I muttered under my breath. I had promised Samantha I'd be at her office by six to pick her up and it was already quarter past. I'd forgotten about the nearby roadworks which had turned the road into one long traffic jam. I hated being late for anything, but especially for her.

Approaching her office, I could already see the blue lights in the distance. It took me a few seconds to realise that they belonged to two police cars and an ambulance, lighting up the street directly outside Donovan Cook.

Shit!

My heart started to beat so fast I thought it might burst out of my chest. Pushing my foot down on the accelerator, I sped towards the scene. My tyres screeched to a halt outside when I got there. Leaping out of the car, I took the couple of steps up to Samantha's office in one stride. As soon as I reached the door I was stopped by a uniform.

'This is a crime scene, Sir.' He said, his arm outstretched in front of me to stop me from moving any further.

'That's my fucking girlfriend in there,' I snapped at him, determined to move him by force if he didn't step out of my way voluntarily.

'Name?' the uniform said as he reached for his radio.

'Gabriel Sullivan,' I seethed. My teeth were clenched so hard my jaw was beginning to ache.

'There's a Gabriel Sullivan here, Sarge.'

The voice on the other end crackled through. 'Let him in.'

I pushed past the idiot at the door and into the hallway. At the sight of blood spattered across the floor, my hammering heart felt like it was going to pack in altogether. I tried to swallow but there was no saliva at all in my mouth.

'Mr Sullivan,' another uniform stepped out of the office doorway. She gave me a half-smile and gestured for me to step inside Samantha's office.

'Gabe!' Samantha shouted when she saw me.

My knees felt like they'd been hit from behind with a sledgehammer. Holding onto the doorframe for a split second, I steadied myself as I looked at her sitting at her desk, seemingly uninjured. I let out a long breath. She was pale and shaking like a leaf, but she was okay.

'Sam, what happened? Are you okay?' I crossed her office in two strides.

She nodded at me and gave me a weak smile.

I felt a firm hand on my shoulder. 'We're just about to take a statement, Mr Sullivan.' I turned to see a tall, bearded man in a brown overcoat indicating the chair next to Samantha. I took a seat and frowned. I wasn't used to co-operating with the law.

I turned to Samantha. 'The blood? The ambulance?'

'Your girlfriend here broke her attacker's nose,' the bearded police officer answered for her. 'And quite possibly a couple of his ribs.'

'And she dislocated his shoulder,' the female officer who had shown me into the room said.

'What?' I said as I stared at Samantha.

'I told you I didn't need a bodyguard, Gabe,' she said with a faint smile.

I shook my head before smiling back. Jesus Christ, just when I thought this woman had run out of ways to amaze me.

'In your own time, Samantha,' the bearded detective said with a smile.

33. SAMANTHA

I took a deep breath. My mouth was dry. My throat felt swollen. I clasped my hands in front of me to stop them from trembling. Gabriel shifted in his seat, moving closer to me and resulting in his thigh being pressed against mine. The heat from his body penetrated the thin fabric of my skirt. I glanced at him and saw the concern in his eyes. Clearing my throat, I started to relay the details of my brush with Mr Garvey, while one of the uniformed constables wrote down my statement.

'I was filing some papers before finishing for the night when I heard the buzzer at the front door. I assumed it was Gabriel and pressed the release to unlock the doors and let him through. It was stupid. I should have checked who it was,' I shook my head. DS Phillips smiled at me and I went on. 'I heard the footsteps coming towards my office and I knew it wasn't Gabriel. The shoes squeaked on the tiles, like trainers do, you know? And Gabriel never wears trainers outside of the gym. I grabbed the letter opener from my desk just as Anthony Garvey walked through the door.'

I paused and reached for the glass of water DS Phillips had given me a few moments earlier.

'He started shouting as soon as he saw me. Calling me a fucking bitch and telling me I was about to get exactly what I deserved. He made a grab for me. He was so close, I could smell the cigarettes and whisky on his breath. He put one hand around my throat and then started to pull at the buttons on my shirt.' I paused as I felt Gabriel tense beside me.

'I tried to jam the letter opener into his ribs but he was wearing a thick coat, and it barely scratched him. He started laughing then and telling me how I was going to pay, how he'd make me suffer. He made a grab for my hand, trying to get the letter opener from me. I knew I had to get out of there and away from him so I grabbed his arm and twisted it behind his back until I heard a pop, and then I made a run for it. I grabbed my jacket off the chair on my way out. My mobile was in it and I managed to dial 999 before he caught up with me and knocked it from my hand. He was screaming by then that he was going to kill me. There was a bit of a scuffle but I head-butted him in the nose and then kicked him in the ribs when he was doubled over. I locked myself in my office then until you arrived.'

I finished my statement and took another sip of water. Gabriel took hold of my free hand and squeezed and I smiled at him. I knew it hadn't been easy for him to stay calm hearing about my assault. I had felt his body tense throughout. 'I'm just relieved you arrived when you did,' I said to the officers.

'There was a car in the area,' DS Phillips replied.

'Thank God,' Gabriel muttered.

'For who?' one of the officers said, smiling, until he realised that nobody else found his joke amusing.

It felt like hours before I was finally allowed to leave the office and go home. Both Gabriel and I were silent during the drive. I knew he'd be blaming himself for being late, and I didn't have the energy to argue about it. I wondered whether to tell him what else I thought Garvey had said to me. I could have sworn he'd said 'we'll make you pay.' But it had all happened so fast and my blood had been thundering in my ears, I couldn't be sure. I hadn't mentioned it to the police and now I wasn't sure why. Maybe because if there was a 'we' it had to be Jackson behind it. And if that was true then the police could do little about it. Jackson had friends very high up in the Met.

Gabriel and my father would have me wrapped in cotton wool and never leaving the house again if they knew. But more importantly, I didn't want either of them on the wrong side of my ex-husband. As tough as the two of them were, Jackson was far too dangerous. No, I would find out what was going on myself, even if that meant speaking to Jackson to find out what the bloody hell he was playing at.

I showered as soon as I got home to my apartment, turning the temperature dial up as far as it could go. I enjoyed the feeling of the hot water running over my face. I recalled the many times I had stood in a scalding shower and desperately hoped that it might wash away a memory. Sometimes, I used to like to imagine it washing me away entirely. Like maybe I could just melt, trickle down the plughole and disappear.

Gabriel didn't join me, as he usually would, and I wasn't sure if I was hurt or relieved. My brush with Anthony Garvey had shaken me more than I would ever admit. I had been stupid to open that door without checking who it was. I'd been so desperate to prove that I could look after myself and didn't need protection, that I'd been reckless. I'd spent years of my life doing all I could to keep myself safe, and now that some crazy person was out to get me, I'd been careless and arrogant. I had thought that surviving Jackson made me invincible. At least now Garvey was going to be behind bars for the foreseeable future. That gave me some comfort at least — and so did having my own personal bodyguard in the form of Gabriel Sullivan, as much as I would never admit that to him or my father.

Padding into the living room in my bathrobe, I found Gabriel sitting on the sofa with a glass of Jack Daniels in his hand. There was another glass on the coffee table.

'I thought you might like one,' he nodded towards the glass and I picked it up before taking a seat beside him.

Taking a large gulp of the dark liquid, I enjoyed the feel of it burning my throat as I swallowed.

'I'm sorry, Sam.' Gabriel said, shaking his head. 'I should have been there.'

'It's not your fault, Gabe. I should never have let him in. Even so, it's nobody's fault, except his. And the police have him now. He'll end up where he belongs soon enough.'

Gabriel drained his glass and started to pour another.

I put a hand on his arm. 'Let's go to bed, Gabe. I'm tired.'

He nodded and followed me to the bedroom. We both undressed silently before slipping into bed. I lay my head on his chest and he wrapped his arms around me, pulling me to him so tightly I struggled to breathe.

'Easy, Tiger,' I laughed, trying to wriggle from his vice-like grip.

'Sorry,' he said absent-mindedly, loosening his hold.

I moved to look at him, leaning my head on my elbow. 'Where are you, Gabe? Come back to me.'

'I'm sorry. It's just that I should have been there.'

'Will you please stop? I am not your responsibility, Gabe. I get that you want to look after me, I do, but I am responsible for my own life. And in case you still haven't realised, I can look after myself.'

'I know that, Sam. But I can't help it.'

'Well, please try. I want my Gabe back. The one who wouldn't dare leave me to shower alone,' I grinned. Needing to anchor him back to me somehow, I ran my hand down his chest towards his groin and he groaned. Taking hold of his stiff cock, I squeezed before bending and running my tongue across the tip. 'Where would you like to come tonight, Sir?' I asked as I looked up at him and fluttered my eyelashes. 'My mouth? Or my hot, wet pussy?'

In an instant, he had me rolled over onto my back and pinned to the bed. 'Both,' he growled as his eyes burned into mine, and then he was inside me, fucking me so hard that I forgot all about Anthony Garvey and Jackson Carver.

. . .

Gabriel and I lay facing each other in bed, our legs entwined.

'You broke his nose, his ribs *and* dislocated his shoulder, Sam?' he raised an eyebrow at me.

'Yes. I told you I could look after myself.'

He shook his head. 'But how?'

'I had a personal trainer for years. I saw her three times a week. She was an excellent yoga teacher, and Jackson thought that was all we did. But she was a champion kickboxer too. She taught me self-defence and part of that was learning the best way to disable an attacker. I was very good at it — an A student,' I told him with a smile.

He kissed my hand. 'I'm proud of you — and maybe just a little bit scared,' he laughed and his green eyes twinkled. 'Have I ever told you, you are the most incredible woman I have ever known, Samantha Donovan?'

'You're pretty incredible yourself, Gabriel Sullivan.'

34. SAMANTHA

The tyres of Gabriel's Jaguar crawled over the gravel path as he pulled up outside his friend's cottage. Climbing out of the car, I smiled as I looked at the place where we were about to spend the weekend. It was beautiful. Old stone walls and huge windows. Standing in the middle of nowhere, in the beautiful English countryside.

Taking our bags out of the car, Gabriel smiled at me. 'What do you think?'

'It's gorgeous,' I replied.

He dropped the bags and pulled me to him. 'Complete privacy.' He grinned wickedly. 'No-one will hear you scream.'

I gave an involuntary shudder.

'Only with pleasure, Sam,' he whispered. Pulling me to him, he kissed me long and hard, as if to remind me of the pleasure he could instil.

The cottage was stunning inside too. An old-fashioned Aga dominated the rustic kitchen and a log fire was the focal point of the living room. The place had two bedrooms and we chose the one with the giant four poster bed. My insides contracted in anticipation at the thought of we would do in it later.

Gabriel had booked us a table at a restaurant in the nearest village that someone had recommended to him. Apparently, they did the best steak in all of England and he couldn't wait to try it. I was brushing my hair in the bedroom and was almost ready to go out, but as usual when Gabriel was around, I was feeling decidedly horny. There was something about being stuck in the middle of nowhere, only me and him, that made me think of nothing but having him rip off my clothes and ravage me in every room of the house. Suddenly, I remembered the surprise outfit I'd brought along. Smiling to myself, I slipped it on and made my way into the living room where Gabriel was reading the newspaper. He looked up as I walked into the room and smiled.

'Jesus Christ, Samantha! What are you wearing?'

'Do you remember this, Gabe?' I asked as I gave him a twirl.

'Yes, I do. And it's even more obscene now than it was fourteen years ago,' he laughed.

I made my way over to him. 'Well, I have filled out a bit since I was eighteen.'

He was right though. The tiny black dress barely covered my modesty. I had found it in amongst some of my old things at my father's house and had known that I'd have to wear it for Gabriel. I straddled him as he sat on the sofa, making him put down the newspaper.

'You can't go out in this, you know that, don't you?' he said.

'Why not?' I said, feigning indignation.

He pulled gently on the fabric and my nipples popped out of the top. 'That's why,' he said, taking one into his mouth and sucking hard, making me squirm with pleasure.

'Well, I'm wearing it. I think it looks fine,' I insisted.

'No, you're not,' he snapped as he nipped at my shoulder blade.

'Are you seriously telling me what I can and can't wear, Gabriel?'

He laughed. 'I wouldn't dare. But I'm asking you politely to please put something else on. For my own sanity. I'm starving and I've been desperate to try this restaurant's steak for ages. And if you continue wearing this poor excuse for a dress, then we will never make it to the restaurant.'

'We could always stay in?' I purred in his ear. 'I can cook us an omelette?'

'An omelette?' he replied with a flash of his eyebrows. 'Do you even know me at all, woman? Besides, I made you come twice before we left, and you still want more? You're insatiable. We've got all weekend. And there'll be plenty of other opportunities for you to wear this tiny little dress. In fact, I'm going to fuck you in it later. But right now, I'm starving. So please get changed.'

I climbed off him and headed back to the bedroom. 'I'm wearing the dress,' I shouted as I made my way down the hall.

I returned ten minutes later, ready to go. I was still wearing the dress, only I had put on a strapless bra and pulled the dress up like a boob tube, pairing it with some skinny jeans and my favourite Louboutins. Gabriel laughed out loud when he saw me.

'Told you!' I smiled.

'You look beautiful,' he said, pulling me to him for a kiss. 'Now, let's go.'

I looked around the crowded restaurant. It was certainly popular. I had ordered champagne from the wine menu and Gabriel had simply smiled when the waiter had told him it cost four hundred pounds a bottle. There was something about the country air that was making me feel giddy. Or perhaps it was the champagne, which I had consumed almost entirely to myself as Gabriel was driving.

'Thank you Paulo,' I giggled at the Spanish waiter whom I had been brazenly flirting with all night as he brought my meal. I had even squeezed his bicep at one point and asked him how often he worked out. I could sense Gabriel getting angrier by the minute, but despite that, I couldn't seem to stop myself. I knew I was playing a dangerous game, but I seemed to be driven by some innate need to see just how far I could push him before he would snap.

My marriage to Jackson had made me suspicious and paranoid. Gabriel was too perfect — he must have a flaw, and it was better that I found out sooner rather than later what that was.

Gabriel asked for the bill as soon as he had taken the last bite of his steak. After paying, he walked to the car in silence, with me trailing after him.

'Are you angry with me, Gabe?' I asked.

'Just get into the fucking car, Samantha,' he growled.

I did as I was told, given that my only other option was to stay where I was and be stuck in the middle of nowhere. Gabriel didn't speak during the drive back. I glanced at him occasionally, noting how his jaw was clenched shut, his knuckles white on the steering wheel. I could feel the anger emanating from his body and as the champagne started to wear off, I wondered if I had pushed him too far and what he would say when he finally spoke to me. Wasn't this exactly what I wanted? To see how far I could push him?

When we arrived back at the cottage, Gabriel collected his things from our bedroom and stomped across the hall to the spare room.

'Gabe, don't do this. I'm sorry,' I said to his retreating back.

He turned to me, his face full of anger. 'Don't you fucking dare! You pretend you don't play games, Samantha. But what the fuck was that tonight? And don't try and pretend I'm overreacting, or convince yourself this is jealousy because that is not what this is about.'

'What is it then?'

'It's about fucking respect. You flirt with the fucking waiter all night, and I'm supposed to just sit there and watch you? Are you out of your fucking mind?'

'I know, Gabe. I'm sorry.'

'I don't want to fucking hear it.' He slammed the bedroom door behind him.

I sat on the sofa for a while, hugging my knees to my chest. God, I had really fucked up now. Gabriel was right. I had behaved like an idiot, trying to prove that he wasn't perfect — and of course he wasn't. But he was a good man. I wondered how I would have reacted if he had behaved the same way.

Finally, I went to bed alone and lay awake for hours, hoping that he would sneak into my room and tell me that he forgave me, wrap me in his arms and tell me everything would be okay. But of course, he didn't.

35. SAMANTHA

The sun was streaming through the window when I finally woke. I had no idea of the time and had left my mobile phone in the kitchen. I could hear Gabriel up and about. Suddenly, the memory of the previous night washed over me in a wave, making me bury my head in the pillow with shame. I couldn't bear to face him. I couldn't stand to hear him tell me that I went too far, and that it was over. While I remained in bed, I could pretend that everything was still okay. I could pretend that he was still my Gabe.

I lay awake, listening to the sound of Gabriel in the kitchen. My head throbbed and my mouth was as dry as the Gobi. Aside from that, the not knowing was killing me, so I dragged myself out of bed — time to face the music!

He was sitting at the kitchen table as I walked into the room. He was drinking a cup of coffee and I could see the remnants from his breakfast on a plate beside him. I sat down opposite him, unsure of what to say, or of how to break the ice.

'I'm sorry, Gabe,' I started.

He laughed and shook his head. 'Well, that makes it all okay then.'

'Well, what else can I say? Tell me what you want me to say.'

He glared at me. 'I want you to tell me why you insist on testing me. You push me, waiting for some sort of reaction. Waiting for me to turn into Jackson. Well, I can save you the trouble. It's not going to happen. It's never going to happen. I'm not him,' he snapped.

'I know. I'm sorry.'

He banged his mug down on the table. 'Stop saying you're fucking sorry. Tell my why you keep trying to push me away.'

I stared at him as I thought about how to answer that question. I wasn't sure I understood fully myself.

'You know what, don't bother — because now you've succeeded,' he said as he looked down at the table.

I felt the tears stinging my eyes, but I would never let him see me cry. I felt like he had stabbed me through the heart. 'Please don't say that, Gabe. I don't mean to push you away,' I said quietly.

'I can't do this anymore, Sam. It's fucking exhausting. I feel like you're always waiting for me to fuck up. Waiting for some excuse to blame me for us not working. I've made allowances for you but I won't anymore.'

'Made allowances for me? Why? Because I'm poor, broken Samantha?' I snapped at him.

'No,' he snapped back. 'Because I want to be with you. Because, God help me, I can't go more than five minutes without thinking about you. I have given up control for you, and you throw it back in my face.'

I sank back into the chair. He was right, of course. Perhaps I owed him an explanation? At least the best explanation I could offer.

'I never really loved Jackson, you know? I thought I did, of course, that's why I married him. But I was nineteen and I had no idea what love was. I was dazzled by him. I loved the person people thought I was when I was with him — at least at first. It was nice to be respected, to be revered by people, instead of sneered at because I came from the wrong area or wore the wrong clothes. Jackson hurt me in ways you couldn't imagine, but he could never break me, because I didn't love him. I found ways to cope with my marriage, I learned how to defend myself, I developed a high tolerance for pain and I threw myself into my work to keep me sane.'

Gabriel looked up at me then, his eyes burning into mine.

'You have the power to hurt me in a way that Jackson never did, and never could, Gabe, and if I'm honest, it scares the hell out of me. I was the person Jackson demanded I be for so long, I'm still trying to figure out who I am without him.'

I didn't tell him that I'd never felt about anyone the way I felt about him. Or that he could shatter my heart into a tiny million pieces, and that I wasn't sure that was something I would ever recover from. Before I was completely lost to him, I needed to test him. I now realised that by doing that, I was bringing about the very thing that I'd been trying to prevent.

'I'm sorry, Gabe. I don't know what else to say. Please just give me the rest of this weekend to show you I'm trying. I don't want to push you away, but it's something I need to work on. You have to cut me some slack here?'

He stared at me and ran a hand through his hair. 'I'm going for a hike. If you want to come, I'm leaving in ten minutes,' he said before pushing his chair away from the table and standing up.

I was ready fifteen minutes later but he hadn't left without me. I hadn't taken longer on purpose, but I couldn't find the toothpaste. I wondered if he thought it had been another test, but if he did he didn't mention it, and I wasn't going to point out the fact that he had waited for me longer than he'd said he would.

We walked mostly in silence, but that was okay. The scenery was breath-taking and I enjoyed the peace and quiet. The fresh air was doing wonders for my throbbing headache. I looked at the green hills rolling into the unending horizon and wondered how a place could be so close to the city, yet be so peaceful and tranquil.

We had been walking for over two hours when Gabriel indicated a crop of rocks we could rest on. Setting down his backpack, he took a packed lunch out of his bag.

My stomach growled at the sight of the food and suddenly I remembered that I hadn't eaten breakfast — or packed myself any food. Gabriel handed me the package before pulling another one out for himself.

'You made my lunch?'

'Of course I did,' he frowned.

'But you waited outside when I was getting ready. I saw you out there?'

'I made it before you got up,' he said and I felt my heart flutter in my chest. He had known I would come with him and he had planned on letting me all along. I knew that all was not forgiven, but perhaps we would be okay?

Gabriel and I took a shower when we get back from our hike — not together, much to my dismay. Gabriel still hadn't touched me, apart from when he'd helped me over some rocks earlier on our hike. He'd grabbed my hand when I'd almost slipped and I had wanted to hold onto him, but he'd let go as soon as I was on solid ground again. I was desperate to touch him, and to make him forget about the previous night, but it would have broken my heart if he'd brushed me off. I wasn't used to him being like this and I missed my tactile Gabriel. The man who was always touching me, kissing me, nibbling at my neck.

He was in the hot tub when I got out of the shower and I walked outside, wrapped in a fluffy robe.

'Mind if I join you?' I asked.

Shaking his head, he signalled me to get in beside him. He was drinking champagne and I noticed there was another glass next to the ice bucket — obviously last night's antics hadn't put him off drinking with me then.

'I don't have a swimming costume though,' I said.

He frowned at me. 'Why would you need one?'

Taking off my robe, I climbed in. The contrast of the hot water and the cold air on my skin making me gasp out loud as I slipped into the water.

Gabriel poured me a glass of champagne and handed it to me, before sitting back with his arms spread out across the back of the tub, giving me a glorious view of him. He still didn't touch me though and I wondered if he was waiting for me to make the first move.

Was he testing me?

I took a swig of the champagne for courage and moved over to straddle him. I could feel his erection between us. He still didn't move a muscle but he smiled at me, a twinkle in his green eyes. I leaned in to kiss him and was relieved when he kissed me back, although he remained otherwise still. I raked my hands through his hair and down his muscular back. I wanted to feel his hands on me though — in my hair — on my body. I started to kiss his neck and he groaned in pleasure, his erection pressing into me further.

'So does this mean we're not over then?' I asked in between planting soft kisses on his throat.

He smiled at me. 'We were never over, Sam.'

'What? So, you were just playing with me? Letting me believe that we were?'

'No. You heard what you wanted to hear, just like you always do. Besides,' he gave me a wicked grin, 'I was interested to know how you might use this weekend to persuade me to give you another chance.'

I hit him playfully on the chest. 'You really are an evil bastard!'

He chuckled and I started to slide myself down onto to his beautiful big cock, stopping before I took the full length of him. I purred into his ear. 'Would this have been enough, Gabe? Or do you want more?' He growled in response and I could feel the familiar tightening in my core. I loved the animal, guttural noises he made. I enjoyed seeing the agony in his face when he was desperately trying to maintain control.

'Touch me, Gabe. Please,' I whispered.

In an instant, I was wrapped in his strong arms. He held onto me, guiding my hips down further onto him, stretching me until I was so full of him I could barely move.

'Does that feel good?' he asked.

'God, yes,' I replied as I bit down on my lip, delighting in the exquisite feeling of being pinned to him.

He continued to guide my hips up and down, rubbing that sweet spot over and over until the whole world fell away around me. All I could feel was him. I realised that my body had been physically aching for him. My breasts felt heavy and tender and when he took my nipple into his mouth I let out a whimper. Then his hand was between us. Rubbing and stroking. Driving me into a maddening frenzy. My whole body vibrated, starting from my feet and working up my legs until every hair on my head felt electrified, every nerve ending on fire.

Then his lips were on my throat, at my ear. He was talking to me then. Telling me how much he wanted me. How he couldn't get far enough inside me. How good it felt to have me riding his cock.

'Come for me, Sam,' he said as he spurted hot and heavy inside me. I shouted his name as he tipped me over the edge. Then he pounded the rest of his orgasm out into me while I melted into him, like a candle in front of an open flame.

'It feels better when you let me take control, doesn't it?' he said as he smoothed my hair back from my face.

I could only nod, my face pressed against his chest.

'Trust me, Sam. Give me that and I promise I'll never use it against you. Can you do that for me?'

I nodded again. 'I'm trying, Gabe. I promise.'

36. SAMANTHA

I was sitting alone in the hot tub after Gabriel had gone inside to make a start on dinner. The scenery was beautiful and I watched the sheep in the nearby field grazing happily. I smiled — happy too after making up with Gabriel. I hoped that he at least understood a little better my need to push him. To test him. Perhaps I wasn't quite ready for a relationship after all — especially one as intense as this one was proving to be. But, I had no idea what to do about that. I couldn't give Gabriel up and I didn't want to. Maybe what was needed was a leap of faith?

Gabriel was chopping mushrooms when I finally got out of the hot tub. Giddy from the bubbles — both the champagne and the Jacuzzi variety, I slipped my arms around his waist and he turned to face me.

'I've been thinking, Gabe,' I said.

'Always dangerous,' he replied with a grin.

'I want you to tie me up. Here, where no-one can hear me scream,' I returned his grin.

'Are you sure?' he asked, although I could already see the fire in his eyes.

'Yes. Absolutely.'

'Are you drunk again?' he asked, his eyes narrowed.

'No. I only had two glasses,' I laughed. 'I promise I am in full control of my faculties.'

He looked into my eyes, searching for some hesitation perhaps — but he found none — there was none to find. 'Go into the bedroom and wait for me,' he said in his signature low growl.

I did as I'd been instructed and was looking out of the window when Gabriel walked into the room. I closed the blinds and walked towards him. He held out his hands to show me my scarf, the belt from his bathrobe, and one of the curtain tie backs from the sitting room.

'I had to improvise,' he smiled.

'Three?' I frowned.

'Four,' he said as took hold of the belt from my bathrobe and slowly pulled it from around my waist. 'You have four limbs, don't you?'

I swallowed. 'I thought it was just arms.'

'Trust me,' he breathed as he kissed my neck.

A few moments later, I was tied, spread-eagled to the bedposts. Unable to move my arms or legs more than a few inches.

'Are you comfortable?' Gabriel asked.

'Yes,' I answered breathlessly. My heart was racing in my chest.

'I'll be right back,' he said with a wink before disappearing out of the room. When he returned a moment later, he set a glass down beside the bed. I strained my neck to see what was inside. It looked like ice cubes, except they were dark in colour. I didn't ask and Gabriel didn't speak. I watched as he undressed until he was standing before me in all his naked glory.

Crawling onto the bed, he took an ice cube from the glass and placed it in his mouth. Then he kissed me, his lips and his tongue cold from the ice. As he did, I realised what it was. He'd made ice cubes using Jack Daniels mixed with water. When had he even done that? God, he was so bloody sure of himself and I loved it.

He trailed the cube down my body, swirling it over my skin before licking it off. Every so often he returned to my lips so I could savour the taste of his whisky filled mouth. Between my hot skin and

Gabriel's hot mouth, the ice melted quickly and soon there was only one left. Taking the last remaining cube, he trailed it down the centre of my body with his fingers and then rubbed it on my clit before licking up the melting whisky. Finally, he pushed the remainder of the cube inside me and I thought I might faint. Gabriel lapped it up from me as it melted. I pulled at my restraints, desperate to touch him and he chuckled at my efforts.

I closed my eyes and concentrated on the feel of Gabriel's cool hands on my body. My skin felt like it was on fire. Soon, his lips were at my neck while his hands touched all the places that made me tremble with the need of him. 'Are you still okay?' he whispered.

'Yes,' I groaned.

'Good. Tell me if you want to stop.'

Then Gabriel spent the next two hours kissing me, rubbing me, biting, licking, sucking, fucking me. I lost count of the number of times he made me come. In the end, it felt like one long, heavenly orgasm. Afterwards he untied my legs and arms, massaging the skin where the restraints had rubbed against me. The skin on my right wrist, where he'd used the rope curtain tie-back, looked red.

'Are you okay? Does it hurt?' he asked as he kissed the inflamed skin.

'No, it's fine. Anyway, you know I have a very high tolerance for pain,' I replied jokingly.

He frowned at me and was about to say something, when I kissed him.

He pulled away. 'Maybe if you didn't struggle so much...' he raised an eyebrow at me.

I laughed. 'So it's my fault then? You tied me up, Gabe. You have to take responsibility for any injuries sustained in your kinky shenanigans.'

He grabbed me and pinned me down on the bed, nipping at my shoulder.

'Kinky shenanigans? Admit it. You love it.'

'Hmm, yes I do,' I agreed.

37. SAMANTHA

I was washing the dishes from the previous night's dinner when I felt Gabriel's strong arms around my waist.

He nuzzled my neck. 'Why didn't you wake me?'

'You looked so peaceful. I didn't want to disturb you,' I answered as I turned in his arms. 'Besides, you worked so hard last night I thought you might need a rest.'

I felt him smile against my neck. 'You enjoyed being tied up then?'

'Just a little,' I teased him and he bit me playfully on the shoulder.

'Sit down,' I told him. 'And I'll make us some breakfast.'

He sat down at the breakfast table. I made coffee and took it over to him. As I placed the mug down on the table, he pulled me between his legs and kissed my stomach through my bathrobe. 'I hope you're naked under here, Sam?'

'I am. Why?' I replied.

'Because there's been something I've been dying to do since I saw this giant table,' he growled as he untied the belt on my robe, brushing his hands over my hips and his lips over my stomach. I ran my fingers through his hair as he lifted me onto the table. He moved the hot coffee out of the way before sitting back down, pulling his chair in as though he was about to sit down to a meal. He pushed me back so I was lying down on the table and then he slowly raised my legs until I had a foot planted firmly on each of his shoulders. Wrapping his large hands around the back of my thighs, he pulled me to him until I was only inches from his face. I could feel his hot breath on my skin. And then I felt his warm tongue, licking the length of my slit before he started to blow on my clit.

'Jesus, Gabe. What are you doing to me?' I groaned, almost panting with wanting him.

'I'm going to take my time eating your delicious pussy, Sam. You taste so fucking good and I'm going to savour every last drop of you,' he growled. The movement of his lips and the vibration of his growling against my tender flesh had me writhing beneath him.

'Please, Gabe,' I whimpered. Having him so close but barely touching me was driving me insane. I thought about putting my hands on his head to hurry him along but I knew that would only slow him down even more.

When I felt like I could bear it no longer, his tongue dipped inside my opening, hot and soft and lush. Soon he was licking me, and then he sucked my throbbing clit into his mouth. I moaned in pleasure. I was bucking like a rodeo bronco but he didn't increase his pace. I begged for his fingers too but his only response was to chuckle softly.

'You're so impatient, Sam. No wonder I have to tie you up.'

'Please, Gabe. Let me come,' I groaned. He'd had me on the table for an age and every time I came close to an orgasm, he re-directed his attention. 'Please, Gabe,' I whispered.

Thankfully he took pity on me. Pulling me closer to him, his touch became more persistent, sucking on the part of me where all my nerve endings came together. When the orgasm finally hit me it was overwhelming. It had been building for so long, I almost passed out. It filled up my body before bursting out through that one, delicious point. The spot where he continued licking and sucking until I was writhing beneath him again, telling him I couldn't take anymore. I was too sensitive. I pulled at his hair to stop him but he kept a vice like grip on my legs, pulling me to his mouth with more force than I could pull him away.

'Just one more, Sam,' he growled. Within a few minutes the sensitivity gave way to ecstasy as he tipped me over the edge again and I was screaming his name, tears rolling down my face.

Gabriel stood up and folded himself over my body. He kissed me, his face wet with my arousal.

'I really want to fuck you, Sam. But I can tell you're sore from last night, and I have plans for later.'

'That's okay,' I panted as I pushed him back down onto the chair and dropped to my knees so I was almost under the table. I pulled his beautiful big cock out of his boxer shorts and took it in my mouth. I lacked the same control as Gabriel had shown and I devoured him like I hadn't eaten for weeks. He tasted so good. It wasn't long before his hands were in my hair and he was pumping into me, hot, sticky liquid sliding down my throat. 'Fuck, Sam!' he hissed as he did.

I straddled him when I was finished and kissed his beautiful lips. 'Thank you,' he breathed when we came up for air.

'You're welcome, handsome,' I grinned as I stood up.

As I was walking away from him, he slapped me on the behind. 'So what's for breakfast then? I'm starving.'

38. SAMANTHA

It had been a week since our wonderful weekend in the cottage and Gabriel and I were in my apartment. I perched on the edge of the armchair in my living room, chewing my thumbnail as I watched him reading the newspaper. I searched his face for a reaction, but as usual, he was completely unreadable. After a few more minutes, he folded the newspaper and placed it on the coffee table before leaning back against the sofa. I continued to watch him intently, looking for any hint of emotion. It had been twelve months since my ex-husband, Jackson had been arrested for my attempted murder. So, one of the national papers had run a piece on him — on both of us. The seemingly perfect couple who were anything but.

A journalist contact of mine had warned me the night before that the rag she worked for was going to run a story. But, despite knowing about it in advance, it still hit me like a twelve-tonne truck that morning when I saw it. Of course, they'd focused on mine and Jackson's relationship, rather than the trial itself.

I was grateful at least that it was a Saturday and I didn't have to go into work. I didn't think I could face other people. I couldn't bear to see their pitying glances. That had been the hardest thing to deal with after Jackson had been sentenced and the case hit the headlines of every newspaper going. It wasn't every day a successful barrister, a Cambridge graduate from Knightsbridge, no less, and the son of a well-known politician, tried to murder his wife with a corkscrew, was it?

'So, what do you think?' I asked as I shifted from one foot to the other and resisted the urge to bite my fingernails.

Gabriel shook his head. 'Just trying to sell papers, aren't they? Shower of parasites.'

'It makes me look like a victim though, doesn't it?'

Gabriel frowned. 'You were the victim, Sam. He tried to fucking kill you.'

'I know that,' I said with a sigh. 'I mean it makes me look like I was this passive, meek little woman throughout our entire marriage, and that's just not true.'

'I know,' Gabriel said. 'Anyone who knows you, knows you are the least passive person on earth. What does it matter what some newspaper article says?'

'That's easy to say when it's not about you, Gabe,' I replied.

He reached for my hand and pulled me to sit next to him. 'It will be old news by tomorrow. I promise,' he said as he tucked a strand of hair behind my ear.

'I hope you're right.'

Gabriel studied my face. 'I don't get you and him. He just doesn't seem your type at all.'

'What can I say? He dazzled me. He was this mature, successful and charismatic man, and I was this naïve girl who hung on his every word. I suppose I was easy prey,' I shrugged. 'It's easy to look back now and see all of the red flags, but I was inexperienced and ultimately, I was flattered that someone like him would choose me. By the time, I realised who Jackson really was, we were married and I was trapped.'

Gabriel hugged me tighter to him. 'You weren't easy prey, Sam,' he said as he kissed the top of my head.

I closed my eyes and leaned my head against Gabriel's chest as he flicked on the television. I had barely slept all night. My mind had been racing with memories of my life with Jackson. Sometimes I questioned my own memories of our life together. Surely, there must have been some happy times? I have no doubt that there were but I couldn't recall any.

Money and power were all my ex-husband had ever known. He was born with it.

Privilege.

It meant that he took whatever he wanted when he wanted it. I was only nineteen when I met him. I'd just got a part-time admin job at a solicitor's firm. He came in one day to meet with one of the partners. Every single woman in the office fancied him. They acted like they were on heat around him. He was already an incredibly successful barrister by then, and he had a smile that could make you forget what you walked into a room for. He wasn't interested in any of the other girls in the office though. He was interested in me. He'd flirt with me, and me being me, I'd flirt back outrageously. But when he eventually asked me out, I was terrified. Flirting was one thing, but actually going out with him was another. But how could I say no? Every woman I knew wanted to date him, and he was so damn charming.

For our first date, he showed up to my student apartment in a brand-new Lamborghini. He showed me a world that I never knew existed. Flash cars, designer clothes, holidays to Monaco and St Tropez. I liked the way people treated me when I was with him — like I was someone special. It was a whirlwind and I was so caught up in it all I didn't see the warning signs. How he chose my outfits all the time. How he was always helpfully suggesting what I should eat or drink. He was a selfish lover, not that I had much to compare him to, but he was only ever interested in his own pleasure. He didn't like me seeing any of my friends but he convinced me that it was because he couldn't bear not spending time with me. He didn't like me talking to my father, because he didn't approve of his criminal lifestyle — and that didn't fit with the image of a good lawyer.

When he asked me to marry him, I thought that to be his wife would mean I would be happy for the rest of my life. We moved back to London as soon as I graduated and got married when I was twenty-one and he was thirty-six. We were on our honeymoon in Sorrento when he first hit me. He slapped me across the face because I'd forgotten to arrange for his favourite shirt to be pressed at the hotel. He was so apologetic afterwards, I thought it was a one-off. But from then on the violence became more frequent and more extreme. He was a sadist and a psychopath. I didn't realise that until I'd been married to him for over a year. He'd managed to keep his tendencies a secret until then. I tried to leave so many times but he always found me. He would never let me go. I was his trophy, and if I left him, it would make him look bad — and him being an egotistical maniac, he couldn't have that.

So, over the years I learned to survive instead. I became very good at tolerating pain, and fighting back when I needed to. My work became my passion – I thought that was all I needed, until one day I realised that I deserved more.

On the night he was arrested, I told Jackson that I was leaving him for good. I told him that I wouldn't run, but I wouldn't be his plaything any more. I'd just made the move into family law and had spoken to a solicitor about a divorce, and I told him so. I knew it was a risky strategy, but I couldn't go on living one more day with him — only living half a life. I think he really would have killed me if he hadn't been interrupted — and I'll bet the slippery bastard would have got away with it too.

'Are you okay?' Gabriel asked, snapping me from my thoughts.

'Yes,' I lied. 'I'm just tired.'

'Well, we can go back to bed if you want?' he suggested.

'And you say I'm insatiable?' I said, giving him a nudge in the ribs.

'I mean to sleep,' he started to laugh. 'We have nowhere to be. And we never got our sleep in.'

That was true. We usually slept late on a weekend, but that morning I had asked him to go to the newsagents at six am to get the newspaper. 'Come on then,' I said with a yawn as I stood up and took hold of his hand, pulling him up from the sofa with me.

A few moments later, I was lying in my favourite place in the world — with my head on Gabriel's chest and with his giant arms wrapped around me.

39. SAMANTHA

It had been three days since the national newspaper had ran the story about me and Jackson, and thankfully, apart from the occasional unwanted stare in the local coffee shop and a few uncomfortable questions from a new client the previous day, the story hadn't brought me too much unwanted attention. So much so, that I had allowed Nick to persuade me to test out his theory that it was already old news, by agreeing to go out for a few drinks to O'Malley's after work.

I was packing away for the day when Gabriel walked into my office, looking as fine as ever, and making me question my decision to go out instead of letting him take me home and doing unspeakable things to me. He walked into the room and over to me before pulling me to him. He kissed me softly and I melted into his arms. A few seconds later, he pulled away, leaving me wanting more.

'Did you miss me, baby?' he asked as he brushed my hair behind my ear.

'Only a little,' I replied with a grin and he knew I was lying.

Then he took off his tie and stuffed it into his pocket before walking across the room and perching himself on the edge of my desk. The sight of him removing any piece of clothing made my womb contract. I closed my eyes as I remembered him restraining me with that very tie only a few days earlier.

'So, what time are you and Nick off out?' he asked.

'In about ten minutes if he hurries up. You sure you don't want to come with us?'

'No. You go and have fun. I'm sure Nick is looking forward to some time with his best mate, and doesn't want her boyfriend tagging along. Besides, it'll give me a chance to check on our clubs. I've been neglecting my duties lately, ever since I started fucking you anyway,' he growled and I felt his voice vibrating through my core.

'Is that all we're doing, Gabe? Fucking?' I smiled and batted my eyelashes at him.

'I suppose not, sometimes we do other things,' he said with a smile.

I walked over to him and he pulled me to stand between his thighs. 'Well, if it's just sex, you won't mind if I consider myself free and single tonight then, will you?' I purred in his ear.

He pulled me closer to him. 'Yes, I fucking will,' he growled. 'Don't even joke about that. You know that you're everything to me, Sam.'

Everything? I didn't know that. He had never told me. I pulled his face to mine for a kiss.

'I'll tell Scott to be on stand-by to drive you home later. I'm not sure what time I'll finish, and besides I don't want to cramp your style, do I?' he said with a grin.

'We can get a taxi, Gabe. I'm sure Scott has better things to do with his time then ferry me around.'

'Scott gets paid, and very well I might add, to do what your father and I tell him to do. He works in security. He protects things — and people,' he added quickly before I could protest that I was not a thing. 'And he knows he is very lucky to be trusted with the most precious person in the lives of both of his bosses. So, stop feeling sorry for him. He will drive you. Phone him when you need picking up. Do *not* attempt to get home on your own, Samantha. Promise me.'

'Okay. I'll phone Scott,' I said with a smile before giving him a long, deep kiss.

A few hours later, Nick and I were suitably drunk in O'Malley's pub, having demolished two bottles of wine in the space of two hours before moving onto Jack Daniels and coke.

'I've missed this, Samantha. Us going out and getting plastered,' Nick said with a grin.

'Me too. Although I don't miss you having to be my wingman,' I replied. 'You were bloody awful at it.'

'Cheek! I haven't been laid for twelve months, Samantha, and I'm the crap wingman?'

I stared at him. 'You haven't had sex for twelve months? Jesus Christ, Nick. Do you even remember what to do?' I laughed.

'Fuck off!' he snapped at me before taking a swig of his drink.

Just as I was wondering who I could set Nick up with, I noticed a familiar auburn head bobbing across the pub towards the bar. I nudged Nick. 'Hey, there's Maria from Kents over there. I swear she's got a thing for you.'

'No, she hasn't,' he blushed. Nick had a thing for her too and had done for a while. She was a legal secretary at another firm we did a lot of business with.

'I'm going over there. I'll show you a real wing*woman*,' I said as I finished my drink and placed my glass on the table.

'Samantha, don't-' he started, but I was already up off my seat and making my over to Maria.

One hour later and Nick and Maria were leaving together in a taxi. Feeling decidedly woozy, I phoned Scott to come and pick me up. Then I texted Gabriel to tell him how much I was missing him, and how horny I was. He replied with one word.

Behave

As I stood outside O'Malley's, I recognised Scott's car weaving its way through the traffic and waved my hand to get his attention. When he pulled up alongside me, I climbed into the back and kicked off my heels.

'Take me to Gabriel's please, Scott,' I slurred.

'Do you have a key for his place, Samantha? Only he's out. There's been an incident at one of the clubs.'

'What sort of incident? Is everyone okay?' I asked, suddenly feeling slightly less intoxicated.

'I'm not sure. Your dad and Gabriel are okay though,' he answered, knowing that their safety would be my primary concern.

'Don't you get fed up driving me around, Scott,' I asked with a smile.

'Not at all, Samantha. It's one of the better jobs Gabriel has given me.' He smiled at me in the rear-view mirror.

'Doesn't your girlfriend mind you being out late at night?' I teased.

'I don't have one.'

'What? A handsome guy like you,' I said, no longer teasing him. He really was handsome. Sandy blonde-hair and rippling biceps — what was not to like? 'We need to sort that out, Scott. I can fix you up if you like. I just fixed my mate, Nick up.'

He laughed in response. 'That's okay, Samantha. Thanks anyway.'

40. GABRIEL

Samantha's apartment was silent as I opened the front door. I'd knocked but there was no answer, not that I'd expected one. It wasn't even 8am yet and given the text she'd sent me late the previous night, I imagined she'd be sleeping off a hangover. I used her spare key to let myself in. After the night I'd had, I couldn't wait to crawl into bed with her and wrap my arms around her warm, soft body. I'd been in the hospital for half the night with one of our bouncers who'd been stabbed. I'd had to hold his wound together until the ambulance arrived.

I pushed open the door to Samantha's bedroom, my eyes taking a few seconds to adjust to the dim light. But even in the darkness it wasn't difficult to see the two naked bodies in her bed. Legs and arms wrapped around each other. Clothes strewn across the floor. I recognised the pattern to them — torn off each other in a desperate need to get to the good stuff. I felt sick. Bile rose in my throat and I forced it back down with a swallow. My whole body shook with anger. How the fuck could she do this to me — to us?

I wondered what her reaction would be if I made my presence known. I was tempted to find out, but also terrified of what I might to do if I didn't get out of there. I could have happily murdered the poor bastard she'd decided to take home for a quick fuck. With my blood thundering in my ears, I slipped quietly out of the room.

Once I was back in my car, I phoned Sebastian. 'Do you fancy a session on the pads, mate?' I asked.

'Yeah, okay,' Sebastian said with a yawn. 'Give me an hour though, I've only just got up.'

'Good. I feel like beating the shit out of someone.'

I could almost see Sebastian smiling on the other end of the line. 'Nice. I'll see you there at nine.'

A few minutes after my call to Sebastian, my phone rang. Seeing Samantha's number on the screen, I pressed the button on my steering wheel to answer.

Her voice filled the car. 'Good morning, handsome. I missed you.'

God, she was a good fucking actress. 'Did you really?' I snapped.

'Of course I did. You seem a bit moody this morning,' she laughed.

'I'm busy. I'll speak to you later,' I said before ending the call, afraid that I would say something that I could never take back if I kept on talking. I needed my head to be a bit clearer before I confronted her. I couldn't believe how deceitful she was being. Phoning me like nothing had happened. As though she hadn't spent the night fucking someone else. I had been in this position before, and I'd promised myself I'd never allow it to happen again. I hated the feeling of not being in control, of being vulnerable. As much as I tried to convince myself that I was in control when it came to Samantha, I knew I was only fooling myself. She had all the power.

She had me by the balls.

But now, I felt like I hardly knew her at all. I couldn't see any way back from this for us. I would never be able to trust her again.

41. SAMANTHA

'Your partner is a moody sod sometimes, do you know that?' I said to my father as he handed me a cup of coffee.

'Why, what's going on?' he stared at me.

Suddenly, I remembered who I was talking to. 'Oh, nothing. Maybe he hasn't had much sleep?'

'Maybe? I think he had a rough night. He's asked me to go for a session on the pads and he only does that when he's either very pissed off, or someone has really done a number on him — or both. We haven't had a good sparring session for ages,' my dad said with a grin.

'Scott did mention he was sorting out an issue at one of the clubs last night?'

My dad nodded. 'Yes, we had a bit of trouble. That's probably it. Although I assumed it was all sorted. He never phoned me back about it.'

'Oh well, maybe he'll tell you what's really bothering him?' I suggested.

My dad laughed. 'Don't be daft. We're going to fight, not talk,' he rolled his eyes as he walked out of the kitchen.

. . .

I was at home putting fresh sheets on my bed when I turned to see Gabriel standing in the doorway of my bedroom. His large frame filled it. He looked like he'd come fresh from his boxing session and I felt a familiar stirring in the base of my abdomen.

'Hello, handsome,' I grinned. 'I hope you've saved some of that energy for me.'

He glared at me. 'At least you have the decency to change the fucking sheets.'

'Pardon?' I blinked at him.

'I saw you, Samantha,' he growled, but it wasn't his usual growl — the one that turned my insides to jelly. There was no hint of anything but anger in his face. His huge arms were folded across his chest. Suddenly, I became very aware of how big his hands were — they were hands that could cause some serious damage. He remained in the doorway and it registered that he was blocking my exit. I could hear my heart beating in my ears. I swallowed. What on earth had got into him? Where was my Gabe?

'Saw me?' I asked, entirely confused by where this was going.

'This morning. In here. The two of you. After you'd spent the night fucking.'

I blinked at him and then the proverbial penny dropped. Suddenly it all made sense.

'That was just Nick-' I started.

'Nick!' He snarled. 'That makes it okay then. You were only fucking your best mate. That's fine then, is it? I hope he was good. I hope he was fucking worth it.'

I walked towards him. 'Will you let me bloody finish? That was just Nick and Maria. They've had a thing for each other for ages. He happened to bump into her last night. They couldn't go back to Nick's because the kids were there with his mum. And Maria is currently staying with her brother. So, I let them use the flat.'

'And where did you stay?' he snarled.

'At my dad's, of course. You've just spent almost two hours with him and he didn't mention that to you?' I said with a shake of my head. 'I was intending to go to your place but Scott told me you were sorting some problem out at one of the clubs and weren't home. I don't have a key for your house, and I was tired anyway, so I went to my dad's.'

I could see him scanning my face — deciding whether I was telling the truth. He uncrossed his arms from his chest and started to frown.

'Ask my dad and Scott if you don't believe me, Gabe,' I snapped.

'Jesus, Samantha,' he said with a sigh. 'I thought...'

'I know what you thought. No wonder you were in a bad mood when I phoned you. But what if I had been with someone else, Gabe? What did you come here to do?' The tension started to creep into my voice. That fear I felt had rankled me.

It was his turn to act bewildered. 'What?'

'You come here, all pumped up from your boxing session, standing in my doorway, scowling at me. Looking like you wanted to go a few more rounds — with me. What were you intending to do?'

'To talk to you.'

'Well, it didn't feel like it.'

'Sam,' he said, stepping towards me. 'I would never hurt you. Never. No matter what. You have to know that.'

'It's easy to say that now, isn't it? Now that you know I didn't do anything wrong. But what if I had?' I pushed him away from me. My head started to spin. Fear was an emotion that I used to feel on a daily basis. And even the slightest hint of it now sent me into fight or flight mode. This was not how I wanted to live the rest of my life. 'I've spent too much of my life scared of doing the wrong thing. I'm not prepared to do it anymore.'

'Sam,' he pleaded.

'I want you to leave, Gabriel.'

'Sam?'

'Please!'

'Okay. If that's what you really want?'

'It is,' I said assertively. 'I need some space.' Although I wasn't sure if that was what I wanted at all. All I knew was that I had been afraid of him — even though it was for the briefest moment, and I had promised myself I would never let anyone make me feel like that ever again.

GABRIEL

I climbed into my car and punched the steering wheel.

Fuck!

Why hadn't I just asked questions instead of assuming the worst? I hated the way Samantha always ran from me, or pushed me away whenever we had a problem. It made me feel like she was still waiting for me to fuck up. I'd told myself that I wouldn't let her do that to me anymore. I would force her to talk to me and deal with our problems like a grown up. And then the first time we'd had one, I'd managed to fuck it up all by myself.

As soon as I'd realised it hadn't been her in that bed this morning, I'd wanted to pick her up and throw her down onto it. I'd wanted to show her my preferred method of solving problems — by burying myself inside her and making her forget why she was so angry with me.

But I fucked up massively. I'd scared her. I had seen the terror in her eyes and it made me feel sick as I remembered how she'd looked at me. She had spent too much of her life living in fear, and now she was scared of me too. I was supposed to be her Angel Gabriel, wasn't I? I was the man who should protect her, and now I was just another man she was afraid of.

42. SAMANTHA

It had been two whole days since I had seen or spoken to Gabriel. I was glad that he'd respected my request to leave me alone, but if I was honest, I was already missing him like crazy. Poor Scott had been designated as my personal chauffeur for the time being, and he refused to engage in any Gabriel related discussion.

I was sitting at my desk, twiddling with a paperclip and staring out of the window when Nick walked in.

'Good God, Samantha. You've been walking around with a face like a slapped arse all day,' he said as he took a seat. 'What the hell is wrong with you?'

I shrugged.

'Come on. It's me. What's up?' he asked, his voice full of concern.

I relayed the details of my fight with Gabriel.

'I'm sorry, Samantha. I feel so responsible,' he said.

'Don't be daft. What we fought over isn't the issue anyway, Nick. It's the fact that I was afraid of him.'

'Well, he does have that menacing quality,' he shuddered.

'Really?'

'Yes. He's huge, and he has that mean and moody thing going on. I imagine he could, and probably does, given his chosen career, frighten the shit out of people on a regular basis. Do you think he was trying to scare you? Or was he just angry?'

'I don't know. He was angry, and I suppose I can't blame him for that after he assumed I'd taken some random home for a quick shag?'

'Maybe his reaction was perfectly normal then? Because of your experience though, it's only natural that you might perceive things differently?'

'Maybe?' I considered Nick's take on the matter. He was probably the only person I ever allowed to pass any comment on my experience with Jackson and how it had deeply affected me. Perhaps because he had been with me through it all? Perhaps because I never felt judged or pitied by him — he was logical and rational and it was one of the reasons I valued his opinion so much. 'It was the way he stood in the doorway, blocking the exit. I started to panic,' I said.

'I imagine he fills most doorways, Samantha.'

'Do you think he would hurt me?'

'You know him much better than I do. I know that he cares for you. Anyone can see that. But that doesn't mean he wouldn't hurt you. Has he ever done anything at all to suggest he would? You know the warning signs. Are there any with him?'

'No. I've never felt like that with him before.'

'You should talk to him, Samantha. You need to decide, one way or another — for both of your sakes. Speak to him, will you?'

I nodded. 'I will.'

'Good. Until then, why not come for a drink with me tonight? I kind of mentioned to Maria I might be at O'Malley's later. At least if you're with me, I won't look like such a desperate case going there on my own.'

'I don't think so, Nick. I'm not sure I fancy being your third wheel,' I rolled my eyes at him.

'Don't be silly. You won't be. She'll be with her work mates. Please, Samantha?' he looked at me with pleading eyes.

'Oh, don't. You know I can't say no to you when you do the puppy dog eyes.'

'Pleeeaaase?' he said again.

'Okay. But just for one or two. Once you're coupled up with Maria, I'm off home.'

'You are a true friend,' he said with a grin.

I perched on a stool at the small table at O'Malley's and watched in frustrated annoyance as Nick and Maria flirted with each other. Maria's work mates turned out to be a single work mate, Neil, the receptionist from her building. I tried to make conversation with him but all he talked about was the gym and how he made sure he hit his macros every day. It was beyond tedious and no matter how many times I tried to change the subject, he changed it right back.

Finally, admitting defeat, I faked a yawn and declared I was heading home.

'I'll come with you,' Neil said. 'I need my beauty sleep,' he said, winking at me. 'We can share a cab.'

Nick laughed. 'Samantha doesn't get cabs. She has her own personal chauffeur service.'

I scowled at him.

'What?' Neil asked.

'Take no notice of him,' I said. 'But, yes I do have a lift. I just need to give him a text. We can drop you at the station if you like though?' Since I had asked Gabriel for some space, Scott had resumed his role as my driver. I knew better than to resist and have my father asking questions. As far as I was aware, he didn't know about my fight with Gabriel and I was happy for it to stay that way, at least until I knew what the future held for us.

'Oh, yeah? Okay then?' Neil said with a grin, as though he knew something I didn't.

I frowned at him. 'I'll text him now and then nip to the ladies. He probably won't be far. Then we can wait outside.'

Neil nodded eagerly and downed the rest of his gin and tonic.

A few moments later, Scott had replied to say he was on his way and I was standing outside with Neil. 'So, is this your boyfriend coming to pick you up or something?' he asked me.

'No,' I shook my head. 'Just someone who works for my dad. It's a long story.'

'Oh,' he flashed his eyebrows at me. 'So, you're free and single then?'

I turned to him laughed. 'That's kind of a long story too.'

'Oh, like that, is it?' he said and then he moved quickly, wrapping his arms around my waist and sliding his hands dangerously close to my behind. 'How about I come to your place then? I can show you my push up form?' he grinned.

I blinked at him. Had I read those signals completely wrong? No, surely he had? What on earth during our past hour of boring conversation had made him think I would even consider that option? I was about to push him away and tell him to get lost when I heard a familiar voice behind me and my stomach sank through my knees and onto the floor.

'Your lift is here, Samantha,' he growled.

I pushed Neil away from me and turned to see Gabriel's face. He was scowling at me — all anger and frustration, and nothing but fury in his eyes. I didn't even have a chance to respond before he stalked off towards O'Malley's. I thought about shouting after him, but then I heard the beep of a car horn and saw Scott holding up traffic waiting for me.

I turned and walked towards the waiting car.

'Hey, what about my lift?' Neil shouted.

'Walk,' I shouted back.

'Hey, Scott,' I said as I climbed into the back seat. 'I didn't realise Gabriel would be coming with you?'

'Yeah. He grabbed a lift at the last minute. He needed to see some of our bouncers at O'Malley's. I'll swing by and pick him back up once I've dropped you off.'

'Oh,' I replied as I sat back against the seat. I wished I'd known he was coming. What must he have thought when he saw Neil standing there with his hands practically on my arse? Not that I had done anything wrong. Neil, it seemed, was not only incredibly boring, but also an entitled prick.

'Who was that guy?' Scott asked.

'Oh, just some knob from the pub. I offered him a lift to the station and he obviously took that to mean, please grab my arse and proposition me. I didn't realise dating had changed quite so dramatically in the last twelve years,' I answered sarcastically.

'Yeah. It's a jungle out there,' Scott replied with a laugh.

GABRIEL

I walked into O'Malley's and straight to the bar. The anger surged through my veins. I didn't usually drink but I ordered a large Scotch on the rocks. I had known it would be a risk catching a lift with Scott. I'd known there would be a chance I would bump into her — perhaps I had wanted to. But I hadn't expected her to be standing there with some fucker's hand on her arse. For fuck's sake, it had only been two days. Was she just trying to hurt me? Maybe she was just like her dad, and subscribed to the belief that the best way to get over someone was to get under someone else?

Had she been planning on taking him home? Using the car and driver that I had sent for her? She would have known that would get back to me. That was just fucking cruel.

But Samantha wasn't cruel.

Maybe she just wanted to hurt me and that was the best way to go about it? I didn't know any more. If she was at home now fucking some other man, then I'd lost her.

'You okay, Boss,' I heard Mickey, one of my head bouncers ask as he walked up to stand beside me.

I knocked back the Scotch in one. 'Yeah,' I said. Mickey was the man I was there to see. He was one of my most experienced bouncers and he was a key figure in my plans for the night ahead. Sebastian and I had told Jimmy Fenton in no uncertain terms that we would never sell Archangel Securities to him. In response, him and his firm has upped the ante and were starting to cause trouble for us all over the place. The stabbing a few nights earlier had just been the start of it all.

Tonight, we were about to put an end to their takeover bid once and for all. And it couldn't be happening at a better time, because I was pumped full of rage, and desperate to vent my fury on someone.

'Just checking you're all set for later? Are you clear what needs to happen?' I asked him. Mickey would be co-ordinating some of the strikes on the Fenton's businesses while Sebastian and I dealt with the Fenton brothers personally.

Mickey nodded. 'Of course, Boss. Shall we go somewhere a little quieter?'

'Yeah,' I agreed as I followed Mickey into the back office.

43. SAMANTHA

Scott pulled his car up outside my apartment block and I looked out of the window. I kept replaying my encounter with Gabriel over and over in my head. Every time I thought about the look on his face I felt a lump in my throat. God, what must he be thinking? I hoped he knew me well enough to know that I wouldn't do that to him. It made me think about the other day too. I remembered him standing in my doorway scowling at me when he thought I'd spent the night with another man. How I had felt the hairs on the back of my neck stand on end when I'd realised he was blocking my exit. All those memories of being trapped in a room by a man who wanted to hurt me came flooding back. He said that he would never hurt me. Until then, I'd had no reason to doubt him. Did he hope that I knew him well enough too?

No matter how hard I'd worked to deal with my past, and how much I insisted it didn't define me, it was also a huge part of me. It coloured every aspect of my life. Maybe instead of fighting against that, I needed to cut myself some slack and allow myself to feel whatever it was I needed to feel? Feeling afraid when Gabriel was standing in that doorway was a natural reaction, just like Nick said. It didn't mean I was afraid of him. And now he'd just seen me in the street being groped by some stranger.

'We're here, Samantha,' Scott said when I didn't get out of the car.

'Take me back to O'Malley's with you, Scott. I need to speak to Gabriel.'

Scott shook his head. 'I don't think that's a good idea. I'm not sure what the boss has on for the rest of the night.'

I didn't care. I'd made my mind up and I had to see Gabriel and explain what he'd just seen. 'I need to speak to him, Scott. I'm not getting out of this car.'

He looked at me and sighed. 'He's really not in the best of moods. Why don't you speak to him tomorrow?'

I shook my head. 'I'm not getting out. If you want me out of here, you'll have to carry me out yourself.'

He frowned at me and I felt a pang of guilt. Scott was a good guy and I didn't want him getting into any trouble.

'Whatever you say,' he said with another shake of his head as pulled away from the kerb.

Half an hour later we were sitting outside O'Malley's in Scott's car. I watched as Gabriel walked out of the bar and over towards us. As he approached the car, he noticed me sitting in the back seat. 'What the fuck is she doing here?' he said as he glared at Scott through the open window.

Scott shrugged. 'She refused to get out of the car, Boss.'

Gabriel climbed into the back seat beside me. 'I don't have time for this,' he growled.

'I need to talk to you,' I said.

'I thought you'd be at home with your date?' he sneered at me.

I could feel the anger coming off him in waves. The tension in the car was palpable.

'He wasn't my date-' I started to say but Gabriel held up his hand dismissively. I was about to protest when I realised it was because his phone was vibrating in his pocket.

'Hey, Seb,' he said when he answered. 'Hang on a minute.' Then he leaned forward and placed a hand on Scott's shoulder. 'Take her back home.'

Then he sat back in his seat and had a conversation with my father about Jimmy Fenton and the spate of incidents that had been happening in their pubs and clubs over the past two nights.

I looked out of the window as Scott drove back to my apartment. I felt like an intruder into their world. Neither of them wanted me there. I should have listened to Scott and just gone home. Gabriel made several more phone calls during the journey and I didn't get a chance to speak to him until we pulled up outside my building again.

'Back again,' Scott said as he turned and gave me a sympathetic smile.

'Thank you,' I said to him before I turned to Gabriel. 'Can we talk?'

He glared at me, his face full of thunderous anger. 'I don't think this is the time or the place.'

'Then come up?' I suggested. 'Just for ten minutes?'

'You've already wasted enough of my time tonight,' he growled.

'Well, then ten more minutes won't kill you, will it?' I challenged him.

He leaned towards me, placing his warm hand on my thigh and squeezing lightly. 'If it's just a quick fuck you're after, baby, I'm sure we could drop you at your new friend's place instead?'

I shrank back from him. He may as well have slapped me across the face. That stung like hell. In a few words, he had made me feel completely worthless. I felt the tears threatening and I choked them down. 'No need. I've got his number. I'll get him to come round,' I lied.

Gabriel scowled at me but didn't respond.

'Goodnight, Scott,' I said and then I got out of the car and walked towards my apartment building feeling like my heart had been torn out of my chest.

I had barely been in my apartment two minutes when I heard the pounding on my front door. I knew it would be Gabriel, but I was still shocked to open the door to a six-foot-two wall of rage. The anger radiated from him like the heat from a furnace.

'You wanted to talk so bad. Well, come on?' Gabriel shouted as he pushed his way past me. 'Tell me why, when you can't bear to be near me, I find you standing outside O'Malley's with some cunt who has his hands all over you! Were you intending on bringing him back here in the car that I fucking sent for you? Do you think I'm some sort of fucking mug?'

'It wasn't what it looked like,' I said.

'So, I didn't see some prick standing there with his hands on your arse?'

'Well, in that case, I suppose it was exactly what it looked like then. But it was entirely unwanted and he was just some guy who thinks a girl being polite to him entitles him to touch her.' I saw his face soften slightly but it was too late, the second half of my sentence was already on its way out of my mouth and I couldn't stop it. 'Are you even bothered who puts their hands on my arse, anyway?' I wanted to push his buttons the way he constantly pressed mine.

He stalked towards me, towering over me, shaking with fury. I had never seen him so angry. He looked like he might explode. I imagined steam might soon start coming out of his ears

'What did you say?' He snarled, his eyes burning into mine. No trace of green remained, they were black, smouldering like the dying embers of a fire.

I swallowed hard. I should probably apologise, but my ego wouldn't let me. 'I said, are you even bothered who puts his hands on me?'

I continued to stare at him, half expecting the anger to have dissipated, as it usually did, but he appeared as fierce as ever and I wondered if this time I had pushed him too far — if he was going to snap.

He didn't. He grabbed me, his hands fisting in my hair, mouth crashing onto mine. He kissed me so hard my lips felt bruised. I kissed him back with the same ferocity, desperate for him.

'I am the *only* man who gets to put his hands on you,' he growled.

'I know,' I breathed.

'You drive me fucking crazy. I should have brought you straight home tonight and fucked you senseless. Because that's what you want, isn't it?'

Pulling my skirt up he pushed his fingers past my underwear and inside me. He groaned against my mouth as he realised I was ready for him. 'Did he make you wet or is this for me?'

His words stung like nettles. 'Of course it's for you,' I answered as he pinned me to the wall. He unzipped his trousers and then pushed himself inside me, fucking me so hard I almost forgot my own name — let alone what we had even been arguing about.

When we had both found some release, Gabriel pressed his forehead against mine.

'He really did just grab me,' I said as I put my hand on his cheek.

'I know,' he breathed. 'And I'm sorry about the other morning. I should have spoken to you before I accused you. I swear though I was only there to talk to you. I would never hurt you like that, Sam. I don't know what I can do to prove that to you. It kills me to think that you were scared of me.'

'I understand why you were angry, Gabe. But you jumped to the conclusion that I was cheating on you without even considering there would be an alternative explanation. Do you really think I would do that to you?'

He looked into my eyes. 'No,' he said softly. 'But, I didn't think. I'm sorry.'

'What would you have done if I had been with someone else, Gabe?'

He frowned at me as though the question pained him. 'I would have shouted. I would have told you it was over. It would have killed me, but I would have done it. I would not have hurt you. When we first got together, I asked you to trust me, and you did. Have I ever done anything to make you question that?'

'No.'

He kissed me deeply before pulling back. 'I really have to get back to work,' he said with a sigh.

'So, you just came up here for a quickie?' I asked him with a grin. I didn't want him to go but I knew he was in the middle of something, and I didn't want there to be any further tension between us. My world felt off kilter when we weren't in sync.

'Well, it had been three whole days since I'd fucked you. I was starting to have withdrawal symptoms,' he smiled at me.

'You know what really annoyed me more than anything else the other morning?' I said as I started to plant soft kisses on his throat.

'What was that, baby?' he groaned.

'You looked so damn fine in that boxing gear. All sweaty and pumped up. And you smelled so good. I was desperate to jump your bones — and then you went and acted like a twat and ruined it all.'

He tilted my chin to look at him. 'A twat?'

I nodded. 'Yes. A prize twat. You ruined a perfectly good shagging opportunity.'

He kissed me softly before he answered. 'You're right. Next time I go boxing I'll make sure to come round and fuck you straight after. Deal?'

'Deal.'

The vibration of his phone ringing in the inside pocket of his jacket interrupted the moment. 'I have to go,' he said.

'Can you come back later?' I asked him.

'I don't know what time I'll be finished. I'll see you tomorrow instead?' he offered.

'Okay. But if you change your mind, you have a spare key.'

He slipped his hands back down to my behind and pressed my body into his before giving me one long, final kiss.

'Goodnight, baby,' he said before walking out of the door.

44. GABRIEL

I walked across the car park and climbed into the passenger seat of Scott's car.

'Feel better, Boss?' Scott asked with a grin.

'You could say that,' I replied, realising that I had a grin on my face too.

'That must have been some talk,' he said with a low whistle and I swatted the back of his head, making him laugh.

'Just drive us to the office. The vans will be there. And we're late.'

'I won't tell them why, Boss. Don't worry,' Scott said with a soft chuckle.

'You'll be out of a fucking job if you do,' I grinned at him. Scott was one of my most trusted employees and I knew he was fucking with me. I also knew that he had a soft spot for Samantha. She was kind of impossible not to like. The look he had given me when she'd got out of the car earlier had made me realise what a bastard I'd been to her. He had seen the exchange between her and that prick outside O'Malley's while I'd been distracted on my phone. He confirmed her version of events. Not that I needed that to believe her. She wasn't a liar.

I leaned back against the seat. There were three vans waiting for us back at our offices. Sebastian and two dozen of our bouncers were in them — armed to the teeth. We were about to put on a display of power to show Jimmy Fenton and his firm once and for all that he could not fuck us over. I ran a hand over my face. I could smell Sam on me and I had to stifle a groan. She smelled so fucking good. I should be in bed with her right now. I should be inside her, instead of having to deal with the Fentons' bullshit.

A few hours later I stood in the shower and washed the blood from my hands, watching the pale red water running down the plughole. Tonight, had been a huge success. We had hit all of the Fenton's main businesses, put at least two dozen of their best men out of action and left our own security in their place. Fenton's Security was no more. There had been no police interference. No innocent bystanders had been caught in the crossfire and our own lads had made it out with nothing more than cuts and bruises.

Sebastian and I had dealt with Jimmy and his brother, Martin ourselves. To Sebastian's delight and amusement, Martin Fenton had pissed his pants when Seb had shoved a gun in his mouth. Eventually, they'd both begged for mercy and against my better judgement, I had left them still breathing, I wouldn't usually be so forgiving when they'd already been warned off. But, they'd drawn too much attention to us all with their amateurish takeover attempt. And I couldn't act without consequences any more. I couldn't risk the possibility of doing life in prison for one of those cunts, because that would mean I had to live a life without Samantha in it — and I wasn't prepared to do that. The Fenton brothers had been spared, and they knew it.

Now that it was all over, I was restless and edgy. There was no way I was getting any sleep. I wanted Samantha. I wanted to feel her soft warm body and bury myself insider her.

I switched off the shower and stepped out before drying myself with a towel. Picking up my watch, from the ledge, I glanced at the time. It was a little after 3am. Samantha would be asleep, but she had said that I could use her spare key. I could be at her place in less than thirty minutes if I left now. I knew it was selfish. But I needed her.

45. SAMANTHA

I'd been in bed for a couple of hours but I'd been restless the whole time. Drifting in and out of sleep and worrying about what trouble Gabriel and my father were dealing with. When I saw the figure of a man walking into the bedroom, I wondered if I was dreaming.

'Gabe?' I asked sleepily.

'Yeah, it's just me, baby,' he whispered.

A few moments later, I felt him slide into bed beside me. He slipped his warm hand beneath the t-shirt I was wearing and onto my abdomen, pulling me towards him and pressing his body into mine. His erection nudged at my back. He nuzzled my neck and I felt the warm feeling spreading through my stomach and down between my legs.

'I know you're sleeping, baby, but I need you,' he breathed in my ear.

I stretched my limbs, pushing my behind even closer against him and rubbing myself on his cock. 'Oh? What is it you need?' I purred.

He slipped his hand lower, under the band of my underwear and between my thighs. 'I think you know exactly what I mean. Open your legs,' he ordered as he nipped my earlobe.

I did as he told me and he slipped his hand further southwards.

'I hope you've been dreaming about me, baby?' he said between kisses.

'Why?'

'Because you're soaking wet,' he growled.

'Oh, that? Well, after you left me earlier, I had to come to bed on my own. So, what's a girl to do when her handsome boyfriend isn't around to take care of her?' I teased.

'So, you took care of yourself?'

'Hmmm,' I groaned as he started to work his fingers on me.

'Then I hope you were thinking of me, at least.'

'I was.'

'Well, I'm glad you don't need warming up, because you're about to be fucked, baby. Hard.'

He didn't even bother taking off my underwear, he just pulled the soft fabric to the side and pushed his cock deep inside me.

'Oh, fuck, Gabe,' I groaned.

'I love how easy you make it for me to slide my cock in you,' he growled in my ear. 'You're going to struggle to walk tomorrow, baby.'

His words made my insides tremble. He rolled on top of me, pinning me down to the mattress with the weight of his body, so that I was lying on my stomach. I could barely move and I realised that I didn't care. I trusted him completely.

'Are you ready?' he growled.

'Yes,' I panted. Because I was always ready for him and whatever he wanted to do to me.

46. SAMANTHA

Despite Gabriel's promise, I'd been able to walk from his car to my office just fine earlier that morning. Although I didn't think my thigh and stomach muscles could ache any more than that time I'd done two spin classes back to back, it seemed I was wrong. Gabriel Sullivan was a machine, and he'd made me late for work. I smiled as I thought about him. Sadie Jones dumped the stack of case files on my desk with a groan, interrupting my daydream.

'I know it's not my place, Samantha. But I'm not sure if we can keep taking on any more clients. Not without an extra pair of hands anyway,' she said as she wiped the beads of perspiration from her forehead. Sadie Jones was one of the best legal secretaries I had ever worked with. She was smart, incredibly organised, had an extensive knowledge of the law and was great with people too. I respected her opinion, and felt a pang of guilt knowing that she was struggling to keep up with the workload.

I had always been a workaholic. It had been the thing I had clung to in order to survive my marriage, but I sometimes forgot that my employees had a life outside of the place. And now that I rarely worked late anymore, and spent most of my weekends with Gabriel, there was no-one to pick up the slack. Maybe it was time we got another solicitor and junior secretary in? We certainly had the workload to justify it. I made a mental note to speak to Nick as soon as possible.

'I think you might be right,' I replied. 'I can't believe we're barely up and running and we're already in the position where we may have to turn clients away.'

Sadie nodded. 'Well, you and Nick make quite a team.'

'And you. We couldn't do it without you. I'll speak to Nick. We'll look at the figures and see what we can do.'

Sadie smiled as she headed out of my office and my phone started to vibrate on the desk to signal a text message. I looked at the screen. It was from Gabriel.

If you don't stop sending me filthy messages I will come over there and bend you over that desk. Behave yourself.

I laughed to myself. I knew he was in important meetings all day and had been sending him texts all morning, telling him what I'd like him to do to me later, and what I'd like to do to him. I was due to leave for court, but couldn't resist teasing him some more. He'd left before I was dressed that morning and hadn't seen the stockings and suspenders I'd put on under my work clothes. I hitched up my skirt and used my phone to take a photograph of the top of my stockings before sending it to him. He sent a reply within thirty seconds.

I'm on my way

I smiled as I tapped out my reply.

Sorry, Gabe. Leaving for court right now. I'll see you tonight xxx

I hadn't even had a chance to put my phone into my handbag before it was ringing in my hand.

'You'd better be kidding me, Samantha,' Gabriel said in that low growling tone of his when I answered.

'Nope. Sorry, handsome. I'm on my way out the door. I did tell you I was in court this afternoon.'

'Yes, you did. Your big case. But I assumed it must have been postponed when you sent me that picture, especially after I told you to behave yourself.'

'You need to learn some self-control, Gabriel,' I teased.

'Do I? Really?'

'Yes,' I purred.

'We'll see about that. I'll pick you up at five.'

'No need. I'll be getting a lift home from Nick. I'll see you at my place. I should be home by five-thirty.'

'Your place it is then. Good luck in court, baby.'

I was in my bedroom taking off my shoes when Gabriel came in. I spun around to face him. The victory in court that afternoon almost made me forget about our flirtations earlier that morning. I looked up at him. His eyes were burning into mine, a wicked smile playing on his lips. I shivered in anticipation.

'Take off your clothes, Sam.'

I stood for a moment, considering whether I should make him wait.

'Now!' he barked.

I did as he instructed and peeled off my pencil skirt and blouse until I was standing in my underwear. All black, all lace — and sheer stockings. I studied his face as he tried not to give anything away, always trying to maintain control, but he couldn't hide the look in his eyes.

'Jesus Christ, Samantha. What are you trying to do to me?' he said. Then he was standing right in front of me in one quick stride, running his hands over my hips and backside. 'You are fucking beautiful,' he said, his breath ragged, catching in his throat. Then he quickly regained his composure. 'Kneel on the floor and bend over the bed.'

I did as he instructed and felt him moving close behind me. I heard the metallic jangle of his belt buckle and then the zip on his trousers as he undid them both. Then he folded over me, pressing his erection into my flesh.

'I've had a hard on for you all fucking day, Sam. Do you know how uncomfortable that's been? Sitting in a room full of nut-cases with my cock straining at the seams?'

I groaned in response, desperate to feel him inside me.

'I hope you're already wet because you're not getting my fingers or my mouth on you today. I don't think you deserve them,' he said with a growl as he pulled my underwear roughly to one side before entering me. He pushed in right to the hilt making me gasp out loud. He knew I would be ready for him. He knew that I couldn't get enough of him and that I counted the hours until I could feel him inside me again.

'You know I love you, don't you, Sam?' he said against my ear.

Did I?

'Because I'm going to fuck you like I don't,' he growled.

Dear God!

He started to pound me. Over and over. His pace relentless. I couldn't breathe. I was so full. Full of him. He drove at that sweet spot inside me, but every time my orgasm threatened, he stopped and changed his angle. Denying me. I started to beg, to plead with him but he didn't relent. I moved my hips against him, trying to get there myself but he realised what I was doing and pinned me to the bed with the weight of his body. He held my hands down too. 'Just in case you try and get yourself off,' he said in my ear.

'You're a monster,' I groaned.

He laughed against my neck. 'Where's your self-control, Samantha?'

Then he came inside me. Fierce and hot, pumping every last drop into me. I was almost frantic. Tender from the hammering he'd just given me, and desperate for the climax that he had threatened, but not delivered.

'Now, get up onto the bed,' he ordered.

I climbed onto the bed and lay down as he straddled me. He slid my thong down over my thighs, past my knees and ankles before throwing it onto the floor. He left the rest of my underwear alone. Smiling at me, he started to unbutton his shirt and I watched him, enjoying the mini strip tease. Taking it off, he tossed that onto the floor too. Then his hands moved to his belt, which was already undone. I assumed he was going to take off his trousers, but he slid his belt off, slowly pulling it through each loop, the leather making a whooshing sound against the fabric as he pulled it off completely. His eyes were fixed on mine the whole time. Then he took the buckle in his palm and wrapped most of the belt around his hand, until there was just about a foot of black leather hanging free.

'Do you still think I need to learn some self-control, Samantha?' He asked, his voice low and husky.

'No, Gabe,' I breathed.

'Did you have fun sending me that picture, knowing it would drive me crazy? Because you knew I would want to peel these stockings off you, didn't you? And that I'd be thinking about it all day?'

'Yes,' I whispered.

He started to trail the leather belt from my neck, over my breasts, my nipples and down over my stomach. 'Maybe I should do the same to you then? Leave you all worked up like this. Keep bringing you to the edge, but never getting you off. What do you think?'

'That would be very unfair. Especially when I was only trying to brighten your day. Liven up your boring meetings.'

He chuckled. 'You certainly did that, baby.'

He brought the leather down between my thighs, trailing it down the length of my dripping cleft. It's touch both delicate and taunting, I writhed beneath it.

'Next time you do anything like that to me, Samantha, I will bend you over the nearest suitable piece of furniture and you'll feel this belt across your backside. Do you understand me?'

I bit my lip and nodded, surprised by just how much the thought of him doing that turned me on. He leaned down to kiss me before moving down the bed to where I was aching to feel him the most. He started sucking and licking at that tender spot before sliding his fingers inside me, rubbing the orgasm out of me. It came slowly, washing over my body, wave after wave of pleasure, all finally reaching that one place, until tears were rolling down my face and I was whispering his name. When I thought I couldn't take any more, he was inside me again, filling me with his magnificent cock. This time he was slow and gentle, whispering how much he wanted me, how much he loved to fuck me, until I came apart around him again.

. . .

Later, neither of us felt like cooking so I ordered us some pizza. When it arrived, we sat on the sofa and I put on one of my favourite films, *Miss Congeniality*. I looked at Gabriel and smiled. This was my idea of heaven.

'Why are you staring at me?' he said.

'Because you're bloody gorgeous, that's why,' I quipped.

'Even with a mouthful of pizza?'

'Especially with a mouthful of pizza.' I leaned over to kiss him.

'I meant what I said before, Sam,' he said, his eyes narrowing, pulling his face into a frown. He pulled me over to straddle him on the sofa. 'I love you.'

I pushed his hair from his handsome face and stared into his beautiful green eyes. Then I leaned down and kissed him. He wrapped me in his arms and crushed me to his chest. We kissed on the sofa until my jaw began to ache and I couldn't remember a time when I had ever been so happy.

47. SAMANTHA

My afternoon court case had been adjourned, leaving me with an unexpected early finish from work, so, I decided to pay my dad and Gabriel a surprise visit. I knew they'd been having some trouble with a rival firm, although Gabriel had assured me it had been dealt with. It had been over a week since the night Gabriel had crept into my bed in the early hours of the morning after dealing with the Fenton situation, but I still worried about them both.

'Sam,' my father smiled as I walked into his office. He stood up and pulled me into a bear hug. 'I hardly see you anymore.'

'I know. Sorry, Dad. I've just been so busy with work.'

I saw Gabriel look up from his laptop and grin at me and I felt the flush creep over my cheeks and hoped my father didn't notice. I resisted the urge to go over to his desk and kiss him. We had agreed to limit our public displays of affection in front of my dad.

'Did Gabriel tell you about the contract we're going for?' he asked me.

'He mentioned something.' I vaguely recalled him telling me about a security contract for a construction company a few nights earlier while we'd been eating dinner, but then he'd dripped some pasta sauce onto his shirt and had taken it off. The conversation seemed to tail off after that for some reason. I couldn't look over at

Gabriel in case my blush deepened further but I could feel his eyes on me and could picture the wicked grin on his face.

I listened intently as my father told me about his and Gabriel's bid to win a contract with Graham Johnson – a big name in construction. He had sites all over the country and was looking for a new security company.

'The contract's worth millions, Sam,' my father said with a huge grin. 'Gabriel has been working on it for weeks now.'

'A restaurant he built is having its big opening on Saturday night,' Gabriel said as he stood up and walked over to me. 'We've been invited, along with some of our colleagues, to give him our pitch and try and win the contract. I assume you'll be my date?'

'Of course I will. I can't wait. Any excuse to get dressed up,' I replied.

'I've really got to go. Kayleigh is waiting for me. I'll see you on Saturday then, love?' my father said before giving me a kiss on the cheek and walking out of the office, leaving Gabriel and me alone. I could tell by the way he was staring at me, his eyes narrowed and his jaw set, that he had something on his mind.

'What is it, Gabe?'

He stepped closer to me. 'I just have a couple of requests regarding Saturday night, and I'm not sure how you'll react, that's all.'

I flashed an eyebrow at him. 'What kind of requests?'

'I have to impress a few people on Saturday, Sam. This contract is a big deal for us. It's bigger than anything we've ever handled before.'

I folded my arms across my chest. I had no idea where he was going with this — did he think I'd embarrass him or something? 'So?'

'I have to focus, that's all I'm saying. I don't want to be distracted. And that's why I want you to do something for me.'

'What's that, handsome?'

'Can you not play any of your ... games?'

'What games?' I asked, feigning my indignation.

'Like wearing no underwear. Like whispering in my ear how much you want to be riding my cock while I'm in the middle of an important discussion?' he said in that low, rumbling tone of his that seemed to vibrate through my body.

I smiled at him as I remembered the occasions when I'd done things just like that. 'Of course, I'll behave. That's just one request though. Do you have any more?'

'Yes,' he said as he grabbed my hips and pulled me to him. 'Could you not wear your hair up?'

'Okay. But why?'

He reached up and pulled my hair to one side, exposing the left side of my neck. 'Because when you wear your hair up, all I can think about is kissing your neck.' He trailed a finger from my cheek down to my collar-bone. Then he started to plant soft kisses along my throat. 'And when I'm kissing your neck, I get a raging hard on, because I'm either fucking you, or about to fuck you.'

'Well, except for right now,' I said.

'But I *am* about to fuck you,' he replied and I could feel him smile against my skin.

'What? Here? But there are people next door,' I said, aware that some of his employees were in the other office.

'So?' he said.

'They might come in.'

'They won't.'

'They might.'

'They wouldn't dare come in here without knocking.'

'How can you be so sure, Gabe?'

'Because they do as they're fucking told,' he said in that low menacing growl. His hands moved lower and he started to lift the hem of my skirt. Suddenly, I wondered how many other women he'd done this with. Was that why his employees always knocked?

'Don't, Gabe,' I said, pushing his hands away.

He stepped back and looked at me. I never told him no. 'What's wrong?'

'How many women have you screwed in your office before me?' I asked.

'None. I don't make a habit of mixing business and pleasure. But,

I've wanted to fuck you on my desk since you first walked back in here six months ago.'

I didn't respond further and he stepped closer to me again until I could feel the throbbing between my thighs building to dangerous levels.

'If you're not already wet for me, I won't fuck you in here. We can go home and fuck in the comfort of my bed instead. Deal?' he said softly.

I nodded although I already knew what the outcome would be. He slid his hand up my skirt and pulled my lace underwear to one side. Sliding one finger inside me, he chuckled. Then he pulled his hand back, and held up his finger, which was glistening with my arousal.

'What do you think?' he said and then he put his finger in his mouth and sucked it clean. 'You taste so fucking good. Have I ever told you that?'

God, I wanted him so much. I always wanted him. And he knew it.

'I'm going to make you come all over my desk, Sam, and then I'm going to fuck your brains out,' he said as he grabbed me by the hips.

He pushed me back against his desk as he pulled my skirt up around my waist before dropping to his knees. Hooking my legs over his shoulders, he started to devour me. Licking and sucking until I was moaning his name, begging him to let me come.

'Okay, come for me, Sam,' he growled against me and my body, as always, obeyed. Then he stood up, undoing his belt buckle and unzipping his trousers before pushing himself inside me.

'I love fucking you, Sam,' he panted as he screwed me to his desk.

Wrapping my legs around his waist, I clung to him, raking my nails down his back, the soft wool of his suit jacket creasing under my fingertips.

'I love the way you fuck me, Gabe,' I replied breathlessly. My words seemed to send him into a frenzy and his pace increased until I climaxed around him again. He followed shortly after, his strong thighs banging against his desk as he buried his face in my neck.

48. SAMANTHA

It was Saturday night. I walked down the stairs of Gabriel's house and saw him standing waiting for me, looking incredible in his tuxedo. I was wearing my hair loose around my bare shoulders as he'd requested.

'You look stunning,' he said as I reached him. 'How about you turn around and go back into the bedroom and I'll see what you're wearing underneath that sexy dress?'

I smiled sweetly. 'You'll make us late. You can have me all to yourself later. Now, let's go.'

My father was already at the restaurant when Gabriel and I arrived. We made our way through the crowd to meet him. I noticed he hadn't brought his newest girlfriend, Kayleigh with him, and wondered whether their honeymoon period had already ended. My father changed girlfriends as often as he changed his sheets.

'So where is this Graham Johnson then?' I asked, craning my neck to scan the crowd.

'Over there. The bald guy with the grey goatee by the window,' Gabriel told me.

'And your main competition?' I asked.

'Gary Mitchell,' my father indicated the man standing directly behind Graham.

I clutched my purse under my arm. 'I'm off to mingle then,' I said before smiling and disappearing into the crowd.

GABRIEL

I had been speaking to all the right people for most of the evening. Sebastian and I had even managed to corner Graham Johnson on his own and given him our best sales pitch. Afterwards Sebastian disappeared to talk to a blonde who'd caught his eye and I stood at the bar with a whisky as I looked for Samantha. It didn't take me long to spot her in the crowd. She was standing with a young woman with flaming red hair whom I'd recently learned was Graham's youngest daughter. The two of them were laughing at something. Not a discreet, polite laugh — they were almost doubled over, clutching their glasses of champagne. I watched as Graham Johnson joined them and soon the three of them were in hysterics and I couldn't help but smile.

Samantha the chameleon.

I loved the easy way she had with people. Nick had told me that she had the ability to fit in anywhere, with anyone and I realised he'd been right. Whenever I would bring my ex-wife, Jennifer, to events like these, she would cling to my arm all night, barely saying two words to anyone. I didn't recall it irritating me particularly at the time — it was probably something I'd sought out in a partner. I wondered why I'd always chosen women like that before — passive, submissive? They had certainly fit with my need to be in control. But they had never worked out. Maybe because they never challenged me? Samantha Donovan drove me crazier than anyone I had ever met in my entire life, but I couldn't get enough of her. I spent almost every waking minute thinking about her.

I finished my drink and made my way over to her, slipping my arm around her waist. It was getting late and I knew she had to spend the following day preparing for a big court case. Samantha introduced me to Graham's daughter, Robyn and I reacquainted myself with Graham. We all exchanged some polite small-talk before Samantha and I made our excuses to leave. I resisted the urge to ask Graham when he'd be deciding who would get the contract for his security, but as we were walking out of the door, he caught up with me and grabbed me by the arm.

'She's an angel. You want to hold on to her,' he winked at me.

'I intend to,' I replied with a smile.

'I'll be in touch soon,' Graham said with a nod before he disappeared back into the crowd.

Samantha kicked off her heels and put her bare feet on the dashboard of my car. She was grinning to herself and her cheeks were flushed pink.

'You and Robyn looked like you were having fun,' I said to her.

'We were. She's nice. We talked about how much we love being strong independent women. I hate talking about myself usually, but I told her all about how well the firm is doing. You're welcome by the way.'

I frowned at her. 'What do you mean?'

'I've just helped you to score the biggest gig of your life, that's what,' she grinned.

'And how do you work that out?'

'For a successful businessman, Gabe, you're a bit obtuse sometimes,' she chuckled.

I let the barb slide given that she was half drunk. 'Oh? Why's that?'

'You really should do your homework. Because if you had, like I did, you would have discovered that Graham has three daughters. His two eldest both have careers in the arts — one is a dance teacher and the other an actress. Robyn, however is more interested in football and golf — just like her dad. But more importantly, she has just graduated with a first class-honours degree in business. Word on the grapevine is that Graham is ready to hand over the reins and Robyn is primed to take over the family business as soon as he does. She will be the one influencing the big decisions now. And do you know how hard it can be being a woman in industry? Robyn doesn't want to be working with Neanderthal's like Gary Mitchell who will question every decision she makes just because she's a woman. She'll want to work with someone who views women as equals. If I'd gone over there and gushed about how wonderful you are, she'd have seen it as a sales pitch. Instead, I showed her what a supportive and empowering partner you are. Like I said, you're welcome.'

She rested her head back against the seat with her eyes closed and a smile plastered across her beautiful face. I smiled at her too and felt my dick twitching thinking about getting her home. I loved her so much sometimes it made me feel like I couldn't breathe.

49. SAMANTHA

I climbed out of Gabriel's car, my heels swinging from my hand. He scooped me into his arms and carried me through the front door, setting me down in the hallway as soon as we were safely inside the house.

'Thank you for tonight, Sam.' He smiled at me. 'You were incredible.'

'Thank you,' I grinned. 'So what's my reward?'

He pushed me back against the front door. 'Are you drunk?' he asked.

'No. Pleasantly tipsy. But in full control of my faculties,' I grinned.

'Okay, I'll give you your reward,' he said in my ear. Reaching his hand around my back, he slowly unzipped my dress until it fell into a pool of green fabric at my feet. Pushing the cups of my strapless bra beneath my nipples he took one into his hot, wet mouth and started to suck gently. His other hand reached to my behind, pulling me to him until our bodies were pressed together. The cool cotton of his shirt, juxtaposed against the heat of my skin. He moved his head to my other nipple, giving it the same attention and making me feel the familiar throbbing and pulsing between my thighs. Then he gave me my reward right there in the hallway.

. . .

I was sitting in Gabriel's home-office wading through piles of information to prepare for my day in court on Monday when I heard him padding down the hallway towards me. He bounded into the room, a smile spread across his handsome face. He'd obviously only just got out of bed and was wearing boxer shorts and nothing else. As always, my breath caught in my throat at the sight of his almost naked body.

'I've just had a very interesting phone call,' he said.

'Really?' I raised my eyebrows at him.

'Graham Johnson has asked for a meeting with me and your dad tomorrow.'

'What? That's wonderful. Does that mean you've got the contract?'

'He wants to go over a few finer details, but providing he likes what he hears, then yes, we'll get the contract.'

I leapt out of my seat and threw my arms around him. 'That's amazing, Gabe. I'm so proud of you.'

'I couldn't have done it without you, Sam.'

'Yes you could,' I blushed.

'Well, maybe. But I wouldn't. Being with you has made me want to make our operation more ... legitimate. I wouldn't have even considered going after a contract like this six months ago.'

'Well, I'm very happy you're trying to become a respectable business-man after all these years, Gabe,' I purred in his ear.

He lifted me up and I wrapped my legs around his waist. 'I know you're busy but can you take half an hour to celebrate with me?' He grinned.

'I can always make time for you, handsome.'

We didn't even make it out of his office. He fucked me on his desk, sending the papers I'd been working on scattering across the floor.

50. SAMANTHA

The big case I'd been working on was finally over after three long days in court. It had gone in my client's favour and had been a massive boost to our firm. I'd decided to reward myself with a rare late start. I lay in bed admiring Gabriel's naked body while he was getting dressed for work. I caught his eye and he smiled.

'I'm just a piece of meat to you, aren't I?' he said.

'Hmm, pretty much,' I agreed.

He was wearing his dark grey suit, the one he wore with his black leather belt. I watched as his deft fingers fed the belt through the loopholes, remembering the last time I'd seen him wearing that belt, and the promise he had made me. I'd bought a new suspender belt and matching underwear at the weekend and had been waiting to try them out.

'You have a very mischievous look on your face, Samantha. What are you up to?'

I fluttered my eyelashes at him. 'Nothing.'

Walking towards the bed, he cupped my face in his hand and gave me a long, lush kiss. 'Hmm. That's a shame. I'll see you tonight then. Scott will be here at ten to drive you to work. Be nice to him!'

'Of course I will.'

. . .

'I'll see you before Court next week, Sarah. We'll do some final prep then,' I said as I squeezed my newest client's hand reassuringly as she stood up to leave. 'It'll be okay. You've been through much worse, I promise.'

Sarah smiled in response. 'Thanks, Samantha. I'll see you next week.'

I had ten minutes before my next client was due to arrive. I had already sent Gabriel three messages. The first one had been fairly tame and I'd told him how much I'd enjoyed the blow job I'd given him that morning. In the second one, I'd told him what I'd like to do to him when we got to his place later. The third was a photograph of the top of my stockings. He'd been on the phone threatening to come over, but I'd told him I had client interviews all day. So, no matter what time he came to the office, we would have an audience of at least one.

I tapped out a fourth message.

Hey handsome. I wish you were here with me. I'm so wet for you I may have to go to the ladies and sort myself out

My phone rang within twenty seconds. 'I thought you had clients all day?' he asked.

'I do. My next one is due in five minutes. Do you think five minutes would be long enough to get myself off?' I asked.

'It'd be enough time for me to get you off,' he growled. 'I told you after that photograph you were walking a very fine line, Samantha. But you keep pushing me. Do you remember what I told you last time you did this?'

'Yes, I do. And I noticed you're wearing your grey suit today.'

I heard him laugh softly before he resumed talking in his trademark menacing growl. 'I'm going to a meeting with your father and Graham Johnson this afternoon. Do you think you can behave yourself for a few hours, at least? I really don't want to be talking to them with a raging hard on.'

'Okay. I'll behave,' I told him. But of course, I didn't.

. . .

The last of my clients had left and I was catching up on some paperwork when a shadow fell across my desk. I looked up to see Gabriel standing in the doorway, filling it with his massive frame. His jaw clenched shut. His eyes burned into mine.

'Hello, Samantha,' he said, his voice low and menacing. If I didn't know him so well I might have been terrified. Standing up, I walked to the other side of my desk, taking my jacket from the back of my chair. 'Hey, Gabe. I'm ready to go.'

He closed the door behind him and I heard the click of the lock. 'What makes you think we're going anywhere?' He walked towards me like a tiger stalking its prey. I took a step back from him, bumping into my desk as I did. He smiled, that wicked grin of his that made my breath catch in my throat.

'Well, this is my office. And I think Nick's still here,' I stammered.

'So? I've locked the door.'

'But he might hear us?'

'Well, you'd better be quiet then, hadn't you?'

'I just assumed we'd be going home.'

'Why would you think that? What did I tell you? The nearest suitable piece of furniture, I said, didn't I?'

He placed his hands on the desk either side of me, pushing me back with his body as he did, so I was perched on the edge. Then he pressed his hands down on it firmly, as if testing it's sturdiness. 'This should do fine,' he said as he looked into my eyes.

I swallowed hard. What the hell had I done? Despite my reservations, I felt the familiar warmth pooling between my legs.

'Turn around and bend over the desk, Sam,' he ordered.

I did as he told me, laying my face on the desk, the cool polished wood soothing my flushed cheeks. He slid my skirt up my legs until it was bunched around my waist. Then he ran his warm hands up the length of my legs, from my ankles to the top of my thigh where my stockings ended.

'I do love you in these, Sam. I've been thinking about peeling them off you all day. But that will have to wait until later, won't it?'

I heard him undoing the buckle on his belt and then the soft whoosh of the leather against the fabric as he slowly slid it off.

'Are you ready, Sam?' He asked as he wound the belt around his hand, until once again there was only a foot of leather hanging loose. He trailed it up the inside of my thighs, and then between my legs and over my backside. So very slowly, prolonging the agony — or building the anticipation? Then I felt him draw back his hand before the leather landed on the fleshy part of my behind. It was a shock more than anything. There was no real pain, just a quick sting followed by a tingling sensation where the leather grazed my skin. Gabriel's free hand rubbed the skin where the belt had marked me, soothing the sting until all I felt was warmth.

'How many of those sexy little texts did you send me today, Samantha?' he asked.

I shook my head. How the hell should I know?

'Six. So, that's the number of times you'll feel my belt.'

The final one was the hardest. It stung but Gabriel's hand soothed my reddened skin before he pulled my underwear to the side and his fingers stroked the length of my cleft.

He leaned over me, his mouth against my ear. 'God, you're so fucking wet, Sam. Do you like feeling my belt?'

I could only nod. All of my senses were heightened and I was desperate for the orgasm which had been threatening since he'd ordered me over the desk. It wasn't long before he had me moaning his name and grinding myself against his fingers. When he'd rubbed the last of my orgasm out of my body, he fucked me so hard that my pen holder toppled off the desk, sending the contents scattering over the floor. His relentless pounding sent me over the edge again. I shouted his name, not caring any longer who could hear me.

51. SAMANTHA

Later that evening, I wrapped my arms around myself as I sat on Gabriel's sofa. The television was on although I wasn't watching it. Instead I watched the light from it dance across the glass coffee table. I was so deep in thought I didn't even hear him come into the room until he sat on the sofa beside me. I could smell garlic and herbs from the kitchen, and it made my stomach growl.

Gabriel's eyes narrowed as he looked at me. 'What's wrong?'

I shrugged.

'Talk to me, Sam,' he said softly.

'I'm not really sure, Gabe. I feel kind of... ashamed? About what happened before, about what we did.'

'Ashamed?' He raised an eyebrow at me. 'I don't seem to recall you actually doing anything, Sam.'

I gave him a gentle shove. 'I mean because I enjoyed it, Gabe. A lot. What's wrong with me? I'm supposed to be a strong, independent woman. I consider myself an advocate for women — but I enjoy getting tied up and spanked with a belt. What the hell is that about?'

He pulled me onto his lap and stroked my hair back from my face. 'Well, for the record, you weren't tied up *and* spanked — although that would be incredible and we'll definitely be giving that a try,' he said with a grin. 'But, seriously, why shouldn't you enjoy those things? Tell me. Do you like what happens when I tie you up?'

I blushed and the memories pulled the corners of my mouth into an involuntary smile.

He laughed. 'I'll take that as a yes then. And when I used the belt. Did it hurt you?'

'No.'

'So, how did it feel?'

I took a few seconds to recall the feel of the soft leather, warmed from the heat of Gabriel's body, as it landed on my skin. 'It stung a little, but no it didn't hurt. It felt ... thrilling ... illicit. It was good.' In fact, the contrast between the belt and the feel of Gabriel's hands immediately afterwards was incredible.

'And then what happened? What did you know would happen?'

I could feel the flush rising again, the heat searing up my chest and across my face, and he laughed.

'Say it,' he said.

'You made me come,' I whispered.

He started to kiss my neck then. 'I tie you up and spank you because we both enjoy it, Sam. It's only about ever about your pleasure. I like to be in control, and when it comes to sex, you like to give it up. And there's nothing wrong with that. I would *never* take advantage of the power I have over you when you let me do those things. So, why wouldn't you enjoy it? Have I ever hurt you?'

'No.'

'And you know I wouldn't, don't you? So, there's no need to feel bad for letting me make you feel good, is there?'

'I suppose not,' I replied. Then he made me feel good again while dinner cooked.

52. SAMANTHA

I had been in court all day and afterwards had needed to console my client who was distraught that her ex-partner had been granted supervised access to their three young children after he had made their lives hell for the past two years. By the time I'd got to Gabriel's house that night, I just wanted to shower, eat and go to bed. He was due to go to Liverpool the following morning to finalise the Johnson contract, and I wanted him all to myself for the night.

But Gabriel had other plans. His aunt, who lived in Cumbria, had paid a surprise visit to London on her way back from her holiday in France and he'd agreed that we'd all go out for dinner together.

'It's only for a couple of hours, Sam,' Gabriel said with a sigh. 'They sprung it on me at the last minute. They're only down here for a night. Besides, I want you to meet them.'

I slipped off my robe. 'Fine. I'll be ready in half an hour.'

Gabriel rarely saw his aunt and uncle but he always made time for them when they visited London. I had never met them before. I had seen photographs of Gabriel's mum, Carol and from what he'd told me of her, she sounded like a lovely woman, so kind and caring — exactly like my own mum had been. Gabriel's parents had died within six months of each other — his father when he was seventeen and his mum when he'd just turned eighteen. Prior to their deaths he had been close to both of them and their loss had hit him hard.

A little over thirty minutes later, I was dressed in what I guessed was suitable attire to meet my boyfriend's relatives for the first time — a turquoise wrap dress. Knee length, and not too much boob on show.

'You look beautiful,' Gabriel said, kissing me as I reached the bottom of the stairs.

'Thank you,' I smiled, my earlier annoyance gone now that I had showered and changed.

We were meeting Maggie and Hugh at a local Italian restaurant and we arrived just as it was starting to rain outside. 'Gabriel!' A woman, I assumed to be his aunt, shouted as we walked through the entrance. She did look like his mum, from the photographs I'd seen of her at least. Just before we walked to join them at their table, I leaned into Gabriel and whispered into his ear.

'I forgot to tell you, I'm not wearing any underwear.'

His hand, which was on the small of my back, skimmed over my backside. I smiled at him as he realised I wasn't joking.

Gabriel introduced me to Maggie and Hugh, who I was surprised to find were delightful company. Maggie clearly adored Gabriel. He was the last link to her sister, I supposed. And after a few wines, she and Hugh told me all about their failed efforts to conceive a child of their own. No wonder they enjoyed seeing Gabriel so much when they visited London. And he always made time for them. How thoughtful of him. It was things like that which had made me fall in love with him. Suddenly, I felt ashamed for sulking about having to go out to dinner with them earlier.

In between laughing with his aunt and uncle, Gabriel glowered at me throughout most of our meal. I smiled sweetly at him. I knew he wasn't really angry with me. He was just annoyed that I wasn't wearing any underwear and he couldn't take advantage of the fact. I wondered what he had in store for me when we get home.

After we'd finished our meals and polished off a third bottle of wine, Gabriel started to make noises about leaving.

'We'll share a taxi,' Hugh said. 'Your place isn't too far from our hotel. We'll drop you guys off.'

'No, that's fine,' Gabriel said. 'It's out of your way. We can a get a taxi on our own.'

'Don't be silly, we can all travel together.' I said and Gabriel shot me a look that sent a shiver through my whole body.

I promised Maggie that Gabriel and I would visit them as soon as we could before getting out of the taxi.

'We should go there at the end of the month, Gabe. I can get the Friday off work,' I said as we walked into his house.

'If you'd like to.'

The front door had barely clicked shut when Gabriel had me pinned to the wall in the hallway. He ran his hands over my backside. 'What the fuck are you trying to do to me, Sam?' he growled.

'Just keeping you on your toes, Gabe.'

His eyes bored into mine. 'Get upstairs. Now!' he commanded and my insides started to melt, dissolving like salt in hot broth. I did as he said, holding the bannister for support as my legs trembled.

Once we were inside the bedroom, he stalked towards me. 'Take off the dress,' he said as he started to loosen his tie and sat down on the bed. I did as he told me until I was standing in just my bra. He stared at me with those beautiful green eyes and I felt the warmth spreading between my legs.

'Now, come here!' he growled.

I walked over to him and without warning, he pulled me across his knee, so I was lying face down with my behind in the air. I gasped out loud.

His hand ran over my skin and I sucked on my lower lip. I knew what was about to happen and my insides trembled at the thought. He brought his large hand down across my backside and the slapping sound reverberated around the room. I had never felt so turned on. I wriggled under his grip and my skin seared with heat.

Then I giggled.

'Do you think this is funny, Sam?'

'No, Sir,' I said before he brought his hand down for a second time. He rubbed his cool hand over the hot skin on my backside before sliding his hand between my legs. He groaned as he found me already dripping wet for him and then he pulled his hand back again. I briefly wondered how many times I was going to feel his hand, but I was also too aroused to care. Lying over his knee, while he was still wearing his suit, and I was practically naked had me almost panting. I could feel the wetness dripping down my thighs. I lost count of the number of times he spanked me, but by the time he'd finished, I was a trembling mess and I was desperate to feel him inside me.

'Now get onto the bed. On your hands and knees,' he instructed as he removed his tie. Once again I did as I was told and watched as he reached into the bedside drawer and took out my vibrator. He motioned me to crawl towards him as he indicated the huge bulge of his erection which could clearly be seen through the fabric of his trousers. 'I've had that all fucking night, thanks to you.'

I unzipped his trousers and took his hot stiff cock into my mouth, my hand fisting him at the root. I loved the taste of him. I licked and sucked and enjoyed listening to the animal noises he made. Then I heard another sound. The buzz of the vibrator coming to life.

He leaned over me. 'Did my spanking you make you wet, Sam?'

I nodded as best I could with my mouth full of him. Of course it had. Everything he did made me wet. I always was when I was around him. He pushed the vibrator inside me, so I had his cock filling my mouth and the buzzing sex toy filling my pussy.

'Does that feel good?' he asked, his voice low and husky. Then he fucked me and my mouth to the same slow, relentless rhythm. He came before I did, spurting hot and sticky against my throat.

'Now lie down on the bed,' he said and I did, desperate for the orgasm which was building.

'Please, Gabe,' I moaned.

'Do you think you deserve to come, Samantha?'

'Yes,' I panted.

He pushed the vibrator back inside me, thrusting it in and out as he sucked on my nipples. Then his mouth moved south and he began sucking my clit with his hot, wet tongue. I came so hard my thighs trembled. As the orgasm rolled through my body, he threw the vibrator onto the floor before filling me with his cock again.

'Christ, you make me so fucking hard, Sam,' he growled. 'I could fuck you like this for the rest of our days, do you know that? You're so hot and wet and so fucking tight,' he said, grinding into me, trying to get as far inside me as he possibly could. I raised my hips up to meet him, desperate to take as much of him as he could give.

'I love the way you fuck me, Gabe,' I said before we both climaxed again.

53. SAMANTHA

I was missing Gabriel like crazy. He and my father were finalising the Johnson contract in Liverpool. I closed my eyes and willed sleep to come but the constant ticking of the clock on my bedside table was driving me crazy. I'd gone to bed early because I'd been falling asleep on the sofa, but now that I was there I couldn't seem to drop off. I wondered what Gabriel was doing, and secretly hoped that he was lying awake missing me too. It was almost midnight but I decided to call him. He answered on the fourth ring.

'Hey, baby. You okay?'

'Hey, handsome. Sorry to call so late. But I miss you.'

'That's okay. I miss you too. I was just about to call it a night.'

Before I could respond, I heard a female voice in the background, and then laughter.

'Who's that?' I asked.

'It's Robyn, she needs me to sign some papers.'

'In your hotel room? At this time of night? Is my dad there too?' I asked.

'No, he went out-'

'So it's just you and Robyn?'

'Yes. But ...'

I hung up the phone. So, he was about to call it a night, was he?

With Robyn? My heart started to thump in my chest. I was lying there, pining for him like some lovesick teenager, and he had another woman in his room. The sound of Robyn giggling echoed in my head. My phone started to ring in my hand and Gabriel's number flashed up on the screen. I pressed the button to cancel the call. One minute later, I received a message to say he'd left a voicemail. He phoned again but I ignored it, hoping he would feel as annoyed as I did. I knew deep down that he wasn't a cheat, but I resented the fact that I was home alone missing him and he was entertaining women in his hotel room.

The following day, I was reading some case files when I saw the shadow fall across my desk. I knew it was Gabriel even before I looked up. His presence in any room set my nerves on edge. I looked up to see him glowering at me.

'Do you have any idea how fucking infuriating it is to be stuck in a city at the other end of the country when the person you need to talk to purposely ignores you? Why the fuck didn't you answer any of my calls?' he snarled.

'Because I didn't want to speak to you. I would have thought that was fairly obvious,' I smiled sweetly.

'You drive me fucking crazy!' He ran his hand through his hair and I had to remind my treacherous body that I was still annoyed with him.

'You were alone with a woman in your hotel room at half-eleven at night, Gabriel, while I was lying awake missing you like some idiot.'

'If you had bothered to answer the damn phone, or listened to your voicemails, you'd have known that she flew to Paris first thing this morning. The papers were drawn up late last night. She wanted to get them signed before her trip. And of course, it fell to me to sign them, because as usual, your father was more concerned with getting laid than he was doing anything else. But you know what, none of it doesn't matter now, does it?'

'What's that supposed to mean?' I said.

'I mean, you don't trust me. So, this — us, it's all fucking pointless.'

I didn't trust him? Was he serious? I felt the anger surging through my chest. I pushed my chair back as I stood up, my palms flat on the desk to steady myself. I felt the skin on my chest and face flush pink. I was literally shaking with anger.

'How dare you say I don't trust you.'

'Well, you assumed I was fucking another woman just because she was in my hotel room,' he snarled.

'Yes, I was annoyed that you were having fun with some woman while I was lying in bed pining for you like a muppet. But, I did not say anything about you fucking her. Were you?'

He planted his hands on the desk now too and leaned towards me. 'Don't fucking push me, Sam. I'm not in the mood.'

'And you think I am? I'm trying to work here and you barge in accusing me of not trusting you. Which, let's be fair, is a bit rich coming from you.'

He scowled at me with one of those thunderous looks on his face.

'Now, I have a case to prepare for. So, kindly, get out of my office and leave me alone,' I snapped.

'You're fucking infuriating,' he snarled before turning around and walking out.

I sank back into my chair. Of all the things he could accuse me of, suggesting that I didn't trust him felt like the biggest insult. How much more trust could I give him? I had laid myself completely bare to him. I had told him things that I never thought I'd be able to tell anyone. I let him tie me up, for Christ's sake — and he just took it all. He expected it. Like it was nothing for me.

It had taken every ounce of courage that I could muster to finally tell Jackson that I was leaving him for good. I had known when I had made that decision, that he may well kill me for it. But, I had been prepared to die. I didn't want to, but I was prepared to. I knew it would have been better than spending the rest of my life with a man who was so cruel and twisted, he could only be happy when I was in pain. I had been right in my assumption too. He had tried to kill me, and would have succeeded if our dinner guest, Nancy, hadn't come back for her scarf.

He'd been charged with attempted murder at first, but it was later reduced to Wounding by the CPS as they believed the lesser charge would be more likely to result in a conviction. Then they had added more and more charges to the docket as I sat in interview after interview detailing the years of abuse he had subjected me to. I never told them everything — things that were too painful, like the time in the house when he'd allowed his friends to rape me. Or about what had happened after I'd lost Alice – my beautiful Alice. Eventually he'd been charged with six counts of Rape and three of Wounding.

Then I'd had to endure the trial, and the media circus around it. For three long weeks, I had to sit in that courtroom and listen to my life and my character being pulled apart by his legal team — like vultures feasting on a rotting carcass. For three days of those weeks, I had been on the stand myself, being grilled by Jackson's barrister — a former colleague of mine, who pulled every dirty trick in the book to try and secure his client's freedom. I knew then I would never go back to criminal defence.

My sex life had been openly discussed in a full courtroom — in front of my poor father! Wasn't it true that I enjoyed rough sex? Wasn't it true that I enjoyed all of it? Wasn't I just out for revenge after I'd discovered his many affairs? Wasn't I just after his money? Our friends were called as character witnesses — for him! It felt like everyone I'd ever known believed his side of the story. Only Nancy was prepared to give evidence on my behalf of what she'd seen that night. She'd insisted that no, it wasn't a tiff that got out of hand, or some sort of twisted sex game — she had found my husband, with one hand around my throat, a corkscrew in the other and a smile on his face, choking me to death and trying to stab me. If it hadn't been for her, Nick, my father and my therapist, I don't know how I'd have coped.

After an intense and lengthy trial, Jackson was found guilty of all three counts of Wounding and two counts of Rape. He was sentenced to sixteen years but would be out in eight. Did I feel like justice had been served? Most definitely not. But, I picked myself up. I dug deep and found strength I didn't even know I had to move back here and start again from scratch. That was why I hated to feel pitied, or for people to think I needed protecting, I had walked through fire and I was still standing.

Then Gabriel Sullivan had walked back into my life and he had turned my whole world on its axis. He had absolutely no idea what it took for me to allow him in like I did.

54. GABRIEL

I drove home from Samantha's office in a rage. My knuckles were white as my hands gripped the steering wheel. Sometimes I wondered if I understood her at all. She wasn't a jealous woman by nature, not usually. I could certainly understand her being pissed off when she'd heard Robyn in my room. But what I couldn't understand was her refusal to listen to my explanation. I'd expected we'd have a bit of an argument, but then I'd thought it would end as all of our arguments did, with some part of my body inside her.

I'd just got out of the shower when I heard the knocking on my front door. Even a run hadn't taken the edge off my fight with Samantha and I was still seething. I opened the door to her and she pushed past me and marched up the stairs without a word. I heard her opening drawers and stomping about the bedroom. My first thought was that she was packing the things she'd left there over the past few months.

Fuck!

I ran up the stairs, taking them two at a time. When I walked into the bedroom, I saw her placing things on the bed. On closer inspection, I could see that she'd laid out a pair of leather cuffs; a couple of my ties; a blindfold, one of her scarves and my belt.

She glared at me. 'What are these, Gabriel?'

Unsure where she was going, I glared back. 'You know what they are.'

'Maybe a better question would be, what do you do with these things?'

'I tie you up with them,' I frowned at her. What the fuck was she playing at?

'Yes. In fact, only last week, you tied my legs and my arms to this bed. And then you blindfolded me. I couldn't move. Do you remember?'

'Yes.' Of course I remembered. My dick started to twitch just thinking about it. But that obviously wasn't where this was heading.

'And this?' she said as she picked up my belt. 'What else have you done with this?'

'I've hit you with it,' I said, realising how wrong that sounded when I said it out loud.

She glared at me. 'Do you have any idea how difficult it is for me to trust anyone that much, Gabriel? Do you have *any* idea how much I have to trust you to allow you to do any of that to me?'

I stared at her. I wanted to argue with her. I wanted to vent some of this pent-up rage that was still coursing through my body. But, she was right. I didn't even think about what it meant for her to give up control to me the way that she did. I just expected it. I took it, without fully appreciating how much it must cost her.

'Don't you *ever* accuse me of not trusting you,' she snapped as she walked past me. I grabbed hold of her arm before she reached the door.

'Sam! You're right. I didn't think about it like that. Don't go.' I pulled her to me, scared that she would shake me off and walk out anyway. To my relief, she didn't. I buried my face in her hair. God, she smelled so fucking good. Everything about her made me hard. She was wearing a wrap dress and it fell apart easily when I tugged on the belt. I slid my hands around to her gorgeous peach of an arse, before pushing the dress over her shoulders and onto the floor.

I laid her down on the bed and pulled off her underwear. Running my hand down the length of her body, she arched her back in pleasure. I knew her better than any woman I had ever been with. I knew that when I moved my hand back up her inner thigh, her legs would fall apart for me. I resisted the urge to push my fingers inside her, although I was desperate to — to push any part of my body inside her. I slid my finger up to her clit instead to find her already soaking wet for me. I rubbed softly at first, because I knew it would drive her crazy. Sure enough, she was soon whimpering and bucking beneath me.

'Please, Gabe,' she groaned.

Taking pity on her, and myself, I sucked on her swollen clit and pushed two fingers inside her. It felt so good to taste her. I loved to feel her come in my mouth. Her whole body trembled. When I'd given her the orgasm she'd begged me for, I fucked her, feeling the relief of finally being inside her.

I often held her hands down when I fucked her, it gave me easy access to her neck and her nipples where I would suck and lick as I nailed her to the bed. But sometimes I liked to feel her claw at my back and my arse, pulling me further into her. I loved that she wanted me as much as I needed her. I loved everything about this woman and the way she made me feel. I came inside her and she rewarded me with another climax of her own, whispering my name as she did.

'I love you, Sam,' I breathed. 'I'll never take your trust for granted again. Can you give me another chance?'

'I thought I just did,' she said with a smile.

'Would you prefer it if I didn't tie you up?' I asked her.

'No. I love you tying me up.'

I smiled. That was good to hear. 'And what about the other stuff?'

'You mean, like when you put me over your knee and spank me like a naughty schoolgirl?' she grinned at me and I felt my cock twitching again.

'Yes, that.'

'I love that too. Can I tell you a secret?' she asked.

'Of course.'

'Sometimes, I try and push your buttons on purpose, just so you'll spank me. Especially when you're wearing that lovely soft leather belt,' she flashed her eyebrows at me and gave me one of her killer smiles.

'Is that why you're always trying to piss me off?'

'I don't try. I succeed,' she replied.

I put my arm around her and pulled her tighter to me. 'That is a very dangerous game to play, Miss Donovan.'

'Well, you know me. I like to live life on the edge,' she started to laugh.

I leaned down and sealed my mouth over hers. I parted her lips with my tongue and she groaned into my mouth. For all her insistence that she would never be my property, when she was with me like this, I owned her. She gave me complete control and I suddenly realised what a privilege that was.

I pulled back and stroked her cheek with my fingertips. 'You know I would never hit you in anger, don't you?' I frowned at her. I needed her to know that was a boundary I would never cross. 'It's only ever for your pleasure.'

She looked up at me with those beautiful brown eyes. 'I know.'

'But, if you ever ignore my calls again and leave me hanging at the other end of the country, I'll turn that peach of yours cherry red,' I smiled at her. 'Understand?'

'Yes, Sir,' she replied.

55. GABRIEL

I was sitting alone in my office when the phone started to ring. I frowned at the offending noise. Who the hell used landlines these days? It was rare for anyone to call us on it. Most people used mine or Sebastian's mobile number.

I picked it up. 'Archangel Securities.'

'I'd like to speak to Gabriel Sullivan,' the well-spoken voice replied.

'Speaking. Who is this?'

The tone of his voice changed in an instant. 'This is Samantha's husband.'

I felt the hairs on the back of my neck stand on end. So, this was the monster who was responsible for causing my girl so much pain and misery. It was a pity I couldn't reach through the phone and smash his teeth down his throat. 'Ex-husband.' I reminded him.

'Well. We'll see about that. I'm giving you a polite warning to stay the hell away from my wife.'

I laughed out loud. 'You're warning me? Is this a joke?'

He didn't speak for a few seconds. 'I'm afraid not. Why don't you find yourself a nice, shiny new girlfriend? I'm sure some young, pretty little thing would be much more up your street? Samantha is too complicated for men like yourself to understand. She needs to be handled a certain way.'

I felt my pulse quickening. It was obvious he was trying to push my buttons and I knew he'd get off on making me lose my shit. 'I don't think you have any idea how she needs to be handled.'

He started to laugh. 'Ah, let me guess. You think because you fuck her well, you can handle her?'

I sucked in the air through my teeth, trying to keep a lid on my temper. But it was becoming increasingly difficult. I had never hated anyone as much as I hated the man on the other end of the phone.

Jackson took my silence as an invitation to keep talking. 'My uncle has a ranch in Montana. Every summer I used to go there for a few weeks. And you know what my favourite thing was? Watching those cowboys break in the wild horses. Some people might say it's a brutal practice. You basically use brute force and dominance to ride the animal into submission. But once they're broken, they will always belong to you. That's exactly what I had to do with Samantha,' he laughed. 'She was a feisty one, I can tell you. I enjoyed breaking her. But, she will always belong to me.'

'You're a sick fuck!' I growled.

'No. I am exactly what she needs. You have no idea what makes her tick. I have done things to her that you couldn't even imagine. I've pushed her to limits you wouldn't even dare to go. I have marked every part of her body as my own.'

I could feel my body shaking with rage now, but I kept my voice calm. 'Maybe. But that was then. I'm the one who gets to push her limits now, aren't I? When you go to sleep in your tiny little cell tonight, know that I will be in a warm, king sized bed with your even warmer ex-wife. And every part of her body will be pressed against mine.'

'Just stay the fuck away from her,' he hissed. 'You have no idea what I'm capable of.'

Then I heard a click and the line went dead. I sat back in my chair and took deep breaths to regulate my heart rate. He was a fucking animal. I felt a pain in my chest when I thought about the life

Samantha had endured with him. One day, I was going to make him feel just as much pain as she had.

I went to the boxing gym after Jackson's phone call. Fighting and fucking were my two preferred methods of working out my rage issues. And I didn't want to see Samantha until I'd calmed down. I would have to tell her about Jackson's phone call. I'd rather not, but she deserved to know. I'd have to choose my moment carefully though. I needed her to know that there was nothing I wouldn't do to keep her safe from that sadistic fucker. There was nothing I wouldn't do to keep her by my side.

56. SAMANTHA

I looked at the huge pile of paperwork on my desk and groaned inwardly. I didn't even know where to start. As if my growing workload wasn't enough, the domestic abuse case I was working on had me rattled. The perpetrator had applied for sole custody of his children, despite being a violent bully, and because of his wife's previous mental health issues — exacerbated by him, no doubt, he might just win. I was going to have to phone Gabriel and tell him I needed to work late.

As though I had conjured him with my thoughts, Gabriel appeared in the doorway. He'd clearly come straight from the gym. His t-shirt, which was already tight-fitting, was stuck to his skin with fresh sweat and his damp hair was stuck to his forehead. He was wearing shorts which showed off his muscular, toned legs. And I thought he looked good in a suit! He smiled at me, his green eyes twinkling.

'Hello, handsome,' I greeted him with a smile.

'As promised, I've just finished a boxing session, so I've come to give you a good seeing to.'

I opened my mouth in mock horror, recalling how I had berated him for being an arsehole when he'd turned up at my house in his boxing gear a few weeks earlier — wasting a perfectly good opportunity for me to jump his bones. 'Unfortunately, I'm busy.'

'Sadie told me you have no appointments this afternoon.'

I pushed my chair back and walked over to him until we were standing less than an inch apart. The smell of his fresh sweat gave me butterflies. 'Just because I have a clear diary, doesn't mean I'm not busy.'

He stepped into my office, closing the door behind him and pushing me back against my desk. 'I'll be quick.'

'Oh, be still my beating heart,' I laughed. 'But, seriously. I am absolutely snowed under here. I cleared my diary for the day so that I could make some headway with all of this paperwork.'

He nodded. 'And how is your case going?' he asked.

'Not good. We have the most unsympathetic judge I've ever known,' I shook my head.

Gabriel pulled me into his arms and kissed me and I melted into his body. Then I remembered all the work I had to do and pulled away from him.

'You'll figure something out. You always do,' he said.

'I hope so. I'm going to have to work late tonight to try and get on top of this.'

'Okay. How late?'

'Eight?' I said.

'I'll pick you up at eight then. Don't let anyone in here while you're on your own,' he warned me.

'I won't,' I replied. 'I learned my lesson. Now please go. You are very distracting, Gabriel. Especially in those shorts.'

'Good,' he said with a smile, then he gave me one last, lingering kiss before he left.

57. SAMANTHA

A few days later, I was getting dressed for work when my phone started ringing on my dresser. I saw DS Philips' name on the screen and wondered why he'd be calling me so early on a Thursday morning. I answered it and listened as he told me that Anthony Garvey had got himself a shit-hot lawyer, and was making a bail application later today.

I was still on the phone when Gabriel got out of the shower.

'Thanks, Carl. I appreciate you letting me know,' I said.

Gabriel sat on the bed beside me. 'What's going on?'

I took a deep breath. I still hadn't forgotten what Garvey had said about him being a 'we' and my suspicion that it might be Jackson. If Garvey had been able to afford himself a top-notch lawyer, then I wouldn't be surprised if it was one of Jackson's buddies. The thought made my skin crawl. But right now, my priority was telling Gabriel what had happened without him quitting his job to become my personal twenty-four hour bodyguard – not that that wouldn't have its perks.

'That was the sergeant dealing with Garvey's case. He's making a bail application today, and could be out later if the Court agrees to it.'

'What?' he frowned at me. 'That's fucking nuts. The guy's a psycho.'

'It's the way the law works, Gabe. He's entitled to apply for bail. And if he's got a suitable address to go to, the judge could well agree it.'

'Then I'm not letting you out of my sight. You'll have to stay off work, Sam. Tell them you're sick.'

'Are you kidding? Don't be ridiculous. I'm not having my life dictated to by Anthony Garvey or by you.' I got up off the bed and stalked to the bathroom and he followed me.

'I can't protect you if I'm not with you.'

I spun around to face him, the skin of my face and chest started to turn red. 'I don't need your protection, Gabriel. I am not a child. How many times do we need to go over this?'

'He wants to fucking kill you, Sam,' he shouted.

'Oh, don't be so dramatic,' I said even though the thought of Anthony Garvey being released bothered me more than I would ever admit. But, I had faith in the criminal justice system. Surely, the judge would look at his antecedent history and refuse bail? Or maybe I was just fooling myself?

'Don't be so bloody reckless then. You are my responsibility, Sam,' Gabriel said. No doubt, it had been said in the heat of the moment, and the look on his face told me that he regretted those words as soon as they left his mouth. But he had said them and he might as well have pushed a giant red button on my forehead that said 'Caution – do not press.'

'Your responsibility?' I shouted. 'Well, let me relieve you of your responsibility. Get out.'

'Sam?'

'I said, get out!'

I was physically shaking with temper. I wasn't really angry with him, I was angry that Anthony Garvey might be out on the streets by the end of the day, but Garvey wasn't standing in front of me and Gabriel was.

He glared at me for a few seconds, his hands balled into fists at his side. 'Okay,' he said eventually. 'I'll have Scott come and pick you up for work. Please don't give him a hard time about it,' he said as he left.

. . .

Later that afternoon, I took a taxi cab to Gabriel's office. I felt bad about our argument earlier that morning and I wanted to make things right between us. The domestic abuse case I'd been working on was getting to me, and that on top of the news about Anthony Garvey had pushed me over the edge. I had taken it all out on Gabriel and I knew that wasn't fair. I had such an issue with people caring about me. I equated their concern with pity and any attempt to protect me made me feel like I was being treated like a possession. I knew why. It was because of Jackson and the person I'd had to become to survive my marriage to him. But Gabriel was not Jackson.

I suppose I couldn't blame Gabriel for wanting to protect me. My ex-husband was a well-connected, sadistic psychopath who seemed hell-bent on destroying my life. And if that wasn't enough, there was a crazed madman, who blamed me for stealing his wife and children from him, threatening to kill me. Not only that, he was quite possibly about to be released on bail. It was like my life had turned into a soap opera.

I hoped that my father wasn't in the office. I didn't fancy telling him about Garvey's bail application right now and having another row. And besides that, I was hoping to find Gabriel on his own. I felt so on edge. My skin prickled with irritation and only Gabriel had the perfect way to soothe me.

I could hear a raised voice when I walked into the reception area, which was unmanned as usual — the pretence of a wholly legitimate business. As I reached the back office I could hear it was Gabriel's voice. He was shouting at someone. It took a second to realise he must be on the phone as I could only hear a one-sided conversation. I pushed open the door to let him know I was there. He was standing with his back to me.

'I will cut off your bollocks and stuff them down your throat, you cunt,' he bellowed. There was a pause and then he continued, 'Oh, really! Well, she belongs to me now. You fucking animal. You will never touch her again. Do you understand?'

My heart sank as I realised he was talking to Jackson, and I suspected not for the first time. He threw the phone onto the sofa and it bounced onto the floor.

'Fucking bastard!' He shouted so loud I thought the people in the next street must have heard him. He turned around and saw me standing in the doorway. The anger dissolved from his face.

'Sam,' he said.

'So I belong to you, do I, Gabe?' I asked.

He walked over to me, reaching out his arms he went to pull me to him but obviously changed his mind and let them drop to his side instead. 'I didn't mean... It was just... He's a fucking psychopath.'

'Jackson?' I said.

He nodded.

'Is this the first time he's phoned you?'

'No. He phoned last week too. I was going to tell you but you were so busy with work and then the timing just never seemed quite right.'

I nodded. I didn't want to know what Jackson had said to him. I could imagine. I had known it wouldn't be long before he found out about us. And I couldn't help feeling that it had sounded the death knell for our relationship. It made me want to burst out crying. Why couldn't Jackson just let me go? Hadn't he taken enough of me already?

'I'm sorry, Sam. For what I said to him. But he-'

'Got under your skin? Pushed your buttons?' I interrupted him. 'That's what he does, Gabe. It's like his super-power.'

Gabriel sat on the sofa in his office with his head in his hands. I couldn't help but want to make him feel better. I, of all people, knew how skilled Jackson was at finding the most vulnerable part of you, and exploiting it. It made me feel sad and happy at the same time, to know that I was Gabriel's weak spot.

I walked over and stood in front of him. Then I slipped off my black lace thong and placed it on the sofa beside him. He looked up at me as though I'd lost my mind.

'Is this what you need, Gabe?' I asked as I hitched up my skirt and straddled him. 'Then take it. I'm all yours.'

'Sam. You don't have to...' he groaned as I unzipped his fly.

I pulled out his hot, stiff cock and squeezed it in my hand. 'Put your hands behind your head,' I commanded. 'And don't move them unless I say so.'

He looked up at me, but did as I told him to and I held onto his muscular shoulders. His biceps bulged in his suit jacket. I looked into his eyes as I slid myself down onto him. As always, I was ready for him and I took him inside me easily, right to the hilt. I could see his eyes burning into mine. I saw the pain there. I saw the struggle. Nobody ever told him what to do.

I moved my hips up and down, riding his cock as he groaned, keeping his hands behind his head as I'd instructed. 'Is this what you want, Gabe? To own me? To claim me? Then why don't you do it?'

He flipped me beneath him in one swift movement and then he started to pound me into the sofa as though his life depended on it. He pulled my blouse open, causing the buttons to pop off and skitter across his office. Pulling my bra down, he allowed my nipple to pop out and sucked it between his teeth, making me cry out. He continued sucking as he reached between us and rubbed that sweet spot until we both climaxed. When he was done, he brushed my hair from my face with his hand. I could feel the dampness of my arousal on his fingertips.

'I fucking love you, Sam.'

'Don't you mean you love fucking me?' I teased.

'I do love fucking you, yes. I love to make you come. I love to make you moan and whimper and scream my name. But more than any of that, Sam, I love you. You are without a doubt the best thing that's ever happened to me. I'm going to fuck up sometimes. But, please can you try a different way of handling it other than pushing me away or running?'

I looked up at him. 'Okay. Any suggestions?' I asked with a flash of my eyebrows. 'Maybe I could resort to the way you and my father resolve disagreements and punch you in the face?'

'Hmm? I think I'd prefer that,' he grinned at me.

'Okay. Or I could refuse you sex?'

'Nope. That's impossible,' he growled.

'Is that so?'

'Yes. And you know it is. I only have to touch you and you're ready to come. Even talking dirty to you makes you soaking wet,' he grinned.

'All that is true, yes. You are a sex God among men, Gabriel Sullivan.'

He kissed me again, almost taking my breath away.

58. SAMANTHA

The letter looked innocuous enough when it had arrived in my in-tray that morning. I opened it as I did any other and unfurled the neatly folded page. I read the first three sentences before I had to stop, my hands shaking as I put it back down on the desk. I hadn't heard from Mr Garvey since he'd applied for, and been granted, bail six days earlier. I had hoped that his bail conditions would be enough to prevent him from contacting me, but it seemed he was back to his old tricks. Although this letter was altogether more sinister — and specific. Most concerning of all was that he mentioned the pink blouse I'd been wearing the other day. It was new so he couldn't have seen it before. I looked around me instinctively, even though I knew I was the only person in my office. A shiver ran down the length of my spine. That feeling of being watched was not a new one to me, but it was one I had hoped I'd never experience again.

I phoned DS Phillips, and he told me he'd stop by to pick up the letter as soon as he could. I realised I'd have to tell Nick and the rest of the team so they could be on alert. I groaned inwardly as I realised I'd have to tell my father and Gabriel too. God, they weren't going to let me move — but maybe that was a good thing?

I was starting to realise that having them to watch out for me might not be such a headache after all. Anthony Garvey was starting to terrify me. The sooner the police picked him up again, the happier I would be. I had already spoken to one of my contacts in my old firm to see if I could get a legal visit set up to speak to Jackson in prison. If I couldn't, I'd have to ask him to send me a Visiting Order himself, and I could only imagine how much the arrogant prick would love that. But I needed to get to the bottom of what was going on sooner rather than later.

I'd phoned Gabriel shortly after Detective Phillips left and half an hour later, he was standing in my office. He walked over to my desk and pulled me up into his arms.

'Are you okay, Sam?' He asked as his eyes scanned my face.'

'Yes,' I said and then I realised that was a blatant lie. 'No, not really,' I added.

He wrapped his large arms around me and kissed the top of my head. 'Where is the letter?'

'The police have taken it.'

'What did it say?'

I told him what I could recall. He listened intently, his face set in a grimace. His jaw working, the way it did when he was trying to maintain control of his temper. He scowled when I'd finished speaking. 'When I get my hands on him ...'

'He's not worth it, Gabe. Let the police handle it.'

He cupped my face in his hands. 'I won't let him hurt you, Sam. I promise.'

'I know that. You're going to be a nightmare now though, aren't you?' I said with a smile.

He nodded. 'Yes, I will, and you'll just have to do as you're told. We'll have to tell your dad too, you know?'

I buried my face in his chest and groaned. 'Let's tell him tomorrow. I feel like going home for the day. Come with me?'

He kissed my forehead. 'Of course. I'm not letting you out of my sight.'

. . .

When we got to my apartment, Gabriel poured us each a glass of wine and we lay on the sofa together watching *Casablanca*.

'I don't know what I'd do if he hurt you, Sam,' he suddenly said, his voice thick with emotion.

'Well, I hope you'll never have to find out. The police will catch up with him. They deal with people like him all the time.'

'Well they better had, because if I do ...'

I kissed him before he could finish his sentence. I didn't want to think about Anthony Garvey.

'Why don't we do something to take our minds off that lunatic? I don't want to think about anything,' I whispered in his ear. He didn't need much encouragement and he started unzipping my skirt before I'd even finished my sentence. Soon enough, I was naked and lying beneath him while he remained fully clothed. I started to undress him and he stopped me.

'Kneel on the floor and bend over the sofa,' he ordered as he stood up.

I did as I was told. He took his tie from the coffee table and then used it to bind my wrists together behind my back. 'You're going to get fucked. Hard. Is that what you want?' he asked.

I nodded. It was. I loved how he always knew exactly what I needed.

After he'd nailed me to the sofa and made me beg to let me come, he untied my wrists and carried me to bed where he kissed every inch of my body. He told me how much he loved me. How much he wanted me. Then he fucked me slowly, gently rocking us both to a long rolling orgasm.

'I love you, Sam,' he whispered as I lay my head on his chest and drifted off to sleep.

CHAPTER 59

It had been a week since I'd received the letter from Anthony Garvey, but thankfully I'd heard nothing from him since. The sound of my office door opening made me look up from my computer screen.

'Gabe! This is a nice surprise.'

'Sadie told me you had a couple of hours with no appointments so I thought I'd take you out to lunch,' he said.

I looked at the pile of paperwork on my desk. I had so much to do, and spending far too much time with Gabriel was the reason why. But I could do with some fresh air, and I realised I was starving. I closed my laptop and grabbed my coat.

We walked to a coffee shop near my office and managed to snag a table by the window. Gabriel was at the counter ordering for us when I heard someone call my name. Gabriel heard too and he looked over. I prayed he didn't notice the look of horror on my face when I realised who it was.

'Stanley,' I said as he approached me. I could feel the colour draining from my face as he stood there, leering at me. If the cafe wasn't so packed I would have stood up and walked out. But if I'd done that, I would have no choice but to brush past him, to touch him, and the thought of that made me want to vomit. He moved closer towards me, his heavy jowls wobbling as he did. His face shining through a sheen of perspiration as his glasses began to slide off his nose.

'Here on your own?' he asked, lips curling back over his yellowing teeth.

'No, she's not.' Gabriel's voice startled him.

Stanley turned around and I couldn't help but smile as he visibly flinched at the sight of Gabriel. A six foot two wall of solid muscle.

'Nice to see you, Samantha,' Stanley squeaked before trying to move through the crowd as quickly as his chubby legs would carry him. I could see his wife waiting in the queue for him, so there was no escape for him. He would have to wait with her, although I would bet, lecherous old Stanley would rather be making a very sharp exit.

'What's wrong?' Gabriel asked. 'You're as white as a sheet. Who is he?'

I shook my head. 'No-one. I'm fine.'

'Who is he, Sam?'

'He's an old friend of Jackson's,' I whispered and I saw the realisation dawn on his face that Stanley was one of the men from the house. His jaw clenched shut as he started to get up from his chair.

I grabbed his arm. 'Gabe. No. Please. Don't make a scene. These people are my colleagues. He's with his wife for God's sake,' I pleaded. The thought of him confronting Stanley, here, in front of all these people made me feel sick again. My heart was pounding in my ears.

'Then she should know what a fucking pervert she's married to,' he snarled. 'That he gets his rocks off raping women who are young enough to be his daughter.'

I felt my face flush bright red. 'Keep your voice down,' I hissed.

His face softened then. 'I'm sorry, Sam,' he said quietly. 'I won't say or do anything. But only because I don't want to embarrass you. Not that you should be embarrassed. He, on the other hand, should be fucking deeply ashamed. I can't believe he has the nerve to even look at you.'

Gabriel was true to his word and he didn't make a scene, although he glared at Stanley the whole time he was in the cafe. An already perspiring Stanley mopped his brow continuously, no doubt sweating from the heat of Gabriel's gaze.

60. SAMANTHA

To escape the drama of the Garvey situation, Gabriel and I discussed getting out of the city for a few days. We both needed a break. It had seemed like the perfect opportunity to take up his aunt Maggie on her offer of a visit. When I'd suggested it to Gabriel, he'd been thrilled at the idea.

Maggie and Hugh were standing on their large driveway as Gabriel's car pulled up to their house. Maggie pulled me into a hug as soon as I stepped out of the car and ushered me inside the house as Gabriel and Hugh got our bags from the boot.

'Samantha, I'm so pleased you're both here,' Maggie beamed. 'Gabriel hasn't visited us for years. You must be a good influence on him,' she said with a wink.

Gabriel walked in behind us and grabbed me by the waist before I could answer. 'She certainly is,' he smiled as he gave me a kiss on the cheek.

Maggie bustled us all into the kitchen where she had laid out a spread fit for a platoon of hungry soldiers. We spent the evening eating and drinking and laughing, mostly at Maggie and her stories about Gabriel when he was a small child.

By midnight Hugh could barely keep his eyes open and we all

decided to call it a night. Maggie showed us to the guest room which I noted was tastefully decorated, much like the rest of the house.

I changed into one of Gabriel's old t-shirts for bed while he pulled back the covers. The conversation had turned to him and Jennifer during the evening and Gabriel had done his best to change the subject each time it did. I managed to glean more information from Maggie about Gabriel's ex-wife when she had shown me around the garden. Maggie and Hugh had got on with her well enough, but they'd only met her on a few occasions as she had usually been busy whenever Maggie and Hugh had visited Gabriel in London.

I noticed that Gabriel had been quieter since the mention of Jennifer's name.

'Maggie told me you and Jennifer came here a couple of times,' I said as I climbed into bed beside him.

Gabriel shrugged in response.

'Did you have sex in this bed?' I asked.

He didn't even acknowledge that question and I knew that it was none of my business, but I was trying to provoke some reaction from him.

'Why don't you ever talk about her?' I asked.

'Why would I?'

'Because she's a big part of your past, and your life. That's why. I want to know about the two of you. How did you meet? How did you propose? What was she like, Gabe?'

'Why does any of that matter?'

'I don't understand why you won't talk to me about her.'

'Because she ripped my fucking heart out, Samantha,' he snapped.

I realised he wasn't going to talk to me and I turned on my side to face the huge bay window. Gabriel pushed his body up against mine, slipping his hand under my t-shirt and onto my bare skin.

'Don't touch me,' I said.

'You don't mean that, Sam.'

'Don't tell me what I mean.'

'Okay. Maybe what I should have said was I hope you don't mean that.'

'Well, that would make sense wouldn't it,' I turned to face him. 'Because as long as I let you touch me, then we're all right. Let's face it, Gabe, that's all we're about, isn't it?'

He sat up in bed. I saw the look of hurt flash across his face. 'Samantha, you know that's not true.'

'Do I? Because if you don't share your past with me, if you won't talk to me, then we are just about the sex, aren't we?'

'So, because I don't want to talk about my ex-wife, I'm only interested in you for sex? That's quite the leap, Sam. Even for you.'

'Even for me!' I snapped.

'Shall I tell you what you want to know then? I met Jennifer at a party. I thought she was gorgeous so I went over and started taking to her. For our first date, I took her to the cinema. I proposed while we were on holiday in Mexico. It was at sunset on the beach and I got down on one knee and proposed. It was fucking perfect. For our first anniversary, I took her back there. Did I fuck her in this bed? Yes, quite a few times, actually. What was she like? She was quiet and thoughtful. In the five years we were together she gave me less grief than you have in the last five months. Is that what you want to hear, Sam?'

I blinked at him. Why was he being so unreasonable? I had told him all about my past, as painful as it was, so why couldn't he do the same? I threw back the cover and climbed out of bed.

'Where are you going?' he said with a sigh.

'Away from you,' I snapped as I stomped out of the room.

I was sitting on the wooden patio furniture in Maggie and Hugh's garden, enjoying the silence, and wondering how on earth I had managed to get into another epic row with Gabriel when I heard the door opening behind me. Gabriel walked out onto the decking in his bare feet before placing two glass tumblers on the table. Then he poured us each a glass of Hugh's finest Scotch.

Gabriel sat on the chair nearest to me and ran a hand though his hair before picking up his glass and taking a large gulp of the golden liquid.

'She was seeing him for six months behind my back. Six fucking months and I had no clue. I was working away and I decided to surprise her so I came home a day early. I found them in bed together, although I heard them first. After I threw him out, she started crying and told me I'd neglected her. I called her some horrible names, and then I threw her out too,' he said as he finished off the last of the whisky.

He looked at me. 'I've never told anyone that before. I didn't even tell your dad the detail. I don't talk about it. Not with anyone. It wasn't my finest hour.'

'Do you still love her, Gabe?'

'No. I love you, and only you. I can't believe you would ever doubt that.'

I blinked at him. 'I ...' I just couldn't say the words.

'You own me, Sam. Everything I am. Everything I have — is yours.'

He stood up and placed his empty glass onto the table. He held his hand out to me and I considered whether to take it. I was still angry with him. He expected openness and honesty from me, but when it came to his own past, he didn't give me the same in return. Part of me also hated that he had once loved someone else so much that she had broken his heart. But, the other part of me knew that he loved me, and I wanted to crawl into bed with him and let him make me feel the way that only he could. I took hold of his hand and noticed how warm it was, despite us being in the cold garden. I loved the feel of his rough skin on mine as his fingertips brushed my palm. He pulled me up from my seat and I followed him silently back to bed.

. . .

Once we were in the bedroom, Gabriel peeled off my t-shirt, his hands working quickly. Then he pushed me onto the bed, and silently removed my underwear before he stepped out of his shorts. He crawled onto the bed and held himself over me before trailing kisses from my jawline, along my throat, down my collarbone and onto my nipples. He sucked one into his mouth while he gently tugged at the other. I pushed my hips into him, grinding myself onto his already rock hard cock. He didn't stop me like he usually would, but after a few moments he moved to kiss my stomach, and then to where I wanted to feel his mouth on me the most. He licked the length of my cleft before settling his mouth over my clit, licking and sucking until I was thrusting my hips to meet his rhythm. When he pushed two of his fingers inside me, I moaned loudly. He made me come quickly, rubbing and sucking on those sweet spots. Then he wrapped my legs around his waist and fucked me — slowly. In and out. So, damn slowly. His lips didn't leave mine the whole time. When I came for him a second time, I groaned into his mouth and he responded by thrusting harder until he found his own relief.

He collapsed on top of me, but he didn't pull out of me as he whispered in my ear.

'I love you, Sam. I love you so much that sometimes it feels like I can hardly breathe.' He looked into my eyes and started to run his right hand down the length of my body, back to my throbbing clit, before he started to rub again. 'I will *never* get enough of your body. Sex will always be a big thing with us, but that doesn't mean that's all we are. That doesn't mean that's all I want from you.'

'I know, Gabe,' I whispered, hoarsely. I could barely focus with his maddening teasing of my over-sensitive flesh.

'Even though you drive me crazier than anyone I have ever known, and you push every single boundary I have, I would rather fight with you, than do anything, with anyone else. You do know that, don't you?'

'Yes,' I panted, desperate for another orgasm, the type that only he could provide.

'Shall I make you come again?' he growled.

'Please,' I whimpered and he obliged.

Gabriel and I lay in bed facing each other. I had my legs draped over his and he ran his warm hand up and down my back.

'Do I really give you that much grief, Gabe?' I asked.

'No, you don't. That was unfair of me.'

'I'm scared too, you know? At least you've done this before. This is all new to me. I've never had a healthy relationship. I've never been in love with anyone else.'

'And are you with me?' he asked.

'What do you think?' I said.

'You've never actually told me.'

I stared at him. It was true, I'd never told him that I loved him, even though I did. I had loved him for most of my life.

'Yes,' I whispered before pulling his face to mine for a kiss.

61. SAMANTHA

Gabriel and I had enjoyed a wonderful weekend with Maggie and Hugh and had driven back to London late the previous night. I stifled a yawn as Nick walked into the conference room of Donovan Cook and handed me a fresh mug of coffee. 'The next one looks suitably nervous, Samantha,' he said with a smile.

'Good. Nerves are good,' I replied. We had been interviewing all day for a new junior solicitor given that our workloads were becoming unmanageable for just the two of us. We'd also hired a new junior secretary the previous week to help Sadie out. We'd had plenty of applicants and had chosen to interview six of them. I was sure we'd get ourselves a good fit.

'Let's get him in and see what he's made of then, eh?' Nick said.

'Yep,' I nodded in agreement and Nick walked back to the open door and called the candidate inside.

Simon Hardaker strolled into the office trying his best to look cool and collected, but failing miserably. I could see his hands were shaking as he took his seat. I liked that he was nervous though, it showed that he cared about making a good impression. Nothing was more annoying than a newly qualified solicitor who thought they knew it all. I should know, I'd been one once.

Nick offered Simon a glass of water and we allowed him a minute to compose himself. He pushed a strand of blonde hair out of his eyes and I noticed how young he looked — or maybe I was just getting old?

Despite his nerves, Simon impressed both Nick and me. He seemed conscientious and had a good knowledge of the law. Most importantly though, he seemed to care about the work we did, and about the people we worked with. None of the other candidates impressed as much as he had. Nick and I argued over who got to give him the good news. We tossed a coin in the end and I won. Simon could barely contain his excitement and his disbelief when I'd phoned him.

'Thanks so much, Samantha. I can't wait. See you Monday.'

I was pleased with our new addition to the team, sure he would be a good fit.

Gabriel picked me up from work as usual. I slid into his warm car and kicked off my heels.

'My place or yours, beautiful?' he asked with a smile.

'Yours,' I said as I laid my head back against the warm leather seat. 'I feel like being waited on.'

He laughed. 'A take-away it is then. How did your interviews go?'

'Good. We've got a new guy starting next week.'

'A guy, eh? What's he like?'

'He's nice. He'll fit right in. He's smart, and friendly. He's very handsome too.'

'Very handsome? Is that so?'

'Yes, Sadie and Beth couldn't stop staring at him.'

'But not you?'

'Why would I stare at some young boy when I've got a gorgeous man like you waiting for me, Gabe?' I said with a grin.

He laughed. 'That's a good answer.'

'I aim to please.'

'You certainly do.'

I looked across as Gabriel and my heart fluttered in my chest.

There had been a time, when I was an awkward teenager, when I had dreamed about moments like these. But they had seemed so far out of my grasp. Gabriel had always been off limits. I had always assumed he was out of my league, and now here we were.

A couple.

In love.

The road we had taken to get here hadn't been an easy one, but for a moment I wondered if all my previous heartache had been worth it just to be right here, right now, with him. Suddenly, I didn't want to go home. I wanted to go out somewhere and act like a normal couple. I wanted people to look at this incredible man and know that he was mine.

'Forget the takeaway. Let's go out to eat. My treat,' I said.

He turned to me and smiled — that one that made my knees feel like jelly. 'Okay. Where to?'

'How about that new steak place that opened on the High Street?' I suggested.

'Deal. You want to go straight there?'

I checked my watch. 'Hmm. Do you think we can get a table?'

Gabriel laughed. 'Yeah. I know the owner.'

I rolled my eyes. 'Is there anyone in London that you don't know?'

'No,' he said as he looked at me. 'I have eyes everywhere, Sam. Remember that,' he said with a fake menacing growl that made me laugh out loud.

Gabriel and I had finished our meal. The waitress had just brought over the dessert menu when I saw the change in Gabriel's face. He was looking at the door.

'What the fuck is that prick doing in here?' he mumbled.

'Who?' I turned in my seat to see a man walking towards the back of the restaurant. He looked about my dad's age. He was tall and stocky like my dad too. But his face was a mess, full of cuts and bruises, and he walked with a limp. A red-haired woman walked behind him. He caught Gabriel's eye and walked over to our table while the woman was shown to their table by a waiter.

'Evening,' he said curtly as he reached us.

'Evening. How's that eye?' Gabriel asked with the hint of a smile.

'Fine, thanks,' the man snapped at him. He had a black eye with a huge cut over it, and obviously that had something to do with Gabriel.

'I didn't know you ate in here. You know this is Turkish Mick's place?' Gabriel said.

'Me and Mick sorted our differences,' the other man replied. 'I hope that we've resolved ours now too?'

Gabriel nodded.

Then the man turned to me. 'Who is this lovely lady?'

'Samantha, meet Jimmy,' Gabriel replied.

'Not Samantha Donovan?' Jimmy laughed. 'Does Sebastian know you're fucking his daughter?' he leered at me as he said the word fucking and licked his lips. It felt obvious to me that his question had intended to make me feel uncomfortable.

I saw Gabriel's jaw clench and wondered whether Jimmy was about to get a cut over his other eye. I didn't want a scene in the restaurant though.

'Oh, of course he knows, Jimmy,' I replied with a smile. 'Although we tend to call it dating around my dad. You know because of that temper of his? But we do fuck a lot, don't we, honey? I mean *a lot*.' I beckoned Jimmy closer to me. 'Sometimes he makes me come so hard, I literally pass out,' I whispered and I saw Gabriel chuckling from the corner of my eye.

Jimmy shifted uncomfortably. 'Yeah, well, he's good at making people pass out, aren't you, Gabriel. I assume she knows all your dirty secrets? Even the ones you buried years ago?'

Gabriel's eyes blazed with fire and he clenched his fist on the table. 'Fuck off, Jimmy. Before I rip your fucking head off.' He made to stand up and Jimmy flinched before backing off and walking away.

'What the hell was that about?' I asked.

Gabriel shook his head and I could see his face still full of anger.

'Let's get out of here before I bury Jimmy too,' he said as he took four crisp fifty pound notes and left them on the table.

'This was supposed to be my treat. And I don't think our meal cost two hundred pounds, Gabe.'

He shrugged. 'Then that waitress will get a nice tip. Come on. Let's go.'

I'd been eyeing up the chocolate fondant for dessert, but it was clear that Gabriel wanted out of there. 'Okay,' I said as I stood up.

Gabriel had hardly spoken during the drive to back his house. Once we were back I showered and changed and he hadn't interrupted me once, which was so unlike him. I pulled on one of his t-shirts and walked downstairs. He was sitting on the sofa staring at a blank television.

'Who was that guy, Gabe?' I asked as I sat down next to him. 'And why has he got you so rattled?'

He turned to look at me. 'That was Jimmy Fenton,' he replied.

I remembered the name now and wondered how I hadn't put two and two together in the restaurant. 'The guy who's been giving you and my dad some trouble?' I asked.

'Yeah.'

'But I thought that was handled?'

'It is.'

This was like pulling teeth. Clearly something else was going on here. 'So, what was this secret he was referring to then?' I asked. I'd hoped he'd explain of his own volition, but clearly he needed a nudge.

He lowered his eyes and shook his head. I had never seen him like this before. He was always so confident and sure of himself. Was this the thing that tormented him in his sleep? The demon that he'd once told me of?

I reached out my hand and stroked his cheek, 'Please, Gabe. Talk to me,' I said.

'If I tell you... I'm not sure I could stand the way you'd always look at me afterwards.'

'Well, you're just going to have to trust that I love you, and nothing will ever change that,' I said.

He looked up at me. 'You sure about that?'

I nodded. I was sure there was nothing Gabriel was capable of that could ever make me fall out of love with him. I knew the man he was. He might be my angel Gabriel but I wasn't naïve enough to think that to many who knew him, he was the devil in disguise.

He didn't look convinced though.

'Do you remember when I told you that I've never been in love with anyone else?'

He frowned at me. 'Yeah.'

'Well, that's true. But the reason that's true is because I've been in love with the same man since I was fourteen years old. And I can't imagine there is anything he could do that would change that.'

Gabriel took a breath, as though he'd been winded. 'Wow,' he said as he let the breath out. 'That man *is* me, right?'

'No. It's my dad's neighbour, Archie. Of course it's you,' I said with a laugh.

He smiled at me then. 'Well, I wish I'd known that before today.'

'Oh, come on. You knew. I used to practically drool whenever you were around.'

'You never drooled, Sam. You used to flirt with me. I knew you had a thing for me. But being in love is an entirely different thing.'

'Yeah. Tell me about it.'

'I came to see you before you left for uni, you know?' he said.

'No?' I didn't know that at all. I'd gone off to uni thinking that I'd made a massive fool of myself and that he'd never want to speak to me again.

He nodded. 'I wanted to say goodbye. And, I wanted to see you. I wanted to tell you that I would miss you and ... Well, I don't know what I was planning to do. But you'd left. Your dad said you were too excited to hang around.'

'Yeah. I told him that. But I was too embarrassed after what I'd done,' I said as my cheeks flushed pink.

'You never have to be embarrassed about anything in front of me, Sam. I love you.'

I smiled at him as he realised our conversation had now come full circle. 'And I love you. So? Talk to me, Gabe.'

62. GABRIEL

I sat on my sofa staring at this incredible woman telling me that she'd been in love with me for eighteen years. I wondered how our lives might have been different if I had asked her to stay in Dagenham that night. No doubt, she would have resented me eventually. I wished I could have stopped all the awful shit that had happened to her. I wished I hadn't been so wrapped in up in my own ego and pride and reached out to her. But despite all of that, in some ways I would change nothing. Because sitting here with her now, I knew that this was exactly where I was supposed to be and I wouldn't change it for anything.

And now I was about to tell her who I really was. This was the thing that still sometimes kept me awake at night. I took hold of her hand and she sat staring at me intently while I told her all about Calvin Stewart. He wasn't the only man I've ever killed, but he was the first. He was the only man I'd never meant to kill and the only one who hadn't deserved it. I call him a man, but he was no more than a boy. Just seventeen.

I'd been a promising boxer when I was a teenager, but I'd had a shit manager and too many people had only seen pound signs in their eyes when they'd looked at me. By the time I was eighteen, I'd given up on my dreams of professional boxing and was fighting in illegal street fights instead. My manager had told me it would be easy money — the way to fund my pro career. Neither of which were true. The money was great, but it certainly wasn't easy. These fights were managed and run by a man named Alfie Cunningham, and Jimmy Fenton had organised them on Alfie's behalf. It had been lucrative for me, and my record was unbeaten.

Before long, me and my trainer had started hearing rumours about this wonder kid from Edinburgh – Calvin Stewart. Apparently, he was unbeatable. Hard as nails and crazy with it. He'd knocked out every opponent who'd faced him stone cold. But from what I'd heard, he'd never taken a good punch.

I'd been eager to fight him. The purse would be my biggest yet and the fight had been the only topic of conversation in our underground circles for weeks leading up to it.

The night of the fight came. I was pumped. Calvin was too. He looked strong and fit. They told me he was eighteen — perhaps they believed he was. We went into the ring and I fought the hardest two rounds of my life. This kid was fast and he was strong — a lethal combination. In round three I decided to go for it. I was sure if I could connect with his jaw, he'd be out. I went into round three feeling like a fucking lion. I missed his jaw and hit his temple instead. No big deal though. But Calvin dropped to the floor like a sack of spanners. His trainer ran over to him with the smelling salts while me and my trainer were celebrating the win. But something had gone wrong. Calvin wasn't coming round.

He was pronounced dead a few minutes later and that was when his trainer told the first aider that he was only seventeen. Everyone scattered into the wind, until the only people who were left were me, Jimmy Fenton, the kid's trainer and of course the dead kid. And I'd fucking killed him — in an illegal bare knuckle boxing match. I wasn't ready to go to prison. My trainer and my manager left me swinging in the wind. Luckily Jimmy Fenton needed Calvin's death covered up as much as I did. Alfie Cunningham wouldn't have the death of some kid ruining his lucrative side-line and he would hold Jimmy personally responsible if it did.

We buried Calvin's body in a deep hole in the middle of a forest near Cumbria and he was registered as a missing person. As far as I knew, his mother still held out hope that one day he would come back home again.

I sat back against the sofa and searched Samantha's face for a reaction. She held on tightly to my hand.

'Is this the secret Jimmy was referring to?'

I nodded.

'But, Gabe. It was an accident. It sounds like Calvin knew what he was getting into. And if he didn't then he was exploited by his trainer and Jimmy Fenton, but not you.'

'But his mother deserves to know that her son is never coming home. She deserves to have a grave to visit.'

Samantha took my face in her hands. 'You are a good man, Gabriel Sullivan. The fact that this still haunts you proves that. Don't you see? Jimmy Fenton is a piece of shit for using this to get to you. But uses it because he knows that you have something he doesn't — a conscience.'

I looked into her eyes and saw nothing there but love. This woman was incredible and I didn't know what the hell I'd done to deserve her devotion, but it made me feel like the luckiest guy on the fucking planet.

I reached for her waist and pulled her onto my lap so she was straddling me. 'I must have done something right in a previous life to deserve you.'

She smiled at me. 'You must have been a veritable Santa Claus,' she said and I pulled her to me and kissed her until I forgot about everything except her.

63. SAMANTHA

I'd just come back from court and was eating lunch at my desk when my office phone started to ring. 'Yes, Beth?' I answered.

'Samantha, there's a Mr Smith on the phone for you. Says he needs a solicitor. He asked for you personally.'

I checked the time on my watch. I had thirty minutes before my next client was due. 'Put him through,' I replied. I often had people asking for me. Nick did too. Personal recommendations generated a lot of business.

I heard the click as my receptionist, Beth hung up the phone.

'Hello, Samantha.' The voice was unmistakeable. It was cheery, almost sing-song. But I knew the coldness and the cruelty it disguised. The hairs on my skin stood on end. My breath caught in my throat and I felt my blood freeze in my veins.

'Hello, Jackson,' I whispered.

'It's so good to finally hear your voice, Samantha.' He laughed. 'Have you missed me?'

'What do you want?' I snapped.

'Well, to be honest, I'm very disappointed in you. I thought at least I'd taught you some class. I assumed you'd have a bit more respect for yourself than to start fucking that Neanderthal, Gabriel

Sullivan. You do know he thinks he's some sort of gangster? But you know what they say, you can take the girl out of Dagenham ...'

'Class?' I snapped. 'Gabriel has more class in his little toe than you do in your whole body, you spineless bastard.'

'Oh no! Please don't tell me you think you're in love with him, darling? For God's sake,' he started to laugh.

'Piss off,' I snapped.

I heard the change in his voice instantly. 'It's not love, Samantha. It's infatuation. Limerence, I believe they call it. Look it up. But trust me, you do *not* love him.'

'What would you know about love?' I hissed.

'I know enough. I know you are the only woman I have ever loved, Samantha, and I expect you to be waiting for me when I get out of here. Did you know my appeal is underway?'

'No,' I said as my heart almost leapt out of my throat. I hadn't heard that yet.

'Yes. I imagine I'll be out before you know it. So, I expect you to conduct yourself with some fucking decorum, because like it or not, you are still my wife.'

'No, I'm not!' I insisted.

'You think those divorce papers mean anything to me? I've let you have your fun and now it's time to remember who you are what I'm capable of, darling. You will stop seeing him, now! I tried to warn him off, but he's a stubborn little bastard, isn't he? Either that or he's plain stupid.'

'He's not-'

'Break it off now, Samantha. Or I will have the police and the tax man crawling up his arse, and your fucking father's too. I'm sure the pair of them have plenty of skeletons in their closets that they'd rather not have found. And if that doesn't work, I have plenty of other people at my disposal. To be blunt, darling, if you don't end it, I will end him.'

Jackson hung up the phone then without giving me a chance to argue or ask about his involvement with Anthony Garvey. Even though we were divorced, Jackson would never let me go. I should have argued my case with him though. I should have pleaded for mercy. But what would have been the point anyway? I had spent years pleading with the monster I'd been married to, and all it had ever served to do was to make him hurt me more. I knew he was more than capable of carrying out his threats. He had the connections, and the money, to see them through.

I wracked my brain for a way around my predicament. I didn't want to give up the best relationship I'd ever had. I was happier now than I had ever been in my life. Perhaps Gabriel and I could meet in secret? But I knew he would never accept that. And despite how careful we would be, Jackson would find out — it was what he did.

I sighed and rested my forehead on my cool desk. Hadn't I known all along that this would happen? That a life with Gabriel was just a dream, an illusion I could hold onto just for a little while. And it had been nice while it lasted — more than nice. But that was all it had ever been — an illusion. I was still Jackson Carver's property — no matter how hard I tried to escape him. That thought both saddened and terrified me in equal measure.

64. SAMANTHA

I took a cab to Gabriel's office before he arrived to pick me up. It would have been cruel to have him drive all the way over to take me home when I was going to send him away. Besides, I had to be the one to walk away, because if it had to be him, and he refused, I wasn't sure I'd have the strength to make him.

He looked up as I walked into his office. Then he smiled at me and it made my heart physically ache.

'Sam.' He stood up and walked over to me, trying to pull me into a hug but I backed away. 'What's wrong?' he said with a frown.

I had been rehearsing what to say all the way over there and each time the words became more difficult to say. And now standing in front of him, I wasn't sure if I could go through with it at all. Except that I had to. For both of our sakes. Jackson would never allow us to be together. One way or another, he would make sure we weren't.

'I've come to tell you it's over, Gabriel. I can't be with you anymore. It's too much. I feel suffocated. I just need to be on my own.'

'What?' he frowned as he stepped towards me.

I didn't respond. I stared at the floor.

'Look at me, Sam!' he growled.

I shook my head. I couldn't look at him. Because then he might see I was lying.

Taking hold of my arms, he said again. 'Look at me.'

I looked up at him. There were tears in my eyes. But I didn't cry. I never cried.

'You don't mean this. I know you don't. It's Jackson, isn't it? Has he got to you? I can protect us, Sam. Just trust me,' Gabriel pleaded.

I shook my head. I wanted to believe him. There was nothing I'd like more than to melt into his arms and tell him that I would never leave him, because he meant more to me than anything in this world. But it was for that very reason I had to. 'I do mean it, Gabriel. This isn't about Jackson. It's about me and you. This is all too much. I'm not ready for it. I don't want this.'

His face crumpled before my eyes. The anger that was there a moment ago replaced with a pain that I couldn't stand to see.

'But you love me, Sam,' he said.

'No. I don't,' I lied. 'I thought I did, but I was wrong. I'm incapable of love.'

He dropped his hands and I took my chance to walk away, out of his office and into the blazing heat of the sun. My heart felt like it had been torn from my chest and trampled by an elephant. But I still didn't cry. I was Samantha Donovan, and I never cried.

65. GABRIEL

I sat at my desk with my head in my hands. My heart raced in my chest and my blood thundered around my body. What the hell had just happened? I had just watched my whole world implode in front of me and there wasn't a single thing I could do about it.

Samantha had just stood right there in front of me and lied to my face. I had to believe she was lying, because the alternative was unthinkable.

Was this about what I told her about Calvin? Surely not? She hadn't had a problem with it. In fact, she had convinced me that leaving that poor kid's mother never knowing what had happened to her son didn't make a monster.

It had to be Jackson. It was the only explanation that I could comprehend, because it was the only explanation that meant she still loved me and the past six months with her hadn't been a complete lie.

I dialled Sebastian's number and he answered his phone on the second ring.

'What's up, buddy?' he asked.

'Remember when you said you'd like to get rid of that scumbag, Jackson Carver, once and for all?'

'Yeah? A year ago — and you talked me out of it. You convinced me that prison was the best punishment for him.'

'Yeah, well now I've changed my mind. We need to wipe him from the face of the earth, Seb. As soon as possible.'

'Why? What's happened? Is Sam okay?' he asked, the panic audible in his voice. 'Has something else happened?'

'Nothing like that. She's not in any danger. Look, I've just got to go and see someone. Meet me at the office later and I'll fill you in.'

'Okay. I'll see you later.'

I stood on the doorstep of the large terraced house as I waited for it to be answered. The light from inside illuminated the doorway when it finally opened.

'Hi, Nick,' I said to Samantha's best mate and business partner.

'Gabriel! What are you doing here? Is everything okay? Is Samantha?—'

'Can I come in?' I interrupted him. The doorstep wasn't the place for this type of conversation.

Nick opened the door wider and allowed me inside. Looking around, I noticed the toys strewn across the floor and piled up under the stairway as well as the empty dog dish by the stairs. It reminded me of a real family home, like the type I'd grown up in myself. Nick had two kids and a dog whom he shared custody of with his ex-wife, Mandy.

'Excuse the mess,' Nick smiled. 'Haven't had a chance to tidy up yet. Mandy only picked the kids up half an hour ago. Can I get you a drink?'

'A coffee would be good,' I replied.

I followed Nick out into the kitchen and watched as he took two mugs from a cupboard before filling the kettle.

'So what can I do for you, Gabriel?' he asked while we waited for the kettle to boil.

'I know you love Samantha,' I started

Nick blinked at me, looking taken aback at first but then he glared at me. 'Yes, I do. She's one of my oldest and closest friends.'

I smiled, realising Nick had misunderstood my intentions. I couldn't help but admire that he was standing up to me. Standing up for her. I suddenly saw why Samantha loved him too.

'I'm not accusing you of anything, Nick. I need your help, that's all.'

I told Nick about Jackson's phone call a few weeks earlier and how he'd threatened me and Samantha if we didn't stop seeing each other. Gritting my teeth, I also told Nick about Samantha's visit to my office earlier that day. It still killed me to think about it, let alone say the words out loud.

'So, I think maybe he's got to her too,' I sighed. 'You worked with him. You know what he's like. There must be someone out there who might have a grudge against him. There must be something we can use as leverage over this guy.'

'I don't think finding people with a grudge against him is going to be a problem, Gabriel. There's plenty of them. It's people who are willing to cross him that you'll struggle to find.'

I nodded. I understood keeping people in line through fear. 'I know that, but there must be something or someone out there, Nick. Can you at least try for me?'

Nick looked at me for a few moments, considering my request, before nodding. 'I'll do it — for Samantha. Because I watched that fucker destroy her and I couldn't do anything to stop him.'

Nick looked at the floor, as though he was ashamed of himself, and I could relate to that. Putting my hand on Nick's shoulder, I said. 'We all wish we could've stopped him. Maybe now we can?'

Nick nodded. 'What if you do this and she doesn't come back to you? What then?'

I swallowed. I'd thought about that question and the answer terrified me. 'I'll respect any decision she makes, as long as I know it's her decision and she's free to make it without that cunt holding anything over her.'

'Then I'll see what I can do,' Nick smiled at me.

. . .

I arrived at our offices of Archangel Securities to find Sebastian there waiting for me. Again, I relived that awful moment this afternoon when Samantha told me she was leaving me, although I spared her father the details. But I told him about my hunch that Jackson had got to her.

'I know I had my issues with you and Sam, Gabriel, but you were good for each other. And I'm sorry, mate. I know how much you love her,' he said as he put a reassuring hand on my shoulder. 'And I agree that we need to get rid of Jackson Carver once and for all.'

'Good,' I nodded, glad that I had him on board. 'So, we'll need a plan.'

It only took a few moments to realise that Sebastian's plan as usual, was to have no discernible plan at all, and go in all guns blazing.

'Let's just kill the fucker,' Sebastian said.

'How? He's inside for another six and a half years, or had you forgotten that?'

'It's never stopped anyone before,' Sebastian snapped. 'Obviously, we would need someone else to actually do the deed. But at least we know where he is.'

I shook my head. 'Jackson is too well connected with far too many people in his pockets. There's too much of a risk. He might get a sniff of a possible hit before it could be carried out. And if that happens, he'll be after us all especially Samantha. No, we have to be smart about this. Jackson is a ruthless cunt and he's bound to have some skeletons in his closet. He must have fucked over the wrong person at one time or other. And all we need to do is find out who.'

'How are we going to do that?'

'You're going to speak to our good friend DI Bullen, and ask him to dig around. And I've already spoken to Nick, he's known Jackson, and worked with him, for years. He's on board. Between us, we must be able to come up with something we can use.'

'What if Bullen's not interested?' Sebastian asked.

'If he isn't, remind him that I still have those photographs — and we'll be getting them sent straight to his wife. And the Chief Constable if he doesn't want to play ball!'

Sebastian nodded. 'Okay. I'll speak to him tomorrow.'

66. SAMANTHA

I couldn't help but fidget as I sat on the plastic chair. The waiting was unbearable and the heat in the large room was stifling. I had been to prison countless times before, having been a criminal defence solicitor for many years, but I had never been on a personal visit. I'd never had any reason to.

I looked up and shuddered as I saw him walking towards me. Despite his prison issue tracksuit and fluorescent vest, he still carried himself like the arrogant, entitled bastard he had always been.

Jackson Carver smiled as he slid into his seat, making my toes curl in my shoes.

'Samantha, darling. To what do I owe this considerable pleasure?' he smiled, baring his teeth.

'Hello, Jackson.'

He tilted his head to one side, appraising me. 'You're looking good, Samantha. Not as good as you used to, but good,' he leered at me.

'Look Jackson, I just came here to speak to you about the letters. About Garvey. I need to know if it's you.'

He frowned at me. 'What letters? Who is Garvey?'

'The threatening letters that have been coming to my office for the past eight months from Anthony Garvey. Him turning up at my office? I'm convinced he said he wasn't working alone. Was it you, Jackson? Are you behind any of it?'

He frowned at me. 'Samantha, I have absolutely no idea what you're on about.'

I studied him. He was an accomplished liar, but I'd been married to him for twelve long years and I knew him well enough to know when he was telling the truth.

'Tell me what's been going on,' Jackson said, his voice full of concern as he reached across the table to take my hand. I snatched it away, his touch like a jolt of electricity through my fingers. How dare he have the audacity to show concern for me, after everything that he had done.

'Tell me,' he repeated sternly.

In spite of myself, I told him all about the letters and Garvey's visit to my office a few months earlier. Jackson shook his head. 'Does that sound like my style, Samantha? Letting someone else have the pleasure of tormenting you? Do you think I would ever let anyone else hurt you?'

I glared at him, remembering all the times he'd done just that.

'That was different,' he said, waving his hand dismissively. 'I got to watch.' He winked at me and I had to fight the urge to slap his face. 'I can't have anyone hurting you while I'm in here, darling. I will be out soon.' He grinned, then, the terror and the threat implicit in his words.

'So, it was nothing to do with you?' I asked again, although I already knew the answer. The letters, paying someone like Garvey to clumsily harass me — it wasn't Jackson's style.

'Of course not.' He shook his head as though it was the most ludicrous suggestion in the world. 'But I'll find out who was responsible.'

'Why?' I frowned at him.

He glared at me. 'Because I love you. You know that.'

'I know nothing of the sort,' I snapped.

He scowled at me. If he wasn't sitting in a prison visiting room, serving time at Her Majesty's Pleasure, he would have slapped me across the face with the back of his hand for such a remark.

'I need to go,' I said as I stood up to leave.

'It was wonderful to see you, darling,' he said.

'I wish I could say the same about you,' I said as I started to walk away.

'Oh, Samantha,' he called after me.

Samantha spun on my heel. 'What?'

'I'm very pleased to hear you're no longer seeing that big ape. That's my good girl,' he grinned.

I swallowed the bile that rose in my throat and walked out of the visiting room.

67. SAMANTHA

I sat in Scott's car as he drove me to my office. Ever since I'd broken things off with Gabriel, my father had insisted that I allow Scott drive me to and from work every day. Anthony Garvey was still at large and as much as I hated to admit it, I had come to rely on the comfort and safety of having Scott around. Now that I knew Jackson didn't have anything to do with Garvey's threats, I was constantly on edge, wondering who else was out to get me.

'Your work routine makes you a sitting duck, Sam,' my father had told me. 'He knows your comings and goings and it's the perfect opportunity for him to act.' I had to agree, but I wouldn't give up my job. I wasn't going to put my life on hold any longer for some lunatic who wanted to control me.

'I've just got to nip in for some files,' I said after Scott picked me up from court. 'Do you mind stopping off there on the way?'

'Not at all,' he'd replied with a smile.

I let myself in through the office doors and was surprised to see the light on in Nick's office. He'd usually left by five on a Friday. I walked towards it to pop my head in and tell him to have a good weekend when I almost bumped into Gabriel as he was walking out.

My heart started hammering in my chest. He was wearing his

dark grey suit — and that belt. God, why did he have to look so bloody good?

'Gabriel?' I gasped. 'I'm sorry, I...'

'Hello, Samantha,' he said with a nod, but he didn't move out of my way. He stood in front of me, his eyes burning into mine. Six feet two of muscle and sex. He made my insides tremble just standing near me.

'What are you doing here?' I asked.

'Just some business,' he replied curtly.

'What business?' I demanded.

'It's personal,' he snapped.

I stood there, staring at him, drinking him in. It had been four weeks since I'd told him I didn't want to be with him anymore. I had missed him so much, and now he was there, right in front of me. I had to resist the urge to reach out and touch him. We stood like that for what felt like an eternity, staring at each other. Then he moved and I wondered if he was going to push me up against the wall and kiss me until I forgot about anyone but him. God, I hoped so.

But he didn't.

'Bye, Samantha,' he said gruffly as he walked out.

I turned and watched him leaving, wanting to shout his name and beg him to stay. I thought that if he only he would turn around and look at me, he would know, and then he would run back towards me and pull me into his arms. But he walked straight out of the door and into the street.

I walked into Nick's office. 'What the hell was Gabriel doing here?'

Nick looked at me in surprise. 'I thought you were at court all day?'

'I was. I had to call in for some papers,' I snapped.

'Oh, you're not working weekends again, Sam?' he said, his voice full of concern.

'It keeps me occupied. And you haven't answered my question.'

'And I can't. You know that. Client privilege.'

'So, Gabriel is your client now?'

Nick nodded.

'You could have at least warned me. I thought you were on my side?'

'I am, Samantha. I always am,' he frowned at me. 'What is going on with you? Talk to me.'

I shook my head. 'Nothing. Have a good weekend,' I said before I walked out of his office. I collected the papers from mine and left the building, feeling betrayed and alone.

68. GABRIEL

I stepped out into the street and let out the breath I'd been holding in since I'd seen her. Nick had promised me she wouldn't be there. We had been discussing his progress digging into Jackson Carver's past. It was the last thing I needed right now to bump into Samantha. I was trying to focus on getting the job done without thinking about her constantly. Then she'd walked in with her hair up and wearing one of those damn pencil skirts and all I could think of was marching her to her office and fucking her senseless.

I shook my head to clear it. I spotted Scott's car waiting outside and jogged over.

'You okay, mate?' I asked as I bent my head down to the driver's window.

'Sound, Boss,' Scott nodded.

'I hope she's not giving you too much grief?'

'Nope. She never does. It's probably not my place to ask, but is she okay?'

'What do you mean?' I asked, needing to know how she was doing.

'She just seems different?' he replied with a shrug.

'Just make sure you look after her,' I said as I placed a hand on Scott's shoulder.

'Of course, Boss,' Scott replied.

I jogged over the road to my car, eager to leave before I bumped into Samantha again. Part of me wanted to run back into her office and forcibly carry her out of there, take her home and make her realise that we belonged together. I could feel the anger welling up inside my chest.

I needed a drink.

Two hours later, I was sitting in a dark booth in the nightclub Sebastian and I had recently bought. It was only eight o'clock and the place was quiet. I looked at the almost empty bottle of whisky on the table in front of me. It had been full when I sat down.

I put my head in my hands. The whisky hadn't helped at all. In fact, it had only made me angrier. I was angry at everyone, including Samantha. Why couldn't she trust that I could keep her safe? Why couldn't she just let me protect her, instead of insisting on her one woman crusade to prove to the world she didn't need looking after? My blood felt like it was boiling beneath my skin. I needed some fucking relief and I needed it soon.

I wondered if I was imagining things when I heard a soft female voice beside me. 'I thought that was you, Gabriel. Are you okay?'

I looked up. 'Jennifer?' I frowned. Of all the people to run into when I was at my lowest ebb, it had to be my cheating ex-wife. She had spent a year begging me to take her back after I'd thrown her out. I suspected she missed my money more than anything else. But I hadn't seen her in three years. 'What the hell are you doing here?' I slurred.

'I was just out for a drink with the girls after work,' she replied with a shrug. 'I thought I saw you sitting here.'

'Well, now you know it's me. You can go back to your friends,' I snapped.

She sat down in the booth opposite me. 'You look like you could use some company,' she smiled sweetly. 'Or something else?' she purred.

My head was spinning and I needed some air. I needed… something. Jennifer looked at me intently. What did she just say? Suddenly a memory of her giving me a blowjob in a nightclub toilet popped into my head. I wondered if she was still any good at those.

'Is there anything you need, Gabriel? Anything at all I can do,' she reached over and squeezed my hand.

'Actually, there is something?' I stood up. 'Come with me.'

I held out my hand and she took it. I led us across the dance floor to the disabled toilet. My bouncers averted their eyes as I walked inside. Ordinarily they would stop anyone who looked like they were going in there for a hook up. But I was their boss, and it was my club. There wasn't much they could say.

Jennifer followed me inside willingly. I consoled myself with the fact that she knew exactly what my intentions were. I had every right to use her body after what she'd done to me.

I closed the door behind us and she pushed herself up against me. 'I've missed you so much,' she breathed in my ear. 'Nobody fucks me like you, Gabriel.'

I pushed her backwards. Maybe she should have thought about that before she fucked someone else while we were married?

'We can't fuck. I don't have a condom,' I growled. I was looking for some quick head and nothing more.

She smiled at me. 'You haven't been in a nightclub toilet for a while then?' she said as she indicated the wall behind me. I turned to see the condom dispensing machine. Fucking hell, it was like we were inviting people to have sex in here. But right now, it seemed like it would serve a purpose.

I pulled some notes out of my pocket and she frowned. 'You need change. Here,' she said as she pulled a few pound coins from her handbag.

I put them in the machine and pulled the lever and a box of condoms popped out of the bottom drawer. I handed them to her. She used her teeth to tear open the plastic wrapping while I unfastened my belt.

When she'd opened the box, she pulled out a condom and

handed the foil wrapper to me. Then she wrapped her hands around my neck and started to kiss me. I didn't want to kiss her. I just wanted to shoot my load inside her and go home to bed. But, I was a gentleman, wasn't I?

I pushed her backwards towards the toilet, lifting her onto the wooden ledge behind the cistern. She pulled down my zip and pulled my stiff cock out of my pants and squeezed until I groaned. I tore open the foil wrapper with my teeth and rolled the rubber over my cock. Pushing her skirt up, I pulled her underwear to one side and pushed myself inside her. She groaned as she held onto my neck. 'God, Gabriel, you feel so good,' she breathed in my ear.

I closed my eyes. This was so fucking wrong. But I was committed now. No point holding back. I put my arms either side of her, pressing my hands against the wall as I fucked her against it. I pulled out as soon as I'd come, staggering backwards. I stared at her. She wasn't Samantha. Not even close. She smiled at me as she slipped down off the ledge and straightened her skirt. I grabbed her hand and pulled her out of the way as I bent forward and puked my guts up into the toilet bowl.

Standing up, I wiped my mouth with the back of my hand.

Shit! What the fuck had I just done?

I could hear my mobile phone ringing on the bedside table beside me. I sat up and groaned. My head felt like it had been hit with a sledgehammer and my temples throbbed. I tried to swallow but my mouth was completely devoid of saliva. I glanced at the screen and saw it was Sebastian calling. I turned the phone onto silent and lay back down against the pillows. I would call him back later. I couldn't face talking to him now. I couldn't face anyone. I winced as I remembered my monumental fuck-up last night.

What the hell had I been thinking? A quick fuck in a nightclub toilet with a woman I could barely stand just to relieve some tension. It was bad enough that I'd gone anywhere near another woman —

but Jennifer! If Samantha found out she would be fucking furious — and heartbroken. Wouldn't she?

Samantha and I weren't together, so why did it still feel like I'd cheated on her? Why did I feel sick to my stomach when I thought about the possibility of her finding out? I felt the bile burning against the back of my throat and swallowed it down.

After I'd thrown up in the toilet last night, I'd told Jennifer that I'd made a huge mistake and that I never wanted to see her again. She'd ran out of the toilet in tears, but hopefully, she got the message.

I should just forget that it ever happened. And the best way I could think of doing that was to throw myself into my work — specifically my work to end Jackson Carver.

69. SAMANTHA

I watched my father as he sat opposite me playing with the hole punch on my desk.

'You looking forward to tonight then?' I asked him. He looked nervous.

He nodded. 'You'll be there, won't you? At eight on the dot?'

'Of course I will. But I don't understand why you're nervous about it. Isn't this engagement number five now, Dad? I'm sure you just do it for the parties,' I said with a smile.

'Not this time. Kayleigh is the one. This time I'll make it up the aisle, I promise,' he said as he flashed me one of his winning smiles right back.

I highly doubted that. My father, as much as I loved him, seemed to have an innate inability to remain monogamous, resulting in four previous failed engagements.

'Will Gabriel be there too?' I asked, despite knowing the answer to the question.

'Of course he will be, Sam. He's my best mate. Is that going to be a problem?'

'No,' I said defensively.

'Good. Because you both promised me things wouldn't get weird if you two didn't work out. We're all adults, you said.'

'It's not weird,' I replied a little too quickly. 'I was just asking. Is he bringing a date?'

'I don't know. Why? Are you?'

'Probably,' I replied with a shrug, although it was a blatant lie. But I didn't want my father to tell Gabriel I was likely spending my nights home alone, reading Mills and Boon and pining away — which I was of course, minus the Mills and Boon.

I smoothed my dress over my thighs as I stood outside the function room. It was a short black halter. Part of me was dreading having to face Gabriel, but the other part of me was desperate to see him. I pushed open the doors to the club and was greeted immediately by my father and Kayleigh. I liked Kayleigh and I hoped my dad didn't mess this one up. After I had congratulated the happy couple, I went to the bar to get a drink.

I was sipping my Jack Daniels and Coke when I saw Gabriel walking through the door, with a tall, beautiful blonde on his arm. I took a deep breath. I felt like I had been punched in the stomach. How could he do be so cruel? Was he deliberately trying to hurt me? It had only been six weeks since we'd broken up.

It was a small function room and as hard as I tried, I was unable to avoid Gabriel and his hot new girlfriend for the whole night.

'Hello, Gabriel,' I said as I eventually came face to face with him.

'Hello,' he replied coolly. His blonde date hung onto his arm, smiling widely. 'Samantha, this is Fiona,' he said. 'Fiona, Samantha is Sebastian's daughter.'

'Oh, Samantha,' she shrieked. 'I've heard so much about you.'

I smiled. Obviously not everything.

'Why don't I get us some drinks?' Gabriel said.

'Oh yes please. What are you drinking, Samantha?' Fiona asked.

'Jack Daniels and coke,' I replied.

Fiona wrinkled her nose. 'Oh, I can't abide spirits. Prosecco for me.'

Five minutes later I was desperately trying to drown out the sound of Fiona's inane chatter when Gabriel handed us our drinks.

'Your Jack Daniels,' he said to me and I swore I saw a twinkle in his eye. I blushed, recalling our weekend at the remote cottage when he had made ice cubes from the same drink and tortured me with them. Unable to stand being near the two of them for a moment longer, I excused myself.

I spent the next hour listening to Kayleigh's cousin talking about the merits of going vegan and began to wonder why on earth I had worn one of my best dresses for this. I stole glances at Gabriel and Fiona when I could and was annoyed to see him looking like he was enjoying himself.

I finally decided I'd had enough small talk and made my apologies to my father and Kayleigh, telling them I wasn't feeling well. I told a further lie and told my dad I had a taxi outside and left. I wanted to walk for a while and enjoy some fresh air.

I wrapped my coat around myself as I strolled down the busy street, full of couples and friends enjoying an evening out. Suddenly I felt incredibly alone.

'Samantha! Wait.' I heard someone calling behind me.

I spun around to see Gabriel running after me.

He grabbed hold of my arm as he reached me. 'What are you doing walking home by yourself?'

I wrenched my arm from his grip. 'What do you think you're doing? Get your hands off me.'

'You told your father you were getting a cab, and here you are wandering about alone. You know that psycho's still out here. How could you be so stupid?'

'Stupid? Me? Do me a favour, Gabriel and fuck off back to Fiona,' I snapped as I turned away from him.

He grabbed my arm again and pulled me into the doorway of the shop we were standing in front of. 'You drive me fucking crazy, do you know that?' he growled as he pushed me against the wall.

He started to kiss me, his mouth clashing with mine. I tried to push him away but he was too strong. I bit his lip but he remained undeterred. Then his hands were inside my coat, on my hips, pulling me to him. I could feel his erection pushing against me and the fight left my body. I wanted him so much. I kissed him back and he groaned into my mouth.

'Come home with me?' he pleaded.

'What about Fiona?'

'She's gone home. Your father knows her. She is no-one to me. I swear.'

I kissed him again, melting into him like hot wax. He pulled me back out onto the street and hailed a passing taxi cab. Once inside we continued kissing on the back seat, rubbing our hands over each other's bodies. The cab driver made a comment about us getting a room but neither of us cared.

When we reached Gabriel's house, we were barely inside the door before he had my dress up and off over my head. He pushed me against the wall so I had the cool plaster against my back, and the heat of a determined Gabriel at my front. He dropped to his knees and started to lick and suck at my tender flesh. His fingers and his tongue working me into a frenzy. He was urgent and fervent, lacking his usual finesse.

'God, Sam. I've missed you so much. You taste so fucking good,' he growled.

The vibration of his growling against my hyper sensitive clit had me climaxing around his fingers and shouting his name.

Then he was standing again, pushing his body against mine and whispering in my ear. 'I'm going to take you to bed and fuck you all night, Sam. I'm going to bury myself inside you. I'll make you come so hard...'

He trailed off as we stumbled up the stairs, his mouth never leaving my body. I returned his ardent passion with my own. I craved his touch, his taste. I felt empty without him. My body physically ached for him. He pushed me through the door to his bedroom and down onto the bed.

He pulled my hands above my head. 'Don't move them, Sam,' he growled. 'Or I'll tie you up.'

'Then you'd better tie me up, Gabe. Because there is no way I'm going to be able to keep my hands off you.'

He groaned. 'God, you are so fucking sexy. I'll leave your hands free then. I love the way you claw at my skin when you're desperate to come.'

Gabriel was true to his word. He fucked me over and over again until I was hoarse from screaming his name. And he made me come so many times I lost count, with his fingers, his mouth and his magnificent cock.

The light was breaking through the blinds when I woke the following morning, tangled in Gabriel's arms and legs. My limbs ached from the previous night's endeavours, in a way they hadn't done for weeks. I tried to extract myself without waking him, but failed spectacularly. He draped one of his muscular arms over me and pulled me back to him.

'Gabriel,' I started, and I knew he could tell from the tone of my voice.

'Don't say it, Sam.'

'Last night doesn't change anything, Gabe. I have to go.'

He moved his arm and let me get out of bed. He didn't say anything else and I was glad, because if he'd tried to make me stay, I just might have. It broke my heart to leave him again — but it was better for both of us. He deserved someone better than me. Someone who could give him everything he deserved and love him the way he needed to be loved. Not some broken shell of a woman who didn't know how to be in a healthy relationship. And I needed to be on my own. As much as I missed him, I knew that I was better off alone.

70. SAMANTHA

I sat on my sofa and stared at the piece of pink and white plastic in my hands.

Two blue lines.

Holy shit!

What the hell was I going to do? What was Gabriel going to say? Oh, dear God, what would Jackson say? What would he do? Although I already knew the answer to the last question — he would kill me!

I had been feeling nauseous for a little over a week, but I had put it down to stress. I hadn't even registered that I'd missed my period until Sadie had been complaining about menstrual cramps the day before. By my calculations, I was about five weeks. The night of my father's engagement party. How could I have been so stupid? I had been on the pill while Gabriel and I had been together, but had only taken it sporadically since we'd split up. Taking that little yellow pill every morning was just another reminder that I didn't have him in my life. And now I would probably always have him in my life — or at least a part of him.

I had no idea how I felt about that. I thought about my beautiful Alice and my heart felt like it was going to break in two. I had always wanted to be a mother, but I had lost my one and only chance when

I'd lost Alice – at least I thought I had. And now I was pregnant, and not with Jackson's baby, a man I despised and who would have been a terrible father, but with Gabriel's. I felt the sob catch in my throat.

The realisation that I was having a baby, Gabriel's baby, started to sink in and despite the circumstances, I felt a sudden rush of happiness. Even if Gabriel wanted nothing to do with me or our baby, we would be okay. Providing I could escape my ex-husband.

I sat in my dad's kitchen and stared out of the patio doors into the garden while I waited for him to come back from the corner shop. It had been a week since I had found out I was pregnant. I'd gone to the doctor's that morning and she had confirmed I was six weeks. Every day since I'd found out, I had picked up the phone to call Gabriel, but I could never quite manage it. Last time I'd seen him I'd been leaving him again, after he'd spent the night inside me, telling me how much he loved me. I remembered the look in his eyes when I'd left, and I wouldn't blame him if he never wanted to speak to me again. Besides all that, I was still just getting used to the idea of being pregnant myself and wasn't sure I was ready to have him sharing that experience with me. That was if he even wanted to share it. I had no idea if he wanted children. He had never mentioned them — although neither had I.

I wondered what type of father Gabriel would be. Would he be strict or would our child have him wrapped around their little finger? Would he rock them to sleep and change nappies? I realised I was smiling as I heard the front door opening.

'Seb?' I heard a familiar voice shout and my stomach flipped over. My dad had obviously left the door unlocked and Gabriel had let himself in.

I heard him walking towards the kitchen and I briefly contemplated making a run for the patio doors. A few seconds later he walked into the kitchen. 'Seb?' he said again and then he saw me sitting by the table instead and took a step back, as though the sight of me had physically winded him. I tried not to be too offended as I looked him over. He was wearing his grey suit — and that belt! God, why did he have to look so damn fine all the time. Couldn't he just once turn up looking as rough as I felt?

'He's just gone to the shop. He'll be back in a minute,' I said.

He opened his mouth to speak but then obviously thought better of it and just nodded instead. We looked at each other and I pulled at the sleeve of my tatty old cardigan, wishing I had worn something a little more alluring.

'I'll just wait outside for him,' Gabriel said.

'Fine,' I snapped and turned back to the table. Now he couldn't even stand to be in the same room as me. How the hell was I going to tell him I was pregnant?

He started to walk out of the room but then he turned around again. 'Are you okay?' he asked.

'Yes. Why?'

'You just look... a bit run down, that's all?'

'Run down?' I snapped, my eyes narrowed as I scowled at him. What the hell! I was carrying his bloody baby and had almost constant morning sickness, and he judges me for being a bit run down.

'I didn't mean,' he said with a sigh. 'You look off colour, that's all. Are you feeling okay?'

'Yes,' I lied.

He rolled his eyes and went to fill the kettle. 'Let me make you a coffee.'

'I don't want a coffee,' I said. I had read that too much caffeine was potentially harmful and given my history, I didn't want to take any chances and had switched to decaf. He placed the kettle on the counter and I heard him sigh.

'I'll have a peppermint tea if you're making a drink though?' I offered.

He nodded and switched the kettle on before opening the cupboard and taking out the box of teabags. His knowledge of my father's kitchen only reminded me of the closeness between the two of them and I felt an acute pang of sadness that I couldn't be a part of that anymore.

'You sure you're okay?' he asked again.

I had been wondering how to tell him about my pregnancy since I'd found out, and this seemed like as good as an opportunity as any. I took a deep breath. 'Actually, I'm glad you're here. I want to speak to you about something,' I said.

He walked towards me. 'Okay?'

Just then, with impeccable timing, my father walked back into the house. 'Not a bloody hob-nob to be found in that damn shop,' he shouted as he walked down the hallway.

'It's okay. It doesn't matter,' I said to Gabriel as I shook my head.

He frowned at me but then my father walked into the room.

'Gabriel,' he said as he eyed him suspiciously, which raised my hackles immediately. 'What are you doing here?'

'I need to speak to you,' he said.

My father nodded and glanced sideways at me.

'I'm going anyway,' I said as I stood up. 'I forgot I have some work to catch up on.'

'Sam, you don't need to go,' my father said. 'Just give me five minutes with Gabriel, and we'll have that brew. I bought custard creams,' he said as he held the packed of biscuits aloft triumphantly.

'Custard creams? Come on, Dad. They're no substitute for hobnobs, now are they?' I laughed as I gave him a kiss on the cheek.

'She's right there, mate,' Gabriel agreed.

'But, I love custard creams,' my dad replied.

'I'll call you later,' I said to him.

'Okay. Bye, love.'

I walked out of the door and left the pair of them to their dodgy business dealings.

71. GABRIEL

I walked through the reception area of my office.

'I'm going to be on an important call from ten o'clock,' I said to our newest employee, Stuart. 'I don't want to be disturbed.'

I had a call with Graham Johnson scheduled. His daughter Robyn was primed to take over from him, but we had some unfinished business to take care of first. We were drawing up plans for the security for the site of the hotel he was building in Liverpool. I had learned that Graham wasn't quite as clean cut as his LinkedIn profile made him out to be. He was a shrewd businessman, but Graham had made his way to the top of his game via any means possible, and that included paying off council officials, bribery and extortion. He wasn't averse to getting his hands dirty to get what he wanted, and that suited me down to the ground, because neither was I.

I walked into my office and fired up my laptop. A few moments later, I connected to Skype and saw Graham's face filling the screen.

'Good morning, Gabriel,' he said with a wide smile. 'How are you?'

'I've been better, Graham. How are you?'

He laughed. 'I'm good, and I'm sure you'll feel better when I tell you about what happened to our mutual friend, Mr Garvey.'

I leaned closer to my laptop. This was interesting. 'Oh?' I said and just then the door to my office opened. I looked up to see Stuart popping his head through. 'What the fuck did I just tell you?' I barked at him.

'Sorry, Boss,' he said and disappeared again.

'Jesus Christ,' I shook my head and Graham started to laugh again.

'You just can't get the staff these days, mate,' he said.

I nodded. 'So, tell me about our friend then.'

'He went for a walk last night and fell off the top of an eight-storey car park.'

'He fell off?' I asked with a flash of my eyebrows.

'With a little help,' Graham grinned at me.

'I thought you were just going to find out where he was for me?' I asked with a shake of my head.

'I did. And then my Robyn told me what kind of man he is, she's always googling people, and so I asked Howie to have a chat with him.'

'Oh?' Howie was Graham's longest serving employee and his own personal protection detail. 'So how did a chat end up with him falling off a roof?'

Graham sucked the air through his teeth. 'Well, it seemed he gave our Howie a bit of lip. They had a scuffle, he fell. End of. No CCTV. Police have it down as an accident. I thought you'd be pleased?'

I shrugged. I most definitely was pleased, but I didn't want Graham Johnson thinking he'd done me some massive favour. We got on well together and I sensed I could trust him, but I didn't know him well enough yet. 'Makes no difference to me if he's alive or dead.'

Graham nodded. 'Good. Now let's get down to some business.'

An hour later, I turned off my laptop and leaned back in my chair. I checked my watch and realised I had a meeting with Nick in half an hour. Grabbing my coat off the back of my chair, I stood up and walked out of my office. Stuart looked up as I walked into the reception.

'Next time I tell you not to disturb me, don't,' I snapped at him.

'Sorry, Boss, but-'

'I don't give a shit why you did it. Don't ever let it happen again.'

He nodded and I walked out of the office. I didn't want to be late for my meeting with Nick at O'Malley's. He was still digging into Jackson for me but we couldn't meet in his office any longer in case Samantha saw us. I felt a tightening in my chest as I thought about her. The last time I'd seen her a few days ago was in Sebastian's house. It had been awkward and she'd looked at me like she couldn't bear to be around me. I was beginning to wonder whether Jackson was behind her decision to end things, or whether she just didn't want to be with me. I didn't want to believe that she didn't love me at all, it was too much to contemplate that our whole relationship had been a lie. But maybe she was right when she said she wasn't ready for a relationship.

I opened my car and climbed inside. I had to stop thinking about her and start to face the reality that she might never come back to me. She wasn't mine any longer — and maybe she never had been.

72. SAMANTHA

It had been two days since I'd seen Gabriel at my father's house. I'd had every intention of telling him about my pregnancy but my dad had come back and then the two of them had started acting strangely. I'd thought about phoning him later that evening but I reasoned that it was a conversation better had face to face.

I'd gone to his office earlier that morning only to find the reception being manned for a change, by a stocky man who refused to let me into the back. He told me Gabriel wasn't to be disturbed. I had insisted and told him, quite assuredly, that his boss would want to see me. The stocky man had disappeared then and I had been sure that he would return with an apology and allow me through, but he only told me that Gabriel had refused to see me. So, I supposed I'd have to wait a little longer. Maybe it was for the best not seeing him right now. I was constantly nauseous and that seemed to make me permanently cranky too.

I walked out of our conference room in Donovan Cook to find Beth waiting for me.

'DS Phillips is waiting in your office for you, Samantha,' she said.

'Oh? Did he say what he wanted?'

'No. I told him you were in a meeting, but he said he was happy to wait.'

'Okay, thanks Beth.'

I walked into my office to see him holding a mug of tea which I assumed Beth had made him.

'Good afternoon, Sergeant,' I said as I walked in. We had been on first name basis but I hadn't seen him for a few weeks, and I also didn't know why he was there to see me.

'Hi, Samantha,' he said with a smile. 'And please call me Carl.'

I smiled back as I took a seat at my desk opposite him. 'To what do I owe this pleasure?' I asked.

'I thought you'd want to know that we've found Anthony Garvey,' he said.

'Oh? Is he back in custody?' I asked.

'Not exactly,' Carl replied. 'He's dead.'

'Dead?' I asked and I felt my stomach drop through my knees, remembering Gabriel and my father's suspicious conversation a few days earlier.

'Yes. We had a call from our colleagues in Liverpool. He was found early this morning.'

'Liverpool?' I asked.

He nodded. 'Yes. Do you know if he had any contacts in Liverpool?'

'No,' I shook my head, but I knew two men who did. 'How did he die?' I asked, trying to keep the tremor from my voice. I felt guilty by association and was desperate not to say anything that might incriminate Gabriel or my father.

'Suicide, apparently?' he said with a shrug.

'Suicide?'

'Yeah. He jumped off an eight-storey car park. Obviously, he decided he could no longer live with being a scumbag and ended it all.'

I sat back in my chair and let out a long breath. My heart hammered in my ears. Had he really jumped off a building, or had he had a little help?

'Are you okay, Samantha?' Carl asked as he leaned forward in his seat.

'Yes. It's just a bit of a shock, that's all.'

'Well, it must be a weight off your mind. I thought you'd want to know as soon as possible. The world is a much better place without him in it as far as I'm concerned.'

I smiled awkwardly. I didn't know how to respond to that statement. Was he interviewing me? Why had he come here to tell me that himself and not sent one of his constables, or phoned me? Or was I just being paranoid and he was simply being nice?

'Anyway, we'll be closing the case now, so I wanted you to know,' he said and then he started to fidget awkwardly in his seat.

'Thank you, Carl. I appreciate you coming to see me.'

'I was wondering, now that we're not involved in any official capacity, if you fancied going for a drink some time?' he asked.

Oh, now that explained it all. I looked at him. He seemed nice. He was handsome and smart, and he seemed kind too. He was just the type of man I should have been thinking about dating. 'I'm sorry, Carl. That's very nice of you, but I'm kind of involved with someone at the moment,' I said. It wasn't a complete lie. I was pregnant with someone else's child.

'Oh, okay. Beth told me you were single,' he said as his cheeks flushed pink.

Beth! I could kill her. 'Well, we've been kind of and off,' I said.

'Well, if you're ever off again, you've got my number,' he said as he stood up.

'Duly noted,' I said with a smile.

73. SAMANTHA

I had spent the whole night tossing and turning. At first I hadn't been able to stop thinking about Anthony Garvey's death. Had he committed suicide or had he been pushed off that roof? Now, I would never know if someone else was behind his attack on me. Unless, that person decided to strike themselves? No! I must have misheard him. It wasn't Jackson, so who else would want to hurt me like that? Then I began wondering how I was going to tell Gabriel about my pregnancy, realising that I'd have to tell him soon. He deserved to be the first to know and as much as we had our differences, it was unfair to keep it from him any longer.

By the time the morning had rolled around, I had decided that I was going to tell him as soon as possible. I entertained a fleeting notion that I'd suggest we move far away and start a new life, just the three of us. Somewhere Jackson would never find us? But that was completely unrealistic. And besides that, I wasn't sure that Gabriel wanted to be with me anymore. He'd dismissed me from his office yesterday when I'd gone to speak to him, without even the courtesy of telling me to my face. I supposed I couldn't blame him after everything that had happened between us.

I showered and dressed quickly. I ate a piece of toast to stave off the nausea and then I grabbed my handbag and walked out of the door, determined to see Gabriel and tell him my news before I changed my mind again. It started to drizzle shortly after I left, the soft droplets bounced off my arms as I walked down the road. I contemplated turning back but hailed a passing taxi instead.

My stomach was in a knot by the time I reached Gabriel's house. The closer I got, the more anxious I became. I climbed out of the taxi and was crossing over the road when I saw the door to his house open. A blonde woman stepped outside. She was clearly wearing clothes from the previous night. Unless mini-skirts, vest tops and six inch heels had become the new normal Saturday morning attire. How ironic — that had been me five weeks ago — leaving after a night of sex. She looked like Fiona, Gabriel's date from my father's engagement party, but I could see even from across the street that she wasn't. Clearly Gabriel had a new type! I suddenly realised why he'd refused to see me yesterday — he was probably screwing her on his desk.

The rain was getting heavier and I regretted leaving the house in such a hurry. I had no coat and no umbrella and was beginning to get soaked, but at least the rain would disguise the tears streaming down my face. I started to run. I had no idea where I was going, but I was desperate to get home. I rounded the corner and almost crashed into him.

'Gabriel!' I said.

'Sam! What's wrong?'

'I was at your house. I saw her leaving...' I started babbling at him, like some sort of lunatic.

'Saw who leaving? Why are you crying? Sam?'

'The blonde girl,' I sniffed.

'She's your dad's latest conquest. He couldn't take her home, could he?'

My father! God bless him and his inability to remain monogamous.

'Wait! Did you think?' he said as he ran a hand through his wet hair. 'God, no! Is that why you're upset?'

I nodded and fell into his arms. He pulled me into a shop

doorway to shield us from the rain. God, what was it with us and shop doorways! He stroked my wet hair from my face and looked at me. His green eyes piercing into mine. I swore that man could see into my soul.

'There's something else. I've never seen you cry in my whole life, Sam. What is it? Is it him again?'

'No,' I sobbed.

'Then what? Tell me.'

I shook my head. It had sounded so rational earlier. That I would just tell him I was pregnant and we would run away together. But, right there, in the dingy doorway, that smelled faintly of urine, it just didn't feel right. As if reading my thoughts, he released his grip on me.

'Let me take you home, and we can talk.'

'Okay,' I nodded as I wiped my cheeks with the back of my hand.

We walked the short distance to Gabriel's car and he drove me home in silence, although I could feel his eyes burning into me as he checked on me frequently, probably wondering why I was acting like such a fruit loop.

I sat at my kitchen table while Gabriel made us both a cup of coffee.

'You on decaf now?' he asked.

'Yeah. Trying to cut down on my caffeine,' I answered with a smile.

Gabriel placed our drinks on the table and sat down opposite me. He looked at me with such concern that I thought I might burst into tears again. But I knew that wouldn't help matters. It must have been my hormones, messing with my ability to think clearly.

'Please talk to me, Sam. It kills me to see you hurting like this.'

'Well, I came to talk to you yesterday,' I sniffed. 'But one of your goons told me you wouldn't see me.'

He frowned at me. 'What? When?'

'Yesterday morning. I came to your office.'

'Nobody told me, Sam. I would never refuse to see you. Who did you speak to?'

I picked up my coffee and wrapped my hands around the mug. The warmth was comforting. 'I don't know. Some stocky guy with a shaved head.'

'Fuck!' he mumbled but then he looked at me. 'That must have been Stuart. He's new. I was on a conference call and I told him not to disturb me. He did pop his head in, but I told him to clear off. I didn't realise it was because you were there. I'm sorry, Sam. If I'd known ...'

I sniffed. 'It's okay. I probably should have called first instead of just turning up like that.'

'Sam! You don't need to make an appointment to see me. You could have just walked into my office yourself, you know?'

'What? And fought my way past Stuart? Besides, you could have had some woman in there for all I knew.'

He shook his head and frowned at me. 'Really?'

I shrugged. I knew he wasn't that guy, but him moving on with someone else who could give him all the things I couldn't, was my biggest fear.

'Well, I'm here now. And I'm listening. So, talk to me.'

'I don't know how to tell you, Gabe,' I said.

'Tell me what?' he asked. I could see his jaw working overtime, the way it did when he was desperately trying to keep a lid on his temper. Trying to maintain the control he so desperately needed. I was about to blow his world apart and I didn't want to hurt him any more than I already had.

'Whatever it is, we can handle it,' he said.

I liked the way he said we. As though we were still a unit. I took a large gulp of my milky coffee. 'I'm pregnant. Almost seven weeks.'

'What?' he stared at me. 'But I thought you were on the pill?'

'I am. I was. But I didn't take it properly after we broke up. And then...' I trailed off, not feeling like discussing our epic sex life at that moment.

'Wow,' he said as he ran a hand over his face. 'Have you decided what you're going to do?'

'Yes. I'm keeping the baby. But this doesn't change anything between us, Gabe. And I don't expect anything from you. This was my mistake.'

'Are you fucking kidding me? It changes everything. And please don't call our child a mistake!'

I blinked at him. 'I didn't mean...' I said before I started to cry again. What the hell was wrong with me?

'Get your things, Samantha. You're coming home with me,' he said.

'No, I'm not. I'm staying here,' I made a feeble protest.

'Nothing's changed for you. I get that. But you are carrying my child. And I won't let you put it in danger because you're too stubborn to accept my help. Jackson will go fucking mental when he finds out about this, and I can't be worrying about you being here on your own. So, pack a fucking bag. Now!'

My lip trembled as I stood up and walked to my bedroom. I threw some things into a bag although I could barely stop snivelling long enough to do it.

Damn pregnancy hormones!

CHAPTER 74

If the car journey to my apartment had been strained, then the drive back to Gabriel's house was ten times worse. I could feel the anger radiating from his body. His arms and hands were rigid as he gripped the steering wheel. And the worst of it was, I wasn't entirely sure why he was so angry with me. Although at least I had managed to stop crying.

Gabriel carried my bag inside and showed me to the spare room. Thankfully my father must have left shortly after his blonde lady friend.

'Towels and stuff are in the cupboard,' Gabriel said gruffly as he closed the door behind him and left me to it. I got the feeling he resented my presence there and wondered why he'd bothered asking me to come. But whatever the reason, I was glad that he had. Just being under the same roof as him made me feel better. Although I wished I was staying in his room with him. I missed him so much. The feel of his hands on my body. The warmth of him. Especially when I woke in the middle of the night, as I often did. I had become so used to him being there, curling into him, worming myself underneath his arm into the crook of his shoulder. Now when I reached out, I felt nothing but the cool cotton sheets.

I put the few things I'd brought with me away and wandered downstairs. Gabriel was in the kitchen making coffee.

'I'm working from home today. Help yourself to anything you want. You know where everything is,' he said.

Then he disappeared into the back room he used as a home office. I padded barefoot around his house searching for something to do, anything to distract me from the memories of the other times I had been there. I flicked through some of the books on his bookshelf but nothing could hold my attention. I drifted back to the kitchen and opening the fridge, I saw there was a fresh chicken. I decided to rustle up a roast dinner. I refused to make one on a Sunday anymore — another little rebellion of mine, but a Saturday roast would be just fine.

Dinner was cooking nicely and I decided to take a shower, enjoying the hot water running over my body, wishing it was Gabriel's hands, as it had been the last time I'd been in there.

After I'd showered I realised I hadn't brought many of my things with me and had nothing comfortable to change into. One of Gabriel's t-shirts was on top of the laundry basket. I picked it up and held it to my nose. It smelled of him and I put it on, feeling closer to him as I inhaled his unique scent. I walked back downstairs, hoping that Gabriel would soon emerge from his office.

As I finished preparing dinner, the house started to fill with the aroma of roast chicken and potatoes. It smelled delicious — even if I did say so myself. As I strained the vegetables over the sink, Gabriel's voice broke the silence.

'What's going on in here?'

'Erm. Cooking. I hope you don't mind,' I said, indicating his t-shirt. 'I didn't bring much with me.'

'Of course not. Have you made a roast dinner?' he walked over to the worktop and looked at the food appreciatively.

'Yes. To say thank-you for looking after me today. I know I'm not easy-'

'Well, that's an understatement,' he said.

I ignored the barb and went on. 'And I wanted to talk to you — about the baby.'

He sighed and ran a hand through his hair, in that way that drove me crazy. 'I don't feel like an argument right now, Samantha.'

'Neither do I, Gabe. But I need to know how we're going to do this.'

'How we're going to do this?' he said with a shake of his head. 'I have no fucking idea, Sam. I suppose that all depends on you, doesn't it? The last time you were here, you left me and you told me you didn't want any of this. So, although you may not want to be with me, I am going to be in our child's life whether you like it or not.'

I choked back a sob. Damn these bloody hormones! They were turning me into a sobbing mess. How could he possibly think that I wouldn't want him in our child's life?

'Of course I want you in our child's life, Gabe. But I know this must have come as a shock to you. It did to me. I wasn't sure you'd even want to do this? We never discussed kids.'

'Well, we never got the chance to, did we?' he snapped.

He must have seen the hurt in my eyes as his face softened again. 'I think the fact that you're here tells you that I want to do this, doesn't it? It's a surprise, yes, but I'm as responsible for this situation just as much as you are. I believe it takes two, doesn't it? Although I never did pay much attention in biology,' he replied with a smile.

I nodded. Satisfied with his response for the time being, I plated up the food.

Gabriel tucked into his food while I picked at mine. I was discovering that feeling nauseous for at least eight hours a day was another wonderful side effect of my pregnancy.

'This is good, Sam,' he said with a smile.

'Thanks. It was another one of the things I had to learn to be good at. A proper wife must be able to cook after all.'

He stopped eating to look at me. 'Are you okay?' he asked.

I nodded. 'I feel better now than I did this morning anyway.'

He smiled and went back to his dinner.

'Why were you so angry with me this morning? Was it because of the baby? Do you think that I've trapped you?'

Putting down his knife and fork he sighed. 'Samantha! I thought we'd just discussed this. Of course I don't think you trapped me.'

'So why were you so annoyed with me then?'

'Because you said that a baby didn't change anything between us. As though it could be anyone's and it wouldn't matter to you. Like I'm just some fucking sperm donor.'

I felt the tears sting my eyes again. 'No, that's not it at all. I didn't want you to think that I was trying to tie you to me. It means everything to me that this baby is yours — ours. But there's Jackson ... You're right, he's going to go crazy when he finds out. I need you to understand, Gabe, that there is nothing that man wouldn't do. When he finds out I am carrying your child ...' I shook my head. I couldn't bear to finish the sentence.

'Let me worry about that fucker. I won't let him anywhere near either of you,' he said.

Suddenly, the emotions of the whole day and the preceding few weeks felt like they completely overwhelmed me and I started to sob.

'Sam,' he said as he started to stand up.

I knew he was going to try and comfort me. I held up my hand to stop him. 'There's something else I need to tell you about,' I said.

He sat back down and nodded. 'Go on.'

'I've been pregnant before, Gabe,' I sniffed. This was the most painful memory I had. 'You and my dad always wondered why I won't drive anymore? It's because the last time I did, I lost my child.'

He stared at me, his eyes full of concern.

'I'd had an argument with Jackson. We were having dinner with some friends and he had berated me in front of them for some minor misdemeanour. Then he'd followed me to the ladies' room and continued his tirade in private. I left and drove home. It was raining, and I was in a state. I probably shouldn't have been driving, but I just wanted to get away from him and get home. I didn't see the car swerving on the opposite side of the road until it was too late. The other driver crashed straight into me, head on.'

'Jesus, Sam,' Gabriel said.

'I was almost five months pregnant.'

He stared at me, blinking as he digested what I'd told him.

'She was a girl. I called her Alice, after my mum.'

'I'm so sorry.' Gabriel whispered.

'I was unconscious and rushed straight to hospital. Of course, Jackson was called, and he enjoyed playing the role of the devoted husband and father, while we had an audience at least. But as soon as we were alone he couldn't wait to tell me that I'd murdered our child. For the next four years, he used it against me every opportunity he could. I've never driven a car since that day.'

'Sam,' Gabriel said softly as looked at me. 'I'm so sorry. I can't even imagine,' he shook his head. 'You must miss her every day.'

I nodded. 'I do.'

He reached out and took hold of my hand and lifted it to his face, brushing my fingertips across his lips. His touch felt like an electric current on my skin. I wanted him so much. I wanted to feel his hands all over my body and taste the sweet saltiness of his skin.

The moment was interrupted by the ringing of Gabriel's phone. He looked at the caller display. 'I'm sorry, Sam, but I really need to take this,' he said as he stood up and walked into the other room. I strained to listen and could hear his side of the conversation.

'You're kidding? Really? This is exactly the kind of thing I was hoping for. And your timing couldn't be better.'

'You're a legend. I owe you one, a very big one.'

'Yeah, well I appreciate it just the same.'

There was a long pause before I heard him speaking again. 'I'll be there in half an hour.'

A few seconds later Gabriel walked back into the kitchen.

'I know the timing is awful, but I have to go out for a few hours. Will you be okay here on your own?' he asked as he was putting on his coat.

I nodded. I didn't want him to leave, and I wanted to know where he was going, but I supposed it was none of my business really. 'I'll be fine,' I said.

'I can ask your dad-'

'No,' I interrupted him. The last thing I needed was my dad fussing over me. 'I wasn't planning on telling him about the baby until I've had my twelve-week scan.'

'Okay. Nobody knows you're here. So, you should be perfectly safe. And no-one knows you're pregnant?' he asked.

I shook my head. 'Just you, me and my doctor.'

'Good,' he nodded. 'I can ask someone to come and sit outside though if that would make you feel better?'

'I'm fine, honestly,' I lied. 'I'm a big girl.'

What I really wanted to do was to throw myself at him, beg him to stay home, take me to bed and fuck my brains out. But of course, I didn't.

'I'll be back as soon as I can,' he said as he checked his mobile phone distractedly. 'Don't wait up though. You need your sleep.'

The closeness that had been there between us just a few moments ago already gone, I watched as he walked out of the door.

75. GABRIEL

I checked the address that Nick had sent me again as I walked up the path to the large house that had been converted to flats. I looked for Flat Number 2A and saw her name beside it – Ms Jayne Hunter. I pressed the buzzer and a few seconds later heard her voice through the speaker.

'Hello?'

'Hi, Ms Hunter. It's Gabriel Sullivan. Nick said you'd be expecting me.'

'Of course,' she answered. 'Come on up.'

I heard the buzz of the door opening and pushed against it. I climbed the stairs to the second floor before I reached Flat 2A. She opened the door as I reached it and invited me inside. I followed her into her sitting room and she offered me a seat.

'Would you like some tea?' she offered. 'I was just about to make one.'

I was desperate to speak to her, but I sensed she didn't get many visitors and she reminded me of my aunt, Maggie. 'Yes. That would be lovely. Thanks,' I replied.

A few moments later, Jayne brought in a tray complete with a plate of biscuits, milk, sugar cubes, a teapot and two china cups and saucers. She poured our drinks and I sat back patiently.

'Help yourself to milk and sugar, dear,' she said.

I poured some milk into the tea before picking up the delicate china cup. I couldn't get my large finger through the tiny handle and had to hold it by its rim.

She caught sight of me and laughed. 'I'm sorry, would you prefer a mug, dear?'

I took a sip of the hot liquid before putting it back down on my saucer. 'No. I'm fine,' I shook my head. 'So Nick told me you could help with my problem?'

She nodded. 'I can. I should have said something years ago, but I couldn't. They are such powerful men, Gabriel. They threatened me. And they ruined my daughter's life,' she added.

'They ruined her life?' I asked. Nick hadn't mentioned this.

She sniffed and nodded. 'She was a promising young solicitor when that beast, Jackson Carver, got his claws into her. He pursued her for months, even thought he was married to that lovely woman. I read about what he did to her. Monster!' she said with a shake of her head. 'Anyway, my daughter and him had an affair. I disapproved, obviously, and I tried to warn her, but she wouldn't listen. But then children never do, do they?' she asked as she took a sip of her tea.

I wouldn't know. But I was about to learn, wasn't I? And that reminder of Samantha's pregnancy made me smile. That had been the best news I'd heard all year. And although it was a surprise to both of us, I knew that it would be the best thing that ever happened to us.

'Anyway,' Jayne went on, 'after he got fed up of her, he dumped her. But that wasn't enough for him, he had to ruin her career too. He told everyone that she was obsessed with him. He made out that she had stalked him and was unhinged. She couldn't show her face anywhere. Poor girl.'

I nodded and took another drink of tea. Had her daughter worried about Samantha being able to show her face while she was screwing her husband? I took a deep breath. I was letting my emotion cloud my judgement, but I could hardly bear to think about the life Samantha must have had with that cunt.

'So, what was the information you thought might be helpful to me, Jayne?' I asked. I hoped that it was valuable, and it wasn't some petty attempt to get justice for her daughter.

Half an hour later, I was walking out of Jayne's apartment and back towards my car. To think I'd been worried that Jayne might simply be seeking revenge for her daughter. Whatever her motives were, she had just given me the key to bringing Jackson Carver down. Now, I needed to speak to Sebastian and put the next phase of my plan into action.

76. SAMANTHA

I was lying in bed reading a book of useless facts I'd found in Gabriel's office and the only thing I had learned was that it is impossible to sneeze with your eyes open. I couldn't concentrate on anything which required actual thought. He'd been out for almost four hours and I was beginning to worry. He hadn't even called me once to check on me. Was he with another woman? Maybe he was telling her all about how his ex-girlfriend had shown up and dropped a bombshell on him, ruining his life?

I heard a key in the lock and then Gabriel's heavy footfall coming up the stairs and past my bedroom door. I held my breath, hoping he would come in — praying that he would. Desperate for the touch of him, the taste of him. To hear him whisper words of lust and longing in my ear. But he didn't and my heart sank. I felt like bursting into tears but took a deep breath and bit my lip instead. I heard the door to his bedroom close seconds later and had to stifle another sob.

I put the book down. Just five weeks earlier he hadn't been able to get enough of me. He had told me that he loved me. Surely his feelings hadn't changed in that short time? Mine hadn't. I still loved him more than I could bear. Even if he was seeing a new woman, I was having his baby. Surely that counted for something? There was only one way to find out. Pull yourself together, Samantha, I told myself. If you want him, go and bloody get him.

He was mine. I knew he was. If I would just get out of my own damn way.

I tiptoed across the landing wondering whether I should knock or just go straight in. What was the protocol for such a situation?

I decided to knock.

'Come in,' I heard him say.

I pushed open the door. I was still wearing his t-shirt — and nothing else. Gabriel was sitting up in bed watching television.

'Is something wrong?' he asked.

'No. Yes. Everything's wrong.'

Confusion flashed across his handsome face.

'Well, for a start, you appear to have put me in the wrong bedroom. We both know I should be in here. Then there's you wearing a t-shirt in bed. Covering up that body is nothing short of criminal,' I smiled at him. 'And I can't sleep. I'm horny. I'm so fucking horny. I'd blame the pregnancy hormones but we both know that's not true.'

He said nothing and I wondered if it was too late. Had I really lost him? Or maybe now wasn't the time for my poor attempt at humour.

Just then he opened his mouth to speak, but suddenly I was terrified of what he was going to say. If he had turned me away, I wasn't sure my heart would cope. I felt so fragile and I hated it. Perhaps honesty should have been my starting point when I'd walked in there looking for him to pull me into his arms and into his bed.

'I'm sorry I left you, Gabe,' I interrupted him. 'I thought I was protecting us both. I do love you. I thought that I was broken ... and then I found you again,' I sniffed. Damn these bloody hormones!

His face was impassive, giving nothing away. For an awful, heart-stopping moment, I thought he was going to tell me to go back to my own room.

'Take off the t-shirt, Sam. And come here,' he said.

I peeled it slowly over my head.

'No underwear?' he smiled appreciatively.

I reached the bed and he pulled me down onto it.

'You know that if you stay with me tonight, you stay, Sam? No more running.'

I nodded and in an instant, his hands were all over me, running over every inch of me. Reminding himself of every crease, every scar, every nuance of my body. And reminding me of his expert touch. I shuddered as he reached my knees and pulled them apart, exposing me to him. His hand slid up the inside of my thigh to where I was already slick for him — dripping with longing.

'My beautiful, Sam. Always ready for me,' he said as his hands started to work. Rubbing at my clit in slow, lazy circles. Then his fingers were inside me too. The rhythmic in and out. Around and around. Over and over, Driving me insane.

'Please, Gabe,' I breathed.

'Soon, baby. Soon. I always take care of you, don't I?'

The tightening in my core was building to a crescendo. It was so intense I could barely stand it. My body was on fire. He brought me to the edge of climax so many times, and then left me hanging there — on the precipice of ecstasy, before starting all over again. It was maddening.

'Gabe, please.' I whimpered.

'Do you want to come, Sam?'

'Yes,' I said, my voice barely a whisper.

'Hang on, baby. Not until I say so.'

Oh, dear God!

'I love how greedy you are for me. Never getting enough.' His hands continued working me while he sucked one of my nipples into his mouth, making me gasp in ecstasy. Then he started to nibble across my shoulders and up to my neck, growling in my ear. I bucked my hips against him, desperate for the orgasm he deliberately withheld, but he held me still with the weight of his body. Then his mouth disappeared, no longer growling in my ear or teasing me with his delicious tiny bites. I realised why when I felt his tongue join his fingers. Now he was rubbing, and sucking, and licking. I knew I couldn't hold on much longer.

'God please, Gabe,' I gasped.

'Come for me then, Sam,' he growled, his teeth grazing my tender flesh as he did. My orgasm burst through my body like a river breaking a dam, making it feel numb and alive at the same time. My legs shook as Gabriel continued to rub the last of my orgasm from me in slow, delicious waves. I was still trembling when he pushed himself into me.

'You know I love you, don't you?' he said.

'Yes,' I breathed.

Then he fucked me, making up for all the time we'd been apart. I knew that he would be relentless and that I would struggle to sit down comfortably for any length of time tomorrow. He was going to nail me to the bed. Taking hold of my wrists, he held me down as he began his assault. But I loved it. I loved him. As much as I hated to admit it, I loved to be dominated by him — to give him complete control of my body. I climaxed again, just before he did, the sound of me screaming his name sending him over the edge.

'Fuck! Samantha! Fuck!' He collapsed on top of me. Completely spent. 'I love you, Sam. I love fucking you. I love making you come.' I felt his smile against my shoulder before he looked up at me, his eyes locked on mine.

'I am sorry,' I said again. 'For leaving ...'

'I know,' he replied as he pushed my damp hair from my face.

'What were you going to say earlier? When I told you I was horny? You looked like you were about say something?' I asked him.

'I was going to tell you to get your sexy, horny little arse over here,' he said with a laugh.

'I thought you were going to tell me go to back to my own room.'

'Sam,' he said as frowned at me. 'There is no argument in this world that we could have that would make me turn you away when you're semi-naked and gagging for it.'

'I didn't say I was gagging for it!'

'Not in those exact words, no,' he grinned. 'Anyway, I hope you know that I'm not letting you go ever again. Even if it means tying you to this bed.'

I smiled. 'Although I do enjoy you tying me to this bed, you don't need to do anything that drastic. I'm not going anywhere. I love you. I belong with you.'

'Good. Because you own me, Sam.' He smiled at me, his green eyes twinkling and I wondered what I had ever done to deserve this incredible man.

77. SAMANTHA

The following morning, I woke early. The overwhelming feeling of nausea rousing me from my sleep. I lay still for a few moments until it passed. Then I turned onto my side, moving under the weight of Gabriel's heavy arm until I was facing him. I stared at him. My whole body ached with the exertions of the night before.

He opened one eye. 'Why are you staring at me? Do you need taking care of?' he asked with a sleepy grin.

'Gabe,' I started and his eyes snapped open.

'Don't you fucking dare, Sam,' he said.

I reached out to touch his face. 'I told you I'm not going anywhere. But I need to tell you something.'

He stared at me impassively but I could tell what he was thinking. What the fuck now?

'That time Garvey came to my office, he insinuated that someone else was behind him threatening me-'

'What?' he snapped as he sat up. 'Why the hell didn't you tell me about this at the time, Sam? For fuck's sake!'

'Because I assumed it would be Jackson, and I didn't want you and my father getting involved with him. You don't know him like I do, Gabe. He would destroy you both just for fun.'

'I'd like to see him fucking try,' he snarled.

'Well, I wouldn't,' I said.

'Don't get me wrong, I'm glad that you have, but why are you telling me this now?' he asked.

'Because Garvey is dead. Did you know that?'

He nodded. 'I heard someone threw him off a roof.'

'I heard he jumped,' I said with a frown. 'Did you or my father have something to do with it?'

'Not exactly.'

'You expect me to believe that?'

'I wouldn't lie to you, Sam. I asked a contact up there to find him for me. He gave them a bit of trouble, and then he *fell* off a roof. I won't pretend I'm not pleased about it though.'

'Well, me neither, I suppose. But now that he's dead, if there was someone else behind it, then we can't find out who it was.'

'It must have been Jackson,' he said with a frown.

'No, it wasn't.'

'How do you know that?' he asked. 'Isn't it just his type of thing?'

'No,' I shook my head. 'Not at all, actually, when I think about it. He's perfectly capable of terrifying me himself, without needing anyone else to do it for him.'

'But he must have been behind it.'

'He said it wasn't him. I could always tell when he was lying, and I looked him in the eyes. It wasn't him.'

'You looked him in the eyes?' he glared at me.

'Yes.'

'When?' he growled.

'I visited him-'

'You visited him? Fucking hell, Sam! When?' he shouted.

'A few months ago. Not long after we broke up. I wanted to make sure he was going to leave you and my father alone, and I wanted to ask him if he knew anything about Garvey. He didn't seem to know what I was on about and like I said, I believed him.'

Gabriel shook his head in annoyance. 'You shouldn't have visited him.'

'Why not? I wanted answers and he could give them. I was perfectly safe. We were in a room full of prison officers.'

'Is there anything else I should know about, Sam?'

I nodded and he rolled his eyes.

'He's appealing his conviction.'

'What? What does that mean?' he asked.

'It means that he may get his day in court and could have his conviction overturned if the court rule in his favour.'

'What? How can that even be a thing?'

'It's our legal system. I told you it wasn't perfect. I expected him to appeal the length of his sentence, but didn't think he'd have any grounds to appeal the conviction too. It seems he has.'

'Fuck!' Gabriel whispered. 'If he gets out ...'

'I know,' I said with a shudder.

Suddenly Gabriel pulled me to him again. 'I will *never* let him touch you again, Sam. I swear to you.'

I nestled my head against Gabriel's chest, wishing that I could believe him.

78. SAMANTHA

I took the folder from my desk as our junior partner, Simon Hardaker, walked into my office.

'You've done a great job on this case, Si. Well done.'

Simon smiled. 'Thanks, Samantha. That means a lot.'

I looked up to see Gabriel standing in the doorway. 'Hello, handsome. To what do I owe this pleasure?' I said.

'I was just driving past and couldn't go by without stopping in to see you,' he winked at me.

Suddenly, I remembered Simon was in the room. 'Simon, I'd like you to meet Gabriel. He's my... other half?'

The two men shook hands. 'Nice to meet you, Si,' Gabriel smiled, using the familiar name that I had.

Simon gathered up the papers he needed from my desk, dropping some on the floor as he did. Gabriel picked them up and handed them to him.

'Thanks again, Samantha,' Simon mumbled as he left the room, closing the door behind him.

Gabriel had me pinned up against my filing cabinet before the door was even closed.

'Your other half?' he grinned.

'Well, you're so much more than my boyfriend, and anyway that makes us sound like a pair of teenagers. And partner is so business-like – Nick is my partner. So, I went with other half.'

'I like other half,' he said before kissing me. 'I think Simon might have a little crush on you,' he chuckled as he started to kiss my neck.

'Don't be daft. He's just a baby! And besides, I think he has a girlfriend.'

'You really are blind sometimes, Sam.' He ran his hand through my hair, grabbing a handful at the nape of my neck, tilting my head up to the perfect angle to silence my impending retort with a deep kiss.

He finally let me up for air and I asked. 'Does it matter anyway? You trust me, don't you?'

'Implicitly. I know you only have eyes for me.'

I smiled at him. 'I love how sure you are of us. Of yourself. Although some might say arrogant?'

I saw the wicked gleam in his eyes. 'Well, I happen to know for a fact that you love me. And I also know that you're well-aware no-one can fuck you as well as I do. No-one else can make you come so easily — can they, Sam?'

I opened my mouth in mock horror. 'It's all about the sex with you, isn't it?'

His hands slid down my body and he started to lift the hem of my skirt. 'We both know I could make you come right now. All I'd have to do is get my mouth on you, and you'd be screaming my name within five minutes.' He whispered in my ear, his teeth grazing my skin. 'I bet you're already wet for me.'

Before I could stop him, he moved his hand inside my skirt and up my thigh. He smiled as he confirmed his suspicion. 'Samantha,' he groaned as he slipped a finger inside. He was about to drop to his knees when my office door opened and Simon bounded back inside.

'Did you say...' he started before he saw us pressed against the filing cabinet. Thankfully, Gabriel's back was to the door, his large frame shielding me from view. He withdrew his hand and straightened my skirt so quickly I was sure Simon couldn't have seen what we were doing. Nevertheless, I flushed bright red. Both from embarrassment and the orgasm that was already building from Gabriel's expert touch.

'I'm so sorry,' Simon sputtered.

Gabriel didn't miss a beat. The fact we were almost caught in flagrante delicto didn't faze him at all. 'My fault,' he smiled. 'I should have locked the door. I'll see you later, baby.' He kissed me and then walked towards the door. Once he was out of Simon's view, he turned to me and sucked his wet finger clean, before winking at me and walking out of my office.

'I'm so sorry, Samantha.' Simon said, his face as flushed as mine was.

'Don't worry, it's fine.'

I wondered whether I should tell him that I wasn't usually in the habit of getting felt up in my office, well at least not every day. My cheeks burned with embarrassment but I thanked God that he hadn't walked in two minutes later and found me pinned to the cabinet with Gabriel's head buried between my legs.

'So, what were you saying, Si?' I asked.

We started to discuss how to proceed with a restraining order he had been applying for when my phone vibrated, signalling a text. I saw the message display on the screen — bright and bold.

You smell so good, Sam

I quickly pocketed the phone and blushed again as I counted the hours until I could be alone with him.

GABRIEL

I smiled as I put my phone back in my pocket and climbed into my car. I'd been at Donovan Cook to see Nick to update him on my very helpful chat with Jayne Hunter. Nick had confirmed the elements of her story that he'd been aware of and we both agreed that this was exactly what we needed to bring Jackson Carver down for good.

I'd stopped into Samantha's office too, pretending I was there to see her. Not that it was any imposition to ever visit her at work, especially when I always found her dripping wet for me and ready for whatever it was I had in mind. If only that new junior partner of hers hadn't interrupted us. I ran my hand over my face and inhaled her sweet scent, feeling my cock start stirring to attention. I felt like going back in there and taking her home. I'd spent too long away from her and as she'd only been back in my bed for one night, I hadn't fucked her even nearly enough to make up for that yet.

But the important thing was that she was back by my side and all was right with the world. Now, I just had to put the next stage of my plan to finally be rid of her psychopathic ex-husband into action.

79. SAMANTHA

I was surprised to see my father instead of Gabriel at five o'clock that evening.

He flashed me one of his winning smiles. 'Gabriel had some business he needs to deal with. And I have finally got my licence back, so I'm here to escort you home and keep you company.'

I tried to smile at him, but I wanted to see Gabriel. Obviously, I didn't hide my disappointment very well.

'Bloody hell, Sam, you don't have to look so miserable about it.'

'I'm sorry, Dad. I was just expecting Gabe, that's all.' I gave him a genuine smile then and linked my arm through his as we headed out of the door. I hadn't mentioned my pregnancy to him yet, and had warned Gabriel not to either — not until I'd had my first scan and confirmed everything was okay.

I walked to my father's car with him and wondered why Gabriel hadn't mentioned earlier that he wouldn't be able to pick me up? I had been on edge since he'd left my office that afternoon. I loved spending time with my father, but I currently had an itch that only Gabriel could scratch. Sitting in the passenger seat of my father's car, I took out my phone and sent Gabriel a text.

What time will you be home? I miss you. I was hoping we could pick up where we left off. Phone me x

I waited for a response but one didn't immediately arrive the way it usually did. Especially when I had mentioned anything remotely sexual.

'Where did you say Gabriel was?' I asked.

'Just taking care of some business,' he answered nonchalantly.

'What kind of business?'

'Just business, Sam,' he said, his tone making it clear that he didn't intend to discuss it any further. 'Don't worry. Everything is fine,' he added as he turned to me.

I sat back in my seat and listened to my father talking about the plans Kayleigh was making for their wedding. I knew he was trying to take my mind off Gabriel and wherever he was, because usually organising a wedding would be the kind of topic that would bore my father to death.

Twenty minutes after I had sent the message, and just as we were pulling up outside Gabriel's house, he responded.

Can't phone. Be home late

Then immediately after.

Love you x

My father came into Gabriel's house with me and insisted he was going to cook us some dinner. He said I didn't look very well and then his over-protective side kicked in. I tried to enjoy spending time him, as I usually would, but my stomach was in knots. I felt incredibly nauseous and wasn't entirely sure whether it was pregnancy related or the worry of where Gabriel was.

I ate as much as I could of the delicious meal my father cooked and then we sat on the sofa together and watched my favourite childhood film, *Hook*.

By 10pm, I could barely keep my eyes open and I decided to go to bed. I was surprised when my father insisted on staying, but he assured me that it was only because he needed to speak to Gabriel when he came home. I didn't believe him. Something was going on. But I didn't have the energy to argue with him.

80. GABRIEL

Alfie Cunningham's scrap-yard was closed when I arrived. Despite that, there was a flurry of activity. One of his boys opened the giant wrought iron gate for me, while another three restrained the dogs which constantly patrolled the site. Vicious little bastards they were — the dogs and the boys. Alfie was the most ruthless individual I had ever had the pleasure of meeting. I'd known him for years and after the incident with Calvin Stewart he'd offered me a job. I'd politely turned him down, but our paths had crossed many times over the years. He and his sons ran East London with an iron fist, although I had always found Alfie to be fair, as long as you didn't try and take the piss. Many a man had walked through those gates and never been seen again. Alfie had lots of friends in very high places and was considered untouchable. Anyone who crossed him would end up either severely maimed — or worse.

His two sons, Alfie junior and Joe, were equally fearsome. However, there was one blot on Alfie's otherwise perfect, landscape. Six years earlier, his youngest son, Mark, had been convicted of the rape and murder of a fourteen year old girl. Mark had befriended the girl in the local park. He used to buy her and her mates cider on a Saturday night and sit drinking with them. But he was a good lad. He was twenty-one but still had the mind of a child — a kid trapped in a man's body. He'd always found it easier to connect with children rather than adults and most of the kids from the local high school knew, and liked him. No-one who knew him believed that he'd done what they said he had, and those who didn't know him dare not admit it if they did think he was guilty. For all his friends and his contacts, Alfie wasn't able to stop his son going to prison for life.

Six months into his sentence, Mark was found murdered in his cell. Rumour had it that he'd been sexually assaulted too, although Alfie made sure that rumour was put to bed before many people could hear it. Alfie knew his son was innocent, and he had been desperate ever since for any chance to find out had who really killed that poor girl — and exact his revenge. It ate him up day and night.

'Gabriel Sullivan,' Alfie boomed as I walked into his portacabin and he pulled me into a bear hug. 'Long time no see, son. In fact, I haven't seen you since the last time you turned down the chance to work for me,' he said with a wink.

'Well, I've been busy, Alfie.'

'Yes, I heard, doing well for yourself by all accounts.'

'Not bad,' I said with a nod.

'Good,' he said. 'I always liked you, Gabriel. Always knew you'd go far. Now, what the fuck are you doing here?'

'It's about Mark,' I said and I could feel the atmosphere in the room change immediately. There were several sharp intakes of breath.

'Tread fucking carefully, son,' Alfie warned me.

'The barrister who defended Mark-'

'The one I paid a shitload of money to?' Alfie snapped.

'Yes, him. He also took a massive pay-out from the father of the real murderer to make sure that Mark went down for the crime. The prosecuting barrister was paid off too. The three of them were old Cambridge buddies. The prosecuting barrister was an odious piece of shit called Stanley Baker – and of course you already know the barrister for the defence.'

'Jackson Carver,' Alfie spat, his face full of venom.

'Who did kill that girl then?'

'Marcus Payne. Spoilt little fucker. Daddy has bailed him out of all kinds of scrapes. He's the same age as Mark, and similar build.'

Alfie nodded. 'Explaining that eye witness who saw someone fitting Mark's description running away from the scene?'

I nodded.

'How the fuck do you know all this?' he asked. 'And what's in this for you? What do you want?'

'I know because I've had lots of people digging into Jackson Carver, and this is what they came up with. What I want, Alfie, is Carver dead.'

'If what you're telling me is the truth, then I will make that happen, without a fucking doubt. He's doing time, isn't he? He'll be easy to get to. But I want some fucking proof, Gabriel. Do you have any?'

'Nothing concrete other than the word of some people who I trust. But I understand you want more than that, so I thought we could pay Stanley Baker a little visit tonight — and extract the truth from him?'

'That sounds like a good idea. But if you're leading me up the garden path,' he pointed his finger in my face. He didn't finish his sentence — he didn't have to.

An hour later and I was sitting in a van with Alfie and his sons, waiting for Stanley Baker to leave the gentleman's club he always frequented on a Thursday night.

'That's him.' I indicated as I saw Stanley's cumbersome body lolloping down the street.

'Fat fucker, ain't he?' Joe sneered. Then he and Alfie junior jumped out of the van. Putting an arm each around Stanley's shoulders, they bundled him into the back of the transit, throwing him onto the dusty floor.

He started to whimper. 'Please. I have money...'

I scowled at him. He had money, did he? I despised how people like Stanley thought that everything and everyone could be bought and paid for. I savoured the look of fear on Stanley's face. He looked up and saw me and at that point, he pissed his pants as his whole body started to shake, obviously remembering our brief encounter in the coffee shop. A part of me wished that Samantha was there to see it.

We drove in silence back to the scrap-yard listening to Stanley pleading with us to let him go, offering money or whatever else we wanted. Eventually Alfie junior punched him in the head and told him to shut the fuck up.

Stanley was strapped to a chair with gaffer tape in Alfie's office within five minutes of us arriving back there. He was crying then, begging us to release him. I wondered if Samantha cried and begged him to let her go? Fucker! I wanted to knock every tooth out of his head, break every bone in his body — but I couldn't. This was Alfie's show.

'Tell me what you know about Marcus Payne, Stanley,' Alfie said to him. His voice low and full of menace.

As soon as Stanley heard the name Marcus Payne, the realisation of why he was there visibly dawned on his face. That told Alfie all he needed to know, and I thanked Christ that Nick and Jayne Hunter's information had been spot on. It only took a few slaps and threats to do unspeakable things to him and his family, to get Stanley to confess everything. He threw Payne and Carver straight under the bus to try and save his own skin. That was when Joe pulled out his specialised toolkit from under the desk. It was a kit full of all manner of torture devices designed to extract the truth from even the most hardened of men.

I doubted that Stanley would last five minutes before his heart gave out. As much as I hated Stanley Baker, I didn't particularly have an urge to watch the man being tortured to death. Just knowing that it was going to happen was enough.

I looked around the room at Alfie and his two sons and knew that they were in their element. 'If you don't need me, I need to get home. I've got some other business to take care of,' I said, feeling guilty for calling Samantha business, but not wanting any of the men in the room to know anything about her.

Alfie nodded. 'Of course, son. Thanks for your help. I'll let you know as soon as I find that little nonce, Marcus Payne.'

'Good. And Carver?'

'He will not see out the end of the month. I promise you that.'

'Thanks, Alfie,' I said.

Alfie walked over to me and put his hands on my shoulders. I saw tears in his eyes. 'No. Thank *you*, Gabriel. I know you have your own reasons, but I owe you. You have...' he choked up.

'You don't owe me, Alfie. I knew Mark. He was a good lad. And that poor girl, and her family — the fucker who did that needs to pay. And the bastards who helped him get away with it.'

Alfie nodded. 'And believe me, they will.'

81. SAMANTHA

I was asleep when Gabriel finally arrived home. I woke as he slipped into bed beside me.

'Where have you been, Gabe? And don't tell me it was just business. What have you been doing?'

He pulled me to him until I was lying in his arms and I breathed in the scent of him. His skin was cool and I could smell the fresh air on him.

'Sam,' he said as he smoothed my hair. 'I promised you that I would never lie to you. But right now, please don't ask me what I'm doing. I will tell you when it's all over. But for now, please just trust me?'

I sat up and turned on the bedside light. 'Why can't you tell me? Is it dangerous? Is it illegal?'

'Please, just trust me,' he said softly, kissing my forehead.

'You're asking a lot.'

'I know I am, baby. But have I ever given you a reason not to trust me? Everything I do is for you. For us. The three of us,' he said as he placed a hand on my stomach.

'I can't say I'm happy about it,' I said with a sigh. 'But I've got a feeling you're not going to tell me anyway, and I'm tired of fighting with you, Gabe. Promise me you're not doing something completely stupid? Promise me you're not going to get yourself hurt.'

'Why would I risk losing you, Sam?' he said before kissing me.

I turned off the bedside lamp and lay with my head on his chest, his strong arms wrapped around me. Despite his assurances, I knew that he was up to something dangerous, and I had an idea it was something to do with my psychopathic ex-husband.

82. GABRIEL

I frowned as I heard the vibration of my mobile phone ringing beside me. It was only 6am and I had to untangle myself from Samantha's beautiful, warm body to answer it.

I saw Alfie Cunningham's name flashing on the screen and groaned inwardly. It had been a week since we had kidnapped Stanley Baker together and his disappearance had been on the news. Thankfully, Samantha hadn't asked me any questions about it and I was glad. She was tired and wrapped up in a case, but I knew she'd want some answers soon enough.

'Now's not a great time, Alfie,' I said quietly.

'I need some back-up, Gabriel. I've found the cunt. My boys are on a job. I thought you'd want to help me sort the fucker out.'

'I do. It's just-'

'Are you fucking scared or something? This is not a request, Gabriel.'

'I'll be there in half an hour,' I said as I put the phone down.

Alfie had found out where Marcus Payne had been holed up and obviously wanted to pay him a visit before he disappeared again. I would rather not get involved. I'd been happy to help give Stanley a good kicking but the type of punishment Alfie had planned for Marcus was not my thing — at least not any more.

. . .

Two hours later Alfie and I pulled up outside a cottage in the middle of nowhere.

'Are you sure he's in here?' I asked.

'Yes, I'm fucking sure. He's on his own in there as far as I can tell. He's a fucking no-mark. He won't put up much of a struggle. We get in, we get him and we get out of there. We're taking him to my lock-up. Understood?'

I nodded. I knew what happened in Alfie's lock-up. Marcus Payne would be begging someone to kill him by the time the day was over.

Alfie knocked on the front door, as though we were polite visitors, and I wondered how stupid Marcus Payne would have had to have been to open it. As I expected there was no answer. Alfie gave me the nod and I kicked the door open. It was old and the wood splintered easily, allowing us easy access. As soon as we were inside, we heard a noise coming from the back of the house and ran towards it. Alfie was leading the charge. I knew how anxious he was not to let Marcus get away. As we rounded the corner into the kitchen, I saw Marcus trying to escape through the back door but he couldn't open it fast enough.

'You're not going anywhere, cunt!' Alfie spat.

Then Marcus turned and in that split second I saw it, the glint of metal as it caught the sunlight streaming through the window. Marcus pointed the gun at us.

There was no time to think, I just reacted. I pushed Alfie out of the line of fire before the crack of a gunshot rang in my ears. Then I heard another shot and watched as Marcus Payne dropped to the floor like a sack of spanners. I turned, everything happening as if in slow motion. Alfie was standing next to me, his right arm outstretched, his own gun smoking in his hand. It took me a few seconds to feel the searing pain. I looked down at my shirt and watched as the white cotton turned to deep crimson.

'Gabriel.' Alfie caught me in his arms before I hit the floor.

83. SAMANTHA

It was late afternoon and I was in my office when my phone rang.

I was given the news quickly and matter of factly.

My hands visibly shook as I put down the phone. My head spun. I felt dizzy and sick. I forced myself to swallow the bile rising in my throat so that I didn't vomit onto the floor of my office.

It couldn't be true.

I could hardly believe it.

Then the tears came, like a river that had been held back by a dam for far too long, forcing their way out of me like a torrent. I wailed. I actually wailed, like some crazed madwoman. I heard myself, but the sound was so alien to me, I wouldn't have believed it was coming from my own body if I hadn't been the only person in the room.

Nick came running in, his face a picture of shock and horror. He crouched down to me as though I was a small child.

'Samantha! What is it? What's wrong?'

Through the snot and tears I managed to mumble. 'He's dead.'

The rest of our team had piled into our office behind him by this point.

I heard Nick speaking quietly to Sadie, asking her to phone someone although I couldn't make out who.

'Yes, of course. I'm on it,' she replied.

Then Nick wrapped his arms around me and I folded into them, sobbing uncontrollably. Struggling for breath. He held me to him and stroked my hair. I didn't know how long I stayed there like that, but then Nick's arms were gone, and someone else was lifting me from the chair, picking me up as though I was made of air.

'Sam. It's okay. I'm here now,' he said.

I looked up into Gabriel's handsome face and felt like I could finally breathe.

'He's dead, Gabe. Jackson's dead,' I said and then I clung to him, burying my face in his neck.

'I know. Come on, let's go home.'

Freshly showered and in one of Gabriel's old t-shirts, I curled up on the sofa. Gabriel brought me a mug of sweet tea and sat beside me, pulling me onto his lap.

He stroked the hair back from my face, in that way that always made me feel cherished and safe. 'Are you okay?'

I sniffled and nodded. 'Poor Nick. He must have got such a fright, seeing me like that.'

'He'll be fine.'

'I can't believe it. Jackson is dead.' I shook my head in disbelief. 'How did you do it, Gabe?'

'Me? I didn't do it, did I? I was here with you last night — and he was in prison. They're as hard to break into as they are to break out of, you know?'

'I know you didn't actually do it. But you had something to do with it. That's what you've been up to. That's what you couldn't tell me?'

He shrugged. 'I gave an old friend of mine some information about Jackson and he acted on it — that's all. I'll tell you all about it — but not right now.' He kissed me on the forehead and sat back in the chair. I noticed him wince as he flexed his right shoulder.

'Are you okay?' I asked.

'I'll tell you about that later too,' he said with a grimace.

I opened my mouth and was about to protest when he frowned at me. 'Will you please relax?' He placed his hand on my stomach. 'You've had a shock, and I don't want either of you getting stressed.'

I placed my hand over his. 'There's no way anything can come back on you?'

He shook his head. 'No way at all.'

'You really are my Angel Gabriel, aren't you?' I said as I leaned my head on his chest.

He pulled me tightly to him. 'Always.'

84. GABRIEL

I held Samantha tightly as she sat on my lap on the sofa. I had put a cheesy romantic comedy on and I was pleased to see her smiling at her favourite part. The searing pain in my shoulder throbbed and I wondered how many hours it had been since I'd taken some of the strong painkillers I'd been provided with earlier.

With Alfie's help I had stumbled out of the cottage earlier that morning and into Alfie's car. I vaguely remembered the drive to the surgeon's house as I'd drifted in and out of consciousness in the back, but I'd heard Alfie organising the clean-up crew to dispose of Marcus Payne's body and any other evidence that he and I had been there.

By midday the bullet had been removed from my shoulder and I'd been patched up by Alfie's surgeon friend as well as given three pints of blood and some heavy-duty painkillers. Then the surgeon's wife had brought in an array of shirts until I had found one to fit me. I had been impressed by their operation and it was obvious that Alfie sent a lot of work their way. Alfie Cunningham paid the bill, thanking me for taking a bullet for him.

Once I was dressed again, it had been hard to tell, from looking at me at least, that I'd even been shot. I certainly felt like I had though. I felt like I'd been put through a clothes mangle. I'd been at home about to sleep off the last of the sedatives I'd been given when I'd received the call from Sadie. I'd known Jackson Carver's days were numbered, but I hadn't known when it was going to happen. He'd been found dead that morning — hanging in his cell by all accounts.

Although Samantha was convinced otherwise, her father and I were sure that Jackson Carver had been behind Anthony Garvey too. Now the two of them were out of the picture.

As soon as I had seen Samantha earlier, adrenaline had kicked in and I'd forgotten all about my bullet wound and how much it fucking hurt. I wondered how the hell I was going to explain it to her later when we went to bed and she saw my shoulder. But for now, I was content to sit with her in my arms. Finally, we were free of Jackson Carver, and Samantha Donovan was all mine.

EPILOGUE

Samantha

I watched as Gabriel hung my favourite piece of art on his sitting room wall — although I supposed it was now my wall too. I'd agreed to move in with him and let my flat go. I'd only been renting the place while I looked for somewhere more permanent. I spent every night with Gabriel anyway, and now that I was fourteen weeks pregnant with his baby, it seemed like the most logical next step.

'Is this okay?' he asked as he took a step back and admired his handiwork.

'Perfect,' I replied with a smile.

'Good,' he said as walked over and flopped onto the sofa beside me. 'Is there anything else I can do for you m'lady?'

'Yes. You can nip to the supermarket and get me some peanut M&M's. The baby needs some.'

'Ah, I am well aware of our child's current addiction to M&M's and there are three bags in the cupboard.'

'Oh, when did you go to the shops?' I asked.

'I nipped to the corner shop this afternoon when you were on the phone to Sadie for an hour.'

'They had none in stock when I asked this morning?'

'What can I say? Susie has a thing for me. She always has whatever I ask for in stock,' he said with a grin.

I rolled my eyes. Susie owned the newsagents at the end of the road. She was in her sixties, wore leather miniskirts and had a beehive, and she always gave Gabriel the eye when he went into her shop. 'I think I'd better keep my eye on you and Susie,' I said as I nudged him in the ribs.

He started to laugh and put an arm around me. 'I only have eyes for you though, you know that.'

'Hmm,' I replied.

'Hmm? What does that mean? You think after what I did to you this morning I could even look at another woman ever again?' he said with a twinkle in his eye.

'What did you do? I can't even recall?' I teased him.

'You don't remember? Really? Even though you almost woke the whole street up with your screaming?'

I kissed his beautiful lips. 'Oh yes, I remember now.'

'Just in case though, I'll take that lasagne out of the oven and then I'll remind you again, shall I?'

'Oh yes, I'd like that,' I said with a smile.

We were interrupted by a knock at the door and we looked at each other

'It's probably my dad,' I said. 'No-one else would call round at six o'clock on a Sunday. You sort the dinner and I'll get the door.'

'If it is your father, tell him to stop being a cock-blocker and clear off,' he said with a grin.

'A cock-blocker? Really? You want me to say that to my father — who likes to think that this little one was conceived via immaculate conception?' I said as I rubbed my tiny bump.

He nodded and then disappeared down the hallway.

I walked to the door and thought, not for the first time that day, how happy and blessed I felt to have Gabriel and our unborn child. I opened the door and almost passed out with shock to see a woman standing there with tears streaming down her face.

'Is Gabriel home?' she asked between sobs.

I had never met her, but I recognised the face of Gabriel's ex-wife from a photograph. 'Jennifer?'

If you've enjoyed reading Dark Angel and want to find out what's next in store for Samantha and Gabriel, you can order Fallen Angel now.

Fallen Angel

ACKNOWLEDGMENTS

A huge thank you to the incredibly supportive women who helped me turn this book into a reality - Edie, for your generosity and your patience with my endless cover changes; Sue and Michelle for your feedback and encouragement; Mary, for your eagle eyes and your ongoing friendship and support.

ALSO BY SADIE KINCAID

He is the King of L.A, and she is his queen. Alejandro and Alana Montoya are hotter than hell in Sadie's L.A Ruthless series. Available on Amazon and FREE in Kindle Unlimited.

Fierce King

Fierce Queen

If you'd like to read about the hotter than hell Irish Mafia, Ryan Brothers and their computer hacker, Jessie, you can order the New York Ruthless series on Amazon now:

Ryan Rule

Ryan Redemption

Ryan Retribution

Ryan Reign

Join Sadie's reader group for the latest news, book recommendations and plenty of fun. Sadie's ladies and Sizzling Alphas

Sign up to Sadie's mailing list for exclusive news about future releases, giveaways and content here

Printed in Great Britain
by Amazon

77692477R00200